# WOOF!

## THREE TALES IN ONE

### WOOF! THE TALE WAGS ON
### WOOF! THE TALE GETS LONGER
### WOOF! A TWIST IN THE TALE

by Andrew Norriss

based on the Central Independent Television series
full-length feature film versions
of WOOF! Series One and Series Three
are available on video

FANTAIL

FANTAIL BOOKS

Published by the Penguin Group
Penguin Books Ltd, 27 Wrights Lane, London W8 5TZ, England
Penguin Books USA Inc., 375 Hudson Street, New York, New York 10014, USA
Penguin Books Australia Ltd, Ringwood, Victoria, Australia
Penguin Books Canada Ltd, 10 Alcorn Avenue, Toronto, Ontario, Canada M4V 3B2
Penguin Books (NZ) Ltd, 182–190 Wairau Road, Auckland 10, New Zealand

Penguin Books Ltd, Registered Offices: Harmondsworth, Middlesex, England

*WOOF! The Tale Wags On* first published 1989
*WOOF! The Tale Gets Longer* first published 1991
*WOOF! A Twist in the Tale* first published 1992
This compilation edition first published in Fantail Books 1992
1 3 5 7 9 10 8 6 4 2

Printed in England by Clays Ltd, St Ives plc
Filmset in Monophoto Baskerville

# THE TALE WAGS ON

by Andrew Norriss

# CONTENTS

Fresh Beginnings 9

Roy's Dream 23

The Money Spinner 36

The Adoption 50

The Road-Runner 63

Mr Blocker's Pipe 80

Mixed Doubles 99

Moving On 117

# FRESH BEGINNINGS

When Eric Banks turned into a dog one afternoon, he was understandably frightened. Any boy in his position would have felt the same. It wasn't the turning into a dog that scared him – that had happened several times before, and he was beginning to get used to it – what was frightening was that he was two-thirds of the way up a very large chestnut tree at the time, and he didn't see how he was ever going to get down.

He had been standing on a branch almost twenty metres from the ground and reaching up for the next hand hold, when he had felt a slight itching and tingling at the back of his neck. He just had time to call out to his friend, Roy Ackerman, that he was feeling rather strange when ... when it happened. He turned into a dog. A mongrel, to be precise, and he found himself clinging for his life to the trunk of the tree with paws instead of hands, while his clothes (which had all fallen off, because he was much smaller as a dog than he had been as a boy) flapped around on the branches beside and below him.

Fortunately, Roy was there to help. Roy was the only other person who knew that this occasionally happened to Eric. He was a couple of branches higher, but he scrambled straight back down, to see what he could do.

When he realized that Eric was stuck, unable to climb either up or down, his first thought was that maybe he could carry him back down to the ground, but he soon realized that wouldn't be possible. Roy was big for his age (like Eric, he was eleven years old), but Eric-as-a-dog was over half a metre long and weighed sixteen pounds. The tree they were in had been quite difficult to climb. Roy had needed both hands on several sections on the way up, and he knew he could never climb down using only one hand. If he slipped, or if he dropped Eric and either of them fell, they could be very badly hurt.

So, in the end, he climbed down on his own and called the fire brigade.

'What I don't understand,' said the Chief Fire Officer, thoughtfully scratching behind one ear, 'is how your dog got that high up a tree in the first place.' He looked at Roy, and then back to where a fireman was carrying Eric down a ladder to safety. 'I mean,' he went on, 'it's the sort of place you might expect to find a cat, but I've never heard of a dog that could climb like that.'

'He sort of followed me up there,' explained Roy. It was at least partly the truth. 'I didn't realize at first, and then I didn't know how to get him down.'

The fireman from the ladder came over with Eric, gave him to Roy, and turned to the Chief Fire Officer. 'I found these up there as well,' he said, holding out the clothes Eric had been wearing.

The Chief looked at the label on the sweater. 'Eric Banks,' he read aloud from the name tag. 'Do you know anything about this?' he asked Roy.

'I know Eric,' Roy said. 'I could get the clothes back to him, if you like.'

The Chief Fire Officer thought for a moment. There was something not quite right here, and he decided he had better find out what it was. At that moment, however, another fireman came over and said the Chief was wanted on the radio.

The Fire Officer turned to Roy. 'You wait here,' he said, 'and your dog as well. I've some questions to ask you.' Then he walked over to the fire engine to answer his call.

Roy gathered up Eric's clothes. 'I think it's time to go, Eric,' he said, and the two of them slid quietly away.

Roy called round to Eric's house the following day to see how he was. Eric was just about to take his sister Emily's puppy round to the vet's for its injection, so Roy said he'd come too. That way they'd have a chance to talk about what had happened.

It had, after all, been something of a surprise. Although Eric had turned into a dog several times before, neither he nor Roy had expected it to happen again. When it had happened before, they had spent a great deal of time trying to find out why it happened, and had eventually discovered that it was Eric's sister, Emily (who wanted a dog even more than she wanted a brother) who was somehow making it happen. But they had cured Emily. Between them, they had bought her a puppy of her own, and Eric's 'changing' had stopped immediately.

'If it's not your sister,' Roy pointed out, 'I don't see who *could* be causing it.'

'I've been thinking about that,' said Eric. 'There is one possibility.'

'Is there?' Roy was puzzled. 'Who?'

'Face it, Roy,' said Eric. 'My sister's not the only person round here who's always wanted a dog.'

It was several seconds before Roy realized what he meant.

'You think it's me!' he said. 'You think it's me that's doing it, don't you?'

Eric looked at him. 'Who else is there, Roy?'

'But . . . but lots of people want dogs!' argued Roy. 'It doesn't mean they go around turning their friends into one.'

'I don't know why it happens,' said Eric, shrugging his shoulders, 'and maybe you don't mean to do it – but you're the one that's causing it. I just know it.'

'Well, what am I supposed to do about it?' asked Roy.

They were standing at the door to the vet's. Eric paused before he went in. 'For a start,' he said, 'you could try and stop thinking about dogs.'

There was only one other patient in the vet's waiting room, a small, dark collie, which the vet was leading away to the surgery. Eric took his sister's puppy over to the reception desk to tell the veterinary nurse who he was and why he had come.

'Would you like to come through and hold him while he has it?' asked the nurse.

'I'll just wait here if you don't mind,' said Eric. He didn't like injections, not even watching other people get them. The nurse took the puppy away, and Eric came and sat down beside Roy.

'What are you doing?' he asked.

Roy had his eyes tightly closed, and his brow was furrowed in concentration. 'It's not easy,' he replied.

'What isn't?'

'Not think about dogs,' said Roy. 'Especially in here. There's your sister's puppy, there's that little black collie, there's posters of dogs on the wall, there's magazines about dogs on the table . . . I thought if I just closed my eyes, I might blank them all out, but it hasn't worked. Even now I can sort of see you in my mind. Like you were when you were sitting on that branch, and the more I try and make you go away, the more you're there.' He paused. 'But I want you to know I'm really trying. Okay?'

'Woof!' said Eric.

Roy opened his eyes. Eric had turned into a dog again, and was sitting on the chair beside him with a somewhat chilly look in his eyes.

'Hey, Eric, I haven't . . . I didn't mean to . . .' Roy tried to apologize, tried to pick up Eric's clothes for him and was trying to apologize again, when the vet came back with Emily's puppy.

'There we are. All done,' said the vet. 'Now the only thing to remember . . .' He looked around the waiting room. 'Where's he gone?'

'Who?' asked Roy.

'Eric Banks,' said the vet. 'Where's he gone? I've got his sister's puppy here.'

'Ah!' Roy thought quickly. 'He couldn't stay, I'm afraid, but he asked me to look after the puppy.'

'I see,' the vet handed the puppy to Roy. 'Well, there you are. The only thing to remember is to bring it back in three months time for a booster shot.' He noticed Eric, still sitting on the chair. 'Is this your dog?'

'Yes,' said Roy. 'Sort of.'

The vet reached out and stroked Eric's head. 'He's a nice looking fellow, isn't he? Been innoculated, has he?'

'What?' asked Roy.

'Has he had his injection?' explained the vet. 'Against distemper and hard pad. They need a booster shot every year, you know.'

Roy thought. 'I don't think he's had any injections for things like that.'

The vet looked rather concerned. 'No?' Well, I think he should, don't you?'

'Woof, woof,' said Eric, who had already realized where this conversation was heading. He and Roy had a code for when he turned into a dog. One 'woof' meant yes, two meant no and Eric DEFINITELY didn't want any injections! He leapt off his chair and scampered over to the door. He couldn't open it himself, the handle was too high, but he looked pointedly at Roy.

'I don't think he likes injections much,' said Roy.

'I don't think he'd like distemper either,' said the vet, seriously. 'It affects the central nervous system, you know. They have fits, they get sick, they can't breathe properly. They usually die.'

Roy hesitated. He knew how Eric felt about injections, but supposing he did get one of those diseases? Presumably he couldn't catch distemper or hardpad while he was a boy, but while he was a dog . . . who knew? Dying sounded pretty serious.

'I could do it for you now, if you like,' said the vet.

'Well . . .' Roy was still uncertain.

'Don't worry,' said the vet, cheerfully scooping up Eric in his arms and carrying him off to the surgery. 'I'll just give him a quick jab in his bottom. He'll hardly know what I'm doing.'

'Thanks,' said Roy, faintly.

'I've worked out what we'll have to do,' said Eric, as he and Roy finished their paper round the following morning.

Roy was a little relieved. It was the first time Eric had spoken to him since the incident at the vet's. 'Do?' he asked. 'Why do we have to do anything?'

Eric looked at him rather coldly. 'I've been nearly killed up a tree, I've been given an injection I'm quite sure I didn't need, I have no idea when I might change, or, if I do, when I'll change back . . .'

'Okay!' Roy agreed, hastily. 'We have to do something, but what?'

'Well,' said Eric. 'We cured my sister of wanting a dog by getting her one, right?'

'Right,' said Roy.

'So why don't we cure you the same way?'

'Get my parents to let me have a dog you mean?' asked Roy. 'But they won't have animals in the house. I've been trying to persuade them for years.'

'I think you should try again,' said Eric.

Roy tried. He talked to his mother, then he talked to his father, then he talked to his mother again, and at meal times, he talked to them both. He told them research had shown that pets were good for your health; he promised that he would do all the looking after; he produced lists of figures to show how little it would cost; he told them that, once they got one, they would wonder how they'd ever managed without, and that if he didn't have one soon he would probably die from disappointment, and that they would be entirely responsible.

Roy could be very persistent when he wanted, and this time he wanted. His parents resisted strongly at first, but more weakly as time went on, and eventually they gave in.

Mrs Ackerman went out to the pet shop one afternoon and came back with a little cardboard box she presented to Roy.

'Oh, you shouldn't have!' he said, as he opened it, to find his parents had bought him a cat.

'In that case,' said Eric, when Roy had admitted defeat. 'There is nothing for it. We have to tell my parents.'

'Are you sure?' asked Roy.

'They're my parents,' Eric said. 'It's only fair they should know if their only son turns into a dog, isn't it?'

Roy nodded. 'I suppose so.'

'The only question,' said Eric, thoughtfully, 'is when do we do it?'

'We?' said Roy. 'Why does it need both of us?'

'I'll need you to do the talking,' said Eric. 'I mean, if I tell them something like that while I'm a boy, they'll never believe me. And if I try and tell then when I'm a dog, I won't be able to say anything except "woof" and they'll just do what they did last time and throw me out of the house.'

'I don't know . . .' said Roy, doubtfully.

'What's wrong?'

'I . . . I can't just go up to your Mum and Dad and

say, "Excuse me, but did you know Eric turns into a dog sometimes?"' complained Roy. 'They'd never believe me. Your Dad would kill me.'

'Don't worry!' Eric assured him. 'I've got it all worked out,' and he told Roy his plan.

It was a very sensible plan, really. Roy was to walk Eric-as-a-dog round to the Banks' house, and first of all show them that his dog was abnormally intelligent, and could understand what people said. They decided the best way of doing this was for Roy to show that he had simply to ask Eric to do something or fetch something, for Eric to do it.

Once they had established that Eric was really too clever to be an ordinary dog, Roy was to break the news that he was, in fact, their son, Eric.

'And to prove that I really am,' Eric explained, 'we'll have to do something that'll show I know things that only Eric could know.'

'Like what?' asked Roy.

'I thought, if you got them to lay out some of my toys,' said Eric, 'that they could ask things like "Which one did Gran give you for Christmas?" or "Which one of these really belongs to Emily?" you see? I'll pick out the right toy, and then they'll know it must be me!'

'Brilliant,' said Roy. 'Okay, I'll do it. You're quite sure your dad won't thump me?'

'I promise, Roy,' Eric assured him. 'Dad's never thumped anyone.' He thought for a moment. 'I should watch out for Mum, though.'

At first, it all went roughly to plan. The next time Eric changed into a dog, he went round to collect Roy and the two of them walked back to the Banks' house where Roy knocked on the door.

Mr Banks answered it. Eric's Mum had gone out with Gran to do some shopping.

'Ah,' he said. 'I'm afraid Eric's out at the moment.'

'I know,' said Roy. 'I was wondering if I could talk to you. It's rather serious.'

'Ah,' said Mr Banks, who'd been looking forward to a doze in front of the television. 'You'd better come in.'

In the sitting room, Roy sat on the sofa, Eric sat on the floor beside him, and Mr Banks sat in his usual arm-chair.

'Mr Banks,' said Roy, 'I have to tell you something about this dog, that will astonish you, but first . . . is there anything you'd like brought to you?'

Mr Banks thought. 'I wouldn't mind a cup of tea,' he said. 'If you . . .'

'No, no.' Roy cut him off. 'No, it has to be something that can be carried, you know, in someone's mouth.'

'Does it?' said Mr Banks, wondering why conversations with Roy were always so difficult to follow.

'Like . . . like a pair of slippers. Would you like me to get you some slippers?'

Mr Banks pointed out that he was already wearing his slippers.

'Okay,' said Roy. 'The newspapers. I'll get you the newspaper.' He looked down at Eric. 'The newspaper for Mr Banks, please, Eric.'

Eric got up, trotted to the coffee table, picked up the newspaper and took it over to his father.

'Thank you,' said Mr Banks.

'And a cushion,' said Roy. 'Would you give Mr Banks a cushion as well, Eric?'

Eric gave his father a cushion as well.

'Thank you,' said Mr Banks.

Roy was rather pleased with the success of stage one and was all set now to move on to stage two.

'Mr Banks,' he spoke clearly and seriously, 'I expect you're wondering how this dog could possibly know what things to bring you . . .'

'He's certainly a bright little fellow, isn't he?' said Mr Banks.

'The fact is, he is no ordinary dog,' Roy leant forward, solemnly. 'Now, this may come as a bit of a shock, but he is in fact . . .'

The front door opened, and Eric's Mum called 'Hello, Charles! I'm back!'

Mr Banks got up. 'We'll have to leave this till later, I'm afraid, Roy,' he said. 'I have to help bring in the shopping.'

Mr Banks went out to help unload the shopping from the back of the car. Roy looked at Eric. There was clearly no point in trying to talk to either Mr or Mrs Banks until they'd finished.

Eric's Gran came into the sitting room. Her feet were aching after a long walk round the shops and she sat down gratefully on the sofa.

'Hello, Roy,' she said.

Roy made an instant decision. 'Would you like anything brought to you?' he asked.

'Well, I wouldn't mind a . . .'

'No, you can't have a cup of tea,' said Roy, hastily. 'It's got to be something like . . . Eric? Bring over a cushion.'

Eric brought over a cushion, and gave it to his Gran.

'And . . . and the newspaper,' said Roy.

When Eric had brought over the newspaper as well,

Roy launched into the speech he had intended to give to Mr Banks. 'I expect you're wondering how this dog could possibly know what things to bring you,' he said.

'Isn't he clever!' said Gran. She was very fond of dogs, and she liked the way this one kept looking at her with its big, brown eyes.

'Now, this may come as a bit of a shock to you,' said Roy. 'But this dog is in fact . . .'

Eric felt an itching and tingling at the back of his neck. He knew what it meant, and without even waiting to hear Roy finish the sentence, he scooted out into the hall and raced up the stairs to his bedroom.

As he dressed, he thought how infuriating it was. The one time he *wanted* to be a dog so that he could prove it really happened, he'd changed back into a boy.

Eric sat up in bed that night, writing down the day's events in his diary. He closed it when his Dad put his head round the door.

'Time this light was out, isn't it?'

'Right, Dad.'

Mr Banks came into the room and sat on the end of Eric's bed.

'I was wondering if you'd do something for me,' he said.

'Sure, Dad.' Eric had a feeling he knew what was coming next.

'I want you to have a talk to Roy.'

'What about?' asked Eric.

'I don't want to be harsh . . .' Mr Banks hesitated. 'Roy has a wonderful imagination, and it's a gift that

I'm sure he'll find very useful one day, but the trouble is that if he uses it on someone like your grandmother . . .'

'What did he tell her?' asked Eric, who knew perfectly well.

'He told her . . .' Mr Banks changed his mind. 'Well, it's not really important what he told her. The thing is, if he'd told me or your mother, it wouldn't have mattered.'

'Wouldn't it?' asked Eric. 'Why not?'

'Because we'd have laughed and told him not to be silly and sent him home,' Mr Banks explained. 'But your grandmother . . . Well, she's rather old and occasionally gets confused, so . . . so I want you to have a word with Roy and ask him not to go telling stories like that again. Alright?'

'No more stories?' asked Eric.

'I think it would be best,' said Mr Banks.

'Okay, Dad.'

Mr Banks smiled. 'Attaboy,' he got up and walked back to the door. 'Night, son!'

Eric lay in the dark, thinking. No more stories. Oh well, maybe it was for the best.

'Sorry I messed things up like that,' said Roy, as the two of them walked home through the park after school the next day. 'If I'd known you were going to change back when you did, I'd never have said all that to your Gran.' He sighed. 'Your Dad'll never believe anything I say again!'

They crossed the bridge over the lake, and headed towards the swings. 'But I was thinking,' he went on. 'It might be more fun with nobody knowing. Except the two of us. I mean, you don't have to worry about food or anything, I mean, I'll look after you. I'll always be here.

And we could have all sorts of adventures.' He looked at
Eric. 'Don't you think?'
    'Woof!' said Eric.

# ROY'S DREAM

It was always Roy's dream that one day he would do something so amazing, so important or so brave, that he would get his picture in the newspapers.

He and Eric did a paper round, and Roy often liked to imagine everyone opening their morning papers to find his photograph splashed all over the front page. He liked to think of their faces when they realized that their newspaper boy had done something ... well, Roy was never quite sure what it was he wanted to have done, but that wasn't important. What was important, was that his picture was in the papers.

This wasn't just an idle daydream Roy had from time to time. He actually dreamt about it when he was asleep, too. In his dream, he was standing on the stage of the Assembly Hall at school, with Eric beside him, looking out at hundreds of people, all clapping and cheering until the Mayor lifted his hands for silence, and addressed the crowd.

'Ladies and Gentlemen,' he said. 'We are here to pay tribute to an act of outstanding heroism, and to acknowledge our debt to Roy Ackerman, who, with the help of his faithful dog, has single handedly exposed and apprehended a dangerous, international criminal.'

All eyes turned to a short, burly man standing between two large policemen. He was handcuffed, and scowling heavily.

'Only a razor sharp mind like Roy's,' the Mayor laid a friendly arm on Roy's shoulder, 'would have realized that the headmaster of his own school was, from his study, leading a gang of other headmasters in a vast diamond smuggling opertion! It is, therefore, with the greatest of pleasure that I now present him, and his dog, Eric, with the Freedom of our City, and with this cheque for thirteen million pounds.'

The best part of the dream wasn't getting the money. It was when the flashguns of the newsmen in the front row popped excitedly and Roy knew that, by morning, his picture would be on the front page of every newspaper in the country.

The worst part of the dream was when the hand on his shoulder started shaking him, and he realized it was his mother, waking him up and telling him he was late for school.

One morning, when Roy had come down to the kitchen for breakfast, he found his sister, Susan, studying the local paper.

'Look, Mum!' she said, excitedly. 'I'm in this one as well!' She pointed to a photograph with the caption 'Beauty and the Beast'. 'It's the one of me leading the donkey.'

'Very nice!' said her mother, admiringly. 'Show it to Roy.'

Susan held the picture out in front of her brother. 'What do you think?'

Roy looked at it. 'Which one's you?' he asked. 'The one with the big ears?'

'Oh, very funny!' Susan snatched the picture away.

'It's not everyone's got a sister who's Carnival Queen,' said Mrs Ackerman. 'You should be proud.'

'What's so special about being Carnival Queen?' asked Roy with a scowl. 'I mean, it's not as if she's caught a gang of international thieves or anything, is it?'

'You're jealous!' Susan was quite unbothered. 'That's your trouble, you're jealous!'

Roy denied it, of course, but even as he did so, he knew that the awful truth was that his sister was right. He *was* jealous. Susan had got her picture in the papers and was famous – well, sort of famous – while he had never even had a mention in the school magazine.

He decided, then and there, that he was doing to do something about it. He was going to do something that would mean they would *have* to put his picture in the papers.

The only question was . . . what?

Roy talked it over with Eric as they walked to school that day.

'What's the point?' asked Eric, who didn't really understand why anyone should want their picture in the papers in the first place. 'And how are you going to do it? It won't be easy, you know.'

'Maybe not,' said Roy, 'but I've got one thing going for me.'

'What's that?'

'You!'

'Me?'

'Exactly,' said Roy. 'I mean, it's not everyone who's got a best friend that turns into a dog, is it?'

'But you can't put that in the papers!' Eric protested,

'I don't want anyone else to know about it. And you promised!'

'I wasn't thinking of telling anyone about you,' said Roy. 'I was thinking of you doing things.'

'What sort of things?' asked Eric.

Roy stopped. They had taken the short cut to school, and were crossing the canal. Roy pointed down into the deep, slime covered waters of the lock.

'Imagine someone in there, drowning,' he said. 'The crowds gather, gasping in horror as the victim screams for help, and then I step forward. "Stand back, everyone!" I say. "Don't worry! My little dog will rescue her,"' he turned to Eric. 'And then you jump in and rescue her. I got the idea from a Lassie film.'

'Rescue who?' asked Eric.

'My sister, Susan.'

'What would Susan be doing in there?'

'You know,' said Roy. 'Drowning.'

'But why would she be in there?' Eric persisted. 'She's never fallen in before.'

'We could push her,' said Roy, hopefully. 'And think of the headlines. "Ackerman's Wonderdog Saves Girl." I could tell them I'd specially trained you for emergencies, and that . . .'

'No,' Eric shook his head, firmly. 'That's a crazy idea.'

Roy sighed. 'You're probably right. Who'd want to see my sister rescued?'

They crossed the canal and continued the walk to school.

'I'll tell you something, though,' said Eric. 'What you said about Lassie has given me an idea,' and he told Roy what it was.

'Brill-i-ant!' said Roy.

*

They had to wait until Eric turned into a dog again before they could put Eric's plan into action, but fortunately they didn't have to wait long.

On Saturday morning, when Roy heard Eric-as-a-dog barking in his front garden, he went and told his mother that he was just going out for ten minutes. Then he went outside to meet Eric, and the two of them set off down the road.

It took them only a few minutes to get to the building site, to crawl through a gap in the corrugated iron fencing, and to pick their way over the piles of rubble to the place they had chosen earlier in the week. They were standing on the bulldozed remains of a row of terraced houses. It was just the sort of place that children should keep away from. Accidents, after all, can happen very easily on building sites, and that is exactly why Eric and Roy had chosen it.

Roy lay down in the dust and dirt and began piling some of the bricks around his legs and body. He pulled a large piece of wood over his chest, and finally took a small bottle of theatrical blood from his pocket. He poured a little round one leg, splashed some more over one arm, and finally put a trickle from one corner of his mouth.

'How does that look, Eric?' he asked. 'Okay?'

'Woof!' said Eric.

'Right,' said Roy. 'You'd better get back and do your bit.' He looked at his watch. 'Twenty minutes since I left, they should be worrying by now.'

Eric's plan was quite simple. While Roy lay on the building site, pretending to be injured, Eric was supposed to race back to the Ackermans' house, bark at the door, and then persuade Roy's mother or someone to come to the rescue. It was the sort of story that newspapers love, and they were sure there would be a headline 'Boy Saved By Faithful Dog' and a picture of the two of them together.

When Eric got back to the house, however, and barked, it didn't work like that at all. For a start, it was a long time before anyone even heard him. Mrs Ackerman and Roy's sister, Susan, were the only people in the house, and they were both upstairs, making beds.

Eventually, Susan opened one of the upstairs windows. 'It's that dog that keeps following Roy,' she told her mother.

Mrs Ackerman looked out of the window. 'Why does he keep barking like that?' she asked. 'What does he want?'

'I know exactly what he wants,' said Susan. Hurrying into the bathroom, she filled a basin with cold water and emptied it all over Eric.

'Well!' she said, in a satisfied voice. 'That seems to have stopped him barking.'

Back on the building site, Roy couldn't understand why Eric was taking so long. He was tired of waiting, and had almost decided to give up the whole idea, when he heard someone coming. He closed his eyes, as if he was barely conscious, and gave a low groan.

The next thing he felt was a large, rough tongue scraping across the side of his face and he opened his eyes to find a dog looking down at him. Not Eric, but a large white bulldog that seemed to like the taste of theatrical blood.

'Rufus. Come to heel, sir! At once!' With a sinking heart, Roy recognized the voice of his headmaster, and a moment later, Mr Blocker came scrambling over the rubble towards him.

'Ackerman?' Mr Blocker stopped in surprise. 'What are you doing here?'

Roy struggled into a sitting position. 'Well, sir . . .'

'Don't you realize it's dangerous to play in places like this? Unless you're very careful, you can have a serious accident and . . .' Mr Blocker's voice trailed off, and his face went white as he stared at the beam across Roy's chest, the bricks over his legs, and the blood over his face and arms. 'Oh, my goodness! You already have!'

'No, sir. It's alright . . .' Roy struggled to get up to show that there was nothing wrong with him.

'No, no!' said Mr Blocker. 'Whatever you do, don't move until we've got help.' He ran back towards the fence and shouted to his wife. 'Martha? Martha, there's been an accident. We need an ambulance. And you'd better call the police . . . and the fire brigade. We've got a boy trapped under a beam.'

He turned back to Roy, who had by now struggled free.

'I'm alright, sir,' he said. 'Really.'

'Alright?' gasped Mr Blocker. 'But . . .' His eyes hardened suspiciously. 'What's going on here?'

'It was just a sort of joke, you see, sir,' Roy smiled, hoping that Mr Blocker might see the funny side of it all.

Mr Blocker did not smile back. 'Monday morning, Ackerman,' he said, grimly. 'Outside my study.'

Later that morning, Roy and a rather wet and bedraggled Eric, were sitting on a bench in the shopping precinct, gloomily wondering why it had all gone wrong.

'It was never this difficult in the films,' sighed Roy.

'Woof, woof,' said Eric.

'There are always plenty of people quite happy to be rescued in films. It must be different in America. I mean, over there they always seem to be falling down mine-shafts or getting attacked by bears, but who needs helping round here? No one!'

But Roy was wrong. At that moment, just in front of them, a man coming out of the chemist's dropped his wallet. He obviously meant to put it back in his jacket – but instead of going into the pocket, the wallet fell to the ground.

Eric barked and dashed over to pick it up, but the man was already walking briskly down the road.

'Eric!' Roy was very excited. 'This is our big chance! If we follow him and give him his wallet back, we might . . .'

But Eric was already chasing off down the road, the wallet gripped firmly in his mouth.

'Hang on!' called Roy. 'Wait for me!'

Eric nearly caught up with the man as he turned out of the precinct and crossed the high street, but just as he was about to follow, the traffic lights changed. He had to wait a full forty seconds before he could get across himself.

By that time, Eric had lost sight of him. (It's not easy to keep track of someone on a busy street when your head is only a foot or so off the ground. Fortunately, Roy had caught up by then. He could see which direction the man had gone, and the two of them dashed off up the High Street in pursuit of their quarry.

They saw him go round into Coleman Street,

followed him as he turned into Tadburn Lane, and then, just as they were catching up with him, he climbed into a taxi, and drove off. Roy and Eric were left panting on the pavement, staring after him.

Eric saw the bicycle first, propped up against the side of the greengrocer's. He ran over to it and barked. Roy recognized the bicycle as well. It belonged to Alison Lewer, a girl in their class at school, and Roy didn't hesitate.

'Hop in, Eric!' He pointed to the basket strapped to the front handlebars, and as soon as Eric was in, Roy swung into the saddle and they were off.

Alison came out of the greengrocer's. 'Hoi!' she called.

'Just borrowing it for an emergency!' shouted Roy. 'We'll bring it right back!' And without waiting for Alison's reply, he pedalled off down the road.

Normally, of course, a bicycle could not hope to keep up with a taxi, but Eric and Roy were lucky. The traffic was heavy through that part of town, and the taxi had to keep stopping, while Roy could weave his way in and out of the traffic jams. He was never quite fast enough to catch up, but at least he managed to keep the taxi in sight. Finally, to Roy's relief (his legs were getting very tired) they saw it turn into the bus station and the man got out.

Gratefully, Roy brought the bicycle to a halt, and leaned against a wall, gasping for breath. Eric leapt out of the basket. Still clutching the wallet in his mouth, he followed the man into the ticket office, and proudly laid it at his feet.

'That'll be three pounds forty,' the ticket clerk was saying.

The man reached into his pocket. 'My wallet!' he gasped. 'I've lost my wallet!'

'Woof, woof!' said Eric.

'You haven't dropped it or anything, have you?' asked the ticket clerk.

The man looked down, and saw his wallet on the ground. 'So I have!' he said.

Roy staggered into the ticket office, his legs still wobbly from all the cycling. 'You dropped your wallet!' he called.

'Yes, I know,' said the man, cheerfully. He picked it up, paid for his ticket, and went out to catch his bus.

Eric and Roy stared after him.

'We'd better face it, Eric,' said Roy. 'We're just not cut out to be heroes.'

After that, Roy decided that trying to get his picture in the papers had landed him in quite enough trouble for one week. He'd had a very uncomfortable half hour with Alison's father, who called round to complain about the bicycle, and there was still Mr Blocker to face on Monday morning.

As he and Eric did their paper round, Roy admitted that he thought, perhaps, they should abandon the whole idea.

'Woof,' Eric barked in agreement.

The fact that Eric was a dog while they were doing the paper round didn't slow them up too much. Most of the letter boxes were still within his reach, and as long as Roy folded them up for him, Eric could carry them up the paths and push them into the boxes. In fact, as Eric later pointed out, it was just as well he *was* a dog that day, otherwise they would never have found Mrs Quilter.

Mrs Quilter lived on her own at number 37. Her front door was mostly made of glass, so her letter box was right at the bottom. This meant that, when Eric pushed her newspaper through the flap, he could see into her hall – and what he saw was Mrs Quilter lying in a heap at the bottom of the stairs.

Eric barked, and Roy came over to see what the trouble was. He called through the letter box to Mrs Quilter a couple of times to ask if she was all right, but she didn't reply. She didn't even move.

'I'll call an ambulance,' said Roy.

Eric was a dog again when they went to visit Mrs Quilter in hospital after school the next day. As the nurse took them along to the ward, she asked, 'Are you the ones that found her?'

'Woof,' said Eric.

'Yes,' said Roy.

'Well, you did a good job there.' She showed them to Mrs Quilter's bed, which had a curtain pulled round it. 'Now don't stay too long. And for goodness sake don't let Matron see the dog.'

Mrs Quilter was propped up in bed on a lot of pillows. She was looking rather frail and tired, but her face lit up when Eric hopped up on to the bed and gave her the bunch of flowers they had brought.

'How lovely!' she said. 'And is this the dog that helped you find me?'

'That's right,' said Roy. 'He's called Eric.'

'Well, I think he must be very clever,' said Mrs Quilter, 'I think you both are, and I want to thank you. I want to thank you both very much.'

'You're alright now, are you?' asked Roy.

'I think I am,' Mrs Quilter smiled. 'Though they tell me if you hadn't found me when you did, it might have been a different story.'

'We brought a jam jar for the flowers,' said Roy. 'I'll get some water.'

Roy fetched the water and Mrs Quilter laughed as Eric picked up the flowers in his teeth and put them neatly in the jar.

'You're very good for me, you two,' she said. 'I wish there was something I could give you in return. I know . . .' She fumbled in her handbag for a moment, and then pulled out a tiny, ivory handled penknife with the initials 'I.Q.' on it in silver. 'Here,' she said, pressing it into Roy's hand, 'I want you to have this.'

'You don't have to give us anything,' said Roy. 'We're just glad you're better.' He looked at the knife. It was very small indeed, but a beautiful knife, nonetheless.

A man put his head round the curtain. 'Sorry to disturb you,' he said. 'The *Daily Echo*. Just wondered if anyone would mind if we took a picture?'

It was a very good picture. It covered half a page and had the words 'Roy's Superdog Saves Pensioner' printed over the top. Underneath was a long column of text saying how Roy and Eric had found Mrs Quilter and raised the alarm.

The funny thing was that it didn't make Roy feel like he thought it would make him feel. It was quite useful – Mr Blocker, in view of what he called Roy's 'initiative and common sense' had decided to say no more about the incident on the building site – but it didn't make Roy *feel* any different, and he'd somehow imagined that it would. He'd thought that, if the newspapers said he was important, then he would *feel* important, but he didn't. He felt like he was ... well, like he was still just Roy, really.

His mother cut the picture out of the newspaper and asked Roy if he'd like to keep it and stick it up on his wall, but in the end, he didn't bother.

He kept the penknife, though.

# THE MONEY SPINNER

It was something Alison said that started it. She said it in the playground, when Eric (who was a dog at the time) and Roy were doing a trick. Well, Roy called it a trick. What he did was to shuffle some cards, lay them face up on the ground and then ask his dog (that was Eric) to pick out the Queen of Diamonds.

Of course, if you'd known Eric was really a boy, you wouldn't have been very impressed. All Eric had to do was walk up and put his paw on the right card. But if you didn't know Eric was a boy (and nobody except Roy did), you'd probably have thought, as Alison did, that he was the cleverest dog you'd ever seen.

'You should enter your dog for competitions, Roy,' she said. 'He might win some money.'

The bit about money stuck in Roy's mind. He had the money he earned from his paper round each week, but just at the moment, most of that went to pay for a new kitchen window. The idea of winning money was very appealing. So, first of all he asked Alison what sort of competitions she had meant, and then he suggested the idea to Eric.

Eric wasn't very keen at first. 'I'd never win a dog competition!' he said. 'My legs are too short. And anyway, I don't want to be shampooed and combed and have to stand around all day being stared at.'

'It's not that sort of competition,' Roy told him. 'It's called an Obedience Trial. You just have to be able to do things when you're told. For someone who can multiply fractions in his head, it'd be no problem at all.'

Eric didn't quite see what multiplying fractions had got to do with it, but he had to admit it didn't sound too difficult. If it was a competition to see who could understand orders best, then Eric, with the brain of a boy, ought to find it quite easy.

'How much money?' he asked Roy.

Roy said that was one of the things they'd have to find out.

The following Wednesday evening, Roy led Eric through the front gates of Collingwood Comprehensive, past a large blackboard on which had been chalked 'Dog Obedience classes – 7.30 p.m.', and into the hall where the class was being held.

In the day time, it was the school gymnasium, but now all the equipment had been put away, and plastic sheeting had been spread over the floor. Along one wall, stood a line of people, each with a dog, and in the middle of the room, a tall woman in a tweed hat was talking to them about whistles.

Just by the door, another woman was sitting at a green baize table, with an exercise book full of names. 'Can I help you?' she asked.

'Yes,' said Roy, giving his best smile. 'I'd like to enter my dog in a competition.'

The woman looked at him.

'Competition?' she asked.

'That's right,' said Roy, and he pointed down at Eric. 'So he can win a prize. Money.' He smiled again.

'Has he done any obedience training?' asked the woman. 'Has he been to classes? Learnt the commands?'

Roy had to admit that he hadn't. 'But he picks things up very quickly,' he said. 'You just tell me what he's got to do, and I'll explain it to him.'

'Anything wrong, Joyce?' The woman in the tweed hat had come over to see what was happening.

'This boy says he wants to enter his dog in a competition, Miss Robson. I was about to tell him it's not quite that easy.'

Miss Robson looked down at Roy, and then at Eric. She was the sort of woman who made you want to check that your shirt was properly tucked in and that you'd pulled your socks up.

'And what's your name?' she asked.

'Roy. Roy Ackerman, Miss.'

'Do you know what dogs have to do in an obedience competition, Roy?' she asked.

'Not really,' said Roy.

'Well, if you want to find out, you'd better follow me,' and with that, Miss Robson turned briskly away.

'Wait here, Eric,' Roy hissed.

So Eric waited, while Roy followed Miss Robson to the middle of the room where she called to one of the people along the wall. 'June! Perhaps you'd be kind enough to show this young man how to do a retrieve,' and she passed over a small piece of wood shaped like a dumb-bell.

June brought her dog into the middle of the floor, while Miss Robson explained to Roy what was going to happen.

'To start with, the dog has to sit to heel, while the dumb-bell is thrown. The dog mustn't chase after it, or you lose points. Then, on the order "Fetch", the dog must run straight to the dumb-bell, pick it up, bring it straight back, present it, and sit to heel again.'

'Do you think your dog could learn to do the retrieve?' asked Miss Robson.

Roy was fairly sure that Eric could do a lot better than the collie. 'No problem,' he said. 'Just let me explain it to him.' He ran back to Eric, who was still waiting by the table, and told him what he had to do. Eric was rather relieved. It certainly didn't sound very difficult.

'Okay?' Roy asked.

'Woof!' said Eric.

Eric followed Roy back to the middle of the hall, and when Miss Robson said they could start, Roy threw the dumb-bell. Eric, of course, did it all perfectly. He didn't move till he was told, he brought the dumb-bell straight back to Roy then went round the back and sat down again. In fact it all seemed so simple that it was a bit of a shock to find everyone clapping. Even Miss Robson seemed rather impressed.

'You say he's never done this before?' she asked.

'No,' said Roy. 'Like I said, he picks things up very quickly.'

Then Miss Robson asked if he'd mind trying a few other exercises, and for the next quarter of an hour, Roy walked Eric to heel, recalled him from a distance, made him sit up, lie down, stay, and then find things by scent. At the end of it all, the audience weren't just clapping, they were cheering out loud, and all sorts of people had come in from other classes in the school to watch what was going on.

'I've never seen anything like it,' said Miss Robson. 'I've been training dogs for thirty five years and I've never seen anything like it in my life. You want to enter him in a competition?'

'We could take them to the Nottingham trials this Saturday,' murmured Joyce, 'and put him in for the Beginners Class.'

'Put him straight in the Novice Class as well, I think,' said Miss Robson. She turned to Roy. 'Perhaps I'd better have a word with your parents, young man. Where exactly do you live?'

Roy told her, and while she was writing it down, he felt Eric nudging his ankle, and remembered the other thing he was supposed to ask.

'Are there prizes at this competition?' he said. Miss Robson looked a little blank, so he added. 'We heard you could win ... you know, money and things.'

'Money?' said Miss Robson. 'Well, nothing to speak of, I'm afraid. The first prize is only five pounds.'

'Five pounds!' said Roy, wondering how rich you had to be before five pounds was 'nothing to speak of'. 'That'd be ten pounds if we won both classes, would it?'

Miss Robson said she thought it probably would.

'Brilliant!' said Roy.

Roy and Eric were watching from Roy's bedroom window, the day Miss Robson called on Roy's father.

'Ten pounds,' Eric was saying for the umpteenth time, 'just for walking around and picking up sticks!' He was rather excited. Until now, turning into a dog had been fun occasionally, but more usually very inconvenient. 'Of course, there's one snag,' he added.

'Snag?' said Roy.

'Well, what happens if I *don't* turn into a dog for the competition on Saturday?'

It was the first time the thought had occurred to Roy, and it was a very alarming one. 'Hey, Eric!' he clutched his friend's arm, 'What happens if you don't turn into a dog on Saturday?'

'I think it'll be alright,' said Eric. 'Remember when we decided to go round to that dog class? We didn't know I was going to turn into a dog then . . .'

'But you did!' Roy said.

Eric nodded. 'I think, as long as it's something we both want . . .'

'Brilliant!' said Roy.

'Here she comes,' said Eric. Miss Robson had parked a battered old Land Rover on the pavement outside the house, and was walking up to the front door.

Roy's father, was a little confused. When Miss Robson had rung to say she wanted to talk to him about Roy, he'd presumed that she wanted to complain about something – but here she was saying that Roy had a 'remarkable rapport' with animals and that she wanted to take him and his dog to Nottingham on Saturday.

'You want to take Roy,' he said, 'and that scrubby little mongrel stray to a dog show?'

Miss Robson stiffened. 'There's no such thing as a scrubby little mongrel in my book, Mr Ackerman,' she said, sternly. 'All dogs have their own personalities, just like people. And yes, I certainly do want to take them.'

Mr Ackerman was still doubtful. He'd always regarded Roy as the sort of boy who could break things just by being in the same room with them, and to let him loose on a kind, well-meaning spinster like Miss Robson, just didn't seem fair.

'Look, Miss Robson,' he begain. 'It's a very generous offer, but my son can be a bit of a handful . . .'

Miss Robson cut him off decisively. 'I've trained Alsatians for the police, Mr Ackerman,' she said. 'I promise you, young boys are no problem at all.'

Mr Ackerman gave up. He'd tried to warn her. 'Well, if you're sure,' he said, 'I'll go and tell him.'

'I shouldn't bother,' said Miss Robson. 'I should imagine he's been listening at the door since I came in.'

Mr Ackerman opened the door, just in time to see Roy and Eric disappearing upstairs. He looked at Miss Robson with a new respect. Maybe, she'd be alright after all.

As far as Eric and Roy were concerned, the competition at Nottingham that Saturday went exactly as planned. Eric did change into a dog, and he and Roy entered the Beginners class, scored 100 out of 100 points – then did exactly the same in the Novices. Naturally, they came first in both, and Roy collected ten pounds. It was all too easy.

Then Miss Robson said there was another show next Saturday in Ashfield, if they'd like to go. Eric said 'Woof!' and Roy said 'Yes, please,' and after that, a sort of pattern emerged. Each Saturday, Miss Robson and her friend Joyce would arrive at Roy's house in the old Land Rover, and take them off to a show.

The things they had to do became more complicated. Roy was only allowed to give an instruction
once, for instance, so Eric had to listen carefully, and
sometimes he was only allowed to use hand signals,
which Eric had to remember, but even so, it wasn't
very difficult. They always came first, and Roy would
go up at the end to collect the prize money, with Eric
trotting beside him.

They won a lot of money – certainly more than
most eleven-year-old boys had, but in all the excitement of being rich, it never occurred to them to
wonder why Miss Robson and her friend Joyce should
give up every Saturday just to ferry them around the
country.

They found out at Wakefield.

At the Wakefield show, Roy had been up to collect his
prize as usual, but when he and Eric returned to the
Land Rover, they found Miss Robson and Joyce setting up a picnic on the grass – both of them buzzing
with excitement.

'Well, Roy,' said Miss Robson, as she offered Eric a
sandwich. 'That was rather a special win.'

'Was it?' asked Roy.

'You've scored over 290 points in a championship show,' said Joyce, barely able to conceal her
glee. 'That means you've won a Kennel Club
certificate . . .'

'And you've already had three wins in an Open
Class C competition,' said Miss Robson. 'You know
what that means?'

Roy shook his head.

'It means,' said Miss Robson, lowering her voice, as
if she were speaking in church. 'It means that you and

Eric are entitled to enter the supreme dog championship of them all . . . Crufts!'

Eric pricked up his ears. Crufts! He'd seen that on television. Was it really possible? Eric had always thought of himself as a rather ordinary boy – and an ordinary dog, come to that. He found the idea very exciting.

'Our little club has never had a Crufts champion,' said Joyce. 'Even Miss Robson only came third, when she entered, but you two . . .'

'You two could win,' said Miss Robson. 'I'm sure of it. Would you like to enter?'

'Woof!' said Eric, without hesitation.

Roy thought for a second. 'What's the prize money?' he asked.

'I believe it's thirty-five pounds,' said Miss Robson.

'Brilliant!' said Roy.

The Crufts championship is held each year at Earl's Court in London. As Roy entered the huge arena for the first time, and stared about him at the thousands of people and hundreds of dogs of every imaginable shape and size, he began to understand why Miss Robson and Joyce had been so excited about it all.

There were dogs being judged for their agility, their grooming, their appearance and their breeding. There were dogs so big they could have eaten Eric with one swallow, and dogs so small they could have curled up in one of his shoes. But above all, there was a buzz, a tingle in the air, a sense of excitement that you could almost touch.

'They've come here from all over the world, Roy,' said Miss Robson. 'The most experienced trainers, the best breeders, the finest dogs – and all of them with just one dream. To leave here as a Crufts Champion.'

'Champion,' breathed Roy. He was already picturing himself and Eric striding across the arena to collect an enormous silver cup.

'You see, Roy,' said Joyce, beside him. 'It's not just the money.'

'No,' Roy agreed. 'It isn't, is it?'

'Come along,' said Miss Robson, 'We must get you registered.' She led the way to the desk where competitors had to sign in.

Roy was the thirty-sixth competitor in the first heats of the obedience trials, and as he stood in the tunnel, waiting his turn to go out into the arena, he was distinctly nervous. He wasn't nervous about the competition. He'd been watching the other competitors and he knew that he and Eric could get through to the finals without much difficulty. He was nervous because he'd lost Eric.

Half an hour before, Roy had gone to buy himself a hot dog. He told Eric where he was going, so that he could come and warn him if they were called early – but when he came back, Eric was gone. He'd tried asking people if they'd seen him, but you get some funny looks when you say you've lost your dog at a dog show, and he didn't want to search too far afield in case Eric came back while he was away. The trouble was, that number thirty five was already out in the arena. Roy and Eric were next and if Eric didn't turn up soon . . .

Suddenly Roy felt a tap on his shoulder, and turned round to see Eric saying, 'Hi, Roy!' His first feeling was of relief at the sight of a friendly face.

'Eric!' he said. 'Look, I've lost . . .' And then he stopped. It had taken him that long to realize that if Eric was here as a boy, then there was no Eric here as a dog, and if Eric wasn't here as a dog . . .

'What are you doing?' he gasped. 'Why have you changed?'

'I couldn't help it,' said Eric. 'I just did.'

'But you said if it was something we both wanted . . .'

'I think that's the trouble, Roy,' said Eric. 'I'm not sure I do want it.'

Roy couldn't believe it. 'Don't you realize what we could win in there?' he said. 'And I'm not talking about the thirty-five pounds. This is Crufts, Eric, a chance to be champion at Crufts! How can you *not* want it?'

Eric sighed. 'I'll try and explain, Roy,' he said, 'Do you mind if I get dressed first, though? It's a bit cold in this dog blanket.'

When Eric had turned back into a boy, of course, he hadn't had any clothes, so he'd grabbed the nearest thing he could find (a dog blanket) and come back to tell Roy. Fortunately, Roy's mother had insisted he take a bag of smart clothes ('just in case he won') and these were back in the Land Rover. Roy and Eric walked out to the car park.

'You see, Roy,' Eric explained, 'winning at Crufts is exactly what mustn't happen. If we won here . . . Well, what would your parents want to do? About me, I mean.'

Roy thought for a bit. His Dad had always said no to having a dog, but if Eric was a Crufts Champion . . . 'They'd probably want to adopt you,' he said.

'And then?' said Eric.

Roy thought a bit more. The first thing his parents would do would be to ask a lot of questions. They'd want to know whose dog Eric was, where he lived, where he'd come from. When that happened, it would get very difficult to hide the fact that Eric the dog was also Eric the boy. 'I see what you mean,' he said.

'I don't want to be a fairground freak, Roy. I don't want to be poked around by scientists so they can find out what's happened to me. I just want to carry on being me. I like it that way. I'm sorry.'

'That's alright,' said Roy.

'Really?' asked Eric.

'Course it is,' Roy grinned. 'What's a Crufts Championship between friends? Here, you'd better get in.'

As Roy helped Eric climb into the back of the Land Rover to get changed, a voice called loudly from the other side of the car park.

'Roy?' It was Miss Robson. 'Is that you, Roy?' She was running between the cars towards him, with Joyce close behind. 'Is everything alright?' she asked, rather out of breath.

'Not exactly,' Roy admitted.

'What on earth are you doing out here?' asked Joyce. 'They've been calling your number for ages.'

'It's Eric,' said Roy. 'He doesn't want to do it.'

Miss Robson looked at him sharply. 'What do you mean?'

'I just mean . . . I just mean he doesn't want to do it,' Roy said, wishing he could think of something that didn't sound so feeble.

'How can a dog tell you something like that!' Joyce asked.

Roy couldn't think of anything to say.

'You've discussed this with him?' asked Miss Robson.

It was an unusual sort of question, but Roy had learnt over the past weeks that, as far as dogs were concerned, Miss Robson was an unusual sort of person. 'Yes,' he said.

'And you're quite sure he doesn't want to enter this competition?'

'Positive,' said Roy. He was feeling thoroughly miserable. He knew how much the championship meant to Miss Robson. He knew how much trouble she'd gone to, how much time she'd given up, and he didn't dare think how much it must have cost. He looked at the ground, half expecting her to tear him limb from limb.

But she didn't. Instead, she said, 'Don't worry, Roy. It doesn't matter.'

Roy looked up. 'You mean you don't mind?'

'Mind? Of course I mind,' said Miss Robson, briskly. 'To have a dog from our little club win a championship at Crufts . . . well, it would have meant a great deal to us, but that's no reason to forget what this is all about.' She put a hand on his shoulder. 'Dogs, Roy. We have no more right to make them do things they don't want to than we have with people. I would never, *never* want to see someone do that, just for the sake of a prize. Even a prize like this. Now, where's Eric?'

Roy drew a deep breath. This wasn't going to be an easy one to explain.

'Woof!' said Eric from the back of the Land Rover, wagging his tail.

'Right.' said Miss Robson. 'Let's go back in and see the rest of the competition, shall we?'

The obedience championship that year was won by a retriever from Hampshire called Corrie. They all watched as the proud owner collected the cup, and held it high above her head so that the newspapermen could take pictures.

Then Miss Robson drove them home.

So Eric never became a champion at Crufts. He'd like to have been one, he and Roy would both have liked that, but in the end, keeping Eric's secret was more important. Anyway, as Eric later pointed out to Roy, they'd been very lucky really. They'd earned some money, they'd seen Crufts, and it had all been a great adventure while it lasted. Neither of them, however, could forget the last thing Miss Robson said when she dropped them off at Roy's house that night.

'Remember, Roy. If Eric ever changes his mind, you let me know.'

'I will, Miss Robson,' said Roy. 'It's a promise.'

'Woof!' said Eric.

# THE ADOPTION

One of the snags about being a dog, Eric discovered, was that you didn't really have a home any more. It was alright if you wanted to walk around town or go for a run in the park, but if, say, you just wanted to sit down and watch television, or make yourself a sandwich because you were hungry, where were you supposed to go?

If you were a dog that was a dog all the time, thought Eric, then your owners gave you somewhere warm and dry to lie down and proper food at meal times, but if you were a boy who was sometimes a dog, as he was, it wasn't that simple.

Eric had a very nice home as a boy, but his parents didn't know that he sometimes turned into a dog. So, if they found a mongrel in Eric's bedroom reading a comic, they naturally thought it was just a stray, and would shoo it outside, whatever the weather.

Usually, of course, Eric could go straight round to see Roy. Roy could make sure he got fed if he was hungry, would smuggle him up to his bedroom, or take him round to visit someone – the trouble was that Roy wasn't always there. He might have been taken out for the day, visiting his relations or shopping, and even when Roy was there, they had to be careful not to be seen by anyone. Roy's Mum and Dad didn't really approve of dogs in the house, and Roy's sister, Susan, would always tell them if she thought she'd seen Eric creeping indoors ... So Eric would sometimes find himself as a dog with nowhere to go, and no one to look after him.

About mid-day one Saturday morning, Eric felt a familiar itching on the back of his neck. He just had time to shout to his mother that he was going round to Roy's and that he might stay there for lunch, before dashing upstairs to change into a dog where no one else would see.

Then he crept out of the house and went round to see Roy.

When Roy saw Eric on the doorstep, he said, 'Hey, Eric! Brilliant!'

'Woof,' said Eric, and he was about to walk in, when Mrs Ackerman called from the hall. 'Is that Eric, Roy?'

Roy hesitated. 'Not exactly, Mum,' he said.

'Well, hurry up,' said Mrs Ackerman. 'We're leaving in five minutes.'

'She's taking me to the cinema,' said Roy. He turned and shouted back indoors 'Mum! Can we bring a dog?'

'No, we can't!' Mrs Ackerman appeared beside him. 'Dogs aren't allowed in cinemas. And you've got four and a half minutes to get changed.' She turned to Eric. 'Off you go!' she said, and closed the front door.

Sitting on the step, Eric could just hear Roy calling from indoors, 'Tell you all abut it tomorrow, Eric!'

And that was that.

Eric walked back down the path and sat on the

pavement, wondering what to do next. While he was sitting there, a baker's van stopped a little way down the road. The baker got out, opened the back doors of the van and started loading his basket.

If you've ever been really hungry yourself, you'll know that the smell of food can make you feel even hungrier. That's what happened to Eric when the scent of freshly baked bread wafted down the street towards him – except that it was a lot worse for Eric, because his sense of smell was so much stronger as a dog.

Almost without realizing it, Eric found himself walking towards the van, just to see what it was that smelt so delicious. When he got there and looked inside, the saliva started dribbling from the corners of his mouth. All along the sides of the van were racks, not just of loaves of bread, but of doughnuts, iced buns, tea cakes, macaroons, chocolate gateaux, Danish pastries . . . and no sign of the baker. He had taken his delivery basket up the path to the house opposite.

Now, under normal circumstances, Eric would never have dreamt of stealing something from the back of a baker's van. But it was coming up to lunch time, he was very hungry, and with Roy at the cinema for the rest of the afternoon, it didn't look as if he was going to get any food for a long time. Maybe, he thought, if he took one bun, just one bun, then maybe another day, when he was a boy, he could meet the baker and pay him for it.

Eric climbed up into the back of the van. He sniffed his way up and down the racks, trying to choose what to eat, and had just decided to have a ringed doughnut, when the baker came back. As he heard the steps, Eric froze, expecting any second to be picked up and thrown back into the street – but it didn't happen. The baker was talking to someone, and didn't even look in the van as he tossed his basket in and closed the doors.

Eric sighed with relief. Then, as he heard the baker get into the driver's seat and start the engine, he began to think that it might have been a good thing if he *had* been thrown out on to the street! A moment later, the van drove off down the road!

At first, Eric thought they'd only be going a little way before the baker stopped for some more deliveries, but that was not to be. They drove on and on and on. It seemed the baker had finished his deliveries in that area and was going somewhere else. Where? Eric had absolutely no idea.

He jolted around in the back of the van, too worried even to eat his doughnut, until, what seemed like hours later, the van stopped. The baker got out, opened the back doors and Eric, who'd been waiting for just this moment, shot out like a bullet and ran off down the road as fast as he could. He had no intention of being trapped in there again.

Eric didn't stop running until the van was completely out of sight. He needn't have worried. The baker was far too surprised to try chasing after him, but when Eric did stop, to catch his breath and look around him, one thing was abundantly clear. He had no idea where he was. He was completely and utterly lost.

Eric walked down the road for a quarter of an hour before he found a sign post which told him that he was seven miles from home – and that he'd been walking in the wrong direction.

It took him another three hours to walk the seven

miles. Seven miles is a long enough distance to walk
even if you have human legs. If you have the little
short legs of a mongrel, seven miles is an absolute
marathon!

It wasn't just the length of the journey that upset
Eric, either. As a dog, he couldn't just look at a map
and check where he was ... he couldn't even ask any
one the way. He didn't have any money to buy food
or drink. Instead, he had the constant worry that at
any moment he might turn back into a boy and find
himself stuck, miles from anywhere, without any
clothes. When he did get home, he was very worried
and thoroughly exhausted.

He told Roy all about it the next day. Roy was just
disappointed that he'd missed it all. He thought being
hauled off into the middle of nowhere sounded rather
exciting, and said he wished he'd been there too. As
Eric pointed out, in somewhat injured tones, if Roy
had been there, the whole thing wouldn't have
happened.

'Sounds like a real adventure to me,' said Roy, who
hadn't realized quite how scared Eric had been.

'Oh, yes,' said Eric. 'It was wonderful. It's tremendous fun to be abandoned in the middle of nowhere
with no money, no map, no idea where you are ...'

'It'll be something to tell your grandchildren,' said
Roy, cheerfully.

'I'm not going to have any grandchildren at this
rate,' muttered Eric.

Roy looked at Eric, and it occurred to him that
while it might *sound* very exciting to be carried off in a
baker's van, if it actually happened to you, it might
just be rather frightening.

'Look, I'm sorry,' he said, 'I'm sorry I wasn't there to help and all that, but I'll be there next time, alright? Next time. I promise!'

But the next time Eric turned into dog, Roy wasn't there again.

To be fair to Roy, it wasn't really his fault. In fact, he'd gone to a lot of trouble to make sure that although he wasn't there, at least he'd done what he could for Eric.

When Eric trotted up the path to Roy's front door, he found a note in Roy's handwriting, pinned to a large cardboard box.

The note said – 'Hi, Eric. Sorry about this, but Mum says I have to go to Grandad's with her. I've left some biscuits on a saucer (smart thinking, eh?) and the box is so that you've got somewhere warm and dry. Anyway, I'll be back about six. Cheerio, Roy.'

Eric could see the saucer beside the box, but there was no sign of any biscuits, and while he was wondering what had happened to them (another dog had already eaten them) it started to rain. Not just a drizzle, but a real drenching downpour. In fact, it rained so hard that the cardboard box Roy had left out for Eric to sit in, collapsed in a soggy heap.

Eric splashed his way back out to the pavement and sat under a hedge, the rain dripping on to the back of his neck, trying to work out where he could possibly go that was dry and warm.

He was still thinking, when a voice said 'Oh, look at him. Poor little fellow!'

Eric looked up and saw an old woman with an umbrella looking down at him. 'Haven't you got a home to go to?' she asked.

Her husband appeared beside her. 'What sort of people leave a dog outside in this sort of weather?' he said.

'Maybe we should take him home?' suggested the woman. 'Get him dry and give him something to eat.'

Eric thought this was rather a good idea.

'You can't do that,' said the man. 'What about his owners?'

'I suppose you're right,' the woman agreed, and Eric watched as they climbed into their car.

Just before the man drove off, he wound down his window and called to Eric.

'If you're ever passing 27 Nelson Close, drop in, and we'll give you a meal.'

'You shouldn't tease him,' said his wife. 'He looks so miserable.'

When Mr and Mrs Potts – the old couple who'd seen Eric under the hedge – arrived back at 27 Nelson Close, they were very surprised to find Eric sitting on the doorstep.

Mr Potts looked at him doubtfully. 'It's the same dog, isn't it?' he asked.

'Of course it is,' said Mrs Potts.

'But it can't be!' Mr Potts was understandably puzzled. He knew Eric couldn't have followed them home, because he'd driven back along the bypass, but if the dog hadn't followed them, how could he have known where they lived?

'What do you think we should do?' he asked.

'We'll do what you said we'd do,' said Mrs Potts, briskly, opening the front door. 'We'll get him warm and dry, and give him something to eat.'

*

And that's what they did. Mrs Potts gave him some left over steak and kidney pudding, and although Eric didn't like kidney as a boy, as a dog, he found it tasted delicious. They let him lie in front of the fire on a towel to get dry, and when they turned on the television, Eric changed channels so that he could watch Blue Peter. They laughed and let him carry on watching.

When the rain had stopped, Eric thought it was time to go home. He went out to the hall, looked first at the front door and then back at Mr and Mrs Potts – and they let him out.

As Eric trotted out to the road, Mrs Potts called after him 'You'll come and see us again, won't you?'

'You can call any time,' said Mr Potts. 'We're usually in.'

'Woof!' said Eric.

From then on, whenever he turned into a dog, Eric trotted round to the Potts', instead of round to Roy's.

All he had to do was scratch at the bottom of their door, and they'd let him in. They gave him food, they talked to him about all sorts of interesting things (Mr Potts had been at Dunkirk, and Mrs Potts had once helped build Lancaster bombers). Then, when he'd eaten as much as he could, he would climb up on to the sofa and doze, while one of them scratched the back of his neck. For some reason, dogs find that very soothing, and Eric was no exception.

Roy couldn't understand it. 'What do you want to go round to them for?' he asked. 'What's special about the Potts? They're a hundred and fifty years old!'

'They look after me,' said Eric. 'They give me food . . .'

'That's more important than friendship, is it?' asked Roy.

'It's better than a cardboard box and an empty saucer,' said Eric, with some feeling.

'That wasn't my fault!' said Roy.

'I know it wasn't,' said Eric. 'I'm not saying it was. It's just that ... well, you've got a sister who hates dogs, a father and mother who don't like me in the house, and sometimes you're just not in. I'll tell you what's special about Mr and Mrs Potts, Roy. They're always there.'

And I suppose it might have gone on like that forever – Roy feeling upset because Eric didn't call round any more, and Eric not calling round because Roy never seemed to be there when he was needed – if it hadn't been for Mrs Potts and the man from the Council.

Eric was round at Nelson Close that morning. Mr Potts was out doing the shopping, and Eric was eating a bag of crisps while Mrs Potts showed him photographs of her daughter's family in New Zealand. There was a ring at the door.

Mrs Potts went to answer it, and found a young man who said he's come from the council to check on the gas leak. He was a smart young man with a pleasant smile and although they didn't have any gas at 27 Nelton Close, Mrs Potts didn't like to just tell him to go away. Instead, she asked him inside.

She pulled open the door to let him in, but then Eric, at her feet, started growling. Mrs Potts told him to stop and then told the young man not to worry, but Eric didn't stop. Every time the man tried to come in, Eric growled even louder, and then started barking. He was only a small dog, but he could look very fierce if he wanted, and just then he looked very fierce indeed. Mrs Potts couldn't understand it, and eventually the young man said he'd call back at another time.

When Mrs Potts had closed the door, Eric rushed back into the sitting room and came back with a copy of the paper that had been lying on the sofa. He dropped it on the hall floor, and tapped at one of the stories on the front page. Mrs Potts looked at it. It was a warning from the police about a young man who went around pretending to be from the Council, checking up about a gas leak, but who, once he was let into people's houses, stole anything he could find.

A lot of things happened after that. Mr Potts came back from his shopping and Mrs Potts cried a lot while she told him what had happened. Then a policeman came round and took notes, while Mrs Potts cooked Eric a huge steak and kidney pudding and cried some more. Then another policeman arrived saying that the young man had been caught, and that he thought everyone should have a dog as brave and intelligent as Eric – which started Mrs Potts crying again – and then Eric fell asleep, because he'd eaten rather a lot of chips as well as his steak and kidney pudding.

When he woke up, he could just hear Mr and Mrs Potts talking out in the kitchen.

'He's a brave little fellow,' Mr Potts was saying. 'I mean, he's only little, and to scare off a full grown man . . . he's a brave little fellow.'

'I don't know what would have happened if he hadn't been here.' It sounded as if Mrs Potts was starting to cry again.

'Anyway, I've decided,' said Mr Potts, 'What we have to do, is adopt him.'

'But he's not ours,' said Mrs Potts.

'So whose is he?' asked her husband. 'Look. I've bought him this. At least it's got our name and phone number, so if he ever gets into trouble, people can let us know.'

Looking through the half open kitchen door, Eric could see that Mr Potts was holding up a smark, new, shiny leather collar.

That's when Eric knew it was definitely time to go home.

When Eric turned back into a boy, later that afternoon, he went straight round to see Roy.

'Don't tell me,' said Roy, when he opened the door. 'I know the face . . .'

'Roy . . .' said Eric.

'I just can't put a name to it,' Roy wrinkled his forehead, as if trying to remember Eric's name. 'Didn't we meet once or twice after school?'

'I need your help, Roy,' said Eric.

'You'd better come upstairs,' said Roy.

It took Roy a little while to understand why Eric was so worried. 'I thought you liked the Potts looking after you,' he said.

'It's not the looking after,' said Eric, 'it's the collar.'

'What's wrong with the collar?'

'Think about it,' Eric said. 'When I turn into a dog, I get smaller, so that all my clothes fall off. If I was wearing a collar when I changed from a dog back into a boy . . .'

Roy suddenly realized what Eric was getting at.

Eric's neck as a boy was a lot bigger than his neck as dog and if he was wearing a collar when he changed back . . . It didn't bear thinking about.

'I see,' said Roy. 'In that case you'd better not go back there any more.'

'It's not as simple as that,' Eric sighed. 'They've been really kind to me. They're nice people. I don't want them to be hurt and yet . . . How can I tell them?'

Roy thought for a minute.

'Leave it to me, Eric,' he said.

The next Friday, Roy took Eric-as-a-dog round to 27 Nelson Close. When Mr Potts came to the door and saw Eric on the front step, he called indoors to his wife, 'He's back, love!'

Then, when Mrs Potts came bustling out of the kitchen, they both saw Roy.

'Hello,' said Roy. 'My name's Roy Ackerman. I think you know my dog, Eric.'

'Your dog . . .?' said Mr Potts.

'I'm afraid so,' said Roy.

'Well.' Mrs Potts straightened her shoulders. 'We always knew he had to belong to someone. You'd better come in.'

'Follow Eric,' said Mr Potts. 'He knows the way.'

Roy followed Eric through into the sitting room, and they sat on the sofa while Mr and Mrs Potts took an easy chair each.

'I've really come round to say thank you,' said Roy. 'Well, we both want to say thank you. For looking after Eric all this time.'

'Woof,' said Eric.

'It was nothing,' said Mr Potts.

'We just gave him a few scraps,' said Mrs Potts.

'And we also came round to tell you ...' Roy hesitated. Now that he was actually here, saying it was a lot more difficult than he'd thought.

'You've come to tell us that you won't be calling round in future, haven't you?' said Mrs Potts.

Roy nodded. 'Well, not quite so often,' he said. 'It's not easy to explain why, but ...'

'You don't have to explain,' said Mr Potts. 'We knew he was never ours.'

'As long as somebody's looking after him properly, that's the main thing,' said Mrs Potts.

'Yes.' said Roy. 'I suppose it is.'

Eric continued to call round to Nelson Close occasionally, though he went with Roy, rather than on his own. Mr and Mrs Potts eventually bought a dog of their own – a short-haired Airedale bitch called Lucy. They grew very fond of it, and it must be one of best looked-after dogs in Britain, but, as Mrs Potts said, it was not the sort of dog you could rely on to recognize a phoney gasman from the Council. They missed Eric, and they knew they always would.

Roy learned two things from the Potts. One was that if you have a dog, even a dog that's really a boy, like Eric, then you have to be responsible for it. The second thing was that a steak and kidney pudding, as cooked by Mrs Potts is the most delicious thing you ever tasted.

# THE ROAD-RUNNER

Roy and Eric were sitting on the top of Monkston Hill, watching the start of a soapbox cart race. Thirty or forty years ago, before bicycles were as popular as they are now, most boys built themselves a soap cart at one time or another. The cart was made from an old wooden box (originally it would have been a soapbox) to sit in, a plank of wood that ran from the box to the front axle and two pairs of old pram wheels. You sat in it at the top of a hill, and let it run down to the bottom, steering it by pulling on a piece of string. With a bit of luck, you didn't fall out too many times before you got to the bottom.

The soap carts that Roy and Eric were watching were rather more advanced than that. They had moulded bodies that you could sit in, some of them even had brakes and speedometers, and they were all smartly painted in bright racing colours. But the basic principle was still the same. There were no engines or pedals. You just sat in them at the top of a hill, somebody gave you a push and you went racing down to the bottom as fast as you dared.

There were five cars in the race down Monkston Hill that day. The smartest and the sleekest of them belonged to a boy called Barry Donohoe, who went to the local comprehensive. Its body was slung low to the ground, it was painted with a broad red stripe up the middle, and everybody knew it was favourite to win the race.

Roy stared at it enviously. 'What would you give to have one of those, Eric?' he asked.

Eric didn't exactly say so, but he wouldn't have given anything. Maybe turning into a dog gave him enough excitement in life. He couldn't really see the point of rushing down a hill in a home made car with every chance of crashing into a tree or something and hurting yourself, just so you could say you got to the bottom first.

'My Dad says, when he was a boy, they used to race soap carts down Dead Man's Hill. It's even steeper than this,' Eric shook his head in puzzlement. 'He must have been mad . . .'

'It'd be worth it though, wouldn't it?' said Roy. 'If you won.'

'What's so special about winning?' said Eric.

Roy got up. 'Come on,' he said. 'Let's watch from the bend halfway down, that's where they usually crash.'

They waited on the bend for the race to start and the soap carts to come down the hill.

'You know,' said Eric, 'I don't mind turning into a dog. In fact it's quite good sometimes, but what I don't like is never knowing when it's going to happen.' He scratched absent-mindedly at the back of his neck. 'I don't like the way it takes me by surprise − like the time it happened when we were up that tree.'

'Yeah,' said Roy. 'It can be a . . .'

But then he stopped, because the soap carts were roaring down the hill and he had to stand up to cheer them on. Barry's machine with the red stripe was well in the lead, as all five cars squealed round the corner, fortunately without upsetting any of their drivers.

When the last car had disappeared from view, Roy was able to finish what he was saying.

'It can be a bit of a shock to me too, Eric,' he said. 'You know, I'm chatting away to you one minute and everything seems perfectly normal, and the next second I turn round and you've . . .'

He paused.

'And you've done it again, haven't you?'

'Woof,' said Eric.

Roy gathered up Eric's clothes, and he and Eric-as-a-dog walked down to the bottom of the hill to see who had won the race.

They met Joan and Alison at the finishing line. They were in their Badger uniforms (they belonged to the Junior St John Ambulance Brigade) and were most disappointed that there was nobody injured who needed to be bandaged up or anything.

When Roy asked, they told him Barry had won the race by miles. There was something about the way they looked as they described how fast Barry had been going, how skilfully he'd driven and how brave he must have been, that Roy found slightly annoying.

'It's not very difficult, you know,' he said.

'No?' Joan looked at him.

'Well,' said Roy, 'you've only got to sit in the thing and steer, haven't you? It's as easy as falling out of a tree.'

'Woof,' said Eric, trying to get Roy's attention.

'If you ask me,' Roy continued, 'Barry makes a bit of a song and dance about it.'

Eric barked again, but Roy still ignored him.

'I mean, all he's got to do is keep his nerve, not bottle out at the corners – I thought he took one or two of them a bit cautiously, but . . .'

Roy stopped. Barry Donohoe was standing right behind him, and had heard every word. That's why Eric had been barking.

'Hello, Barry,' said Roy, and noticed that Barry was very big for his age. Very big. Very big indeed.

'Making a bit of a song and dance, was I?' said Barry, stepping ominously close to Roy.

'Ah . . .' said Roy.

'Bottling out on the corners, was I?' asked Barry, stepping even closer.

'Just a little joke, Barry!' Roy gave a nervous laugh.

'Well, let me tell you . . .' Barry poked a finger at Roy's chest.

'Grrrrr!' said Eric.

Barry looked down at Eric. 'What's wrong with him?' he asked.

'Sorry, Barry,' said Roy. 'He gets very strange if people come too close to me. Took a bite out of my uncle's leg the other day, just because we shook hands. He's alright really.'

Barry took his finger away from Roy's chest. 'Any time you want a real race,' he said. 'Instead of talking big to impress girls, just let me know.' And he turned and walked away.

Eric was very relieved. If Barry looked big to Roy, you can imagine how he looked to a dog twelve inches from the ground. Growling like that had been very brave. But then, just when everything seemed alright, Roy shouted.

'Okay. You're on!'

Barry was back at his soap cart, but turned round. 'You want a race?' called Roy. 'I'll race the lot of you.'

'Woof, woof!' said Eric beside him, but Roy was not to be stopped.

'I've got to,' he hissed at Eric. 'I can't let him talk to me like that.'

'When?' shouted Barry.

'Last Monday of next month?'

Barry nodded, and then pointed up at Monkston Hill. 'Think you can cope with that?' he asked.

Roy looked as casual as he could. 'What about Dead Man's Hill?' he said.

There was a long silence. Then Barry nodded.

'Okay,' he said.

Eric sighed. It looked as if Roy had done it again.

The real problem, as Eric pointed out to Roy the next day, wasn't Dead Man's Hill. If Roy wanted to kill himself, Eric explained, that was his business. The real problem was how to build a soap cart, in six weeks, that would go anywhere near as fast as Barry's. What shape should it be? What should it be made of? How much money would it cost?

Rescue came from an unexpected source. Roy and Eric were in the school library one lunchtime, trying to draw a plan of a car that looked good and that they might be able to build, when Mrs Jessop, their form teacher stopped to see what they were doing.

'What's this for?' she asked.

'It's a race,' said Eric.

'I've been challenged by Barry from the Comprehensive,' Roy explained. 'He's already built his.'

'Lucky Barry,' said Mrs Jessop.

'You don't know anything about designing soap-boxes, do you?' asked Eric, hopefully.

''Fraid not,' said Mrs Jessop. She smiled. 'But I might know someone who does. What are you two doing on Saturday?'

On Saturday, it turned out, Mrs Jessop was taking the top form on a trip to a car factory.

'A car factory?' Roy was still a bit puzzled as he climbed into the coach.

'If anyone's going to know about building soap carts,' said Mrs Jessop. 'I'd have thought it would be them.'

'She's brilliant!' Roy whispered to Eric. He had to whisper it because Eric had turned into a dog again that morning, and the only way he could come on the trip was smuggled in Roy's duffle bag.

When they got to the factory, a big man who said his name was Mr Espiner was in charge of showing them round.

He showed them assembly lines that seemed to stretch for hundreds of yards, with huge machines that pressed sheets of steel into various shapes, cranes that lifted engines onto chassis, and robot arms that welded panels onto doors. The more Eric saw, as he peered out of the bag on Roy's shoulder, the more he was convinced that none of these people could possibly be interested in helping them to build a soap cart.

But then Mr Espiner led them into a different building which he said was for Planning and Design. Here, in the biggest room Eric had ever seen, hundreds of people sat working at desks with drawing boards and computers.

'This is where the design teams work on ideas for new cars, and modifications of designs already in production,' Mr Espiner told them. 'I believe you said your children were particularly interested in this section, Mrs Jessop?'

Mrs Jessop smiled, and nodded.

'If you'd like to come this way,' said Mr Espiner, 'I think we can give you a demonstration.'

He took them all to a room that was shaped like a theatre, but on the bit where the stage would have been, there was a woman sitting at a desk with a computer.

When everybody had sat down, Mr Espiner stood by the computer.

'This terminal,' he said proudly, 'is attached to a Prime CDS4201, and in case some of you don't already know, that is one of the most powerful computers in the world. With this machine it is possible to design a car, any sort of car, from start to finish, without ever leaving your seat.'

Eric pricked up his ears, and Roy leaned forward in his seat.

'Let's say,' said Mr Espiner, 'that you want to design a four seater saloon . . .'

Mrs Jessop put up a hand. 'Could we go for something a bit smaller?' she said.

'Sorry?' Mr Espiner wasn't used to being interrupted.

'I think the children might find the whole thing easier to grasp,' Mrs Jessop explained, 'if you showed them something a little closer to their own experience. Like . . .' She thought for a moment. 'Like a soapcart.'

Mr Espiner looked puzzled. 'A soapcart?'

'Yes,' said Mrs Jessop firmly. 'You know, something about two metres long, a metre wide, and able to seat one person.'

Mr Espiner looked at the woman sitting at the computer, who smiled, shrugged and nodded.

'Alright!' he said. 'Alright. We'll just let Jenny feed the main parameters into the machine . . '

Jenny started typing busily at the computer keyboard.

'No engine,' said Mrs Jessop, 'and we want it to go as fast as possible.'

'No engine,' repeated Mr Espiner, and Jenny tapped some more.

As Roy and Eric watched, a shape began to emerge on the computer screen. It didn't look much like a soap cart at first, and it kept somersaulting so that it wasn't even easy to see which part was the bottom and which the top, but as Jenny typed in more and more information, they could make out which bits were to cover the wheels, and where the driver was supposed to sit.

There was a lot of talk then, which Eric and Roy didn't really understand – about tyre profiles, weight ratios, heat bearings and stress values – but all the time, the shape of the soap cart was getting clearer and clearer. Sometimes the shape got rounder and fatter, then thinner and sleeker. Sometimes the screen only showed one part of it, and then that bit would shrink and you could see the whole thing, until finally, from a printer on the other side of the stage, emerged three very large pieces of paper. The plans for the perfect soap cart.

Mr Espiner rolled them up and put them into a

cardboard tube, which he gave to Mrs Jessop 'as a memento of the visit'. As they walked back to the coach, Mrs Jessop passed them to Roy.

'Have you thought how you're going to build it?' she asked.

'Not really,' said Roy.

'Hmmm,' said Mrs Jessop. 'I think you'd better meet my father.'

Mrs Jessop's father, Mr Dunford, was a retired engineer who spent most of his time making scale models of steam engines. His garage had been converted into a workshop whose walls and benches were covered in tools and machinery of every imaginable shape, size and purpose.

When Mrs Jessop brought round the boys, and Roy asked Mr Dunford if he could help with the soapcart, Mr Dunford humphed and harred for a bit, saying he might be prepared to give them some advice, but when Roy showed him the plans that the computer at the car factory had drawn up, a curious light came into his eyes. In no time at all, he had the drawings spread out over the floor, was scribbling little notes, and had put Eric and Roy to work cutting sections of tubular steel with a hacksaw.

It looked like they were in business.

The car took over a month to build, and it was hard work. It meant spending every Saturday and Sunday, and almost every evening after school at Mr Dunford's garage, but it was worth it. Every day, before their eyes, the soap cart took shape.

They built the chassis of tubular steel, welded into a frame strong enough not to buckle in a crash (Mr Dunford did the welding). They built plywood moulds from which they could make the fibreglass hull and the driver's seat. There were disc brakes and a speedometer, which came from an old motorbike that had belonged to Eric's Dad, and there was a temperature gauge that told you if the bearings were overheating.

It had roll bars and a safety harness to protect the driver if he hit something and over-turned. It had wing mirrors to let you know if the opposition were coming up from behind, a drag vane (Roy was never quite sure what that was for) – and you could tell just by looking at its sleek, curving lines, that the whole machine was designed to cut through the air like a high velocity bullet.

It was painted blue, with just the words 'Road-Runner' printed down each side. As they wheeled it out of Mr Dunford's garage into daylight for the first time, even Eric couldn't help being impressed.

'Not bad, is it?' said Mr Dunford.

Roy couldn't reply. It was, quite simply, the most beautiful thing he had ever seen.

'Thanks, Mr Dunford,' he said.

The Road-Runner didn't just look good, it went like the wind. They did trials with it, first down the slopes in the park and then, the Sunday before the big race against Barry, Roy took it down Monkston Hill. He did the run three times, with Eric standing at the bottom with a stopwatch to record his time.

They knew how long Barry had taken to do the run, so now they'd have a chance to tell whether their machine was as fast as his. On his first run, Roy beat Barry's time by four seconds, the second time it was five point four seconds, and the last time (Roy's confidence was growing) by a full fifteen seconds.

After the last run, Roy stayed sitting it the car, glowing with pleasure.

'We're going to do it, Eric,' he said. 'We're really going to do it.'

'But can you do it without killing yourself down Deadman's Hill?' asked Eric. 'Winning isn't everything, you know. I just hope it's worth it.'

'Don't worry,' said Roy. 'It'll be as easy as falling out of a tree.'

The next afternoon, Eric stood at the top of Dead Man's Hill, looking down the path that, in half an hour, would be the race course. Everything was ready. Road-Runner was in position (it had caused quite a stir when Eric hauled it up the hill). Its bearings and controls had been checked, just as Mr Dunford said they should be, and Eric had given it a final polish.

The other racers were making last minute checks and adjustments. He could see Barry Donohoe putting on a crash helmet, and tightening the strap under his chin. Joan and Alison were there in their Badger uniforms with a large supply of splints, slings and bandages, and standing by to help give Roy a good push down the first part of the hill. Everyone and everything was ready – except for one small item.

Roy hadn't turned up.

Eric couldn't understand it. They'd arranged to meet at the top of the hill three hours before the race was due to start, so that they'd have a chance to look over the course. He knew Roy could sometimes be a little vague about time, but surely not today – not after all the work they'd put in?

One or two of the other racers had noticed that Roy

wasn't there, and Eric couldn't help overhearing one of them suggest that maybe Roy was too frightened to turn up. Eric didn't believe that for a moment, but all the same, he was very relieved when Joan shouted, 'There he is!'

He turned to see Roy limping out of Mr Ackerman's car, which had driven him to the top of the hill. Limping? Eric looked again. Roy was limping, and Eric could see why. His entire left leg was covered in a fresh, white, plaster cast.

'Sorry, Eric,' said Roy. 'I did it falling out of a tree.'

They stood, miserably, either side of the Road-Runner.

'You're sure you can't fit in it?' asked Eric.

'Not a chance,' said Roy. 'Not without breaking it again.'

'But you've got to!' Eric insisted. 'All that work — we can't just waste it!'

'Maybe we could find someone else to drive it,' said Roy.

'Come off it!' said Eric, fiercely disappointed that Road-Runner would never have a chance to show her paces. 'Where are we going to find another driver? The race starts in three minutes.'

Roy looked at Eric without saying anything. Joan and Alison looked at him as well.

'No!' Eric shouted in surprise. 'I can't drive it. I don't know how! And anyway, I don't want to. No, absolutely, definitely, no!'

As Roy helped buckle him into the driver's seat and Joan and Alison were pushing him to the start line, Eric was still complaining. 'This is a very bad idea,

Roy . . . Why don't we ask them to put the race off for a couple of months, and then . . .'

The starting pistol went off.

'Good luck!' shouted Roy, and he, Joan and Alison started pushing the Road-Runner as fast as they could to the top of the path.

And even as they shoved him, even as he crossed the line with his hands on the wheel, Eric felt a tingling down the back of his neck, and before he'd reached the first bend, the hands on the wheel in front of him had become paws.

Eric's first thought, as he steered for the bend, was that he must stop the car and get out. But then he realised that he couldn't. As a boy, the brake pedal would have been immediately under his foot, but as a dog, his legs weren't long enough. They didn't reach.

By the time he had realised he couldn't stop, he was going too fast to jump out. The first part of the course steepened with deceptive speed, and then led into a series of hairpin bends. Somehow, he had to slow down or, as soon as he tried to turn, he'd find himself spinning straight off the track.

Suddenly he remembered. The drag vane! Situated just behind the driver and over the rear wheels, the drag vane was designed to allow wind pressure to push the car a little more firmly onto the road. Eric slammed the control right over until the drag vane stood up vertically. It acted almost like a sail, and the car slowed just enough for him to turn the corner without over-turning. The next corner followed almost immediately. Eric could feel the back wheels spinning slightly but he managed to keep the car under control, and then the ground rose slightly and the worst danger was over.

Not everyone had been as lucky. One of the other drivers had spun in a complete circle on the second hairpin, and was now facing back up the track, at a complete standstill. A second driver had obviously decided to slow down so that the same thing didn't happen to him, and Eric, who was in no position to slow down at all, flashed past him on the way to the river.

The river was Eric's chance to stop and get out. This was the point where the track became shingle, which slowed the cars to a halt, and the racers were supposed to get out, pull their cars across the river, and then drag them up a short hill before pushing themselves off onto the second section of the course.

Even before he got there, Eric knew that he wasn't going to stop racing. Something had happened as he overtook those other two drivers. There was something about the speed and the excitement that made him forget everything else. He forgot about being frightened, he forgot about Roy, he even forgot about being a dog. He forgot about everything except a deep, burning desire to win this race.

As the car slowed to a stop at the river, Eric leapt out, rushed round to the front, seized the tow rope in his teeth and started hauling it up the hill. It was tough going. Mr Dunford and the designers at the car factory had ensured that the Road-Runner was as light as it could be made, but it still felt very heavy to a small dog trying to pull it up a steep incline. In fact it was too heavy. Eric heaved, but he could feel the weight pulling him back . . . and then suddenly there was no weight at all. Looking up, he saw a large black labrador had taken the rope between its teeth. The labrador's owner was shouting to him to come back, but it took no notice. With its powerful shoulders and legs, it hauled the car straight to the top – overtaking a third racer on the way, who was so surprised to see it that he let go of his own rope so that his car fell back into the river.

Eric had no idea why the labrador had done it. Maybe it thought it was just joining in a doggy game, but there was no time to do more than give a quick 'Woof!' of thanks before jumping back into the Road-Runner as it started down the hill, picking up speed.

This was the steepest and probably the most frightening part of the race. The hill was a one in four at some points. There were no bends to slow you down, you just went faster and faster while the car shook and your teeth rattled, but it was important not to use your brakes, because the last part of the course was a long series of shallow bends to the finishing line with very little slope at all. If you slowed down too much in the first section you might not have the speed to carry you through the second.

Eric wouldn't have slowed down, even if he could. On the steepest part of the hill, he overtook a fourth car which had slithered to a halt when its front axle snapped under the strain. Eric gave a fierce yelp of pleasure as he flew past, suddenly realising there could be only one person ahead of him now. All the other racers were behind him, and as he rounded the bend into the final section, he could see ahead of him, the car with the red stripe. It was Barry, and Eric was gaining on him, gaining all the time.

It was just a question of mathematics now. Who

had built up the most speed on the hill? Who's car ran the smoothest? There was no doubt that Eric was going the faster of the two, but was he going fast enough to catch Barry before the line?

Slowly, the gap between them grew less and less. It was ten yards, five, just a few feet, and then Eric's wheels were almost alongside.

Barry suddenly looked over his shoulder and saw what was happening. He was an experienced racer and knew that what he had to do was swing his car over in front of Eric's to stop it overtaking. He was about to do it, when his hands froze for a second on the steering wheel. The other car appeared to be being driven by a dog! He blinked. It couldn't be!

And in that second of indecision, Eric swept past.

Eric crossed the finishing line almost ten seconds in the lead, and with enough speed to carry him fifty yards past the line. The crowd of watchers hurried after to congratulate him.

He was a boy again by the time they caught up with him. A boy who was hastily scrambling back into his shorts and T-shirt before they could thump him on the back and tell him what a great race it had been. Roy was there, hopping up and down on his good leg with a smile on his face that threatened to split it in half, and Joan and Alison had abandoned a real patient so that they could come over and cheer.

Barry Donohoe came over as well. He seemed to have decided that he must have imagined what he saw earlier, because he didn't say anything about it. He just held out a hand to Eric – it was a very big hand – and said, 'Well done.' Then, as Eric shook it, Barry grinned and said. 'It was a good race.' You didn't get many words out of Barry, but when you did, it mattered.

Winning might not be everything, Eric decided, but when it did happen, it felt good. It felt very good indeed.

# MR BLOCKER'S PIPE

It was Monday morning, and Mrs Jessop was telling the class about what they'd have to do on their Nature Trail Outing the following day.

Eric gave Roy a nudge. 'We could win that,' he said.

'Win what?' It was a warm day and Roy had been looking out of the window, thinking about food.

'The competition she's just told us about,' hissed Eric. 'For the team that finds the most animal tracks.'

'Really?' Roy knew that Eric read books about all sorts of things, but he'd never mentioned being interested in tracks before.

'We don't know anything about animal tracks, do we?' he asked.

'I know we don't,' said Eric. 'But if I was a dog . . .'

'Brilliant!' said Roy. If Eric was a dog, with a dog's sensitive nose, he'd be able to sniff out an animal's trail in no time. They'd be bound to find more tracks than anyone else.

A girl knocked at the classroom door with a message from Mr Blocker, the Headmaster.

'Please, Miss,' she said to Mrs Jessop, 'Mr Blocker says everyone's to be in the Hall in five minutes.'

*

As Eric and Roy followed the class down the corridor to the Hall, Roy had a thought.

'Hey, Eric,' he said. 'Supposing you don't turn into a dog? Tomorrow, I mean.'

'We'll just have to concentrate,' Eric told him. 'If we really want it to happen, imagine it happening as strongly as possible, you know . . . it'll be like when we went to the dog shows. It'll just happen.'

Roy knitted his brows in thought. 'Concentrate . . .' he murmured.

'Yes. But not now,' said Eric, who could feel a faint itching at the back of his neck.

'Want it to happen . . .' Once Roy got an idea, it wasn't easy to stop him.

'Roy!' said Eric.

'Imagine it as strongly as possible . . .' Roy turned the corner in the corridor. 'You know. You know,' he said. 'This might work.'

He looked round. 'Eric?'

But Eric wasn't there. Eric, fortunately out of sight of the rest of the class, had turned into a dog again.

Eric dragged his clothes into a changing room. It seemed the best place to leave them ready for whenever he changed back into being a boy.

The school seemed oddly empty with all the children in the Hall. Eric decided to go along as well, and find out what it was all about. By the time he got there, the rest of the school was inside, waiting for the Headmaster, while just outside the doors, Mrs Jessop was talking to a new teacher called Miss Cable.

'What's all this about, Paula?' she asked.

'I'm afraid Mr Blocker's all set to cancel our outing tomorrow,' Miss Cable told her.

'Cancel it?'

Miss Cable nodded. 'Someone's stolen his pipe.'

'Good grief!' said Mrs Jessop. 'Not again.'

Eric knew what she meant. Everyone except Mr Blocker knew there was a society amongst the fourth years that you could only join if you'd stolen Blocker's pipe. It wasn't quite as bad as it sounded. They always gave it back, but it was a way of showing that you were clever enough not to get caught, or brave enough not to mind if you did.

'It seems a shame to have our trip cancelled just because of that,' Miss Cable was saying. 'Couldn't we try and find it or something?'

Mrs Jessop shook her head. 'I'm not sure it's even worth looking,' she said. 'You'd need a tracker dog to find anything the fourth years have hidden.'

A tracker dog, thought Eric. It had given him an idea.

Mr Blocker addressed the assembled school from a lectern up on the stage.

'Someone . . .' he spoke in his fiercest voice, 'someone, during second period this morning, stole the pipe from my office. I've no doubt that many of you think stealing what doesn't belong to you hardly matters at all, but I do! And until the criminal comes forward, owns up, and returns my property, I shall be cancelling all out of school activities. There will be no Nature Trail outing tomorrow, no visit to the Science Museum . . .'

He was going to go on and list all the other things that would be cancelled, if nobody owned up and gave his pipe back, when he was interrupted by a flurry of movement at the back of the hall. To the astonishment of the people sitting there, the swing doors had been pushed open, and a small dog had come in carrying something in its mouth.

'What is it?' asked Mr Blocker.

'I think it's a dog,' said Mrs Jessop.

The dog (it was Eric, of course) trotted up the centre aisle between the children, then up the steps on to the stage, and over to Mr Blocker.

'What is a dog doing in my assembly?' he said.

'He seems to be delivering your pipe,' Mrs Jessop replied.

And sure enough, the dog dropped the pipe from its mouth at Mr Blocker's feet, turned round, and headed back the way it had come.

For a moment, Mr Blocker was too astonished to say anything. Then, 'Come back here!' he shouted. 'I demand an explanation!'

Eric wondered what sort of explanation he expected from a dog, but he had no intention of waiting to find out. He was back out of the swing doors and away, before anyone could stop him.

Only Roy knew what had really happened. He grinned to himself. 'Well done, Eric!' he thought. It looked as if they'd be going on the Nature Trail outing after all.

Mr Blocker watched morosely as the children climbed aboard the coach the next morning. He didn't like Nature outings. He didn't like Nature very much. He thought fresh air and exercise made the children wild and giddy.

'All aboard, Headmaster,' said Mrs Jessop. 'Lovely to be getting out for the day, isn't it?'

'Is it?' sighed Mr Blocker. 'Come on then, let's get it over with.'

He walked over to the coach, muttering to himself 'There must be people who'd love this job. Retired prison warders, off-duty military police . . .'

He climbed on to the coach.

'No smoking,' said the driver.

Mr Blocker took the pipe out of his mouth, and scowled.

At the picnic site on the edge of Dawlish Forest, Mrs Jessop checked that everyone had their pencils, their worksheets, their lunchpacks and a matchbox to collect any interesting insects. She reminded them not to pick any flowers or eat any mushrooms, and told them several times when they had to be back at the bus.

Mr Blocker said that if anyone caused any trouble, he would be down on them like a ton of bricks.

As soon as they were allowed to go, Roy and Eric separated themselves from the others and took a path that led up through the woods and away from the coach.

'We'll just make sure we're out of sight of anyone else,' said Roy, 'And then I'll start concentrating properly. Imagining you're a dog.'

'Woof!' said Eric, and wagged his tail.

It had all been even easier than he'd thought.

Roy put Eric's clothes in a plastic carrier bag, which he hid under an old tree trunk, and the two of them set off to find animal tracks.

Eric had been absolutely right. With his super sensitive nose, he could work his way through the woods and over fields to just the point where an animal had passed. In only ten minutes, they had found and identified four different sets of prints. As far as Roy was concerned, the competition was in the bag.

Eric found a fifth set. They were larger than the others, and when Roy saw them, he wondered at first if they'd been left by a badger.

'Woof, woof!' said Eric.

'No?' said Roy. 'I'll look it up.' He took the guide book from his bag, and flicked through the pages.

'Wow!' he said. 'It's a fox.'

'Woof,' said Eric – and just then, they both heard a hunting horn.

It was coming from the field to their right, and Eric scrambled up the bank and peered through the bottom of the hedge.

In the distance, coming along the valley was a hunt in full gallop. It was a magnificent sight. About forty hounds were whooping along in the front, noses to the ground, tails in the air, and spread out behind them there must have been at least sixty people on horses, all splendidly dressed in smart black or red coats and shiny black hats.

Roy had scrambled up the bank beside Eric, and was looking over the top of the hedge. He'd never seen anything like it in his life.

'Hey, Eric!' he said, 'they're going to come right past us!'

Eric had already seen. Instead of travelling along the valley, the hunt had veered to the left, and were coming up the hill.

'We're going to be able to see them right up close!' Roy had never seen a hunt before, and was very excited at the prospect.

'Woof, woof!' said Eric, scrambling back down the bank.

'What's the matter?' said Roy. 'Don't you want to watch?'

'Woof, woof!' said Eric, again.

Roy turned back to the hunt. They were a lot closer now, and still heading straight towards him. Forty dogs and sixty horses, thundering straight towards him . . .

'Come on, Eric!' shouted Roy, scrambling down the bank. 'Run!'

They ran. Eric led the way along the side of the hedge, over a stile, and then diagonally across the field beyond. As Roy climbed the gate into the next meadow, he paused to look back. The dogs were just bursting over the stile and through the hedge, and he was horrified to see that, instead of going straight on, they had turned and were following exactly the route he and Eric had taken.

He looked ahead. Eric, despite his short legs, was well in front and might be able to run to safety, but the dogs were only fifty yards away from Roy now, the sound of their baying growing louder every second. He made a decision. Climbing to the top of the gate, he could just reach the bottom branch of an ash tree that grew beside it. His fingers closed on the branch, and he swung himself upwards into the safety of the tree.

Beneath him the dogs rushed past, without even an upward glace.

'I hope Eric's alright,' thought Roy.

Eric didn't look back. He didn't need to. He could hear the hunt was still after him.

He needed somewhere to hide. He'd managed to run fast enough to keep ahead of them so far, but he was getting tired. Cresting the brow of a hill, he found himself looking down the other side where, straight ahead, was a small group of farm buildings.

Eric headed for the largest of them, a barn. Its big main doors were ajar, and he ran through the gap, turned, pushed desperately at the door until it swung closed, and then struggled with his paw to push across the bolt.

He was only just in time. As the bolt snapped across, he could hear the baying and snuffling of the foxhounds as they scrabbled at the doors outside. He sat down, gasping for breath. 'Why on earth were they chasing me?' he wondered. 'Why were they following me?'

Looking round the barn for somewhere to hide in case the dogs managed to break in, he found his answer. Crouching behind a bale of straw, and panting almost as much as Eric himself, was a fox. The hounds hadn't been chasing him at all, Eric realized. They'd been following the path of the fox.

Outside, he could hear the dogs had been joined by men and horses. One of them was pushing at the door of the barn to see if it would open, and someone else was shouting that he'd go and check the other side.

Eric felt an itching on the back of his neck.

The Master of the hunt was just wondering if he should force the barn door open and see if the fox had gone to earth inside, when the door opened and a small boy came out.

He was an odd sight. For a moment, the Master thought he was a scarecrow. He certainly seemed to be dressed in scarecrow clothes. His corduroy trousers had holes in the knees and were held up by string, while his jacket was many sizes too big and had straw poking out of the sleeves.

'Hello,' said Eric (who thought he'd been very lucky to find the scarecrow in the barn).

'Ah! Good afternoon,' said the Master. 'You haven't seen a fox, have you?'

Eric thought for a moment. 'Yes,' he said. 'Yes, I did.' He pointed up the hill. 'It was going that way.'

'Thank you very much,' said the Master. He gave a few orders, and some of the huntsmen started moving the dogs off in the direction Eric had indicated. The Master looked back at Eric.

'You're alright, are you?' he asked.

'I was just wondering where the car park was,' said Eric, who had rather lost his bearings in all the rush.

'You mean the National Trust place?' asked the Master. 'It's a couple of miles over there,' he pointed.

'Thanks,' said Eric.

As he watched the hunt move off, a somewhat breathless Roy came running down the path.

'You alright, Eric?' he asked.

'I think so,' said Eric.

'I came as quick as I could, but . . . I'd no idea you could run that fast.'

'Nor did I,' said Eric.

It was time to be getting back to the coach, but there was one thing Eric had to do first. He opened the barn door and called inside. 'It's alright. You can come out now.'

Roy watched in astonishment, as a fox put its head out the door, sniffed the air, and then trotted off down the path.

*

By the time Roy and Eric got back to where they'd left Eric's proper clothes, and he'd got cleaned up and changed, they were running late.

Eric was expecting trouble. They only had five animal tracks, and in all the rush they had done nothing of the worksheet Mrs Jessop had given them. They only had an insect in their matchbox because Eric had found a spider in one of his trainers when he was getting changed.

Mrs Jessop was not impressed. 'What have you been doing all this time?' she asked.

'We thought this was pretty interesting,' said Roy, holding up the matchbox in the faint hope of distracting her attention.

'It's a spider, Roy,' said Mrs Jessop, frostily.

'Can I have a look?' asked Miss Cable. When Roy passed her the matchbox, she gave a low whistle.

'My word!' she said. 'Argiope Runnicheii . . .'

'Is that something special?' asked Mrs Jessop.

'It certainly is,' Miss Cable was nursing the spider in her hand. 'You normally only find them along the south coast and even then they're very rare.'

It turned out Miss Cable had collected spiders since she was eleven, that she had a large collection of them at home, and her cry of excitement when Eric and Roy said she could keep their Argiope Runnicheii was so loud that Mr Blocker came over to see what was happening.

'Are these two causing trouble?' he asked.

'Not at all,' said Miss Cable. 'Look what they've just found.'

She held out her hand to Mr Blocker, who took one look at the spider under his nose and fainted clean away.

'I should have warned you about that,' said Mrs Jessop. 'The Headmaster's not very keen on spiders.'

The good thing was that, in all the fuss of bringing Mr Blocker round, and getting him on to the coach, nobody bothered about Eric and Roy not having done their worksheet.

Nobody noticed either, that Mr Blocker's pipe had fallen out of his pocket when he fainted. As the coach drove back to the school, the pipe was still there on the ground.

Roy was reading from a notice on the main school notice board.

'All school trips will be cancelled till further notice ... there will be no school play, no away matches for the football team, no film at the end of term . . .' Roy sighed. 'He's really gone for it this time.'

'But nobody's stolen his pipe,' said Eric. 'I've asked everyone. He's just lost it, I'm sure he has.'

'Someone,' said Roy, ominously, 'should teach that man a lesson.'

'Maybe,' said Eric, as the two of them headed out to the playground. 'But let's face it. There's nothing we can do.'

'I'm not so sure about that,' said Roy.

He had had an idea, and it was brilliant!

After school that afternoon, Eric and Roy called round on Miss Cable. She lived in a flat in Cromwell Terrace, and was rather surprised to see them. Surprised, but flattered. She had no idea they were so interested in spiders.

Enthusiastically, she showed them her collection. A large part of her sitting room was filled with glass vivariums containing over a hundred different species of spider, including a pair of tarantulas, and Eric and Roy listened to her descriptions of what they ate and how they lived, with faces showing rapt attention.

Miss Cable was very gratified. 'I must say,' she said, 'it's very encouraging to come across people your age who are interested in spiders. So many people these days just seem to be frightened of them.'

'Strange, isn't it, Miss?' said Roy.

'We were rather hoping,' said Eric, 'to start a collection of our own one day.'

'What a wonderful idea!' said Miss Cable. 'If there's any way I can help — you know, books, that sort of thing — just let me know.'

Roy sighed. 'I suppose some of these are rather expensive, Miss.' He gestured to the spiders around them.

'I'm afraid some of them are,' Miss Cable agreed, 'but if you're really keen . . .'

'Oh, we are, Miss, we are . . .' Eric assured her.

Miss Cable made a decision. 'I owe you something for Argiope Runnicheii,' she said. 'How about I help you start your collection? Now, which one would be the most interesting for you . . .?'

'I think we'd like a big hairy one,' said Eric.

'Definitely, Miss,' said Roy. 'We like the big hairy ones best.'

They spent a lot of time trying to decide where exactly they should leave the spider for Mr Blocker to find. Eric thought they should post it to his house, but Roy pointed out that, unless they left it somewhere in the school, they'd never hear the screams. On the other hand, if they *did* try and leave it in his office or something, there was always the risk of being caught.

Then Eric had a brainwave. If he planted the spider while he was a dog, it wouldn't matter if he got caught. Nobody would know he was Eric. He'd just get shooed outside.

So, they put the spider in a box, and the plan was that Eric-as-a-dog would put the box in Mr Blocker's sports bag, which he kept in the staff room. Then, when Mr Blocker went to get changed for cricket, he'd see the box . . .

'Just think of his face when he opens it!' chuckled Roy.

Up to a point, it all went perfectly. Eric-as-a-dog, carrying the box in his teeth, pushed open the door of the staff room and then checked through all the bags until he found the one that belonged to Mr Blocker. It wasn't difficult to find, as it had a large label on it which read 'This bag is the Private Property of J. G. Blocker.'

Eric pulled open the zip with his teeth, put the box with the spider inside, and then closed the bag again. It couldn't have been simpler, except that, just as he was about to leave, he heard voices in the passage outside.

Eric wasn't too worried, but he thought it might be simplest if he hid under one of the armchairs, and waited for whoever it was to go away.

A moment later, Mr Blocker himself came into the staff room, closely followed by Mrs Jessop.

'I'm sure you're wrong, you know,' Mrs Jessop was saying.

'Am I?' asked Mr Blocker, gloomily. 'So why do they keep doing these things to me?'

'That's just children,' came Mrs Jessop's voice again. 'They get high spirited, they do silly things . . .'

'The fact is they don't like me,' said Mr Blocker. 'They never have.'

He sat down in the chair right over Eric, and the springs sank ominously low under his weight.

'To be honest, John, you don't always give them a chance,' Mrs Jessop sat down beside him.

'How can I?' protested Mr Blocker. 'How can I, when they steal my property and don't give it back?'

'Are you sure they've stolen it?' asked Mrs Jessop.

'Of course they have! They're doing it just to spite me!'

'To Eric's relief, Mr Blocker got up then and started stacking a pile of exercise books on the table. 'Did you know it was my birthday next Tuesday?' he asked.

'No, I didn't,' said Mrs Jessop.

'The children made you a birthday cake on your birthday, didn't they?' Mr Blocker's voice was low and gloomy, not like the way he shouted in class at all.

Mrs Jessop didn't say anything.

'Miss Cable's only been here a term, and her class bought her a bottle of sherry,' Mr Blocker went on. 'I've been here twenty years, and the children have never bought me a single present.' Picking up the exercise books, he walked to the staff room door.

'Never,' he said, as he left the room.

'Oh dear,' sighed Mrs Jessop, and she got up and followed him.

When they'd gone, Eric crawled out from under the chair, went over to Mr Blocker's bag, unzipped it and took out the box with the spider.

*

Roy couldn't believe it. 'You what?' he said.

'I'm sorry, Roy,' said Eric. 'I just couldn't do it. If you'd seen him ... It was like he was a normal person.'

'Normal?' Roy was incredulous. 'Blocker?'

'I just thought,' said Eric, 'that maybe that's why he's always so horrible. Maybe if we show him that we like him . . .'

'But we don't, said Roy.

'I know,' said Eric, 'but if he thought that we did . . .'

'You want us to tell him lies?' asked Roy.

'Not exactly,' said Eric, 'but, well, how about if we get him a birthday present? You know, we could collect money from everyone, like they did for Miss Cable.'

'Seriously?' asked Roy.

'It might make all the difference,' Eric assured him.

'I'll tell you one thing,' said Roy. 'It's not going to be easy.'

Roy was right. It wasn't easy. When they asked Alison, for instance, she said why should you give money for someone who'd just cancelled all the fixtures for your hockey team? The Headmaster was not a popular man.

Still, they persevered. They got a few pence here and a few pence there, and had one very successful afternoon when Eric-as-a-dog sat outside the school gates with a tin round his neck. A lot of the parents, waiting for their children to come out, put money in it, though Eric suspected that most of them thought they were contributing to Guide Dogs for the Blind.

By the end of the week they had managed to get

enough money to buy something. Roy suggested getting pipe tobacco, but Eric thought, in the circumstances, it might be a little tactless, and they settled instead on buying a box of chocolates from Mr Patel's newsagents. Roy took the chocolates home, so that his Mum could wrap them up in proper paper.

On Mr Blocker's birthday, they left his present in the basket strapped to the handlebars of his bicycle. Eric had thought they ought to take it to him in his office, but Roy was very insistent that it would be nicest if he got the present straight out of the blue, as a complete surprise, without even knowing where it had come from.

'But I want to see his face when he gets it,' argued Eric.

'So do I,' said Roy, 'but we can hide in the bushes and watch.'

When, at the end of school, Mr Blocker walked over to his bicycle and saw what was in his basket, he was so surprised, he dropped his bicycle clips.

'Ah!' he gave a brief cry.

Mrs Jessop was unlocking her car. 'What is it, John?' she called.

'It's . . . it's a present!' said Mr Blocker.

Mrs Jessop smiled, and came over. Sure enough, there was a box, wrapped in shiny silver paper and held with a large blue ribbon.

'I wondered when it was going to appear,' she said.

'What d'you mean?' asked Mr Blocker.

'They've been doing a collection for you,' Mrs Jessop explained, and because Mr Blocker still looked rather blank, she added 'The children have. For your birthday.'

'Really?' Mr Blocker was suspicious. 'How did they find out?'

Mrs Jessop shrugged. 'I didn't tell them, I promise you. I saw them collecting though – they've been at it for days. Well? Aren't you going to open it?'

Mr Blocker tore off the wrapping paper and the ribbon, revealing the box of chocolates.

'Isn't that nice of them,' said Mrs Jessop.

'Yes . . .' said Mr Blocker.

'Maybe you'll feel a little more kindly disposed to them now,' she suggested, gently.

'What?' Mr Blocker looked up.

'I just thought,' said Mrs Jessop, 'that, in view of this, you might be lifting your ban on school trips and so on tomorrow.'

'Good heavens, no!' said Mr Blocker. He took a deep breath of satisfaction. 'No, no, this just proves the view I've always held that what children really respect is tough discipline.'

'Ah,' said Mrs Jessop.

'Oh, yes,' Mr Blocker nodded firmly. 'Firm discipline, that's what children like, you see, an authority they can respect.'

Mrs Jessop sighed. 'I'll see you tomorrow, John,' she said, and went back to her car.

Mr Blocker didn't seem to notice. He was still clutching his chocolates, saying. 'I knew I was right. Firm discipline . . .'

From their vantage point in the bushes, Roy and Eric had heard every word. Eric was furious.

'I don't believe it!' he spluttered. 'After all the trouble we went to. He thinks we *like* him like that! I've a good mind to go down there and make him give them back.'

Roy laid a restraining hand on Eric's arm. 'I did warn you, Eric,' he said. 'You can't change a man like Blocker with a box of chocolates.'

'I wish we'd never done it now,' Eric was deeply disappointed. 'Come on, Roy.' He got up. 'I'm going home.'

'Hang on!' said Roy. 'I think he's going to eat one.'

Mr Blocker had opened the box, selected a chocolate from the top layer, and put the rest of the chocolates back in the basket on his bicycle. Then, swinging himself up into the saddle, he pedalled out on to the road.

'Follow me, Eric,' said Roy.

Puzzled, Eric followed Roy through the bushes to a hole in the fencing that led out on to the road. They got there just as Mr Blocker cycled by, humming cheerfully, and helping himself to another chocolate from the box.

A suspicion was growing in Eric's mind.

'Roy?' he said. 'What have you done?'

'Sorry, Eric. It was too good an opportunity to waste,' Roy gazed down the road after Mr Blocker. 'Any second now . . .' he murmured.

The spider stirred. It had been quite content, trapped in the dark, but now it could sense movement and light. There was noise and vibration, and something was rocking it from side to side. Its little brain decided that it was time to try and move somewhere safer and quieter.

It stretched its hairy legs to their full five inch span, pushed, and heaved itself up from the bottom layer of the box.

Keeping his eyes on the road, Mr Blocker fumbled

with one hand for another chocolate. The one he lifted out felt rather soft and squishy. He glanced down . . .

A quarter of a mile away, back at the school gates, Eric and Roy heard Mr Blocker's yell with perfect clarity. They watched as his bicycle swerved violently from side to side and then disappeared from view. Then there was another yell, cut off a moment later, by a splash.

'Nice one, Roy,' said Eric. 'I'd forgotten about the canal.'

# MIXED DOUBLES

Roy was hunting under his bed for a pair of plimsolls. He'd managed to find some white socks, white shorts, and a nearly clean white shirt, but he couldn't find the plimsolls.

He and Eric were going to the Tennis Club that afternoon, to be ball boys for Finals Day. It meant they'd get a first class view of the game, a very large tea, and five pounds each at the end of it all, but Mrs Jessop had said that they must be dressed properly, in whites. Maybe someone had put his plimsolls in the chest of drawers.

'Going out?'

Roy's sister, Susan, was standing in the doorway.

'Do you mind?' said Roy. 'This is a private bedroom.' He turned his back on her, and pulled open a drawer.

Susan, it seemed, did not mind. 'You're going to the tennis club, aren't you?' she asked. Then, when Roy made no reply, she went on, 'I just wondered if you were taking that dog?'

'Dog?' Roy rummaged through the drawer. 'What dog?'

'You know . . . your dog.'

'I'm going with Eric.' Roy said, coldly, pulling open the next drawer down. Why couldn't his sister leave him alone?

'Eric . . .' Susan showed no signs of leaving him alone, 'It's funny, isn't it?'

'Is it?' asked Roy. The plimsolls weren't anywhere in the chest of drawers. If only his mother hadn't gone out for the day, he could have asked her where they were.

'Well, I've seen you with Eric,' Susan was still talking, 'and I've seen you with that dog, but I've never seen you with both of them at the same time.' She smiled, innocently. 'And they're both called Eric. Funny, isn't it?'

Roy stopped. He didn't like the way this conversation was heading. 'What's that supposed to mean?' he asked.

'Nothing!' Susan smiled again. 'I just said it was funny, that's all.' She turned to go. 'Oh!' she said. 'You left these by the back door. Mum said to give them to you.' And she dropped Roy's plimsolls onto his bed.

Cycling up to the tennis club, Eric was looking forward to the afternoon's work.

'You know she gets to keep it if they win this time?' he said.

'What?' Roy was a little distracted.

'Mrs Jessop,' said Eric. 'If she wins it three years running, she and Mr Jessop can keep the cup.'

'Oh, yeah,' said Roy.

'Mind you, I don't think there's much doubt about it,' Eric went on. 'If you've ever seen how fast she plays. Half the time her opponents don't even see the ball.'

Roy didn't reply. He was still wondering what his sister could have meant. She couldn't have found out, could she? He decided he'd better tell Eric what had happened, just in case.

Eric was distinctly alarmed. 'You mean she knows?' he said.

'No,' said Roy. 'No, I'm sure she doesn't.'

'If she found out . . .' said Eric. He had a sudden vision of being handed over to scientists who wanted to find out exactly why he turned into a dog, of being taken away from his family and friends, of earning his living in a circus freak-show. All the old nightmares welled up inside him.

'She'll never find out!' said Roy, reassuringly. 'But I think we should be a bit careful for a few days, you know? Keep out of her hair and that.'

'Yes,' said Eric. 'Yes, you're right.'

The two of them turned, and cycled up the gravel drive to the tennis club, where, at the main entrance, they were met by Mr Hudson, the club secretary, who showed them where to change.

Neither of them thought to look over his shoulder, though even if they had they probably wouldn't have noticed Susan. She had been very careful, as she followed them, to keep well out of sight.

There was not a lot of love lost between Roy and his sister Susan, and it has to be said that this was probably as much his fault as hers. She was four years older than her brother, and they did not have much in common. Roy, for instance, thought it was very amusing to leave a frog in her wellington boots, to put sand in her bed, and to tell her boyfriends that she was an adopted orphan, while Susan didn't think any of these things were funny at all.

She did not, as Roy had guessed, know anything for

certain, but she knew her brother well enough to know he was hiding something. There was some sort of secret connected with Eric and the dog that kept turning up at the house, and she was determined to find out what it was. If Roy wanted it kept secret, then as far as she was concerned, it was a very good reason for making it as public as possible. What Susan wanted, was revenge.

At a discreet distance, she followed the boys into the tennis club building. On Finals day, the place was full of visitors, so nobody stopped her. Outside the door to the changing room, she stopped and listened. Eric and Roy were talking inside.

'The thing that annoys me most about my sister,' Roy was saying, 'apart from the fact that she's ugly and stupid. . . .'

Susan grimaced. 'You wait, Roy!' she thought. 'Just you wait.'

'The thing that annoys me most,' Roy repeated, 'is that she's so pigheaded. The only person she ever thinks about is herself . . . Eric, are you alright? . . . Eric?'

'Woof!' said Eric.

There was a moment's silence.

'You know,' said Roy, 'it's not going to be easy explaining this to Mrs Jessop.'

Outside in the passage, Susan was still trying to work out what had happened, when Roy pushed open the door, and nearly squashed her against the wall.

But Susan didn't worry about being squashed. Hidden as she was, behind the door, Roy could not see her, but she could see Roy, still chatting to Eric as they walked down the passage.

Except that Eric wasn't a boy. He was a dog.

Susan shook her head. It wasn't possible! Maybe the real Eric was still inside the changing room? She decided to look, and had just reached out a hand to the door knob, when a voice from behind nearly made her jump out of her skin.

'Can I help you?' said Mr Hudson. The club secretary sounded deeply disapproving. 'This is the men's changing room, you know.'

Susan recovered quickly. 'I'm so sorry!' She smiled apologetically. She was a pretty girl who knew that her smiles could get her out of trouble most of the time. 'I was just looking for my brother, and I was told he's in there.'

Mr Hudson opened the door of the changing room and looked around. 'Nobody in here, I'm afraid,' he said.

Susan followed him inside and looked carefully around the empty lockers and benches.

'No,' she said, thoughtfully. 'There isn't, is there?'

As Roy, with Eric-as-a-dog beside him, walked out of the club building and over to the tennis courts, he met Mrs Jessop.

'There you are, Roy. Jolly good,' she said, and then looked round. 'Where's Eric?'

'He couldn't make it, Miss,' said Roy.

Mrs Jessop frowned. 'We need two ball boys for this match,' she said. 'Why couldn't he let me know?'

Roy evaded the question. 'I thought we could use my dog, Miss.' He pointed at Eric.

Mrs Jessop raised an eyebrow. 'Come on, Roy! We can hardly expect a dog to . . .' She stopped, and looked closely at Eric. 'Is this the dog that played cricket?'

'Yes, Miss,' said Roy.

Mrs Jessop could remember a school cricket match where Roy's dog had not only done some rather impressive fielding, but caught out two of their opponent's batsmen.

'You really think he'll be alright as a ballboy? she asked, still a little doubtful.

'I've taught him everything I know, Miss,' Roy assured her, solemnly.

'Well . . .' Mrs Jessop gave a shrug. 'It won't do any harm to try him out. Let's go and find someone who'll give us a practice knock-up.'

On a court on the far side of the club, they found Mr and Mrs Morgan. At first, Mr Morgan was a little reluctant to play.

'Are you sure that would be wise?' he asked.

'Why ever not?' said Mrs Jessop.

Mr Morgan frowned. 'I need hardly remind you,' he said, 'that we are about to cross swords in the finals of the mixed doubles. Shouldn't we maintain a certain distance?'

'I don't want a game, Mr Morgan,' Mrs Jessop explained. 'I just want to see how these two manage as ball boys.'

Mr Morgan looked around. 'Which two?' he said. He could only see Roy.

'Roy and his dog here,' Mrs Jessop said, cheerfully. 'Is that alright?'

'You can't have a dog as a ball boy!' said Mr Morgan.

'That's what we want to find out,' Mrs Jessop explained, patiently. She turned to Roy and Eric. 'Okay, you two, into place.'

'But this is ridiculous!' protested Mr Morgan. 'A

dog wouldn't even know where to stand, he'd just . . .'
His voice trailed off as he watched Eric trot over to the
ball boy's position at one side of the net, and sit down.

'He's a very intelligent dog,' said Mrs Jessop. 'We'll
give him a try, shall we?' She turned to Mrs Morgan.
'Can I borrow your spare racket, Elaine? My stuff's
still up at the club.'

Eric-as-a-dog was a great success as a ball boy. He
could catch the ball, flick it back to the server, then
trot back to his place by the net, even faster than Roy.
As Mrs Morgan said, he was so good, you'd almost
think he was human. In a very short time, Mrs Jessop
was more than satisfied that he and Roy would be
perfectly alright for the finals.

'Well, I think we know he can do it now,' she said,
breathing heavily after the last rally.

'He's amazing, isn't he!' Mrs Morgan agreed. 'Can't
we go on? I was rather enjoying that.'

'I'd better get my bag first,' Mrs Jessop said. 'I find
it very difficult playing with someone else's racket, and
these shoes are killing me.'

Mr Morgan stepped forward. 'I'll get the bag for
you,' he volunteered, 'while you carry on playing with
Elaine.'

'That's very kind of you,' said Mrs Jessop. 'Are you
sure?'

'Yes, positive!'

'Well, thank you. I left it inside the club entrance.'

Mrs Jessop didn't say so, but she was rather surprised. Mr Morgan wasn't usually the sort of man to
do things for other people like that. Maybe she'd
misjudged him.

*

As Mr Morgan walked back to the clubhouse, his heart was pounding inside his chest, not from the game he'd just played, but at the thought of what he was about to do.

Mr Morgan desperately wanted to win the mixed doubles finals, but he knew, as everyone else did, that he didn't really have a chance. He and his wife were good players, and they practised hard, but Mrs Jessop was better, and always would be. People said she could have been a professional if she hadn't decided to be a teacher.

Mrs Jessop herself had given him the idea, when she said how difficult it was to play with someone else's racket, and that her shoes hurt. In normal circumstances, he knew, he had no chance of winning, but if Mrs Jessop had to play with a borrowed racket, if she had to play in the wrong shoes . . .

He found her bag inside the club entrance, just where she'd said it would be, and carried it outside. He knew that what he was about to do was wrong, but somehow he couldn't stop himself. It would be just this once, he kept saying to himself, it wasn't fair that she always won!

He looked carefully around. No one was in sight, and with a sudden heave, he threw the bag with all his strength into the air. He watched it arc, high above the ground, and then disappear from view as it fell into one of the rhodedendron bushes that lined the drive.

When Mr Morgan got back to the tennis court, he found his wife delightedly crowing that she had won! She had actually won a game against Mrs Jessop!

'I know it's only because she didn't have her own racket,' she said. 'But . . .'

'Not at all,' Mrs Jessop assured her, generously. 'You were playing very well. Mind you,' she added, 'I'll be glad to have my proper stuff back.' She turned to Mr Morgan. 'Did you get the bag?'

'I'm afraid it wasn't there,' Mr Morgan found it easier than he'd thought to tell the lie.

'Wasn't there?' Mrs Jessop was puzzled.

'Not a sign of it,' said Mr Morgan. 'I looked everywhere, but – not a trace. Sorry.'

'Perhaps someone's picked it up and handed it in,' said Mrs Morgan. She liked Mrs Jessop, and was quite unaware of what her husband had done.

'Perhaps,' Mrs Jessop agreed.

'Not a very sensible place to leave it, I'm afraid,' said Mr Morgan.

'Thank you,' said Mrs Jessop. 'Well, if you'll excuse me, I think I'd better go and make a few inquiries.'

'Don't forget we're playing in fifteen minutes,' Mr Morgan called after her.

Roy turned to Eric. 'You could do that,' he murmured.

'Woof?'

'You could track down the bag,' Roy explained. 'If someone's taken it, you could follow the trail, couldn't you? With your nose?'

'Woof!' said Eric.

'Wait for me!' said Roy, chasing after him.

Mrs Jessop was on her way to find Mr Hudson, the club secretary, when she heard a voice.

'Mrs Jessop?' Susan came running up to join her.

'Yes?'

'I'm Susan. Roy's sister,' She held out a hand. 'I

was wondering if I could ask your advice about something.'

Mrs Jessop said that she could, as long as Susan didn't mind walking while they talked, but five minutes later, she was rather regretting the decision. Susan wasn't very good at explaining exactly what she needed advice about.

'Let me try and get this straight,' said Mrs Jessop. 'You're saying that if you knew something that nobody else knew, but if they did know they'd be very shocked by it, should you tell someone?'

'That's it,' said Susan.

'Is it anything criminal or illegal?' Mrs Jessop asked.

'Not really,' Susan admitted.

'In that case,' said Mrs Jessop, firmly, 'I think you shouldn't. My limited experience of telling people things they don't need to know, but which someone thinks they ought to know, is that it just causes a great deal of misery and suffering. Unless you want that to happen, I should just keep whatever it was to yourself, alright?'

Mrs Jessop walked into the club house.

'Misery and suffering,' Susan thought. It sounded perfect, absolutely perfect.

At the club entrance, Eric wasn't having a lot of luck looking for Mrs Jessop's bag. He'd found the place inside the door where she'd left it, easily enough, and there were faint traces in the air that suggested it had been taken back outside, but after that he lost track of it altogether. The trouble was, of course, that Mr Morgan had thrown it up into the air, but Eric didn't know that.

He had just decided to zig zag across the drive a few times to see if he could pick up the scent that way, when he felt an itching on the back of his neck.

'Woof, woof, woof!' he barked.

Roy immediately recognized this as the code that meant Eric was about to change back into a boy.

'Alright, Eric,' he said. 'Don't panic!' He thought quickly, and pointed to the rhododendron bushes that lined the drive. 'The bushes! You hide in there, and I'll get your clothes.'

It was a sensible plan, and Eric ran gratefully to the bushes, while Roy disappeared inside the club house, to get Eric's clothes from the changing room.

Eric waited, shivering, for Roy's return, and while he waited, a car drove up and stopped at the entrance. A woman got out. 'You stay there!' she called to her dog in the back of the car, before going inside.

Carefully peering through the leaves of the rhododendron bush, Eric could just see the car – and the dog in the back. There was something oddly familiar about it. He was sure he'd seen it somewhere before, but he couldn't think where. Then he suddenly realised. The dog was exactly like himself! Or at least, it looked exactly like he looked when he was a dog. There wasn't quite as much white around the mouth perhaps, and the tail was a touch longer, but otherwise the resemblance was uncanny. Eric chuckled. He must remember to tell Roy.

Roy came out of the club house a few minutes later, clutching Eric's clothes, and saw was the dog that looked exactly like Eric, sitting in the back of the car.

'Eric?' he said. 'What are you doing in there? I thought you were going to hide in the bushes.'

'Woof, woof, woof!' said the dog. It always barked at people who came near the car.

'Alright, alright!' said Roy, 'I know you're going to change, but you can't change in the car, can you?'

'Woof,' said the dog.

'Okay,' said Roy. 'Whatever you want.' And he opened the car door to give Eric the clothes.

Over in the bushes, it took Eric a moment to understand what Roy was doing. Then he realized, Roy must think the other dog was him! He stood up to call, to shout, anything to tell Roy his mistake, but as soon as he stood up, he saw two old ladies had sat down on a bench on the grass just in front of the bushes where he was hiding.

Eric, you will remember, had no clothes on, so he couldn't exactly leap out and run over to Roy, and if he shouted, the two women would turn round and see him, which would land him in all sorts of trouble. All he could do was wave his arms above the leaves, and hope that Roy would notice.

Unfortunately, Roy was facing the other way, watching the dog he thought was Eric, tearing up the shirt he'd just been given. It seemed very odd behaviour. 'Your Mum's not going to like that, Eric,' said Roy, and then the dog jumped out of the car, and ran off round the side of the club house.

'Eric!' called Roy. 'Where are you going? What about your clothes?'

Eric watched Roy chase after the dog, and sighed. There was nothing to do except settle back in the bushes and sit this one out. Maybe, when the old ladies got up and moved away, he could risk dashing over to the car to get his clothes back.

Then he saw it. Mrs Jessop's bag was hanging in one of the branches above his head. He reached up and pulled it down. Inside it, were not only the racket and shoes Mrs Jessop needed, but a large white tennis sweater.

Two minutes later, Eric emerged from the bushes, carrying Mrs Jessop's bag and wearing a sweater that came down to his knees. He smiled cheerfully at the two ladies, walked briskly over to the car, and rescued his clothes.

Breathing several sighs of relief, he carried them back into the clubhouse to get changed.

Meanwhile, out on Court Number One, Mr Hudson had arrived to umpire the finals of the mixed doubles. Mr and Mrs Morgan, and Mr and Mrs Jessop were already on court.

'Any luck finding your bag?' he called to Mrs Jessop.

' 'Fraid not,' she answered. 'I'll have to borrow a racket from someone.'

'You can have mine again,' said Mrs Morgan.

'Thanks,' said Mrs Jessop.

'Right,' Mr Hudson looked round. 'Where are the ball boys?'

'They're just coming,' Mrs Jessop pointed to where Roy and the dog were running in their direction. 'Come along, Roy!' she called. 'You're late!'

Roy couldn't understand why Eric was behaving so oddly. He'd spent the last ten minutes rushing aimlessly all over the gardens, barking furiously, and had been in a fight with two other dogs. Roy had tried to tell him that, if they couldn't find Mrs Jessop's bag, they ought to get back to the tennis courts, and it was with some relief that he heard Mrs Jessop call, and the dog he thought was Eric darted onto the court. Roy followed, closing the gate behind him.

Mr Hudson looked askance at the dog as it raced round and round the net.

'Don't worry,' Mrs Jessop told him. 'That's one of the ball boys.'

'But it's a dog!' said Mr Hudson.

'It's all right,' said Mrs Morgan. 'We tried him out earlier, he knows what he's doing. He's extraordinary, he really is!'

'Well,' said Mr Hudson, 'I suppose if you're all happy . . . I've got the balls here.'

Mr Hudson was opening a brand new box of tennis balls, when the dog caught sight of them, came leaping over, knocked the box from his hand, picked up one of the tennis balls that spilled onto the ground, and started eating it.

'What on earth's got into your dog, Roy?' asked Mrs Jessop.

'I don't know, Miss,' said Roy, who was as puzzled as she was.

'It's your dog, is it?' asked Mr Hudson.

Roy was just wondering how to reply to that, when a loud voice shouted, 'No! It's not his dog. It's not anyone's dog.' And Susan came striding on to the court.

'As a matter of fact,' she went on, rather enjoying the stares of amazement from all around her, 'it's not a dog at all. It's a boy called Eric Banks.'

'D'you think she's had a bit too much of the sun?' Mr Hudson murmured to Mrs Jessop.

'I can prove it,' said Susan. 'Ask my brother here. Go on, ask him if this is Eric Banks or not. He knows.'

Everyone looked at Roy, who hesitated only for a moment. He wasn't going to give Eric away to anyone.

'Of course it isn't Eric!' he said. 'It's just a dog I . . . I found.'

'So where's Eric?' asked Susan.

'Was that the boy I saw you with earlier?' asked Mr Hudson.

'Yes,' said Roy, and realized almost immediately that he shouldn't have done.

'I thought you said Eric wasn't here today,' said Mrs Jessop.

'Yes, I know I did,' said Roy, 'But . . .'

'But I showed you both into the changing room, didn't I?' asked Mr Hudson.

'Yes,' said Roy. 'Yes, you did, but . . .'

'But Eric didn't come out, did he?' said Susan, triumphantly. 'Only that dog came out, and Eric wasn't anywhere to be seen, because the dog *was* Eric!'

Roy was feeling distinctly trapped, but at that moment Eric himself walked onto the court, carrying Mrs Jessop's bag.

'Sorry, I'm late, Miss,' said Eric, 'but I was looking for your bag.' He passed it over. 'Everything alright, Roy?'

Roy looked at Eric, then looked at the dog, and then looked back at Eric. 'Fine,' he said. 'Just fine.'

Susan opened her mouth several times, as if she was about to say something, but then changed her mind and closed it again.

A large woman came running down the bank at the side of the court. 'Poppy!' she called, 'Poppy, you naughty dog! Where have you been?' She grabbed the dog by the collar and apologized to everyone, several times. 'I left him in the car,' she said, 'I've no idea how he managed to get out.' And she dragged him away.

Mr Hudson was distinctly confused by all the things that had happened in the last few minutes, but made an effort to get one thing clear.

'This is Eric, is it?' he asked, pointing at Eric.

'We think so,' said Mrs Jessop.

'And he's going to be a ball boy, is he?'

'Yes,' said Eric.

'Right,' said Mr Hudson, 'Let's get on with some tennis, shall we?'

So the finals of the mixed doubles finally got under way. Mr and Mrs Jessop won, of course. Mr Morgan didn't know if Mrs Jessop suspected that he had done something to her bag, but she certainly showed him no mercy. Her serves whistled past his knees with such speed that on some occasions he barely saw them, let alone had any chance of trying to hit them back over the net, while her smash volleys and rapid returns seemed to hit him on the head or body with such regularity that he actually became rather frightened.

Eric and Roy were splendid ball boys, though some of the crowd were a little disappointed that it wasn't the remarkable dog that a few of them had seen earlier. However, they all cheered heartily as Mr and Mrs Jessop went up to collect their cup at the end, and Eric clapped louder than any of them. He felt, perhaps justifiably, that he had played some part in their victory.

After tea, Mrs Jessop walked the boys over to the secretary's office, so that they could be given their

'Thank you both for all your help,' she said. 'Particularly for finding my bag.'

'I just sort of stumbled across it, Miss,' said Eric.

'Hmmm.' Mrs Jessop looked thoughtful. 'Quite an eventful afternoon one way and another, wasn't it?'

'We enjoyed it, Miss,' said Roy.

'Yes,' said Eric. 'It was a brilliant win, Miss.'

'I was thinking more of that incident with Roy's sister,' said Mrs Jessop. 'It was rather odd, wasn't it?'

'She's always been a bit strange,' said Roy.

They got to the office, where Mrs Jessop counted out their money, and then, as she walked them out to their bicycles, she said 'Have either of you ever heard the story of St Cecilia of Calahorra?'

'No, Miss,' said Eric.

'She lived in Spain in the twelfth century,' said Mrs Jessop. 'The Moors were fighting the Christians then, and she was a young girl who tried to smuggle food to the Christians in prison.

'One day, the guards stopped her and asked what she'd got wrapped in her apron. It was bread, but if she'd admitted that, she'd have been executed, so she told a lie. She said that all she had in her apron was rose petals.

'But then the guard asked to see them, and she had to unfold her apron – and you know what fell out? Not bread. Just hundreds and hundreds of rose petals.' She looked at Eric. 'It was a miracle, you see.'

She turned and walked back to the club house. 'See you both on Monday,' she called.

Eric climbed thoughtfully onto his bike. 'Why did she say all that?' he asked.

'All what?' said Roy.

'All that about the rose petals.'

Roy considered this as they cycled down the drive. 'Teachers don't need reasons, Eric,' he said. 'They're always telling you things you don't want to know. It's their job.'

# MOVING ON

Even before he walked up the path to Roy's house, before he'd even turned into the gate, Eric knew that something was wrong.

It all looked the same, same house, same garden, same front door, but it was too tidy. There was no saucer for the cat, no note for the milkman, and none of Roy's toys or Mrs Ackerman's gardening tools lying around in the garden.

Eric rang the door bell and waited. There was no reply, so he rang it again, then pushed open the letter box and shouted, 'Roy! Hi! It's me, Eric!' His voice sounded lost and echoey.

He walked round to the back and peered in through the kitchen window. It was empty. Not just empty of people, but of furniture. The table, the chairs, even the fridge, had all gone. It was the same when he looked in the dining room. There was nothing but the bare floorboards and some old newspapers. Roy's house was completely deserted. It was as if nobody lived there.

Eric wandered back to the front of the house, wondering if perhaps he was having a bad dream. He'd been away for two weeks on holiday – two weeks with his parents and his Gran in a caravan in Wales, – and he'd come back to find that his best friend and his best friend's family had disappeared off the face of the earth.

He looked down at the face mask and snorkel he was carrying. His Dad had bought them for him, and he'd brought them round to show Roy. It had been a really good holiday, and the first thing he had wanted to do when he came back, was come round and tell Roy about it. He hadn't even stopped to unpack. But Roy had disappeared.

He rang the door bell again, not because he thought it would do any good, but because he couldn't think of anything else to do.

'It's no good. There's nobody there.'

Eric looked round. It was Mrs Paterson, calling over the hedge from next door.

'Oh! Hello, Eric!' she said. 'I didn't recognize you, all brown like that. Have you come round to see Roy?'

'Yes,' said Eric. 'Do you know where he is?'

'Like I said, dear,' said Mrs Paterson. 'There's nobody there. They've moved.'

'Moved?' said Eric. How could anyone move in a fortnight? 'Roy didn't say anything about moving!'

'It all happened very quickly,' said Mrs Paterson. 'Inside of a week, the whole thing. They just upped and went.'

'Went where?' asked Eric.

'Amsterdam,' said Mrs Paterson. 'It's in Holland. They caught the boat, day before yesterday.'

Mrs Banks looked up as Eric came in the kitchen door. 'Roy's family has moved!' She was holding a letter.

'I know,' said Eric.

'I've got a note here from his father. The company he works for had an emergency. Someone fell ill, and

he's had to go out and take over. You'll never guess
where they've gone.'

'Amsterdam,' said Eric.

Mrs Banks looked at him. 'Here,' she said. 'There
was a letter for you, as well. From Roy.'

Eric took the letter upstairs to his bedroom. It said:

Dear Eric,
How can they do this to me? I cannot believe it!
How can my Dad drag me off to some foreign
country just because he cares more about his career
than he does about me? I have begged and pleaded
with them to leave me behind. I have told them I
am quite old enough to look after myself and that if
they will just give me the money for a hotel or
something I will be perfectly alright here, but they
will not listen. We leave tomorrow.

It'll only be for a year, Dad says, then we'll be
back. Back in England somewhere, anyway. But
what'll happen about you? Will anything happen?
And if it does, who's going to look after you? I feel
awful. I shall never talk to Dad again, even if he
does buy me a new bike.

You will write, won't you? I still can't believe it.

Thanks for the postcard.

Cheerio,
Roy.
P.S. I am leaving you Mrs Quilter's penknife.

Eric sat on his bed after reading the letter, and stared
at the little penknife in his hand. Roy had kept it as a
sort of lucky charm, ever since that day at the
hospital.

With a sudden clarity, he could remember exactly

how Mrs Quilter's hands had rummaged for it through
her handbag, and Roy's face when she'd taken it out
to give to him.

He put the penknife in his pocket and walked over
to his bedroom window.

He felt thoroughly miserable.

In the weeks that followed, Mrs Banks noticed, Eric
was not his usual self. He was subdued and quiet,
hardly spoke at all, and spent most of his time going
for long walks on his own.

Wisely, Mrs Banks, did not interfere. Roy and Eric
had been best friends since their first day at school, so
it was hardly surprising that Eric missed him. She
thought he was entitled to feel a bit out of sorts, and
firmly believed that, given time, Eric would be his old
self again.

To a certain extent, Mrs Banks was right. What she
didn't know was that Eric had lost more than a friend.
When Roy had asked in his letter 'Will anything
happen?' Eric knew exactly what he meant. They had
always believed that it was Roy wanting a dog that
caused Eric to change into one. Now that Roy was
several hundred miles away in Amsterdam, would it
still happen?

The short answer was that it didn't. It hadn't
happened while Eric had been on holiday in Wales,
and it hadn't happened in the weeks since he'd been
back. Eric was just Eric-the-boy now. There was no
more Eric-the-dog.

What surprised Eric, was how much he missed it. At
the time, he'd often thought that turning into a dog
was more trouble than it was worth. It had got him
into some very frightening and dangerous situations,

but over the last few months, particularly with Roy around to join in, he'd got used to it. No, more than just used to it, he'd got to *like* it. It may have been scary that day up at the tennis courts, for instance, but it had been tremendous fun as well. And now . . . now it had all stopped. There were to be no more adventures. No more creeping out of the house on four paws, no more sneaking in and out of all those places where boys couldn't go but dogs could, no more . . . no more Eric-the-dog.

'Isn't there anything we can do for him?' asked Mr Banks over breakfast.

'He'll be alright when he gets back to school,' Mrs Banks assured him. 'He misses Roy, that's all. Roy and that dog of his. They used to spend a lot of time together, you know.'

'Ah,' Mr Banks poured himself some more tea. 'It's funny, but I miss him too. Sort of.'

'Roy?' Mrs Banks was puzzled.

'I was thinking more of the dog,' said Mr Banks. 'He was a bright little fellow, wasn't he?'

Mrs Banks smiled. 'And we never did find out how he kept getting into Eric's bedroom, did we?' She thought for a moment. 'Did Roy take the dog with him?'

'I don't know,' said Mr Banks. 'I must ask Eric.'

When the new term started, Eric was in a new form at school. He still had plenty of friends. There were Kenny and Dobbo, Alison and Joan, Mark and Christopher, and in class he sat next to a new boy called Brian. He was nice enough. But he wasn't Roy.

Alison and Joan came up to him at break.

WOOF! THE TALE WAGS ON  122

'Where's that dog then?' asked Joan.

'Dog?'

'Roy's dog,' said Alison. 'The one that does tricks. I wanted to show my Mum.'

'Oh, that dog,' said Eric.

'Roy didn't take him to Amsterdam,' said Joan. 'I asked him and he wrote and said.'

'So who's looking after him?' asked Alison. 'Where is he?'

'I wish I knew,' sighed Eric. 'I wish I knew.'

Mr and Mrs Potts asked Eric the same question when they saw him walking home from school that day. Their little puppy was almost full grown now, and when it saw Eric, it jumped up at him in delight, straining at its lead.

'Roy's moved,' Eric told them.

'Moved?' Mrs Potts was aghast. 'Moved where?'

'To Amsterdam,' said Eric.

'Is his dog alright?' asked Mr Potts. 'You know - Eric. Has he taken Eric?'

'We miss him, you see,' added Mrs Potts. 'He hasn't called round for ages. Has Roy taken him with him?'

'I don't really know,' said Eric. 'But I think it looks as if he has.'

Mrs Jessop saw Eric as she was heading into the supermarket.

'How's it going?' she asked.

Eric shrugged. 'Oh . . . alright.'

'I heard about Roy leaving,' Mrs Jessop smiled sympathetically. 'It's not easy, is it?'

'It's alright,' said Eric. 'We still write.'

'I miss that dog of his as well,' Mrs Jessop laughed.

'I'll never forget the day he walked into the school assembly. I hope he's still around. Somewhere.' She turned through the glass doors and went into the supermarket.

Instead of going straight home, Eric walked out towards Monkston Hill. He felt he needed to be alone. He needed a chance to think.

Halfway up the hill, he found a clearing in the trees that gave him a bit of privacy and sat down. He had the feeling there was an important idea in the back of his head, and if he could just concentrate hard enough, it might float out to the front.

It was very strange. All day, people had been telling him how much they missed Eric-as-a-dog. Mr and Mrs Potts, his parents, the children at school, Mrs Jessop – even Miss Robson from the Dog Club had sent him a card that morning saying she'd heard Roy was abroad and she wondered if his dog needed looking after at all. So many people had liked 'that dog' as Joan called him. Eric wasn't sure if it made it better or worse to know that other people missed him as much as he did himself.

An insect landed on the back of his neck, and Eric reached up a hand to brush it away. The idea was still there at the back of his brain, but it wouldn't quite come out. It was ridiculous. All those people wanting to see Eric-the-dog again, and he wanted to *be* Eric-the-dog again, but because Roy wasn't there any more, wanting it, it would never happen again.

The insect must have bitten him, Eric thought, because the back of his neck was still itching, even when he scratched it quite hard . . .

*

If you had been out on Monkston Hill that afternoon, you would have seen a quite extraordinary sight. A dog, a mongrel to be precise, was doing somersaults down the hill. It was bouncing. It was leaping into the air. It was throwing itself over and over for all the world, as if it had just been told it had been given a butcher's shop for its birthday.

When it got to the bottom, it ran along the path so fast that, when it rounded the corner, it knocked Mrs Jessop's bag clean out of her hand, so that her shopping spilled all over the ground. The dog stopped, apologetically, and started picking up the groceries and putting them back into the bag.

'My word!' Mrs Jessop stared down. 'I didn't expect to see you again. We thought you'd gone off somewhere for good.' She bent down to look more closely at the dog wagging its tail in front of her. 'It *is* you . . . isn't it?' she asked.

'Woof!' said Eric.

# THE TALE GETS LONGER

by Andrew Norriss

# 1

Rachel Hobbs was staring rather miserably out of her bedroom window, while outside, her mother was directing the removal men as they carried the furniture into their new house. Rachel knew she ought to be down there helping, but at the moment, she didn't care about furniture or removals or helping – or anything except that she didn't want to be there. In fact, she was feeling so sorry for herself that, at first, she didn't even notice the dog.

It was a scruffy sort of dog with shaggy hair, short paws and a little stubby tail, and for some reason, it seemed to be trying to get into the house. It had started by walking straight in through the front door, but one of the removal men had seen it and sent it back out again, so then it had gone round to the back of the house where, to judge by the voices, exactly the same thing had happened.

Then, and Rachel wouldn't have believed it if she hadn't seen it, the dog had dragged a wooden crate into place just below the sitting-room window and used it to climb into the sitting-room – only to be discovered by Rachel's mother, who had marched it firmly back out on to the road, saying, 'Go on, out! Right out! You don't live here. Just go away!'

But the dog hadn't gone away. It had waited until the removal men were all busy carrying in the piano, and then jumped up into the van. There, it had pushed open one of the sliding doors of a sideboard, climbed inside, pulled the door shut behind itself and waited until the men came back and carried the sideboard indoors. It was such an extraordinary thing for a dog to do that Rachel forgot for a moment how miserable she was. The dog must have wanted very badly to get into the house, she thought, and she couldn't help wondering why.

She didn't have to wonder very long. A minute later, her bedroom door was pushed open and the dog came in. It didn't see Rachel, who was standing by the window, half-hidden by some packing cases. It went straight over to the far corner of the bedroom and started counting – well, that's what it looked like to Rachel – counting the floorboards from the wall.

When it came to number five, the dog stopped and pushed down with one of its paws so that a section of floorboard about a foot long flipped up. The dog pushed it to one side with its nose, then peered down into the gap between the joists.

'What are you doing?'

At the sound of Rachel's voice, the dog gave a little jump of surprise and stepped back.

'Looking for something, were you?' Rachel was understandably curious to know what it was the dog had been searching for, but when she came out from behind the packing cases and peered into the gap under the floorboards, the only thing she could see was a rather battered, leather-bound diary, with the name 'Roy Ackerman' Sellotaped on to the cover. It was one of those big five-year diaries with a lock on it, otherwise I think she might have been tempted to open it and look inside.

'You wanted this?' Rachel was puzzled.

'Woof!' said the dog and, for a moment, Rachel actually thought he was saying 'yes'. But she knew that was silly, so she just said, 'It's no use to you, dog. Better let me look after it.'

She had already worked out that the diary must belong to whoever had lived in the house before, and she put it carefully on top of the wardrobe. Tomorrow, when everyone was less busy, she'd decide what to do with it.

'Want to go for a walk?' she asked the dog.

The dog looked at her for a moment, looked at the top of the wardrobe and then back at Rachel.

'Woof,' it said.

So they went for a walk.

They went to the park, and Rachel took her bicycle. It was different from the sort of bicycle you probably ride. The wheels and tyres were thinner, the handlebars were set very low although the saddle was rather high, and it had more gears than you get on an ordinary bike. It was in fact a racing cycle and, as she and the dog sat on the grass, Rachel checked it over carefully, to make sure it hadn't been damaged at all in the removal van.

Now it is a strange fact, but something you may have noticed yourself, that people will often talk to animals as if they were really another person. Sometimes, they will even tell animals things that they wouldn't dream of telling anyone else in the world. And that is what Rachel did now.

While she carefully polished the chrome on her

bicycle with an oily rag, she told the dog how her mother worked for a building society, how the branch where she worked had closed down, so they had to move – and about how awful it was to leave your home and your friends and the school where you'd been all your life, and move to a place where you didn't know anyone at all.

She told the dog about how her dad had got her interested in cycle racing, before he died, about the cycle club she belonged to back in Exeter, and about her dream of being the first girl ever to win the National Juveniles Circuit Championship.

'Not that there's any chance of that now,' she added, gloomily. 'You can't do that sort of thing on your own – and who's going to help me with training? Working out schedules? Let alone equipment. Who's going to lend me the stuff I need? I can't afford to buy it.' She gestured to the cycle in front of her. 'I mean, I need a Dura-Ace chain set, Shimano toe rings – and what am I supposed to do about it? Hope they turn up as a birthday present three weeks on Sunday?'

Almost despite herself, a tear trickled out of the corner of one eye. 'Mum says I'll make new friends, but I know I won't. I'm no good at that. I never have been.'

The dog looked up at her, barked softly, and put its chin on her knee.

'It's all right for you,' said Rachel, scratching the back of its neck. 'You're different.'

While the dog watched from a park bench, Rachel took her bike for a practice spin round some of the paths in the park, shifting easily through the gears, steadily building up speed.

As she cycled, a boy on another bike came up

alongside. He was bigger and older than Rachel and I think he had some idea in his head of showing her how fast he could go. But to his surprise, when he moved out to overtake, Rachel speeded up as well. He pedalled faster, then faster again, but it was no good. Every time he tried to get past, Rachel went just fast enough to stop him.

As the race progressed – and it had become a race – the boy found it harder and harder to keep up. He was getting red in the face, the sweat was pouring down into his eyes, and his breath was coming in ragged pants. Rachel, on the other hand, hardly looked as if she was trying. You'd have thought she was out for a Sunday stroll.

Then finally, just when he was wondering how long he could keep this up, Rachel turned to him, winked and said, 'That'll do for a warm-up. Let's go.' Unbelievably, she then shifted the bike into another gear and leapt ahead. The boy stared after her, admiringly.

Rachel was a good cyclist. She might not have looked very large or strong, but she was tough and wiry. Above all, she had what people call 'willpower'. It meant that when everyone was getting tired and wanted to drop out of a race, Rachel didn't stop, she just kept going – even when it hurt, even when you knew she must be so tired you didn't see how she could keep going.

When Rachel cycled back to the bench where she had left her kit and the dog, she felt a lot better. There was nothing like cycling really hard to clear the head. Her kit was still on the bench, but the dog had gone. There was no sign of him anywhere.

She was rather disappointed about that.

*

The next day, Rachel started at her new school. Her teacher was all right, an energetic woman with frizzy hair called Mrs Jessop, but every time Rachel looked round the classroom, she couldn't help thinking of all the friends she had left behind at her old school.

When the bell went for afternoon break and Mrs Jessop told the class to put away their books before going out to the playground, a boy made his way through the tables to the desk where Rachel was sitting.

'Hi,' he said. 'I'm Eric Banks.'

He was a red-haired boy of about her own age, with freckles.

'You've moved into Roy's house,' he said. 'Roy Ackerman. He used to be my best friend.'

'Oh, yes?' Rachel looked at him.

'It's just that I had this letter from him a few days ago, and he says he left a diary under a floorboard in his bedroom, and I wondered . . .'

'We found it,' said Rachel. 'We're going to send it on to his new address.'

'Great,' said Eric. 'Only it's a bit private, and he was worried that someone might read it.'

'I don't read other people's diaries,' said Rachel stonily, and left.

Eric was still wondering what he'd said wrong when Mrs Jessop appeared beside him.

'Is that girl all right?' she asked. 'I know it's not easy, joining a new school in the middle of term, but you're the first person I've seen her talk to all day. Is something bothering her, do you know?'

'Well . . .' Eric hesitated.

'It's just that if we knew what it was,' Mrs Jessop went on, 'we might be able to help.'

Eric came to a decision. 'Well, Miss,' he said, 'I think she's upset because she's a really keen cyclist and what she wanted was to be the first girl to win the National Juveniles Circuit Championship, but now that she's moved, she hasn't got anyone to help with the training or looking after the bike, so . . . so she's not very happy.'

Mrs Jessop looked at him. 'You seem to have picked up quite a lot in a thirty-second conversation,' she said.

'I heard her talking to someone,' Eric explained.

'I see,' said Mrs Jessop. 'And is she any good at this cycling?'

'I saw her in the park,' said Eric. 'I think she's brilliant.'

'Cycling, eh?' Mrs Jessop looked thoughtful. 'Well, we'll have to see what we can do about that.'

In the days that followed, Rachel still found it difficult to make friends at school, but she saw quite a lot of the little dog that she'd found burrowing under the floorboards the day they'd moved into the house.

She never knew where he came from. He would just appear, either at her house or while she was out walking, and once he even turned up at school. When Rachel saw him there, he was trotting down a corridor during the lunch break. She was about to call to him when Mr Blocker, the headmaster, unfortunately saw him as well.

Mr Blocker didn't like dogs, and for some reason he didn't like this one in particular. With a great shout of 'Hoi! Stop, you!' he leapt after it. He chased it down the corridor, in and out of the classroom where Mrs Mitchell was giving a recorder lesson, and then chased it so fast through the dining room that he spilt a plate of spaghetti into Brian Richardson's lap.

Rachel watched from a window as the dog came racing out of the main doors and round the corner. Then it stopped, picked up a skateboard and put it carefully into place just where someone coming round the corner in a hurry would tread on it.

And that, of course, is exactly what Mr Blocker did. He came round the corner at ninety miles an hour, put one foot on the skateboard, took off down the path like a rocket, and ten seconds later, landed head first in the goldfish pond. Everyone rushed round to help pull him out, trying not to laugh while they were doing so; only Rachel, watching from her window, saw the dog peer round a corner of the building, as if to make sure no one was still chasing him, and then trot calmly into the boy's changing room.

Rachel didn't know much about dogs, but she did know that an animal that could deliberately trip up a headmaster by putting a skateboard under his feet was a very unusual one. She went down to the boy's changing room, knocked on the door, then looked inside. There was no sign of the dog. Just Eric Banks, putting on a T-shirt.

'You haven't seen a dog, have you?' asked Rachel.

'Dog?' Eric shook his head. 'No. Why?'

'Oh. Nothing.' Rachel closed the door.

Two things puzzled her as she walked away. One was, if Eric *hadn't* seen the dog, where on earth had it gone? And the other was, what was Eric doing getting changed on a day when there were no sports?

The next Saturday, the dog appeared at Rachel's

house again, soon after breakfast, and the two of them set out for a walk.

'You want to be careful, dog,' Rachel was saying, as she followed him down a tree-lined avenue of large houses. 'Mr Blocker's told everyone that if he ever catches you on school premises again, he'll have you minced up and served as a school dinner.'

She stopped. The dog had just turned off into someone's drive and was trotting up to the front door.

'Hey, dog! You can't go in there,' Rachel called, but it was too late. The dog had already jumped up and rung the front-door bell. Rachel ran after him, grabbed him by the scruff of the neck, and was just hauling him back to the road when the front door opened.

'Ah, well done, Rachel,' said Mrs Jessop. 'You found us all right, then?'

'Mrs Jessop?' Rachel stared.

'Well, don't just stand around on the doorstep.' Mrs Jessop ushered her inside. 'I imagine Eric told you what this was all about.'

'Eric?' Rachel was getting more confused by the minute.

'Eric Banks.' Mrs Jessop smiled. 'Or perhaps he wanted this to be a surprise. Anyway, come along. We haven't got all day . . .'

And she led Rachel through into the sitting-room.

It was a surprise, all right. It seemed that Mrs Jessop had been in touch with Rachel's cycling club back in Exeter and between them, they had worked out an entire training schedule for Rachel to follow if she wanted to carry on racing. There was a timetable of things she should practise each day, times and speeds she should aim for, entry forms for the races she should enter with details of how to get to them – everything had been worked out.

While a part of Rachel kept wondering how on earth Mrs Jessop had known about all this, most of her was just overwhelmingly happy at the prospect of proper training again. If you've ever really wanted to do something and suddenly been told that you can do it after all, you might have some idea how she felt.

'Now . . .' said Mrs Jessop, putting a large pile of papers to one side and reaching for a cake knife, 'the one other thing you'll need is someone with a stopwatch to help you keep a record of your times, how many laps you've done, that sort of thing. Got anyone in mind?'

Rachel said the trouble was she didn't really know anyone.

'Hmmm.' Mrs Jessop cut three slices of cake. 'What about Eric Banks?' she suggested.

'He's a boy,' said Rachel.

'He's still a human being,' said Mrs Jessop. 'Most of the time.' She looked at Rachel. 'You two have something in common, you know. You've lost all your friends by moving away, and Eric's best friend has just moved away from him.'

'You mean Roy Ackerman?' asked Rachel. 'We've taken over his house.'

'Yes, I know.' Mrs Jessop smiled. 'And I see you've taken over his dog as well. I am glad. Eric needed someone to look after him once Roy had gone.'

Rachel looked down at the dog beside her. 'He's called Eric? You mean this was Roy's dog?'

'Well, we were never quite sure of that.' Mrs Jessop broke a slice of cake into chunks and passed it down to the dog. 'Roy always said Eric didn't actually belong to him, but the two of them were always together.' She bent forward to scratch Eric's head. 'Look after him, won't you? He's a very unusual dog.'

'Yes,' said Rachel. 'I've noticed.'

Rachel was a lot happier after that. She trained most days, and most days Eric Banks was there to help her – to time her speed over set distances, to keep a record of how many laps or miles she'd done, and to write it all down so that Mrs Jessop could go over it at the end of the week.

And now that she was cycling again, she started to enjoy school and to make friends. She met a lot of people through Eric Banks, but she made even more friends through Eric the dog. It was astonishing how many people seemed to know him. You could hardly walk down the street without someone coming up to say hello, to ask how Eric was and to say how pleased they were that he was being looked after properly. Slowly, Rachel began to realize that although moving house might be hard, it wasn't necessarily the end of the world.

She had always known that Eric was a special sort of dog, but she might never have found out just how special he was, if it hadn't been for what happened on her birthday.

It was a Sunday morning, about three weeks after Rachel had moved in. She was sitting in the garage, adjusting the spokes on her front wheel with a spanner, when Eric Banks stopped off on his newspaper round. He stayed and talked for a bit and then, just as he got up to go, he gave her a parcel, wrapped in newspaper. 'Here. Happy birthday,' he said.

Rachel opened the parcel, and found a pair of Shimano toe rings inside (in case you didn't know, toe rings are what cyclists use to stop their feet slipping off the pedals during a race).

'Wow, Eric!' she breathed. 'These are brilliant. Just what I wanted – how did you know? Come to that,' she added, 'how did you know it was my birthday?'

Eric just laughed and said she must have mentioned it some time, but after he'd gone, when Rachel thought about it, she realized that wasn't true. She *hadn't* told Eric about her birthday. She was quite sure she hadn't told anyone. The only time she'd even mentioned it was that first day she arrived, out in the park, and she'd told Eric the dog that . . .

An idea flashed into Rachel's brain that was so silly she almost threw it straight out again. Eric Banks. Eric the dog. You never saw them together, but . . .

All sorts of things suddenly fitted into place. Eric the dog had run into the changing room at school that day, but only Eric Banks was there when she went in. Mrs Jessop had asked Eric Banks to bring her round to the house, but Eric the dog had been the one to do it. She'd told Eric the dog about her birthday and now Eric Banks had come round with a present.

Suddenly she got up, ran back into the house and straight up to her bedroom. She pulled the chair from her desk, put it in front of the wardrobe, climbed up and felt with her hand along the top. It should still be there, if her mother hadn't . . . Aha! Found it.

She climbed back down, clutching a five-year diary with the name 'Roy Ackerman' Sellotaped on the cover. She'd been meaning to post it to Amsterdam for days, but had never quite got round to it.

She paused. She knew it was very wrong to read

someone else's diary; it was none of her business. But she had to know, she just had to, so, taking a screwdriver, she wrenched open the lock and started to read . . .

'February 12th. Took Eric up to Crufts today. We would have won, but Eric turned back into a boy and . . .'

Rachel blinked and read it again.

'We would have won, but Eric turned back into a boy . . .'

That's why he wanted to get the diary back, thought Rachel. It was true. Eric was a boy who turned into a dog.

'Wow!' she breathed. 'That is brilliant!'

At that exact moment, Eric did not think that turning into a dog was brilliant at all, particularly when it happened in broad daylight while he was walking along the road.

He had been about to deliver the last newspaper on his round, which happened to be Mr Blocker's, when he had felt a familiar itching at the back of his neck and had to dive for cover into the bushes of somebody's garden. He emerged a few moments later with twice as many legs and a tail. Leaving his clothes in the bushes, to be collected later, he picked up Mr Blocker's newspaper in his teeth, and carried it round to the headmaster's house.

Unfortunately for Eric, Mr Blocker had decided to spend the morning in his front garden, weeding the rose bed. When he spotted the dog that had caused him so much trouble at school trotting up the path, he saw the perfect chance to get his revenge. First, he bolted the garden gate so that Eric couldn't get out, then he called to his wife to phone the RSPCA and tell them he'd trapped a dangerous mad dog, so could they come to deal with it.

When the RSPCA man arrived, he soon saw that Eric was not dangerous at all, and when Mr Blocker started rambling on about how Eric had forced him into a goldfish pond, the man had his own opinions about who should be locked up – but none of that helped Eric. The fact was, he had been reported as a stray dog, and it was the RSPCA man's job to take him away and look after him till someone claimed him.

'If nobody claims him, he'll have to be put down, won't he?' said Mr Blocker hopefully.

The RSPCA man said that was only a last resort, but even so, it sent a shiver down Eric's spine. He knew, of course, that nobody could come and claim him, because, as a dog, he didn't belong to anyone. Presumably he would turn back into a boy before anything too awful happened, but even that was small consolation. If he became a boy again while he was locked in a cage with half a dozen other stray dogs and no clothes, explaining how he got there could be more than a little embarrassing.

As Eric was being loaded into the dog van, he was wishing for the millionth time that he still had Roy to help him out of situations like this, when a shout came from down the road.

'Hey! Wait for me!' It was Rachel, pedalling like fury and then screeching to a halt just beside the van. 'Thank goodness you've found him,' she said breathlessly. 'I've been looking for him all morning.'

The RSPCA man got out of his van. 'This is your dog, is it?' he asked.

Rachel nodded. 'He just ran away. I'm ever so sorry.'

'That's not your dog,' said Mr Blocker, who could see that Eric might go free and didn't like the idea.

Rachel insisted, politely, that it was.

'But it can't be!' said Mr Blocker. 'That dog belonged to Roy Ackerman and he doesn't live here any more.'

At that point, the RSPCA man stepped in. 'We can very easily tell if it's the young girl's dog or not,' he said firmly. He opened the door of his van and said, 'Would you like to call him, Miss?'

'Come on, Eric,' said Rachel and, of course, Eric jumped down from the van, trotted over to her and sat at her feet as if he was the best-trained dog in the world.

'Not a lot of doubt about that,' said the RSPCA man, more than satisfied. 'Just try and keep him out of trouble in future, will you?'

Rachel looked down at Eric, and grinned. 'I'll try,' she said. 'But I don't think it's going to be easy. Eh, Eric?'

'Woof, woof!' said Eric.

And that is how it all began.

# 2

If you were to ask Eric what was the most exciting thing that had happened to him while he was a dog, he would probably have to think very hard before deciding. But if you asked him when, as a dog, he had been most useful, I think he would tell you that it was the time he worked as a sheepdog.

It all started when Rachel's mother had to go away on a training course for a week, and Rachel was sent to stay with her Uncle Matt in Derbyshire. She liked staying with her uncle, but she thought it would be more fun with a friend, and asked Eric if he wanted to come with her.

Eric did. He had never been away from home without his parents before, and he had never been to Derbyshire. But he did have one worry. Supposing he turned into a dog while he was there? It was embarrassing enough when that sort of thing happened at home. If he became a dog while he was staying somewhere strange, it could be disastrous.

Rachel persuaded him that it didn't matter. She pointed out that he didn't usually change unless he wanted to and that, even if he did, she would be around to sort things out. So the two of them were put on the train at New Street by Mrs Hobbs. Rachel's

Uncle Matt was to meet them at Hagley, and they would stay with him for a week.

Eric changed into a dog on the train.

It happened about eight miles out of Hagley. Rachel had gone down to the buffet car to get a drink and when she came back, there was Eric-as-a-dog sitting on the seat by the window, with Eric-as-a-boy's clothes scattered all around him. Fortunately, no one had actually seen it happen.

'Why?' she asked Eric. 'Why here? Why now?' But of course, even if Eric had known, he wouldn't have been able to tell her. The only conversations you could have with Eric when he was a dog were those in which he said 'yes' or 'no'. They had a sort of code for that. It was one woof for yes, and two woofs for no. You couldn't really have a code for saying 'I don't know why it happened, but what are we going to do now?' It would be too complicated.

Rachel looked at her watch. In ten minutes they'd be at the station. Her Uncle Matt would be there. He was expecting to meet his niece and her friend and if he didn't, there'd be phone calls home and explanations and panics and ... It didn't bear thinking about.

'Don't worry,' she told Eric. 'I'll think of something.' But when the train pulled into Hagley, she still hadn't thought of anything; as she carried their luggage out on to the platform, it looked as if they were done for.

Uncle Matt saw them, waved and walked towards them. He was a big, jolly-looking man with whiskers and he scooped Rachel up in his arms and hugged her before looking down and seeing Eric.

'Hello,' he said. 'Who's this?'

'This is Eric,' said Rachel.

Uncle Matt paused. 'Eric? You mean this is Eric ?'

'Yes.' Rachel nodded. Then, seeing her uncle's face, she had a flash of inspiration and added, 'Didn't Mum tell you that I was bringing him?'

'But I thought...' Uncle Matt looked back at Rachel. 'I thought she meant ... I mean ... You see...' And then he stopped and gave a great laugh. 'You'll never believe it,' he said, 'but when your mother rang and said could you bring Eric, I thought she meant Eric was a boy!' He laughed again.

Rachel tried to join in. 'Ha ha ha.'

'I must be getting old,' said Uncle Matt. 'You know, I made a proper bed up for him and everything. Never mind.' He picked up a suitcase. 'Come on. Let's take these out to the car.'

They had a slightly sticky moment at the barrier when the inspector asked for Eric's ticket. Eric had a ticket, of course, but Rachel didn't know where it was. Eventually she opened the bag in which she'd put Eric's clothes and let him burrow in it for a moment. Eric pulled the ticket out from his jeans' pocket with his teeth.

Uncle Matt was most impressed. 'Clever little dog you've got there,' he said, as he strapped Rachel's bicycle to the roof of his car. 'I'm not surprised you wanted to bring him along. Must make life a bit more exciting, eh?'

'He certainly does that,' Rachel agreed.

The view from Uncle Matt's house, looking out over the valley and up to the hills beyond, was particularly beautiful, but Eric was in no mood to notice it as he sat on the window-sill of Rachel's bedroom, while she unpacked.

'Come on!' said Rachel brightly, sliding a dress on to a hanger in the wardrobe. 'It's not that bad. We've been really lucky so far.'

Eric did not think he had been lucky at all. How was he going to survive the rest of the week? What would happen when he changed back into a boy?

'As far as I can see,' said Rachel, 'the only tricky bit is going to be when you change back.'

'Woof,' said Eric. It was the first thing she'd said that he agreed with.

'I don't suppose you could stay like that for the whole week?' she asked.

'Woof, woof,' said Eric.

'No,' Rachel sighed, 'I didn't think you could. Don't you worry, though. I'll think of something.'

If anything, that made Eric feel even gloomier. That was what Roy always used to say in a tricky situation, just before he came up with a brilliant idea that made everything worse. As far as Eric could see, they were trapped. There was no way he could stay in someone's house as a dog for a week, without being found out. No way at all.

Under normal circumstances, I think Eric would have been right, but things stopped being normal just then, when Uncle Matt shouted up from the drive below.

'Rachel!'

Rachel opened the window.

'We've got to go.' Uncle Matt looked serious. 'There's been an accident up at Holt Farm.'

Holt Farm was about three miles out of the village. The farmhouse itself was very old, having been built of grey stone in the seventeenth century, and it belonged to a Miss Varley. Uncle Matt, Rachel and Eric arrived just in time to see Miss Varley being carried on a stretcher to an ambulance.

She had been loading bales of hay on to a trailer to take out to the sheep, when one of them had fallen from the top of the stack on to her head. A bale of hay may not sound very serious, but they weigh about a hundredweight each, and when they fall from thirty feet, as this one did, they can hurt. Miss Varley had been found unconscious on the ground by a visiting neighbour, and was lucky to have escaped with concussion.

Her main concern, as they put her in the ambulance, was what was going to happen to her sheep.

'There's no one to look after them if I'm not here,' she groaned.

Uncle Matt did his best to reassure her. 'Don't you fret,' he said confidently. 'I can look after a few sheep. You just concentrate on getting better.'

Then the doors of the ambulance closed, and Miss Varley was driven off to hospital.

Uncle Matt stared after it for a while before turning back to Rachel and Eric. 'You don't by any chance know anything about sheep, do you?' he asked.

'No,' said Rachel.

Uncle Matt sighed. 'Unfortunately,' he said, 'neither do I.'

In the end, Uncle Matt did what any sensible person does when they don't know what to do. He asked someone who did. He rang Mr Sleight, the local vet, who came straight out to Holt Farm as soon as he heard what had happened. When Uncle Matt told him he wanted some advice on looking after sheep, the vet soon made it clear that it wasn't that easy.

'You see, Matt,' he said, as they all sat round the big kitchen table in the farmhouse, 'the situation is this –'

'You just tell us what to do, Gordon,' said Uncle Matt cheerfully, 'and we'll get on with it. Young Rachel here has kindly offered to help.'

'Woof,' said Eric.

'Oh, yes,' said Uncle Matt. 'And there's Eric as well.'

'That's very kind of them,' said the vet, 'but I'm afraid it's not that simple. Looking after sheep is a complicated business. Your Miss Varley only has a flock of about two hundred and fifty, but they'll need drenching, they'll need dipping against foot-rot, they'll need injections against pastoral pneumonia, they'll need . . . Well, they'll need expert attention.'

'There must be *something* we can do,' said Uncle Matt.

'You can go to Mr Painter,' said the vet. Mr Painter had the neighbouring farm to Miss Varley's.

'But he'll want money,' protested Uncle Matt. 'You know Helen can't afford that. If we can't look after the sheep for her, she'll lose this place; it's as simple as that !'

Mr Sleight was sympathetic, but firm. 'If it was just a matter of treating the sheep, I could help,' he said. 'I could show you what to do. But the real difficulty is bringing them in. You have to bring in two hundred and fifty sheep, spread out over a dozen fields, then you have to take them back out again, and you can't do that without a dog.'

'Woof,' said Eric, helpfully.

'I mean a sheepdog,' said the vet.

'Helen's got a sheepdog,' said Uncle Matt. 'It's tied up outside.'

'Sheepdogs only obey one owner,' Mr Sleight explained patiently. 'You don't even know what calls it works to.' He made a note on his pad. 'I'll ask Mr Painter to look after the dog as well.'

That night, after everyone had gone to bed, back at Uncle Matt's house, Rachel crept downstairs to the kitchen. Uncle Matt had arranged a cardboard box with an old blanket in it for Eric to sleep in, and Rachel wanted to check that he was all right.

But Eric wasn't there. Rachel looked round all the likely places, and called for him – softly, so as not to wake Uncle Matt – but there was no sign of him. Then she went back upstairs, saw the door to the spare bedroom was slightly open and realized what must have happened.

She walked inside and found Eric, a boy again, wrapped up in a counterpane and staring out of the window at the moonlight.

'Is everything all right?' she whispered.

'Well,' said Eric, 'I could do with some clothes.'

'Right.' Rachel went and got Eric's case from her own room and put it on the bed. 'What do we do if you're still a boy tomorrow?' she asked.

'Who knows?' Eric shrugged.

'I'm sorry.' Rachel sat down beside him. 'It's all my fault. I should never have persuaded you to come down here with me.'

Eric's mind, however, was on other things. 'Your uncle,' he said.

'What about him?' asked Rachel.

'He really wants to help Miss Varley, doesn't he?'

Rachel grinned. 'He's soft on her. He always has been.'

'I was wondering,' said Eric. 'What the man said this afternoon, about needing a dog to bring in the sheep. I think I could do it.'

'But you're not a sheepdog,' said Rachel.

'I don't think it's that difficult,' said Eric. 'I've seen them on television. Sheep run away from dogs. You just have to make sure they run in the right direction.'

Now it has to be said that, although Eric wanted to help, it was not his only motive for saying all this. If he had to spend the next six days trying to hide the fact that he was really a boy from Uncle Matt, he thought he had a much better chance of doing it out at the farm. With a bit of luck, out there, everyone would be too busy to ask 'Where's Eric?' and even if they did, Rachel could just say he was out somewhere in the fields.

'I think it's worth a try,' he told Rachel. 'Don't you?'

Rachel had the job of persuading Uncle Matt to agree to this, and it was perhaps fortunate that her uncle knew as little about dogs as he did about sheep. When Rachel told him she was quite sure that she and Eric could drive a few sheep wherever they were wanted, he was willing – and perhaps desperate enough – at least to let her try.

So the next morning found Uncle Matt and Rachel, with Eric beside them, leaning on the gate to one of the fields at Holt Farm, looking at the sixty or so sheep it contained. Now that they were this close to the sheep, Eric was not as breezily confident as he had been. The field was a very large one, the sheep were scattered all over it, and the idea that he could some-how persuade them all to come out of the gate and go down the path to the farm didn't seem quite as simple as it had the night before.

Apart from anything else, the sheep were very big. Rachel had the feeling that if she tried to push one of them in the right direction and it didn't want to go, that would be that. It would be quite strong enough to resist her. And they had to try and move not just one sheep, but two hundred and fifty.

'I don't know about you, Eric,' Rachel murmured, 'but they look a lot bigger than I'd remembered.'

'Woof,' said Eric.

The sheep were quite peaceful as they stood grazing out in the field, but Eric thought any one of them looked big enough to pick him up in its mouth and eat him for breakfast. They had big teeth as well. He could see them in the nearest sheep, grinding grass.

'You're quite sure you want to go through with this?' asked Rachel.

Eric wasn't sure at all, but it seemed a bit late to change his mind, so he just said 'Woof,' and, as Rachel pushed open the gate, he trotted into the field.

When they had been talking about it the night before, they had worked out a plan that seemed very simple. Rachel would stay by the gate and make sure that when the first sheep came out, they went down the path to the farm rather than up it to the next field, while Eric would run round to the far side of the field and drive the rest up towards the gate. Once they were all on the path, Eric would stay at the back of the flock, pushing them along, while Rachel would be up at the front to make sure they took the right turnings.

As Eric made his way round the edge of the field, his confidence sank lower and lower. The idea that he could somehow frighten these sheep through the gate seemed downright silly. The more he thought about it, the more likely it seemed that they would turn and walk all over him, leaving him squashed and trampled in the mud.

Once in position on the far side of the field, Eric waited a moment. He could see Rachel as she swung open the gate, and hear her voice faintly as she called, 'OK, Eric! Ready when you are.'

Taking a deep breath, Eric started walking towards the sheep. They took no notice of him. He walked a bit further. Still nothing happened. Heart pounding, he took a step further; then one of the sheep, the nearest one, lifted its head and looked at him. Eric stopped. The sheep thought for a moment and then moved away. Eric stepped forward again, and the sheep moved on a little further. Then, Eric noticed, several other sheep started moving in the same direction. And, of course, that is the whole secret of herding sheep, and explains why one person and a dog have always been able to move large numbers wherever they want. If one sheep starts heading in a certain direction, the others will tend to follow. Get enough of them moving in the direction you want, and *all* the others will follow.

It wasn't quite as easy as I've made it sound. Eric made some mistakes. He discovered, for instance, that barking was not very helpful. It just made the sheep over-anxious and likely to dart in the wrong direction. Again, if he pushed forward too fast, a group of sheep would split off and run back round behind him. The real trick was just to keep nudging gently in the right direction, never to push too hard, but always to be watching so that if stray sheep seemed inclined to break away, he could move to the side and just stand there; eventually it would change its mind.

In no more than ten minutes, all sixty sheep were out through the gate and heading down the path. Rachel looked down at Eric as he emerged from the field.

'That was brilliant, Eric,' she said. 'Brill-i-ant.'

Uncle Matt looked very pleased as well. 'I don't know what that vet made such a fuss about,' he said. 'It all looks quite straightforward to me.'

When Uncle Matt rang Mr Sleight, asked him to come out to the farm, and then showed him the sheep, the vet found it all very hard to believe.

'Are you seriously telling me,' he asked, 'that all these sheep were brought down by your young niece and that little mongrel?'

'That's right,' said Uncle Matt. 'I had a feeling it wasn't that difficult, you know.'

'But it's impossible,' said Mr Sleight. 'It just can't have happened, it can't!'

At that moment, Rachel appeared with the next lot of sheep, Eric trotting along behind and making sure that all of them got safely into the farmyard.

The vet stared at them in astonishment. 'How does she do it?' he asked. 'I haven't even heard her using any calls.'

'Calls?' asked Uncle Matt.

'To tell the dog what she wants it to do,' explained the vet. 'I mean, I haven't heard her whistling or anything. How does the dog know what to do if she doesn't whistle?'

'Ah. I'm not sure about that,' said Uncle Matt, 'but it should be easy enough to find out.'

He called over to Rachel. 'Mr Sleight wants all these sheep in the holding pen, Rachel. Can you get Eric to take them round?'

'OK,' said Rachel, and called to Eric, 'The vet wants these in the holding pen, Eric. All right?'

'Woof,' said Eric, and set to work.

'There you are, Gordon,' said Uncle Matt to the vet. 'That's what she does. She talks to it.'

The vet said nothing.

'Quite an intelligent little dog, isn't he?' added Uncle Matt.

The vet still said nothing. In twenty years of veterinary work, he had never seen anything so extraordinary as a dog that could be told to move sheep. But he knew it wasn't worth trying to explain that to Uncle Matt.

Instead, he started rolling up his sleeves. 'Come on, Matt,' he said. 'We've got work to do.'

Over the next week, they all worked extremely hard. Sheep need a lot of looking after. They need dipping, which means putting them one at a time in a sort of bath to kill off any insects in their wool; their feet need checking regularly for foot-rot; they need to be drenched, which involves squirting medicine into their mouths with a sort of water pistol, so that they don't get worms in their stomachs. And for all of these and lots of other operations, the sheep needed to be brought into the pens at the start of the day, and then taken back out to the fields at the end of it, so that they could carry on grazing. That was Eric and Rachel's work.

As if all that wasn't enough, Uncle Matt had also decided that it would be very nice if, when Miss

Varley came back from hospital, she were to find the farmyard and the farmhouse looking clean, spick and span. So, when they weren't looking after sheep, they were busy mowing the grass, cleaning the house, dusting, polishing, hoovering, sweeping, wiping down and washing up. At the end of each day, they were all very glad to get to their beds.

All the hard work did have one advantage, though. As Eric had suspected, it meant Uncle Matt was far 'too busy to take much notice of him, and this made hiding the fact that he was really a boy that much easier. In fact, if Uncle Matt hadn't been so busy, I don't think Eric could have got away with it.

The trouble was, you see, that he wasn't a dog all the time – or even most of the time. And, as a boy, Eric would have to creep up to one of the upstairs rooms of the farmhouse, or out to one of the barns, and sit and read a book. Then, if Uncle Matt asked where he was, Rachel could just shrug, say she didn't know, and explain that one can never keep track of a dog on a farm.

At the end of the week, Miss Varley came home from hospital, and her face, when Uncle Matt showed her round and explained all that had been done, made the hard work more than worthwhile. Uncle Matt introduced Rachel, and Miss Varley hugged her a lot and thanked her, and then he explained how Eric had brought in the sheep. At first Miss Varley didn't believe it and they all had to troop outside while Eric gave a little demonstration, and Miss Varley said it was the most amazing thing she'd ever seen and started hugging everyone again, particularly Uncle Matt. That evening, they had a big party to celebrate.

When Eric went to bed that night (as a boy, in a

bed), he couldn't help congratulating himself on a very successful week. They had helped Miss Varley keep her farm, they had helped Rachel's Uncle Matt, he had learnt to be a sheepdog, and above all, they had survived the entire week without his secret being discovered. All they had to do was get on the train tomorrow and head for home. Eric gave a sigh of relief.

Over breakfast the next morning, Uncle Matt produced a letter from Rachel's mother. Mrs Hobbs was driving home from her course, and said she would like to stop off at Uncle Matt's to pick up Rachel and Eric in the car, instead of letting them go home by train.

Eric was in despair. If he was a dog when Mrs Hobbs got there, she would want to know where Eric the boy was, and if he was a boy, Uncle Matt would want to know where he'd come from. He was doomed, he just knew it; they were both doomed.

It was Rachel who saw the solution. Uncle Matt and her mother must not meet. So she told Uncle Matt (and I'm afraid it was quite untrue) that Miss Varley urgently needed his help up at the farm. Nothing else could have persuaded him to leave the two of them alone in the house for his sister to collect, but as Rachel had already noticed, where Miss Varley was concerned, Uncle Matt could be remarkably single-minded.

So when Mrs Hobbs arrived at Uncle Matt's, she was greeted by Rachel and Eric-as-a-boy, both of whom assured her that they had had a wonderful holiday. There was a note from Uncle Matt saying he was sorry he couldn't be there himself, but that Rachel and 'little Eric' had been the nicest possible guests. Mrs Hobbs was a bit puzzled by the 'little' as a description of Eric, but of course she never guessed the real story.

A month later, Uncle Matt wrote to say that he had got married. He said he wanted Rachel to know that she could come and stay any time at his new address at Holt Farm and that they had bought a proper basket for Eric so that he could sleep comfortably in the kitchen. Mrs Hobbs was very puzzled by that. 'Why would Uncle Matt want Eric to sleep in the kitchen?' she asked, but, as Rachel pointed out, Uncle Matt had always been a bit different, and Mrs Hobbs had to agree.

That week is the only time that Eric has worked as a sheepdog — or rather, I should say, the only time so far, because I think one day he might like to try it again. He occasionally watches the sheepdog trials on television and wonders what would happen if he and Rachel entered a competition like that. I think they'd probably do rather well. So who knows, maybe one day they will.

# 3

Rachel was doing well with her cycling. She was entering races almost every weekend, and the long hours of training she put in with Eric during the week were paying off. She had already had two impressive wins in events organized by the English Schools Cycle Association, she had won the March Hare Meeting at Eastway, and now she had set her sights on the Divisional Championships. She had a good chance of doing well, she knew that, but she also knew that she badly needed a new bicycle.

Cycle racing is an exciting sport, but it can also be an expensive one. As Rachel explained to Eric, the fee to enter a cycle race might only be a pound or two, but on top of that, you had to pay to get you and your bike to wherever the race was being held, you had to buy all the special clothes that cyclists wear, and then there was the biggest expense of all − paying for and maintaining the bicycle itself. That could cost hundreds of pounds.

The bike Rachel had was a good one, but even good bikes don't last for ever. The frame had been badly strained after a crash she had had in a race at Hawkley, the gearing had been second-hand when she bought it and was becoming noticeably worn, and if she wanted to fit the new tyres that everyone had started using, she would need new wheels as well. Altogether, Rachel had worked out that a new bike, one that would give her a real chance of winning, would cost six hundred pounds.

'Six hundred?' said Eric in astonishment. 'For a bicycle? Where are you going to get that sort of money?'

'I don't know,' said Rachel. 'I thought maybe I could earn it. What if I got a newspaper round like you?'

Eric thought of how much money he got on his newspaper round, did a few sums in his head and told Rachel it would take nearly two and a half years for her to earn six hundred pounds that way. If she was to have the new bike in time for the Divisional Championships, she needed the money in the next few weeks.

In the end, they took the problem round to Mrs Jessop. Mrs Jessop's first suggestion was that they organize a bank raid and that Rachel drive the getaway car, but Rachel said her mother wouldn't let her do anything like that, and Eric explained that what they really wanted was some sort of job. It could be anything, he added, as long as it was part time (because they were still at school) and would earn them six hundred pounds in the next couple of weeks.

'I'm looking for a job like that myself,' said Mrs Jessop, but then she added, 'I know who could earn that sort of money, though.'

Rachel and Eric waited expectantly.

'Eric,' said Mrs Jessop.

'Me?' asked Eric. 'How?'

'No, not you, Eric,' said Mrs Jessop. 'I mean Eric.' She looked at Rachel. 'Your dog.'

'You mean Eric?' asked Rachel.

'Yes.' Mrs Jessop poured herself another cup of tea. 'I've often wondered why Roy never thought of it.'

'Never thought of what?' asked Eric.

'Films,' said Mrs Jessop. 'Television. They need smart animals all the time, and they don't come much smarter than that dog.'

Both Rachel and Eric saw the possibilities at once. Films! It was such an obvious idea, that Eric could only wonder why he had never thought of it himself.

'How do you get a dog into films?' asked Rachel.

'I'm not sure,' Mrs Jessop picked up her address book and started thumbing through it, 'but I have a friend who could point us in the right direction. I'll give him a call if you like.'

Rachel hesitated. She certainly wanted Mrs Jessop to go ahead and call her friend, but she had just remembered that it wasn't really her decision, any more than Eric was really her dog.

'Well?' asked Mrs Jessop, her hand poised over the telephone.

'I was just wondering,' said Rachel, 'whether it was the sort of thing that a dog . . . that Eric would really want to do.' She looked over at Eric as she spoke.

'I think it'd be all right,' said Eric.

'You're quite sure?' asked Rachel

'Yes!' Eric grinned. 'I think dogs probably enjoy being in films.'

So Mrs Jessop went ahead and dialled the number.

Mrs Jessop's friend was very helpful. He found out that they were auditioning dogs early the next week to use in an advertisement, and got permission for Mrs Jessop and Rachel to go along and watch. Auditions in case you didn't know, are often held before making a play or a film. They give a chance for actors and actresses (or in this case, dogs) to show what they can do, so that the people making the film can see who would be the best person (or dog) for the part.

So the following Saturday, Mrs Jessop drove Rachel and Eric over to Dudley, where the director, a very tall man called Mr Atkinson, was holding the auditions in a football stadium.

Mr Atkinson explained to Rachel that he needed a particularly athletic and intelligent dog for the advertisement he had in mind, and that was why the playing field had been laid out with all sorts of things the dogs had to do. There were ladders they had to climb, tunnels they had to crawl through, planks they had to walk along, doors they had to open and barriers they had to jump. At the end of the course, the last thing the dogs had to do was pull open a drawer in a desk, take out a tin of dog-food, and carry it away.

Mrs Jessop and Rachel spent the morning watching with interest while all sorts of dogs tried to complete the course. Most of them were very clever, though several of them couldn't climb the ladder, but all of the dogs had problems with the last part of the course – taking the tin out of the drawer. Unfortunately, Mr Atkinson seemed to think that was the most important task of all.

Some of the dogs went to the wrong drawer, some went to the right drawer but then couldn't open it, and of the two dogs that did manage to open the right drawer, one forgot to pick up the tin and the other had a brainstorm and started chewing the drawer to pieces.

That was when Mr Atkinson said he thought they should all take a break for lunch.

'Could Eric have a go?' asked Rachel.

Mr Atkinson looked in surprise.

'Eric is the dog,' explained Mrs Jessop.

'Oh, I see.' Mr Atkinson smiled at Rachel. 'I'm afraid all this is rather more difficult than you'd think, Rachel. The dogs you've been watching this morning have all been specially trained, some of them for years. You can't get ordinary dogs to do this sort of thing.'

'It wouldn't do any harm to let him try, though, would it?' suggested Mrs Jessop.

Mr Atkinson thought for a moment. The course wasn't actually being used during the lunch break, and Eric didn't look the sort of dog to cause too much damage.

'All right,' he said. 'You take him down and let him have a play.'

Mr Atkinson had been intending to go and have his lunch at that point, but there was something about the confident way in which Eric trotted straight over to the start of the course that made him pause, and he watched as Eric set to work.

The obstacle course was quite easy for Eric. He'd been watching the other dogs on it all morning, and it was just a matter of remembering the right order to do things in. He trotted up the first ramp, pulled a lever with one paw so that a tennis ball came out of a hole, caught the ball, carried it in his mouth down the steps and dropped it into a tube.

Watching with Mrs Jessop, Mr Atkinson could hardly believe his eyes. 'Are you sure he hasn't been trained to do this sort of thing?' he asked.

'I don't think so,' said Mrs Jessop, 'but he seems to pick things up very quickly. He's a clever little dog.'

'He certainly is,' murmured Mr Atkinson. 'He certainly is . . .'

Out on the course, Eric was now well in his stride. He had been through the tunnel, climbed the ladder, crossed the high wire, opened and closed the trap-door – and now all he had to do was jump the wall, cross the plank, and get the tin of dog-food out of the desk. It all seemed easy enough. He pulled open the drawer with his teeth, reached inside and took out the tin, and carried it back to Rachel.

From all around him came the sound of clapping. Eric blinked. Along the edge of the field, all the people who had just seen what Eric had done were applauding and cheering.

'I've never seen anything like it!' said Mr Atkinson. 'I've been filming animals all my life and I've never seen anything like it. Never!'

'Was he all right?' Rachel called. She was still standing with Eric at the end of the course. 'If he got anything wrong, I could ask him to do it again.'

'No,' Mr Atkinson shouted back. 'No, it's all right. He didn't get anything wrong.'

He turned to Mrs Jessop. 'Tell me,' he said, 'do you think young Rachel would be interested in letting her dog work for us? We'd pay her, of course.'

'I think she might be interested,' said Mrs Jessop.

Half an hour later, they were all sitting in the caravan that served as Mr Atkinson's office.

'We'd like your dog for two days' filming the week after next,' Mr Atkinson explained. 'You're sure you can make him do all those things whenever you want, are you?'

'You just have to ask him something, and he does it,' Rachel assured him confidently.

'Good,' said Mr Atkinson. 'Good. Now, you probably haven't thought about money at all, but –'

'As a matter of fact, we have,' Mrs Jessop interrupted him. 'We thought six hundred pounds would be about right.'

'Six hundred...' Mr Atkinson chewed his bottom lip. 'It's only two days' work, you know.'

'It has to be six hundred,' said Mrs Jessop.

'What about four?' said Mr Atkinson.

Rachel and Eric looked at each other in disbelief. Would someone really pay four hundred pounds just for Eric to trot up and down in front of a camera? Rachel was about to open her mouth and say she accepted, when Mrs Jessop interrupted again.

'It's six hundred or nothing, I'm afraid,' she said firmly.

Mr Atkinson shrugged. 'All right,' he said, 'I give in. Six hundred it is.'

'Good.' Mrs Jessop winked at Rachel. 'So, where does he put his paw-print?'

Rachel still worried that it wasn't quite fair – Eric doing all the work, while she collected the money – but, as Eric told her, he honestly didn't mind. The money wasn't that important. He still had quite a large sum in his savings' book from the time he and Roy had won all those dog competitions with Miss Robson. What *was* important to him was the excitement of being on a film set, and even better was the idea that he would one day see himself on television. Admittedly it would be as a dog rather than a boy, but even so, Eric was looking forward to it.

When it came to the day of the filming, two weeks later, Rachel and Eric-as-a-dog listened carefully while Mr Atkinson explained what he wanted Eric to do.

The advertisement was for a dog-food called

Wundadog and the main slogan for the advertisement was 'Wundadog – the dog-food dogs insist on'.

'You see,' said Mr Atkinson, 'we start off with Eric at home, in the kitchen with his master and mistress, and they're supposed to be giving him breakfast, but they've run out of Wundadog. The woman tries to give him something else, some other sort of dog-food, but that's not good enough for Eric. He wants Wundadog and nothing else will do.

'So he runs off into town,' Mr Atkinson went on, 'to where there's this enormous warehouse full of tins of Wundadog, but they won't let him in. So he gets into the building next door, climbs up to the roof, uses a plank to get across to the warehouse, then gets some dynamite to blow a way through –'

'Dynamite?' asked Rachel.

'Don't worry,' said Mr Atkinson, 'it's perfectly safe. Then, after he's broken his way into the store with explosives, he gets his tin of Wundadog, carries it back home to his master and mistress, they put it in a dish for him, and he eats it. OK? Any problems with that?'

Rachel looked at Eric.

'Woof, woof,' said Eric.

'No problem,' said Rachel.

And it really all did seem to be very easy. They had to spend quite a lot of time just standing or sitting around, but when it came to the actual filming, Mr Atkinson told Rachel what he wanted the dog to do, Rachel told Eric, and Eric went ahead and did it.

In the first scene, he looked wonderfully appealing while he waited for his master and mistress to give him breakfast. He turned up his nose in disgust when they tried to give him something that wasn't Wundadog, and then trotted determinedly out of the room.

All the other scenes went just as smoothly – racing round to the warehouse, breaking into the next-door building, walking across a plank between the two buildings (which wasn't as dangerous as it looked) – and Mr Atkinson was particularly pleased with the way Eric did the explosion scene.

He had to carry what looked like several sticks of dynamite, place them at the bottom of the door to the storeroom, then run back round a corner and push down a plunger with his paws. As soon as the doors had blown open, Eric was back, dashing in through all the smoke and dust to pull a box from a shelf, take out one of the tins of Wundadog, and then carry it triumphantly back with him. It looked wonderful.

And because Eric didn't make any mistakes, the whole thing was filmed in record time. There was only one scene left to do and Mr Atkinson, who had thought the filming would take at least two days, now realized that he would be able to finish it all in one – which would save him a great deal of money.

The last scene, you will remember, was the one where Eric had to come back to his master and mistress in the kitchen and give them the tin of Wundadog, which they then put out in a dish for him to eat. It was, in many ways, the easiest scene of all. The only trouble was that Eric refused to eat the dog-food.

He sniffed at it for a bit, looked as if he was about to take a bite, but then backed off, sat down and looked at Rachel.

'Something wrong, Eric?' she said.

'Woof,' said Eric.

Mr Atkinson came over. 'What's happening?' he asked.

'I'm not sure,' said Rachel, 'but I think he doesn't like it. Do you, Eric?'

'Woof, woof,' said Eric.

'What d'you mean, you think he doesn't like it?' asked Mr Atkinson. 'It's dog-food. He's not supposed to like it. He's just got to swallow it.'

'But he won't,' said Rachel.

'But it's the whole point of the film!' shouted Mr Atkinson. 'You can't have an advertisement for dog-food where the dog refuses to eat the dog-food. Tell him he's got to eat it. I don't care if he –' He looked round. 'Where's he gone?' he asked.

Everyone looked round. Eric had disappeared.

Rachel found him first. In fact, Rachel was the only one who could have found him, because by then he'd turned back into a boy. He was sitting at the bottom of some stairs, dressed in a fire blanket, the only thing he'd managed to find to wear.

'Are you all right?' she asked.

'Fine,' said Eric. 'I'm sorry about all that, but I just couldn't eat it. I'd have been sick.'

Rachel sat down beside him and nodded sympathetically. 'I must say, it didn't look very nice.'

'No, it wasn't that,' said Eric. 'I usually like dog-food – when I'm a dog, anyway – but that stuff was . . .'

'Was what?' asked Rachel.

'It smelt of something,' said Eric. 'I'm not sure what it was, but it reminded me of hospitals.'

Mr Atkinson picked up an opened tin of Wundadog dog-food and sniffed it, gingerly.

'I can't smell anything,' he said.

It was early the next morning, and they were sitting in the main office of Mr Bradley, the managing director and owner of Wundadog Foods Ltd. Mr Bradley himself, sitting behind his desk, had a bald head, bushy whiskers, and at the moment looked very depressed.

'I can't smell anything either,' he said.

'I think dogs have more sensitive noses than us,' Rachel explained. 'It's not an obvious smell. Just enough so they don't like to eat it.'

'Woof,' said Eric.

'How d'you know all this?' asked Mr Bradley.

'Well, Eric sort of . . .' Rachel stopped. 'It's not easy to explain.'

'No. Well, you don't really have to.' Mr Bradley gave a sigh. 'It all fits.'

'What fits?' asked Rachel.

It was Mr Atkinson who replied. 'About three months ago, the sales of Wundadog started to fall.'

'They didn't fall,' interrupted Mr Bradley. 'They plummeted. That's why I wanted an advertising campaign, but it's no use advertising something that dogs refuse to eat. This company's done for.' He walked over to the window and looked gloomily out at his factory.

'But it's just something getting into the food,' said Rachel. 'Can't you find out what it is?'

'You think I haven't tried?' Mr Bradley sighed again. 'I've been over that factory a hundred times with a fine toothcomb and, nothing! There's nothing getting in to those tins, I'd swear it.'

He sat back down at his desk, and for one awful moment Rachel thought he was going to cry.

'We just have to face it,' he said. 'We're finished.'

Rachel had been thinking. 'Mr Bradley,' she said, 'could Eric help?'

'Help?' Mr Bradley looked at her. 'How?'

'I just thought, as he's the one that knows what's wrong with the food, maybe if you let him take a walk round the factory, he could bark or something when he smelt whatever it was that was wrong.'

'Could he do that?' Mr Bradley turned to Mr Atkinson. 'Could he?'

'I don't know.' Mr Atkinson turned to Rachel. 'Could he?'

'Well . . .' Rachel turned to Eric. 'Could you ?'

'Woof,' said Eric, confidently.

'He can do it,' Rachel said, firmly.

For a moment, Mr Bradley didn't move. Then, 'Come on,' he said. 'Follow me.'

For the next hour, Mr Bradley led Rachel and Eric round every corner of the Wundadog factory. Through the bakery where the dog biscuits were made, through the meat-processing plant where the joints of meat were brought in, past all the huge vats where the meat was cooked – and every so often, Rachel would ask Eric if he smelt anything odd. But she always got the same reply.

'Woof, woof,' Eric would say.

Then, just as they were going past the point where the cooked food was put into the tins, Eric stopped, his nose sniffed the air and he suddenly darted off up a stairway to the right.

'Where's he going?' asked Mr Bradley. 'We don't do anything to the food up there.'

'I've no idea,' said Rachel, 'but I think we ought to find out.'

They followed Eric up the stairs, along a corridor, and finally into a room that looked like a cross between a chemistry laboratory and a storehouse.

At the far end of the room, a young man carrying a bucket was standing, rather frightened, in the corner, while Eric barked at him furiously.

'All right, Harold,' said Mr Bradley, 'don't worry. The dog won't hurt you.'

But Eric was still barking.

'He thinks something's wrong,' said Rachel.

Mr Bradley looked at the bucket young Harold was holding. 'What have you got in there?' he asked.

'It's just sterilizer, Mr Bradley,' said Harold. 'It's for cleaning out the tins.'

'Woof, woof, woof, woof!' barked Eric.

'How much water have you mixed with that?' demanded Mr Bradley suddenly.

'Water?' Harold looked rather confused.

'You have to mix it with water, lad, don't you?' said Mr Bradley.

'Do I?' Poor Harold was now looking flustered as well as confused.

'Of course you do!' Mr Bradley was almost shouting. 'Otherwise it won't wash out and all the tins of food'll taste of . . . taste of . . .' He slowed, and looked down at Eric. 'Otherwise the food will taste revolting, won't it?'

'Woof,' said Eric.

They filmed the last part of the advertisement later that day, and Eric cheerfully munched away at his Wundadog – the first tin of the new batch that no longer tasted of sterilizer. A big cheer went up as he finished. The story had very quickly got round of how Eric had sorted out what was wrong with Wundadog, and he was a very popular figure as a result.

Mr Bradley was very grateful. He insisted on personally handing over Rachel's cheque for six hundred pounds, and was very interested to hear that she wanted it to buy a bicycle and that her ambition was to be the first girl ever to win the National Juveniles Circuit Championship. In fact, he made a speech in front of the whole film crew, saying how he thought if everyone was as sensible and intelligent as this young girl and her dog, the country wouldn't be in the mess it was today.

'Don't you forget,' he told Rachel and Eric as he led them out to where Mrs Jessop was waiting to drive them home, 'I owe you one for this. Anything I can do, anything at all, you just call me, all right?'

'Right,' said Rachel.

'Woof,' said Eric.

Eric has had several offers of film work since then. He was even invited to America by someone who heard about him from Mr Atkinson, and you wouldn't believe how much money they were prepared to pay. But Eric turned it down.

The fact is, he has his school work at the moment, he has his friends and his family and he thinks it would be silly to give up all that just for money. But it's the sort of thing he might try when he's older. It's always nice to know that you could be a millionaire filmstar, if you wanted to be.

And Rachel got her new bicycle. She used it the next Saturday at the Divisional Championships and only missed winning by a hair's breadth because of a fall in one of the early laps. She made up for it a week later, though, with a win at the Ravensthorpe Circuit that was so decisive that her picture appeared in *Cycling Weekly*. The paragraph underneath said, 'Young Rachel must now be considered a hot contender for the National Championships later this year.'

Rachel showed the piece to Eric. 'A hot contender . . .' she breathed, reading the article for the umpteenth time, 'for the National Championships!'

But that, as they say, is another story.

# 4

Rachel may have been a hot contender for the National Championships that year, but she very nearly didn't race in them at all – and for the silliest of reasons. Her mother didn't post the entry form in time.

It was one of those awful things that isn't really anyone's fault; it just happens. Rachel had given the form to her mother to post that morning. Mrs Hobbs was just leaving the house when she got a phone call to say Rachel's grandad had been taken to hospital. Of course she went straight round to the hospital, waited there till she knew Grandad was going to be all right, and then had to go round and see if Grandma needed any help. What with one thing and another, she completely forgot she'd left her coat at the hospital, and it was over a week before she remembered and went back to try and find it.

When she did find it, she also found the letter Rachel had asked her to post, still in the pocket. She sent it straight away, but they all knew it was too late.

'Isn't there *anything* you can do?' asked Eric. He had just heard the news from Mrs Hobbs downstairs, and he thought he had never seen a grown-up look so miserable in his life.

'Nothing.' Rachel stared blankly out of her bedroom window. 'Closing date for entries was yesterday. That's it. Those are the rules. I'm not in it.'

She sounded quite calm about it, but her face was very white and she was gripping the window-sill so hard that her fingernails were actually biting into the wood.

Eric came over and stood beside her. 'I know what it's like,' he said, 'wanting to win. I nearly won at Crufts once.' He put a sympathetic hand on her shoulder. 'Come on,' he said, 'let's go out for a walk and have a think about it.'

It was raining quite hard as they set off up Monkston Hill, but Rachel didn't seem to notice.

'How about writing them a letter?' suggested Eric. 'Explaining what happened, apologizing, and asking them to make an exception.'

'It wouldn't work,' said Rachel. 'They're very strict – they have to be. It's the only way they can be fair.'

They walked a little further in silence, and then Eric said, 'There is one thing.'

'What?'

'If the closing date was yesterday, that was a Friday . . .' Eric pulled out his pocket diary. 'Offices close over the weekend. They probably won't even look at the entry forms until Monday.'

Rachel shrugged. 'So?'

'So, supposing someone sneaked into the offices on Monday morning and put your entry form into the pile? Nobody would ever know it hadn't been there all the time.'

Rachel said nothing.

'I mean it. I think it could work,' he added.

'I know you want to help, Eric,' said Rachel, 'and that's really nice, but I don't think breaking into a building in broad daylight is a very good idea.'

'Well, actually,' said Eric, 'it would have to be two buildings. We'd have to do the Post Office first. Your mother posted that entry form this morning, so the first thing would be to steal it back.'

'Don't people get put in prison for doing that sort of thing?' asked Rachel.

Eric just smiled. 'Remember the day you moved in here?' he reminded her. 'When I came into the house to get Roy's diary? I got caught then, but nothing happened. Nobody called the police or anything.'

'That was different,' said Rachel impatiently. 'No one bothered about you because you were a –' She stopped. 'Because you were a dog!'

'Precisely,' said Eric.

Eric led Rachel round the back of the Post Office and up to a set of large double doors. He pushed one open and the two of them peered inside. Rachel had never seen a sorting office before. It was an enormous room, about two hundred feet long and nearly as wide. It was full of people and tables and shelves and sacks, but mainly, it was full of letters. Thousands and thousands of letters.

'We're never going to find mine in that lot!' said Rachel. 'It would take years.'

But Eric didn't seem to be worried at all. 'What did it look like?' he asked.

'It was a letter, Eric!' said Rachel. 'It looked like the other five million they've got in there!'

'I meant what colour,' explained Eric patiently. 'Was it brown, white . . .?'

'It was pink,' said Rachel.

Eric nodded. 'Good. That makes it a bit easier.'

'Easier?'

Eric just grinned. 'My dad works here, remember? Posted yesterday evening, second class, for London, postal area W11. I could take you straight to it.'

'You could?' Rachel was impressed.

'All we need now,' said Eric, 'is somewhere to get changed.'

Mr Groves had just finished his lunch break – postmen have lunch very early because they get up before most of us – and he was heading back to his table to finish sorting the letters for London, ready to catch the mail train at 2.30, when he stopped in astonishment.

'Hoi!' he shouted. 'What are you doing?'

There was a dog sitting on his table, starting up at all the pigeonholes above him.

The dog turned round when it heard him shout, but instead of running away, it stood up on its hind legs, reached forward with its teeth and took one of the letters out of a pigeonhole.

'You can't take that!' shouted Mr Groves. 'Come back here!'

But the dog had jumped back on to the floor and was racing for the door. He would have got clean away, too, but just then another postman with a trolley came in and blocked his escape. Instead, the dog veered round to the left and disappeared down one of the aisles.

Mr Groves was in hot pursuit. 'Stop that dog!' he shouted. 'It's stolen one of my letters!'

Half the sorting office was chasing the little dog in the end, but they didn't catch him. The dog seemed to know all the ins and outs of the building as well as the postmen did themselves and every time they thought they had him cornered, he would scramble under a table or over a pile of mailsacks and disappear again. Finally, he darted between the legs of someone coming through the main doors and was away to the outside and freedom, the letter still gripped between his teeth.

The supervisor came down to see what all the noise was about. 'What's the trouble?' he asked, and was very puzzled when they told him. 'What would a dog want with a letter?' he said. 'Are you sure?'

'Positive,' said Mr Groves. 'D'you think we should tell the police?'

The supervisor thought for a moment and then decided that there wasn't really anything the police could do.

'Just make sure it doesn't happen again,' he said firmly, and went back to his office.

The next part of Eric's plan involved taking the entry form that Monday morning to the headquarters of the British Cycling Federation, in London.

They thought for a long time about the best way to get down there, and it was Eric who suggested they get in touch with Mr Bradley.

'He's got lorries delivering dog-food all over the country,' he said. 'We could ask him if there's one going to London that could give us a lift, and there might even be one that could bring us back.'

Rachel made the telephone call because, of course, Mr Bradley didn't know Eric-as-a-boy. She got his secretary first, who said Mr Bradley was in a meeting and couldn't be disturbed, but when Rachel said who she was, the secretary asked her to hold the line for a moment, and a few seconds later she heard Mr Bradley's voice saying, 'Hello, Rachel. What can I do for you?'

'I'm sorry to disturb you, Mr Bradley,' she said, 'but I've got a bit of a problem.' And she explained about wanting to get down to London with Eric the dog.

'Our vans and lorries aren't allowed to take passengers,' said Mr Bradley. 'It's against the law.'

'Oh.' Rachel was understandably disappointed.

'But if you and your dog want to get to London, why don't I lend you my car?'

'I can't drive,' said Rachel.

Mr Bradley chuckled. 'You'll have to let Arnold do the driving,' he said. 'Just tell him where you want to go. Monday, you said?'

'Yes,' said Rachel faintly. 'Look, I didn't mean to –'

'He'll be round at your house, eight o'clock, Monday morning. You'll want him to bring you back as well, I take it?'

'Thank you,' said Rachel. 'This is very kind of you.'

'It's nothing,' said Mr Bradley firmly. 'I told you, I owe you. Anything else I can do, you just let me know. Give Eric my best wishes, will you?' And he rang off.

Mr Bradley was as good as his word. On Monday morning, a large black Daimler drew up outside Mrs Hobbs's house at exactly eight o'clock, and a chauffeur in a peaked hat knocked on the door to ask if Rachel and Eric were ready.

They were and, while Eric-as-a-dog and Rachel sat in the back, Arnold (that was the name of the chauffeur) drove them down the motorway to London, eventually stopping outside a large, grey building, which housed the headquarters of the British Cycling Federation.

'I'm not sure how long we'll be,' Rachel told Arnold. 'Can you wait?'

The chauffeur smiled cheerfully. 'I'll be here,' he said. 'You go ahead.'

Rachel got out and led Eric over to the main doors.

'Right, Eric. The offices are on the third floor,' she reminded him, 'and the man in charge of the entries is Mr Macrossan.' She looked down at him. 'You're quite sure you want to go through with this?'

'Woof,' said Eric.

'Right.' Rachel reached for the door. 'All set?'

'Woof, woof,' said Eric, and Rachel suddenly remembered she hadn't given him her entry form.

'Not much point going in without that,' she said, taking it out of her pocket and holding it for Eric to take in his teeth.

Then she pulled open the main doors, whispered 'Good luck!' and Eric disappeared inside.

'What do we do now?' asked Arnold, when she got back to the car.

'Now?' said Rachel. 'Now, we just wait.'

Inside the building, Eric, the entry form still firmly between his teeth, trotted across the foyer and up the stairs. He had decided to use the staircase rather than the lift, partly because the buttons in the lift might be difficult for a dog to use, but mainly because he knew the stairs were safer.

Eric had discovered from experience that the best thing for a dog in a strange building was not to get trapped in one place, but to keep on the move. When anyone in the building saw him trotting along a corridor, their first reaction would probably be just to stop and stare. By the time they had decided to do anything – like pick him up and put him outside – Eric's plan was to be round the next corner and out of sight. The great trick was to look as if you knew exactly what you were doing – and keep going.

It all worked perfectly. Eric got to the third floor, marched purposefully down the corridors, looking at all the doors, till he came to the one with Mr Macrossan's name on it. Then he hid himself, just outside, behind a large pot-plant.

He waited. It was quite a long wait, almost half an hour, but eventually the door opened and Mr Macrossan came out with a sheaf of papers, followed by a woman who was presumably his secretary. The two of them walked off down the passage.

The office door was left open, so Eric seized his opportunity and darted inside. He could see at once what he was looking for. On a long table by the window, under a big sign that said 'Entries for BCF Nat. Champs.', were five wire baskets. Each tray had a label on it, marked 'Race Officials', 'Seniors', 'Juniors', 'Third Category' and 'Juveniles'. All Eric had to do, he thought, as he jumped up on the table, was to leave Rachel's entry form in the Juveniles basket, and get out as fast as he could.

It was only then that he realized there was a snag. What he needed was for Rachel's entry to look like all the others, but he could see at once that it wouldn't. For a start, the form he carried in his mouth was folded up, and with only dog paws, Eric wasn't sure that he could unfold it and lay it flat like all the others. Worse, he could see that all the entries in the tray had been put in alphabetical order. If Rachel's was just left on top, anyone would be able to see that it had been added later. Worst of all, though, he could already hear Mr Macrossan and his secretary coming back down the corridor.

And then Eric had a rather clever idea. He dropped Rachel's form on top of the others, but then pushed the whole tray with his nose until it, and all the entry forms, crashed off the table on to the floor.

As Mr Macrossan's secretary came in, the forms were still spilling over the carpet, while Eric himself had just enough time to jump down and hide behind a filing cabinet.

'What on earth happened?' asked Mr Macrossan.

'I think it must have been the draught from the window.' His secretary was already bending down to gather up the entry forms. 'I hope we haven't lost any. How many were there supposed to be?'

'Twenty-nine,' said Mr Macrossan.

The secretary counted the entry forms. 'You've got thirty here.'

'Thirty?' Mr Macrossan was rather puzzled. 'Are you sure ?'

His secretary counted them again. 'Definitely thirty.'

Mr Macrossan shrugged. 'I must have miscounted,' he said, making a note of the new number on his pad. 'OK. Thirty it is.'

And while they got on with their work, neither of them noticed Eric, creeping silently back out into the corridor.

The letter saying that Rachel's entry had been accepted arrived at her home three days later. Mrs Hobbs showed it excitedly to Eric.

'You see?' she said. 'It's got her racing number. Official pass. Her name's in the programme and everything !'

'Great,' said Eric.

'I'm so relieved,' Mrs Hobbs went on, 'that they didn't mind the entry being posted late. If Rachel hadn't been able to enter just because I ... She takes that race very seriously, you know.'

'Yes, I'd noticed,' said Eric.

He went up to see Rachel. 'You'd better win, you know,' he told her, 'after all this trouble.'

'Don't worry,' said Rachel. 'I intend to.'

And Rachel did win her race. She says it was the toughest she's ever ridden, and she crossed the line just three-tenths of a second in front of her arch rival, Mark Highland. Her knees and one hand were still bleeding from a fall she'd had in the second lap, and her legs were so tired that when she got off the bike and tried to stand, she fell over. But she won. The first girl ever to win the National Juveniles Circuit Championship; all the papers agreed, the next morning, that it was a very remarkable achievement.

Everyone thought, after a victory like that, that Rachel would become more serious about cycling than ever – that she would want to enter more and more races and try and win more and more trophies. In fact she was invited to an international cycling event in Belgium the next weekend, but she turned it down. To everyone's surprise, the National Championships were almost the last race she ever entered. She didn't exactly give up cycling after that, but she gave up serious racing and training.

Mrs Jessop was rather disappointed, but Rachel was

very firm about it. She had done what she set out to do, and said that, while she enjoyed cycling, she also wanted time for other things in life, like ... well, like going for walks with a dog.

They keep a photograph of her, though, in the British Cycling Federation's hall of fame. If you ever go to London and call in at their headquarters, you will find it in a long corridor on the third floor. It's about halfway along, on the right-hand side, a black-and-white photograph of Rachel Hobbs holding the Championship cup above her head.

They have photographs there of all the people who have ever won Federation championships, but although Rachel's picture is only one among so many, visitors often stop for a closer look, just at that particular one.

It happened while I was there. Mr Macrossan himself was giving a little group of us a guided tour. We were walking down the hall when the woman in front of me stopped and pointed at the photo of Rachel.

'Well, look at that,' she said. 'Isn't that extraordinary!'

'Ah, yes!' Mr Macrossan agreed, warmly. 'Rachel Hobbs, the first girl ever to win the National Juveniles Circuit Championship and, interestingly, the only time we've ever had a father and daughter win the same trophy.'

'I didn't know that,' I said.

'Oh, yes. Her father won the same race in 1964,' said Mr Macrossan. 'I gather that's why she was so keen to win it herself.'

'Is it really a girl?' The woman peered closely at the photo. 'I hadn't noticed that. No, I was looking at this,' and she stabbed with her finger at the cup Rachel holds triumphantly above her head.

We all looked more closely, as I hope you will if you ever go there. The cup Rachel is holding is a large one and inside it, his head peering cheerfully out of the top, is a dog.

'It's the way the two of them are looking at each other,' said the woman. 'It's as if they were having a conversation.'

Looking at the picture, we all agreed.

'I wonder what they're saying,' somebody said.

Mr Macrossan laughed. 'I'm afraid I've no idea,' he said, as he led us down the hall.

But I do.

As she lifted the cup high above her head, Rachel said, 'Nice bit of teamwork, Eric.'

And Eric said, 'Woof!'

It had not been a good week for Eric. At the start of it, he had been thrown out of the swimming pool again, then there had been the trouble with the sausages and, on top of all that, there was the business with Miss Priskett's cat.

He was thrown out of the swimming pool on Monday, for being a dog. They had just installed one of those long chutes that you slide down for miles before splashing into the water, and Eric had gone in one end as a boy, and come out of the other as a dog.

It caused a lot more trouble than you might have expected, quite apart from just getting thrown out. Rachel had been there and had somehow rescued Eric's clothes from the changing room for him. She even remembered to get his swimming trunks from the bottom of the pool (they had followed Eric down the slide, of course), but she hadn't known that he had also been wearing a pair of flippers, borrowed from Kenny Biggs. When Eric went back to the pool later that afternoon, there was no sign of the flippers. So first he had to tell Kenny, and then he had to tell his mum that he had to buy Kenny a new pair, and she gave him a long lecture on looking after things properly . . . All in all, it was not a good day.

\*

And two days after that, there was the business with the sausages. Mrs Banks had asked Eric to get a half-pound of sausages from the butcher's, which would have been simple enough if Eric hadn't turned into a dog on the way home. Unfortunately, there are certain hazards in carrying sausages when you are a dog, and Eric had barely turned out of the High Street before an ugly-looking bulldog nosed up to him and tried to take the sausages.

Eric ran. He knew the area well by now, and there was a hole in the fence at the bottom of Garston Mead that he knew was just big enough for himself, but too small for the bulldog to follow. He got there just in time, but the bag of sausages tore open on the way. They trailed out all over the ground and, try as he might, Eric found it quite impossible to wrap them up again, using just his front paws and his teeth.

This meant the only way he could get the sausages home was by dragging them along the pavement. It wasn't much fun. People pointed at him and laughed, and it didn't do the sausages a lot of good, either. After being pulled through three hundred yards of dirt, they were grey rather than pink, and even after Eric had washed them with soap and water in the bathroom, they still didn't look quite right.

Knowing what had happened to them, Eric didn't fancy sausages for lunch and told his mum he wasn't hungry. Mrs Banks said he'd better have a lie-down, so Eric spent lunchtime up in his room, starving hungry, while downstairs he could hear Mr Banks saying it was a shame about Eric not feeling well, he was missing his favourite pudding – chocolate sponge with chocolate sauce.

*

Then, on top of all that, there was the business with Miss Priskett's cat. Miss Priskett lived next door to Eric. She lived alone, she had no children, and the apple of her eye was a large white Persian cat called Yum Yum.

Unfortunately, Yum Yum was a nervous animal, and particularly nervous of dogs. Whenever she saw Eric-as-a-dog – which was quite often, since he lived next door – she would dash, panic-stricken, up the nearest tree and sit there, yowling loudly with fear. Miss Priskett would hear the noise and come rushing out to see what had happened. Naturally, she formed the conclusion that her cat was being terrorized by Eric.

It wasn't true, of course. Eric had never tried anything beyond the occasional snap or a snarl, but Miss Priskett decided the little mongrel that appeared so often next door was a vicious cat-hater and the sooner somebody dealt with it, the better.

She complained, in fact, so often and so strongly that even Mr and Mrs Banks began to wonder if there wasn't some truth in what she said. They had always rather liked the little mongrel, but if it *was* attacking cats, then maybe it shouldn't be encouraged to hang around the house.

As if that wasn't bad enough, Eric now found (this was two days after the sausage incident) that he was accused of murder. It happened like this. Yum Yum had gone missing. Miss Priskett had let her out in the morning and she hadn't come home for her lunchtime fish finger. Increasingly anxious, Miss Priskett spent most of the day out in her garden, calling desperately for Yum Yum and holding out a saucer of tinned salmon.

It was very bad luck for Eric that he should walk by at just that time, as a dog, and with a large white toy rabbit in his mouth. The rabbit had fallen out of a little girl's pram and Eric, wanting to help, had picked it up and was chasing after the pram to give it back.

Miss Priskett's eyesight was not particularly good, and when she saw Eric with something large, white and fluffy hanging out of his mouth, she instantly concluded that the reason her cat was missing was that Eric had caught it, killed it and was carrying it back to his lair.

The first that Eric, innocently trotting down the pavement, knew of this was when a brick whistled past his head, to shatter like shrapnel on the path in front of him. He turned in dazed horror to find it had been thrown by Miss Priskett. To look at her, you wouldn't have believed Miss Priskett could throw bricks with such force, but the thought of what Eric had done to her beloved Yum Yum had given her a demonic strength and she was, even now, tearing another brick with her bare hands from the wall at the front of her garden, ready to do it again.

Eric turned and ran.

Rachel, of course, knew nothing of all this when Eric trotted into her house, the sound of breaking bricks still ringing in his ears. If she had, she would probably not have said the things she did. She had spent the morning reading Eric's scrapbook, which he had lent her. She had seen the pictures of Eric winning dog shows, the newspaper cuttings of the time he had raised the alarm for old Mrs Quilter, and saved Mrs Potts from the conman – and the thought had struck her that Eric had led a very exciting life.

'You know, Eric,' she said, as they sat together in the garden, 'I think you're really lucky.'

Eric, picking the shards of brick from his fur, was not convinced.

'I mean,' Rachel continued, 'all these amazing things that happen to you.'

Yes, thought Eric, like being stoned by old ladies, getting attacked by bulldogs and thrown out of swimming pools – wonderful!

Rachel, quite unaware of how Eric felt, just carried on talking. 'And all because you turn into a dog,' she said. 'I mean, you're just . . . just so lucky.'

Eric couldn't take any more of it. How could anyone think that turning into a dog was exciting or lucky? Turning into a dog didn't do you any good. It didn't do anyone any good. All it did was cause trouble. He got to his feet and, without so much as a woof to Rachel, walked gloomily back out to the road.

'Eric?' she called after him. 'Are you all right?'

But Eric had gone.

Now it's a funny thing, and something you may have noticed yourself, but when you are feeling depressed, the sight of someone feeling even worse is often the one thing that can make you feel better. I suppose it helps you realize that your own troubles aren't necessarily as bad as you thought.

That, anyway, is what happened to Eric. He was walking down the High Street, quite convinced that he had to be the most unfortunate boy (or dog) in the world, when he saw a tramp. The man was sitting on the ground in the pedestrian precinct, sleeping with his head on his chest, and he looked dreadful. His hair was long and uncombed, his skin was dirty and his body looked as worn-out and frayed as his clothes. It was as though he'd been all used up and was waiting for somebody to come along and throw him away.

Beside him on the ground was an old-fashioned wind-up gramophone, a box of records and a hat. Obviously the tramp had hoped, by playing music, to persuade people to put money in his hat, but at the moment no record was playing and there were no coins to be seen. It looked as if he was just too tired to bother.

Looking at the man, at the dust on his trousers, the holes in the elbows of his coat, and the string instead of laces in his boots, something inside Eric stirred. How could people just walk by and leave him lying there? As a dog, Eric had no money to give, but it occurred to him that he could do one thing for the tramp. He could put on a record, and hope that when people heard the music, they might dip into their pockets.

It wasn't easy to wind up the gramophone with a paw, but Eric managed it. Then he opened the box of records, looked through the titles (he didn't recognize any of them), and chose one called 'Bells across the Meadows'. He put it on the turntable, set it going and gently lifted the needle on to the record.

Behind him there was a smattering of applause, and Eric turned round to find that quite a crowd had gathered to watch what he was doing. It hadn't occurred to him before, but of course the sight of a dog choosing a record and putting it on to a gramophone was such an odd one that a lot of people had stopped to watch.

While the music played, Eric had an idea. Picking up the tramp's hat, he trotted over with it to the crowd and presented it to a large cheerful-looking woman at the front. She laughed, bent down, and put some money in it – and to Eric's amazement, so did almost everyone else.

By the time Eric had been round them all with the hat, the music had finished, and he trotted back to the gramophone to choose another record. He was just nudging it into place when he noticed that the tramp had woken up and was looking at him with deep-blue eyes that stood out against his grimy face. Eric paused.

'No, no, please ...' said the tramp, with a gentle wave of his hand. 'Carry on, do.'

Eric carried on. The crowd was even bigger now, and when he had taken the hat round again it was actually too full of money for Eric to lift. He had to drag it over to the tramp, who looked at its contents in astonishment.

'Goodness gracious,' he murmured. Then he looked at Eric. 'Is this really all for me?'

'Woof,' said Eric.

'You know,' said the tramp, scooping out a few handfuls of the money and putting it in his pocket. 'I think we could be on to something here.' He handed the hat back to Eric. 'I wonder, could you bear to do all that again, dear boy?'

Eric did it all again. In fact, altogether he did it eight times, and then the tramp said they had to stop because he hadn't got any pockets left to put money in. When the last of the crowd had finally gone, the tramp packed up his gramophone, looked at Eric and said, 'I think it's time for a partner's meeting, don't you?'

Eric wondered what he meant.

'Lunch, dear boy,' said the tramp. 'Are you hungry?'

'Woof,' said Eric.

'Of course you are,' the tramp agreed. 'I know a rather nice little place just round the corner.' He loaded his gramophone into an old pram and led Eric out of the precinct.

'If the dustbins are anything to go by, this should be pretty good,' said the tramp, and he led Eric inside a very expensive-looking restaurant.

'It was the most amazing meal!' Eric told Rachel excitedly the next day. 'I've never eaten food like it, and Mortimer told me –'

'Mortimer?' asked Rachel.

'That's his name,' said Eric. 'Mortimer Fitzherbert. He used to be a solicitor.'

'Well, he certainly seems to have cheered you up,' said Rachel.

Eric realized that she was right. His gloom of the morning had completely vanished.

'It's not just being cheered up, exactly,' said Eric. 'It's . . . it's knowing I can help, that I can do something useful, that being a dog isn't just something that gets me into trouble.'

Rachel nodded. 'You get a lot of money for him, do you?' she asked. 'Just for putting on records?'

'You should see it!' said Eric. 'It comes pouring in.'

And in the days that followed it continued to pour in, in ever-increasing quantities. Most mornings, Eric-as-a-dog would trot down and join the tramp somewhere in the precinct. The tramp would get out the gramophone, and Eric would put on a record and pass the hat round. Sometimes, he would dance or try to sing as well, and in half an hour or so they'd have more than enough money to buy food and drink. They'd either go and eat in a restaurant, or just buy some sandwiches and take them out to the park.

The tramp began to look better. He still wore the same old clothes, but they were cleaner. He still didn't sleep in a proper bed, but he had a new thick coat to keep him warm at night, and eating regular meals probably did more than anything to make him stronger and healthier. He no longer looked as if a gust of wind could blow him back down the road

The trouble was, as Eric knew, that it couldn't last. As Rachel put it, 'What happens to him when you go back to school?'

The holidays were almost over, and once term started, Eric wouldn't have time, however much he wanted, to sit with a tramp in the shopping precinct, holding out a hat for money.

Eric thought about it, and eventually decided he would have to explain things to Mr Fitzherbert. He couldn't do that as a dog, of course, so he went as a boy, and took Rachel with him to help with the talking.

They found Mr Fitzherbert dozing quietly on a bench.

'Excuse me,' said Eric.

The tramp eyed them cautiously. 'Yes?' he said.

'You don't really know us,' Eric explained, 'but we've come about your dog. The one that works the gramophone.'

'Ah.' The tramp sat up. 'He's not my dog, really, you know. Just calls round occasionally. Very pleasant it is, too.'

'We've come to say that he won't be able to come any more,' said Rachel.

'Oh,' said the tramp.

'And I've brought you these,' said Eric, holding out a lot of leaflets. 'I've been talking to people and we've found out that if you go to the social security offices, they'll give you money.'

'They'll find you a hostel to live in, as well,' said Rachel.

'They'll even help you get a job,' said Eric, 'and then maybe you could get a house.'

'You could get married,' added Rachel. 'Have babies . . .'

The tramp didn't say anything for quite a long time. 'You're quite sure the dog's not coming back?' he asked eventually.

'Quite sure,' said Eric. 'It's not easy to explain, but he's only free in the school holidays.'

'Ah,' said the tramp. 'Well.' He stood up. 'It's time I was moving on, anyway.' And he started packing all his belongings into the old pram.

'Aren't you going to try the social services,' asked Eric, 'or the hostel?'

Mr Fitzherbert smiled briefly. 'It's not easy to explain,' he said, 'but . . . no.'

'I see,' said Eric, who didn't see at all.

The tramp finished his packing. 'If you ever see that dog again, could you tell him that I'm extremely grateful for his help, and that I enjoyed his company?'

'Yes, of course,' said Eric.

'And tell him I'll be around here again one day, eh?'

'I'll tell him,' said Eric.

Sadly, they watched him go. Eric had liked Mr Fitzherbert; he had liked being able to help. As Rachel had said, it had cheered him up, and now that the tramp had gone, he was left feeling rather empty.

'There are plenty of other people that need helping,' said Rachel. 'You could help Miss Priskett find her cat, for a start.'

Eric remembered the way Miss Priskett had thrown a brick at him. The idea of helping her didn't fill him with much enthusiasm.

'I think you should,' said Rachel firmly. 'Whether you want to or not. You may not have heard, but she's telling everyone that her cat's missing because you ate it.'

'Oh, that,' said Eric.

'You didn't eat it, did you?' asked Rachel.

'No, of course I didn't,' said Eric. 'But she's not going to believe me, is she?'

'You'd better think of some way to make her,' said Rachel. 'It's getting serious.'

When they got home for tea at Eric's house that day, they found out just how serious it was.

'She told me she's planning to kill him,' said Mr Banks.

'Kill who?' asked Eric.

'The dog that's eaten her cat,' Mrs Banks explained. 'But don't worry, she probably only wants to frighten him.'

'No, kill him,' said Mr Banks, cheerfully. 'She was very definite about it. That's why she's bought the gun.'

Eric choked on his tea. 'She's got a gun?' he spluttered.

'Only an airgun, of course,' said his dad. 'I don't expect she can do much damage with that.'

'I don't know,' said Mrs Banks thoughtfully. 'It's only a little dog. If you shot it in the head . . .'

Eric didn't feel very hungry after that. He left the

rest of his tea, and he and Rachel went upstairs. From his bedroom window, Eric could actually see Miss Priskett next door, practising with the air rifle on a target set up in her garden.

'She's getting better,' said Rachel. 'I think she nearly hit it that time.'

'What am I going to do?' Eric groaned. Nobody else seemed to take this shooting business seriously, but personally he found it very alarming.

'Only one thing to do,' said Rachel decisively. 'You've got to find her cat.'

'Find it? How?' said Eric. 'She's been looking everywhere for days.'

'It shouldn't be too difficult,' said Rachel. 'Not for a dog, anyway. You just have to track it down, don't you?'

Rachel was right, of course. As a dog, Eric could use his nose to track almost anything. All he needed was something to show him which scent he had to follow, and there was a cat basket outside Miss Priskett's back door which would do perfectly.

So, Sunday afternoon found Eric-as-a-dog creeping round to Miss Priskett's back door. He caught the scent, carefully memorized it and then set about casting for the trail. The difficulty here was that the garden was full of trails, and Eric had to sort out the most recent of them. The fact that this took rather longer than he'd thought, combined with the fact that Miss Priskett woke up early from her afternoon sleep, very nearly spelt disaster.

The first Eric knew of the danger was a buzzing sound just above his right ear. It was followed by another buzz and a shower of dust blew up from the soil ahead of him. He turned round to see Miss Priskett at the dining-room window, hurriedly loading another pellet into her air rifle. He was being shot at!

Eric had never moved faster in his life. He dived for cover into a flower-bed, ran down along the fence to the bottom of the garden and found a hole which led out of the garden and through to safety.

Five minutes later, when he'd recovered his breath and his paws had stopped shaking, he also noticed there was a very strong scent of cat by the gap he'd just come through. Carefully, he followed the trail and a little while later, it led him straight to Miss Priskett's cat.

As soon as he saw her, Eric realized why she had not been seen for the last few days.

Rachel walked up the path to Miss Priskett's front door and rang the bell.

'My name's Rachel Hobbs,' she announced when Miss Priskett answered the door, 'and I've come to tell you Eric didn't eat your cat.'

'Eric?' said Miss Priskett.

'That's the dog's name,' said Rachel. 'And he didn't do it.'

'But I saw him,' said Miss Priskett. 'I saw him with my own eyes, carrying poor Yum down the road, the blood dripping from his jaws –'

'Eric never touched your cat,' Rachel interrupted, 'but what he has done is find her for you.'

Miss Priskett's jaw dropped. 'Found her? What d'you mean?'

'Look,' said Rachel, 'if you promise not to throw any bricks or anything, I'll call him and Eric can show you himself.'

'Of course, of course.' Miss Priskett was wringing her hands. 'I'll promise anything.'

Rachel turned. 'It's all right, Eric,' she called. 'You can come out now.'

Very cautiously, Eric-as-a-dog put his head round the garden gate.

'Right,' said Rachel. 'We follow him.' She set off down the path but then stopped. 'I nearly forgot,' she added, 'you'll need a cardboard box.'

Rachel and Miss Priskett followed Eric out of the front gate, along the street and down the path that led by the side of the houses to the playing fields at the back.

Eric led them along one edge of the field, then down a steep bank to a small patch of wasteland, before stopping in front of a rusty old sheet of corrugated iron.

'Is this it?' said Miss Priskett.

'Woof!' barked Eric.

Gingerly, Miss Priskett lifted the corrugated iron and there, underneath, was Yum Yum, surrounded by six tiny black-and-white kittens.

Miss Priskett treats Eric-as-a-dog very differently these days. She always gives him a wave when she sees him, and usually invites him in for food. And if any of her cats — she has three now, because she kept two of the kittens — if any of her cats make a fuss or complain, she ticks them off severely. That dog, she tells them, is an honoured friend; with time, I think they've actually come to like him.

She sold the air rifle as well. She was going to give it to Eric at first, as she thought it was the sort of thing a boy might enjoy, but Eric told her that he didn't really want it, thank you all the same. I think being shot at himself had rather put him off air rifles.

But he's glad Miss Priskett hasn't got it any more.

# 6

Eric had spent the evening babysitting for Mrs Jessop.
It wasn't actually her baby he was sitting for – Mrs
Jessop didn't have any children of her own – but she
had a niece called Elizabeth, who was two and a half
years old and had come to stay for three days.

Elizabeth was not an easy child to look after, but
Eric had one advantage over anyone else when it
came to babysitting: he turned into a dog – and
Elizabeth, like most small children, adored dogs. As
long as Eric didn't mind having his ears pulled and
being dressed up in doll's clothes, he could keep Elizabeth happy for hours.

Even so, it had been an exhausting evening before
Eric finally got Elizabeth off to sleep. He was just
heading back downstairs when a pile of newspapers on
the landing caught his eye. To be precise, it was a
headline on the top newspaper that took his attention.
It said 'Super Dog Saves Three in Plane Drama'.

Eric stopped to read the full article. It certainly was
an extraordinary story. A Mr Muller, a German millionaire, had been flying his private aeroplane with his
two sons and the family dog, when he had had a heart
attack. Neither of the two boys knew anything about
flying but, just when it looked as if nothing could stop

them crashing to the ground, the Alsatian had moved into the pilot's seat, taken over the controls and landed the aeroplane safely back on the runway.

The story gave Eric an idea. It was, he thought modestly, one of the most brilliant ideas he had ever had, and he was still turning it over in his mind when Mrs Jessop came back.

'Everything all right,' she asked, 'with Elizabeth?'

'Fine,' said Eric. 'She fell asleep.'

Mrs Jessop was relieved to hear that. She found life with Elizabeth rather tiring, and the thought of looking after her for another day and a half was distinctly daunting.

'Any chance you could come round again tomorrow?' Mrs Jessop asked.

'I'm afraid I'm busy tomorrow,' said Eric.

'The evening?' asked Mrs Jessop, hopefully.

'The evening as well,' said Eric, firmly.

He was still thinking about his idea. Maybe he could call in on Rachel on the way home and see what she thought about it.

Rachel read the story about the German Alsatian and looked up.

'So a dog flew an aeroplane,' she said. 'Why all the excitement?'

'Dogs *can't* fly aeroplanes,' said Eric. 'Not really. Everyone knows that.' He pointed at the newspaper. 'Either they've got the story wrong in some way, or . . . or it wasn't really a dog at all. It was someone like me.'

'Someone who turned into a dog?' said Rachel.

'Right.' Eric grinned. 'I've always thought it couldn't just be me. I can't be the only person this has ever happened to.'

'But if it's happening all over the place, wouldn't we know about it?' asked Rachel doubtfully.

'Why?' said Eric. 'I kept quiet about it. Supposing all the others did the same?'

'Well, how can you find out if it's true, if they're all keeping quiet?' Rachel demanded.

'That's the whole point,' said Eric triumphantly. 'Newspapers! Stories like this get into the newspapers. I know I can't get to Germany to meet this Alsatian, but supposing we checked out the local newspaper office? Found all the stories they've had recently about dogs behaving in an unusually clever manner. Then we could go and see.'

Rachel thought about it. It seemed a very good idea. If there was anybody else like Eric, then it was quite likely that stories about him or her would have appeared in the paper. There had already been several stories about Eric himself.

'How would we get into a newspaper office?' she asked.

Eric didn't know, so he went to ask Mrs Jessop.

'Newspaper offices? You wouldn't,' she said abruptly. If she sounded a little brusque, it was possibly because she had been up since five o'clock that morning playing 'I Spy' with her little niece, Elizabeth.

'You have to be over eighteen,' Mrs Jessop explained. 'Anyway, why do you want to know?'

'I want to do . . . sort of research,' said Eric.

'I see.' Mrs Jessop looked at him over the top of her glasses. 'And what are you sort of researching?'

Eric hesitated. 'Nothing really, Miss.'

'Nothing could be tricky,' said Mrs Jessop. 'But if you're serious, I have a friend who's a journalist on the *Birmingham Post*. I could give her a ring; see if something can be arranged.'

'Would you, Miss?' said Eric. 'We'd be ever so grateful.'

'I'll try and fix up something for this afternoon,' said Mrs Jessop. 'There's just one condition . . .'

Eric told Rachel the good news when he called round to her house after lunch.

'It's all fixed,' he said. 'We just go to the newspaper offices, ask for Miss Shapiro – that's the person in charge of the archives – and she'll tell us how to find whatever we want.'

'Brilliant,' said Rachel. 'But why do we have to bring her?' She pointed to Elizabeth, sitting in the buggy Eric was pushing.

'That was the deal,' Eric explained. 'Mrs Jessop fixed up about the newspaper offices, but in return, we have to look after Elizabeth for the afternoon.'

'A whole afternoon?' Rachel was worried.

'And a couple of hours in the evening,' said Eric. 'She wanted it to be the whole day, but we sort of compromised.' He reached into his pocket and pulled out some Smarties. 'I've stocked up with these to keep her quiet,' he said. 'Ten packets.'

'We'd better get some more on the way,' said Rachel.

In the archive office of the *Birmingham Post*, they keep records not just of every newspaper they have published, but copies of every story under separate subject headings.

Miss Shapiro explained the system while she showed them round. 'If you want to know about ghosts, for instance, you come along here to the Gs,' she moved along the shelves, 'until you find the right box. Then you take it out, open it, and there you are.'

The box marked 'Ghosts' was brim-full with newspaper cuttings of ghost stories that had once been printed in the *Birmingham Post*.

Miss Shapiro put the box back on the shelf. 'So,' she asked, 'what did you want to know about?'

'Dogs, please,' said Eric.

They followed Miss Shapiro back along the shelves to the Ds.

'Here we are,' she said, pointing not to one box, but to a whole row. 'You can have "Dogs, vicious", "Dogs, pets", "Dogs, amusing", "Dogs, various" . . . take your choice. Let me know when you're finished, won't you?' And she was gone.

Eric and Rachel very quickly realized that they would never be able to read all the newspaper stories about dogs in one afternoon. So they decided, instead, that Eric would skim through the files for anything that looked interesting, and that Rachel would then take those cuttings over to the photocopier. That way, they could look at the stories later, at their leisure.

In the next hour and a half, they found twenty or thirty possibles. Rachel was just putting the last of them through the copying machine when Miss Shapiro came over.

'Is your friend Eric all right?' she asked. 'Only he seems to have taken his shoes and socks off.' She was holding them in her hand as she spoke.

Rachel realized at once what had happened, as you probably have yourself, and tried to act calmly. 'Oh, yes,' she said. 'It is hot in here, isn't it. I'll look after those, shall I?'

Taking Eric's shoes and socks, and collecting up all her bits of paper, she hurried back to the table where Eric had been working. She found him on the floor, putting the rest of his clothes into a bag with his teeth. 'Everything OK?' she asked.

'Woof, woof!' said Eric.

'Never mind.' Rachel grinned. 'We'll get you out of here. And look on the bright side. You've cheered up Elizabeth.'

Elizabeth, who had been getting rather bored in her buggy, despite the Smarties, was very happy to see the little dog that had played with her the day before. She chuckled and smiled contentedly, and pulled Eric's ears whenever he came within reach.

'Good thinking, Eric,' said Rachel. 'You keep her amused, and I'll work out how to get you out of here.'

She sat down and thought. It wasn't going to be easy. Dogs are not allowed inside newspaper offices and if she tried to just walk out with Eric, the security men at the doors would be asking a lot of awkward questions about how he had managed to get in.

She thought of trying to hide him under her clothes, and then of trying to fit him in the buggy with Elizabeth, but he was rather big for both of those possibilities.

In the end, she put him in a waste-paper bin. It wasn't an ordinary waste-paper bin. It was very large, ran on wheels, and was pushed by a man whose job it was to collect up all the rubbish from the offices and take it downstairs.

'I think this is your best chance, Eric,' she whispered as she lifted him inside. 'It's all going down to the basement, and you should be able to get out from there. Good luck. I'll meet you round the front.'

Unfortunately, what Rachel didn't know was that all the waste paper taken downstairs was shredded, so that it could be recycled. The bins were emptied into an enormous machine that chewed up the paper into tiny pieces before pushing it out at the other end.

Eric managed to avoid being shredded, otherwise this story would be rather shorter than it is, but it gave him a very nasty scare. Once he had realized what was going to happen, he had tried desperately to get out of the bin down in the basement, before it was emptied into the shredder, only to find the sides were too steep and slippery.

He barked. He barked as loudly as he could, but even so, with all the noise of the machinery, somebody only heard him at the very last minute and pulled him out.

He managed to wriggle free of his rescuer, dart out of one of the exits and meet up with Rachel at the front of the building, but the incident left him badly shaken. It also made him more determined than ever to find out if this dog business had ever happened to anyone else. If it had, and he could find them, they might be able to help him. They might be able to tell him how to stop changing into a dog when he didn't want to, so that he wouldn't wind up getting nearly killed in shredding machines.

Eric and Rachel had their first chance to study the stories they had collected while they were babysitting that evening at Mrs Jessop's – at least, they had a chance after they had eventually persuaded Elizabeth to go to bed.

Little Elizabeth had made a big fuss about it, insisting that before she went up she wanted to say goodnight to Eric. It was a while before they realized that she meant Eric the dog, not Eric the boy, and even longer before they could convince her that saying goodnight to the dog just wasn't possible. Only when Eric told her, firmly, that the little dog had flown off into the air with the fairies, did Elizabeth reluctantly agree to climb into bed.

At last, the two of them sat downstairs at the dining-room table and started reading the photocopies Rachel had made. It wasn't long before Eric was convinced he'd found something.

'Look at this,' he said, holding up a picture of a black Labrador. ' "Dog found at football match in children's playground." '

'Nothing special about that,' said Rachel. 'A lot of dogs like football.'

'Maybe,' said Eric, 'but this one was acting as a referee. It had a whistle and everything. Keep your eye out for stories about a black Labrador, OK?'

Rachel found one. It was a cutting, two years old, about a back Labrador called 'Bruce the Memory Dog', who had provided the entertainment at an RAF base dinner. It had been able to answer true or false to any FA Cup winner since 1911.

'It's the same dog!' said Eric excitedly. 'See? The pictures match. They've both got that little scar over the nose and that kink in the tail.'

Then Eric found the clincher. It was a story about a black Labrador, also called Bruce, who had raised the alarm about a bomb left outside a railway station. The witness who spoke to a reporter said that she could understand the dog knowing it was a bomb and barking like that to keep everyone away, but what puzzled her was how it had known to pick up the bomb and put it in a bucket of water.

'And they've got an address this time, as well,' said Eric triumphantly. 'It lives near Northcliffe Priory.'

'That's just outside Kidderminster,' said Rachel. 'We could get over there and find him!'

'Yes.' Eric paused. 'It's gone very quiet, hasn't it?' he said.

Rachel listened. Eric was right. You normally got a lot of background noise if you were in the same house as Elizabeth. The air was usually full of the sound of toys thrown against walls, taps turning on and off, or heavy furniture being dragged across the floor. At the moment, though, the house was completely silent.

'Maybe she's gone to sleep,' said Rachel.

But she hadn't. Elizabeth had gone. Not just from her bedroom either, but gone from the house. They searched it from top to bottom, and there wasn't a trace of her.

It was Rachel who pointed out that their best (if not their only) chance of finding Elizabeth before anything happened to her, would be for Eric to turn into a dog and track her down.

'She could be anywhere,' said Rachel. 'We don't even know where to start looking, but you could find her. Look how you found Yum Yum and those kittens.'

Eric said he wasn't sure he could turn into a dog just like that, but Rachel insisted it was worth a try. She said she thought anything was worth a try if it meant they didn't have to explain to Mrs Jessop that they'd lost her niece.

Eyes closed, they sat together at the bottom of the stairs and concentrated. Eric had always thought that someone wanting him to be a dog was what caused it to happen, and it has to be admitted that Rachel had never wanted him to be a dog quite as much as she did at that moment; but even so, I think they were lucky.

Eric gave a bark, and Rachel opened her eyes. She could actually see his clothes falling to the ground now that there was no body there to hold them up, and Eric the dog emerged from the heap to go scampering down the hall, tacking from side to side, already trying to pick up the scent. Rachel hurriedly scooped up his clothes and shoes before following.

It took Eric some minutes to pick up Elizabeth's trail. Elizabeth had been all over the house in the course of the last two days, and what Eric had to do, as he had done with Miss Priskett's cat, was pick out which of the scents was the most recent. Once he had found that, and particularly once he'd found it led out of the back door through the cat flap, it got a lot easier.

The trail led straight down to the bottom of the garden.

Eric says he still has nightmares about what followed. How a two-and-a-half year old child in pink pyjamas could have climbed the garden fence, crossed a busy road and then wandered on to a building site, apparently without anyone noticing, he has never understood. But that is what Mrs Jessop's little niece had done.

He never understood, either, why she had done it — though that was really very simple. Elizabeth wanted to say goodnight to the little dog. She was a determined girl and, because Eric had said the dog had gone off with the fairies, and because she remembered being told that fairies live at the bottom of the garden, that is where Elizabeth went to find him.

Again, it was possibly the fact that Eric had said the fairies had *flown* off with the dog that gave Elizabeth the idea of climbing the ladder on the building site. I think she had some idea in her head that if she got high enough, she might actually see them flying around.

Anyway, whatever the reason, when Eric and Rachel arrived at the site, they found Elizabeth about sixty feet above them, trotting along a section of scaffolding with no safety barrier, singing cheerfully to herself.

What they should have done, of course, was call the police immediately. Building sites are very dangerous places, and Eric and Rachel were well aware that children should not play on them. At the time, though, they were both too frightened at the thought of what was going to happen to Elizabeth even to think of getting help.

Neither of them hesitated. Rachel led the way straight up the ladder, and the two of them climbed to the top. They emerged sixty feet up (and I promise you, sixty feet can feel like a mile if you're just standing on a couple of planks with almost nothing to hold on to), in time to see Elizabeth go trotting off along some scaffolding round the corner.

'Elizabeth!' shouted Rachel. 'Come back here!'

'Woof!' called Eric.

It was the woof that did it. Elizabeth put her head back round the corner; as soon as she saw Eric, a big smile spread over her face, and she started running back towards him. She had only gone a few steps when she slipped and disappeared. Just disappeared. Straight over the side of the scaffolding.

Rachel screamed. Eric ran forward. Hearts in their

mouths, the two of them peered over the side – and saw Elizabeth hanging by a loop in her pyjama top from a pole just under the planking. She was still smiling happily.

'Eric!' said Elizabeth. She reached up and started pulling at his ears, and for once, Eric didn't really mind.

Rachel carried Elizabeth carefully down the ladder and back to the house, and by the time Mrs Jessop got home, she was safely tucked up in bed.

'Fast asleep,' said Mrs Jessop. 'That's a relief. I do hope she wasn't a nuisance.'

'Not really,' said Rachel.

'Didn't cry once,' said Eric.

'Well, my sister's picking her up first thing tomorrow morning,' said Mrs Jessop, 'and I can't say I'm not relieved. Not that I've had to do a great deal, thanks to you two.'

'That's all right, Miss,' said Eric.

Mrs Jessop walked them to the front door. 'So what can I do in return?' she asked.

'How d'you mean, Miss?' asked Rachel.

'Well, I thought perhaps a treat was in order. Where would you like to go? The seaside? Alton Towers? Zoo World ?'

Rachel had never been to either Alton Towers or Zoo World and was just trying to decide which she would prefer, when Eric said, 'Northcliffe Priory, Miss.'

Mrs Jessop was rather surprised. As a teacher, she spent a lot of her time trying to persuade children that historical ruins were interesting places to visit, but she knew Northcliffe Priory wasn't much more than a few pillars in a patch of grassland.

'Are you sure?' she asked.

'I think so,' said Eric. 'We've been reading about it.'

'Definitely the place,' said Rachel, loyally.

'All right,' said Mrs Jessop. 'Northcliffe Priory it is.'

The next Saturday afternoon, Mrs Jessop dropped them off at the Priory grounds and said she would pick them up in an hour, after she'd done her shopping in Kidderminster.

The address from the newspaper was that of a farmhouse a little to the north of the Priory. It only took a few minutes to walk there. Eric and Rachel let themselves in the gate, and walked up to the front door. There was no reply when Eric knocked. They waited, then knocked again several times, but it was clear that no one was home. A little disappointed, but not entirely surprised, Eric reached into his pocket for the letter he had written with just this possibility in mind.

The letter was addressed to 'Bruce the Labrador' and it said:

> Dear Bruce,
>
> We have reason to believe that you and your owner, Mr Bentley, are one and the same person. My name is Eric Banks and I also turn into a dog sometimes. If you suffer in the same way, please let me know. I'm sure you do, having checked up everything about you in the papers.
>
> Yours sincerely,
> Eric Banks.

Eric left the letter underneath a milk bottle, and the

two of them were returning to walk back up the drive, when Rachel stopped and nudged Eric with her elbow.

'Look,' she said. 'Over there.'

Sitting quietly on the grass under a tree was a black Labrador, with a small scar just above its nose and a kink in its tail.

Together they walked over to it.

'Excuse me,' said Eric. 'Are you Bruce?'

The dog looked at him.

'We've just delivered a letter for you,' said Rachel.

'You don't know me,' said Eric, 'but I've read about you in the newspapers and things and, well, I think you may be the same as me.'

'Eric turns into a dog quite a lot,' Rachel explained.

The Labrador still hadn't moved.

'Do you understand?' asked Eric.

'Woof. Woof, woof,' said the Labrador.

'He could be saying "Yes. Yes, yes," ' said Eric.

'He could just be a dog,' said Rachel.

The Labrador got up, bounded off over the grass and came back with a stick, which it left at Eric's feet. Eric picked up the stick and threw it. The Labrador chased after it, brought it back and Eric threw it again.

'You're right.' He turned to Rachel. 'It's just a dog. Just an ordinary dog.' He was more disappointed than he cared to admit. 'Come on,' he said. 'We'd better get back to the car.'

'Successful day?' asked Mrs Jessop. 'Saw all you wanted to see, I hope?'

'Yes, thanks,' said Eric.

'We learnt a lot,' said Rachel.

'Good,' said Mrs Jessop, as she started the car.

They drove past the farmhouse on their way home, but neither Eric nor Rachel bothered to look; which was a pity. If they had, they would have seen a rather unusual sight.

Just outside the front door of the farmhouse, a black Labrador was lying on the step with a piece of paper held firmly to the ground by one paw, and looking, for all the world, as if it was reading a letter.

# 7

Eric had suspected for some time that he was being followed.

'Followed?' asked Rachel, when he told her. 'Who by?'

'I don't know,' said Eric.

It was a feeling more than anything. On several occasions over the last few days – on his way to school, doing his newspaper round, or just around town – he had felt a prickling up and down his spine and an overwhelming sense of being watched.

'Is it happening now?' asked Rachel.

Eric nodded.

They stopped and turned round. The High Street precinct was full of people out doing their shopping or just sitting on benches in the sun. Rachel looked at their faces. No one seemed to be taking a particular interest in Eric but, in all that crowd, it wasn't easy to tell.

'What do they look like?' she asked.

'I've no idea,' said Eric. 'I've never actually seen them.'

'If you've never seen them,' said Rachel, 'how can you be so sure?'

Eric hesitated. 'I just am,' he said. 'I know somebody's following me. I just know it.'

If it had been anyone else but Eric, Rachel would have suggested they went to see a doctor, but Eric wasn't just Eric. He was Eric the dog as well, and he had instincts about these things that weren't easy to dismiss.

'What are you going to do?' she asked.

'I suppose I should try and find out who it is and why they're doing it,' said Eric. 'But I don't see how.'

It was Rachel who suggested using a camera. 'You want to take photographs,' she said. 'Lots of photographs.' She gestured to the crowd behind them. 'If you took a photo of that lot today and another tomorrow and another the day after, you could look at them and see if one of the faces was in all the pictures. Then you'd know who was following you.'

'Brilliant,' said Eric.

And that's what he did. Using a black-and-white film, because it was cheaper, he walked round for the next two days with a camera under his arm, pointing backwards, and took pictures at various times of whatever was behind him.

Then they asked Mrs Jessop if they could use the darkroom at school to develop the film. She said they could, as long as they cleared up properly, and they arranged to meet at the school at ten o'clock the next morning, which was a Saturday.

It was just ten o'clock when, as Eric turned into the school grounds with the roll of film in his pocket, he felt an itching at the back of his neck. It took him rather by surprise, and he barely had time to dive for cover before the familiar transformation took place.

As he tugged his clothes behind a bush and dragged

the film out of his trouser pocket, to carry in his teeth, Eric reflected that it could have been worse. He didn't have far to go. All he had to do was nip across to the school entrance. The handle on the door was just low enough for him to be able to push it down and let himself in; once inside, he could find Rachel, give her the film and let her get on with the developing.

Unfortunately, he was seen. Mr Blocker, the head-master, had come into school that morning to write some reports. He happened to look out of his study window, just as Eric was trotting across the grass to the main entrance.

You may remember that Mr Blocker did not like dogs, and that, in particular, he did not like the little mongrel everyone seemed to call Eric. In fairness, he had good reason. He had not forgotten that day when the dog had used a skateboard to make him fall into the goldfish pond, and there had been other incidents since then that were as bad, if not worse. The time at the school chess club tournament, for instance.

The chess club met in Miss Staple's classroom on Tuesday lunchtimes, and Mr Blocker frequently looked in for a game. He wasn't a bad player and he enjoyed winning against the children. He always said it was good for discipline for them to realize how much better he was, but on this particular Tuesday he was challenged by one of them to play against a dog.

He had known instantly which dog it would be, and had refused at once. The very idea of playing a dog at chess was too ridiculous for words. But then he heard someone say something about him being frightened, so he sat down and told the dog to get on with it.

To Mr Blocker's horror, the dog did get on with it, and had him checkmate in five moves. It was a set of moves called fool's mate (anyone who plays chess will be able to explain it to you) and normally, the headmaster would never have fallen into so simple a trap. You have to understand, though, that he was badly distracted.

From the moment Eric had picked up a pawn in his teeth, moved it two squares forward and then pressed the button on the timer at the side of the table, Mr Blocker's brain seized up. He just couldn't believe what was happening. He was sitting in a classroom in his own school, playing that wretched dog at chess, with all the other children grouped round watching – it was ludicrous. In a daze, he moved his pawn in reply. Eric moved a knight, Mr Blocker moved another pawn, Eric moved up his queen, and that was it. Checkmate.

The word went round the school like wildfire that Blocker had been beaten at chess by a dog. For days afterwards, whenever he walked into a class or passed a group of children in the corridor, one of them would be sure to whisper 'Woof, woof!' just loud enough for him to hear. It drove him wild, which was probably why the children did it.

When he asked Mrs Jessop what he should do, she suggested he should laugh about it and forget it, but Mr Blocker couldn't forget. He brooded, and a deep resentment at being made a fool of by a grubby little mongrel dog burned in his soul. He vowed that if he ever found that dog on his school premises again, there would be trouble. Big trouble.

Now it seemed that Mr Blocker would have his chance at last, and he rubbed his hands together in glee, pushed back his chair, and stood up. He would need something to keep the dog in once he'd caught him; that large carton would do. He'd need to defend himself if the dog turned nasty – it had growled at him very strangely once – so he picked up a walking stick as well.

Thus armed, Mr Blocker turned to the door and promptly tripped over his briefcase, badly bruising an elbow as he fell to the floor and barking his shin on the desk as he got up again. He was limping slightly when he got to the door. It's that dog again, he thought bitterly, nothing but trouble wherever it goes.

By the time he got round to the main entrance, Eric had gone, but Mr Blocker noticed with relief that there was a trail. It had rained recently, and a faint gleam of damp from Eric's pawprints could be seen on the tiled floor of the corridor. The box in one hand, the stick in the other, Mr Blocker tiptoed down the corridor, following the tracks. They stopped just outside the photographic darkroom, which was rather puzzling. What would a dog want in a darkroom? He shook his head. With a dog like this, one never knew.

In one quick movement, he wrenched open the door and, holding the stick above his head, shouted, 'Stay where you are and don't move!'

'You're supposed to knock before coming in here,' said an aggrieved voice. 'You've just ruined Eric's film.'

Mr Blocker stared. The darkroom contained no trace of a dog, not even of somewhere a dog might be hiding. There were just Rachel Hobbs and Eric Banks. Eric was holding up a strip of film, most of which had now been exposed to the light, and both of them were wearing the brown labcoats that all the children had to put on in the darkroom, to protect their own clothes from the chemicals.

'I'm s-s-sorry,' stammered Mr Blocker. 'I thought that I ... I ...' He stopped, walked out and closed the door behind him. It was unbelievable. There had been a dog, hadn't there? He couldn't have imagined it, the tracks led straight to the door, but now ... Why did it always happen to him?

Shoulders slumped and muttering to himself, he headed back to his study. Maybe, he thought, he needed a bit of exercise. A good run might clear his head, get the blood circulating – and stop him thinking about dogs.

In the darkroom, once they had finished congratulating themselves on a very narrow escape, Rachel and Eric set to work on developing what was left of the film.

It was rather disappointing. They checked the faces in all the photographs, but none of them seemed to appear with any regularity.

'As far as I can see, Eric,' Rachel said, 'the only thing following you is a black blob.' She pointed at a small dark blur which seemed to have cropped up in several of the photos.

Eric had presumed it was a fault on the film, but something made him pick up a magnifying glass and take a closer look.

'Let's do a blow-up of that,' he said.

You probably know that when you take a photograph, the negative is very small, and that the photo itself is made larger by shining a light through the negative on to special photographic paper. The further away you have the light and the negative, the larger the picture you get, and it is possible in this way to take one section of the photo and make it very large indeed. This is called 'blowing up' the picture, and that is what Eric and Rachel now did.

The result was quite astonishing. The picture they got revealed that the black blur was not a fault in the film, but a dog's head. Blown up still further, it was possible to make out that the dog was a black Labrador, and in the final enlargement, they could even see that the Labrador had a small scar just above its nose.

'It's the dog from the Priory, isn't it?' said Rachel.

'Yes,' said Eric, 'and when we find him, I think he owes us an explanation.'

They found him sooner than they thought. They had been to pick up Eric's clothes from where he'd left them in the bushes and were coming back to collect the photos they had left to dry, when Rachel froze and pointed at the window of Mr Blocker's study.

Eric looked. Just inside, they could see a large black Labrador, standing on its hind legs and pulling open a drawer in the headmaster's filing cabinet, before rifling through the files with one of its paws.

As they watched, it pulled out the file it wanted, took it over to the desk, opened it and started to read. It was too far away to see the name on the top of the file, but there was a photo in the right-hand corner, and Eric knew from that whose file it was. It was his own.

'Come on, Rachel,' he said.

The two of them ran back round to the main entrance, into the school, and then along the corridor to the headmaster's study.

'What happens if we see Blocker?' asked Rachel.

'We'll tell him we saw a dog in his study,' said Eric. 'It's the truth.'

Arriving at the study, he knocked briefly and pushed open the door. The room was empty, but the door to the cupboard on the right was quivering slightly, and Eric went over to it and knocked again. There was a pause, before the door opened to reveal a man of about thirty, wrapped in a tartan travelling rug that, Rachel noted, usually hung on the back of Mr Blocker's chair.

'Eric Banks, I presume,' said the man, holding out a hand. 'Bruce Bentley. Pleased to meet you.'

Eric did not take the hand.

'You've been following me,' he said.

'Yes . . .' said the man.

'I think you owe us an explanation,' added Rachel.

'I quite agree,' said the man cheerfully, 'and I was going to suggest we all went back to my hotel – I'm staying at the Grosvenor – and had a talk over coffee or something, but I wonder if either of you could lay hands on some clothes for me first? If I'm found in a school looking like this, I could be in real trouble.'

Eric thought. He knew what it was like to be stuck with no clothes, but the lab coats would be too small and they didn't have . . . He had an idea.

'Wait here,' he said.

Mr Blocker was feeling a lot better. The run had done him good, he thought, and now he was in the staff changing room, having an invigorating shower. As the water hurtled down on him, he felt so much better that he started to sing. Indeed, he was singing so loudly that he didn't notice the two figures that crept into the changing room behind him and took the tracksuit from the bench where he had thrown it down.

'Won't your Mr Blocker need this himself?' asked Mr Bentley, when Eric gave him the tracksuit.

'He's got his ordinary clothes,' explained Rachel. 'This is just what he used for running, and we can give it back later.'

'Well, I'm very grateful to him,' said Mr Bentley.

'We have to clear up the darkroom,' said Eric, 'so we'll leave you to get changed, and meet you outside the main entrance, all right?'

Mr Blocker was still singing as he came out of the shower and started towelling himself dry, but then he noticed his tracksuit had gone. He looked all round the changing room but, to his horror, there was no sign of it anywhere.

Now when Rachel had said that Mr Blocker had his own clothes to get into, she had not realized one thing. When he went for a run, Mr Blocker put all his own clothes in his locker and locked it with a padlock. The key to the padlock was, unfortunately, in the pocket of his tracksuit trousers.

When under stress, the headmaster developed a tic in his right eye. It started twitching now. He knew, he just knew, that the reason he was stuck in his own school with nothing to wear but a towel was due to that dog, and when he found it . . .

Mr Blocker searched feverishly through all the other lockers in the changing room for clothes, any sort of clothes – there had to be something he could wear. Aha! Hanging in one of the lockers was a green games skirt and a shirt. Not ideal, he admitted, but it would have to do.

Mr Bentley was waiting patiently in the corridor for Rachel and Eric to come back from tidying the darkroom, when he heard a shout.

'Hoi!' said a loud voice.

.He looked up and saw what he thought at first was a woman running towards him. As the figure got closer, however, he realized it was a man wearing a skirt.

'Hoi!' shouted Mr Blocker. 'You're wearing my tracksuit.' By now, he was running at full tilt.

Mr Bentley considered the matter. He could stay where he was, try to apologize to Mr Blocker and perhaps offer some sort of explanation. Two things, however, made him decide against that. The first was that, at the moment, Mr Blocker didn't look like a man who'd be very interested in explanations or apologies, and the second was that he had just started to get an itching sensation on the back of his neck.

Mr Bentley turned and ran. He ran down the corridor, turned a corner, ran down another corridor and then, hoping to throw off his pursuer, darted into a classroom. He had some idea of climbing to freedom through a window, but of course, all the windows were locked.

A moment later, Mr Blocker came thundering into the classroom after him.

'Right!' he shouted. 'I want to know what's going on here, and I want to know –'

He stopped, gulped and stared. There was nobody there – nobody at all. But his tracksuit was lying on the floor and, emerging from it, was a large black Labrador.

'Grrr . . .' said the Labrador.

It was too much for Mr Blocker. Earlier that morning he had followed a dog into the darkroom, only to find it contained two children, and now he had followed a man into a classroom, only to find it contained a dog. It was more than his brain could take.

'Aaaaa . . .' he said faintly. His eyes closed, and he collapsed gently to the floor.

Mrs Jessop was in the Assembly Hall with Police Sergeant Bingham. He had been invited to give a talk on road safety at the school, the next Monday, and sensibly wanted to check beforehand where he could set up his displays.

Mrs Jessop was just showing him where he could plug in his projector when Mr Blocker burst in.

'Where's he gone?' he shouted.

'Ah, John,' said Mrs Jessop, 'come and meet Sergeant Bingham.' She looked closely at Mr Blocker as he came over. 'Is that my hockey skirt you're wearing?' she asked.

Mr Blocker ignored the question. His eyes probed wildly at every corner of the room. 'Have you seen it?' he asked the policeman. 'It was a big black Labrador. It must have come through here.'

'It *is* my skirt, isn't it?' said Mrs Jessop. 'And that looks very like my games shirt as well.'

Mr Blocker was still talking to the policeman. 'It took my trousers, you see,' he said.

'The dog took your trousers?' Sergeant Bingham was wondering what on earth was going on.

'Are you quite sure?' asked Mrs Jessop.

'Of course I'm sure,' said Mr Blocker. He strode over to the equipment room and started rummaging through the lockers. 'I saw him wearing them. And he's around here somewhere . . . They both are.'

'Both of them?' said Sergeant Bingham.

'The other one's here as well,' Mr Blocker told him briskly. 'The one that beat me at chess.'

'Oh, I see!' said the policeman. He sounded friendly

and sympathetic now. 'Chess. Yes, I quite understand!'

He turned to Mrs Jessop and asked in a low voice, 'Do you know who this man is?'

'That's our headmaster,' said Mrs Jessop. 'He's been under a lot of strain recently,' she added. 'It's the National Curriculum.'

At the Grosvenor Hotel, Eric, Rachel and Mr Bentley sat over coffee and doughnuts at a table in the dining-room.

'Why didn't you tell us when we came over to the Priory?' asked Rachel.

'I couldn't be sure who you were,' said Mr Bentley. 'You might have been reporters or anything. That's why I came here and started following Eric. As soon as I saw him change into a dog outside the school, I knew he was one of us. I just thought I'd check his school file, make sure he wasn't in any trouble.'

'And you belong to an organization,' asked Eric, 'of people all over the world who turn into dogs?'

'That's right,' said Mr Bentley. 'There's not that many of us, but we like to keep in touch, for protection mostly. You probably know it's not easy being a dog. We had a vicar recently who was falsely accused of worrying sheep.'

'All those other people,' breathed Eric. He wasn't alone any more; there were others. It was as if a great weight had been lifted from his shoulders.

'If you want to help each other,' said Rachel, 'why do you keep it a secret?'

'Ask Eric,' said Mr Bentley. 'How many people has he told?'

'I don't want anyone to know,' said Eric. 'I don't want to be a freak show.'

'Exactly,' said Mr Bentley, passing him another doughnut. 'Look, I have to be getting back soon,' he added, 'but I wanted to give you this.'

He gave Eric a card with a phone number on it.

'If you're ever in real trouble, you ring that number. Someone from the organization should be able to help.'

He scratched the back of his neck. 'Right. Any other questions?'

'Well, there is one thing,' said Eric. 'Has anyone found out how to control it yet? I mean, the one thing I find really difficult about turning into a dog is that it can happen at the most embarrassing times.'

Mr Bentley smiled sympathetically. 'I know what you mean,' he said, 'but I think you'll find that comes with growing up.' He was still scratching his neck. 'When you get to my age, for instance, you'll find that you're much better at controlling when it happens and . . . Excuse me.'

Mr Bentley disappeared under the table. Rachel and Eric looked nervously around the dining-room for a moment before Eric lifted up the tablecloth and peered underneath.

'Would you like us to take you back to your room?' he asked.

'And bring your clothes?' added Rachel.

'Woof!' said the black Labrador.

It was announced in school the next Monday that the pressures and demands of his work had unfortunately made Mr Blocker ill, and that he would not be coming into school for the rest of that term. Instead, he would soon be leaving for a long holiday in a special rest-home by the sea.

As he listened to Mrs Jessop explaining how Mr Blocker had devoted nearly thirty years to teaching at the school, Eric felt a stab of guilt. Mr Blocker might not have been a very pleasant man, and he certainly hadn't been nice to Eric, but, even so, it hardly seemed fair.

'You don't want to worry about Blocker,' said Rachel cheerfully. 'We've got Mrs Jessop as headmistress now. It's brilliant!'

'I think I'll get him a card,' said Eric.

'You'll have to hurry,' Rachel told him. 'They're driving him down to Bournemouth this evening.'

Mr Blocker sat in the passenger seat of the car, a scarf round his neck and a rug wrapped round his knees. He was waiting for his wife and Mrs Jessop to finish locking up the house before they set off together for the rest-home.

Maybe everyone was right, he thought to himself. Maybe the strain had been too much and he just needed a holiday. After all, when you started thinking you'd seen men turn into dogs, you were obviously going slightly strange in the head. You had to be. He was going to get away from it all. Particularly, away from dogs; all dogs.

At that moment, to his horror, a small mongrel appeared at the car window with a greetings card in its mouth. It was Eric. Mr Blocker stared at him and then, with a trembling hand, reached out and took the card. The dog hopped down and disappeared.

'What's this?' said Mrs Blocker, when she saw it. 'A get-well card? Isn't that nice!'

'Who's it from?' asked Mrs Jessop as she climbed into the driving seat.

'What?' said Mr Blocker in a small voice.

'Who's it from?' Mrs Jessop repeated, slowly and carefully. Mr Blocker thought for a moment. 'Nobody,' he said firmly.

And in fact the card he held was not signed. There was nothing written inside to say who it was from. Not a word.

Just a small, firm pawprint.

Eric was spending the day at his gran's. Mr and Mrs Banks had gone to a wedding; Eric could have gone with them, but he had decided he would rather spend a nice quiet day over at his gran's house, with Rachel for company.

He liked staying at his gran's. She seemed to spend most of the day dozing in a chair, only stirring at mealtimes to organize some food. This meant Eric and Rachel could do pretty much what they wanted, which was how they liked it.

They started by sitting at the bottom of the garden, trying to decide what to do.

'We could walk down to the shops while we're thinking,' said Rachel.

'Mmmm,' said Eric, idly scratching the back of his neck.

'Then we could buy a Mars bar and eat it while we were thinking,' said Rachel.

'Mmmm.' Eric was still scratching.

'OK,' said Rachel. 'I tell you what. You turn into a dog, then we go into town, buy a Mars bar, then we think of something.'

'Woof,' said Eric.

*

They strolled down to the tobacconist's, and Eric waited outside while Rachel went in to get the sweets. Dogs aren't allowed in shops – not even dogs that can point to what they want, pass over the money with their teeth and check that they've got the right change – so Eric had to wait on the pavement while Rachel bought his Mars bar for him.

While he waited, a van drew up just in front of him. It had 'EL and BEE Decorators' written on the side and two men in overalls got out. One of them patted Eric on the head.

' 'Allo, doggie,' he said. 'Nice little doggie.'

The next thing Eric knew, and the whole thing happened almost before he could blink, the other man had thrown a sack over Eric's head, scooped him up and thrown him into the back of the van. As he landed with a thud on the van floor, Eric could already hear the engine starting up, the bang of the doors closing and then he could feel the van being driven off. The whole thing had taken no more than fifteen seconds.

When Rachel came out of the shop a few moments later and found Eric had gone, she was not as worried as you might have thought. Eric not being where you expected him to be was quite a normal occurrence. It was one of the things you had to accept when your best friend kept turning into a dog. Eric could have seen someone he knew, he might have needed to hide because he was changing back into a boy, or he might just have gone off chasing a cat.

The first thing Rachel did, very sensibly, was to have a good look round to see if Eric was hiding anywhere as a boy. She knew that if he had changed back, he would need some clothes. However, there wasn't any sign of him, as a boy or as a dog, and she eventually decided to go back to his gran's house, and wait for Eric there.

She still wasn't worried. She was sure he would turn up.

But if Rachel wasn't worried, Eric certainly was. Jolting about in the back of the van, kept in complete darkness by the sack, he was, quite understandably, thoroughly frightened. He wasn't the only dog in the van, though. He could feel warm bodies around him and he could hear odd whimpers and yelps, so it didn't take him long to work out what had happened.

He had been dognapped.

Dogs, particularly the pedigree breeds, can be worth a lot of money. Eric had read about people who stole dogs from the streets to sell them, though he had certainly never expected it to happen to a mongrel like himself. He wriggled around in the sack, trying to find some way to get himself free, but it was no good. It was securely tied at the top and, in the end, he settled down to wait.

He didn't have to wait long. It was about a quarter of an hour before the van halted, the doors were opened, and Eric felt himself being picked up and carried along. Then the sack was opened, he was tipped out on to a concrete floor and had a chance to take stock of where he was.

He was in a wire mesh enclosure on one side of what looked like an old farmyard. All around, in dozens of other pens, were dogs. All sorts of dogs. There were large and small, short and long, smooth-coated and rough, and all of them seemed to be barking as loudly as they could, while the two men Eric had last seen

outside the sweet shop unloaded yet more dogs from
the van. Finally, their work complete, they disappeared inside the farmhouse and Eric settled down
to think.

He wasn't so worried now. He knew, from listening
to the men talking while they worked, that all the
dogs were going to be left in their cages till nightfall at
least, and he could see that the catch on the front of
his cage was only a loop and a nail. As soon as he'd
turned back into a boy, he would have no difficulty
setting himself free. But all around him were dogs who
were not so lucky. They had been snatched from their
comfortable homes, with no idea why or what was
going to happen to them, and they yelped and howled
miserably.

Eric felt an itching start behind his right ear. He
was thinking, even while he changed into a boy, that
he would have to help these dogs in some way. But
first, he had to find something to wear. The last time
Eric had been caught like this in a farmyard, he had
found some clothes on an old scarecrow, and it was
with this idea in mind that he crept out of his pen,
towards one of the farm outhouses.

On his way, though, he found something even
better. On the front seat of the van were the painter's
overalls that one of the men had been wearing earlier.
They were too big, of course, but once Eric had rolled
up the legs and the sleeves, they didn't look as odd as
you might think.

His next problem was getting home. Apart from the
fact that he was somewhere out in the countryside, he
had no idea where he was, or which direction to go in.
He just knew that it would take him a very long time
to walk.

He sighed. All he had wanted was a quiet day, a chance to sit about and –

'Hoi! You!'

Eric spun round. It was the bigger of the two men, the one with the stomach hanging over his trousers and a spider's web tattoo on his elbow.

He looked suspiciously at Eric. 'What're you doing round here?'

'I was just admiring your dogs,' said Eric. 'They're really beautiful. Are they –'

'Is that your bike?' said the man. Luckily, he didn't seem to have noticed the overalls Eric was wearing.

'Bike?' Eric looked in the direction the man was pointing. There was a brand-new bicycle leaning against the gate, just by the farm entrance.

'Just get on it and get out of here,' said the man. 'All right? And don't let me see your face here again.'

'Right,' said Eric. He got on the bike and pedalled off.

'What was the trouble, Len?' The other of the two men had come out of the farmhouse. He was smaller, thinner, and kept fingering a large boil in his nose.

'Nothing, Brian,' said Len confidently. 'Just some kid snooping around. I got rid of him.'

'Good.' Brian looked over at the gate. 'Where's my bike gone?' he said.

'Bike?' Len sounded rather nervous.

'I left it there by the gate.' Brian pointed. 'You can't trust anyone these days, can you? I only nicked it yesterday.'

Back at Gran's house, Rachel had started to worry. Eric had been gone for nearly two hours and she didn't know what was the best thing to do. Wanting to keep Eric's secret, she hadn't told anyone that he'd gone, but as time went by, she began to wonder if she was right. If something *had* happened to Eric and he was really missing, then the sooner she told someone, the better. But how would she describe what had happened? And which Eric would she say was missing – Eric the boy, or Eric the dog?

She was still trying to decide when Gran called her from the house.

'Rachel? Your mother's on the telephone.'

Rachel went indoors and picked up the receiver.

'Hi, Mum.'

'It's not your mum,' said a voice. 'It's me.'

'Eric?' Rachel nearly dropped the phone in surprise. 'What are you doing? What happened? Where are you calling from?'

'It's a long story,' said Eric. 'But I'm all right. Look, has anyone noticed I've gone?'

'Not yet,' said Rachel.

'Good,' said Eric. 'I'll be back in about three-quarters of an hour, all right?'

'Right,' said Rachel, and before she could ask anything else, the pips went and she had to put down the phone.

'You and Eric ready for lunch yet?' asked Gran.

'Oh. Thank you,' said Rachel, then added, 'Could we have it in the garden?'

'Yes, of course,' said Gran. 'I'll bring it out on a tray.'

'No, no, don't worry,' said Rachel helpfully. 'I'll do it.'

Eric got back to his gran's house hot and tired. While

he changed back into his proper clothes, he told Rachel what had happened to him from the time she had left him outside the sweet shop.

He wasn't so much frightened by the day's events now, as angry. Angry not just at what had happened to him, but at the thought of all the dogs he had left behind at the farm. They had been taken from their homes and everyone they knew, without any idea where they were being taken or why. The noise they had made would have told anyone how miserable they were, but those men hadn't been bothered by it at all.

'They're planning to ship them out of the country tonight,' he told Rachel. 'So if we're going to help, it's got to be soon.'

'Help?' said Rachel. 'Us? If they're thieves, why don't we just tell the police?'

Even as she spoke, she realized it wasn't that simple. If Eric told the police about the dogs at the farm, they would want to know how he had found out, and that would not be easy to explain. It would be even harder explaining to his parents how he had got to a farm six miles away, when he was supposed to have spent the whole day with his gran.

'We can't do much on our own,' said Rachel doubtfully. 'Can we?'

'I know,' said Eric, who had been thinking it all out on the long cycle journey back from the farm. He reached into his pocket and pulled out a card with a phone number. 'But we've got this.'

'Mr Bentley!' breathed Rachel. 'Of course!'

Eric's mum called from the house. 'We're back, Eric. Time to go home!' She turned to Gran. 'I hope he hasn't been any trouble.'

'Not at all,' said Gran. 'You'd hardly know he'd been here.'

Eric spent the rest of the afternoon round at Rachel's house, and when he got home for supper that evening, Mrs Banks noticed that he seemed very thoughtful, not his usual cheery self at all.

'Anything wrong?' she asked.

Eric thought for a moment. 'I'm just a bit tired,' he said. 'Do you mind if I go to bed early?'

Mrs Banks didn't mind, but she was rather surprised. She was even more surprised when Eric was in his pyjamas by half past seven and climbing into bed.

'I hope you're not sickening for something,' she said and insisted on taking his temperature, which turned out to be normal.

She looked into his room a little later, but Eric seemed to be fast asleep in the darkened room, tucked under the bedclothes, so she didn't disturb him. As she came back downstairs, she saw the dog.

'I don't know how you keep getting in here,' she murmured, 'but you can go outside now.' She picked him up and dropped him outside the front door. 'I'm not having you wake up Eric, now he's asleep.'

It was nearly dark as Rachel crept out of the back door of her house and gently pulled it shut behind her.

'Eric?' she whispered. 'Are you there?'

'Woof,' said Eric quietly, appearing at her feet.

'Great.' Rachel buttoned up her coat. 'No problems getting out of the house?'

'Woof, woof,' said Eric.

Rachel picked up her bike and wheeled it down the path towards the road.

'I've put a basket on the handlebars,' she said. 'You can ride in that if you want.'

'Woof,' said Eric.

Len drove the van into the farmyard and parked it just outside the cages, before getting out and walking back to the farmhouse.

He pushed open the door and called inside, 'I got the petrol, Brian. Van's all ready.'

Brian appeared at the top of the stairs, a bottle of beer in his hand. 'Right,' he said. 'Time to load up.'

Pouring the last of the beer down his throat and tucking his shirt in his trousers, Brian followed Len out of the front door and round to the van. It was not a large enough van to carry so many dogs, but Len and Brian were not the sort of men to worry about whether the dogs were comfortable or not.

'Gone very quiet out here, hasn't it?' said Len.

Brian listened a moment. It had gone very quiet. The dogs, who had been howling and moaning most of the day, were silent now, and the only noise in the night was the thud of their own footsteps on the path.

Turning into the farmyard, the two men stopped. Sitting on his own in the middle of the yard, bathed in a great pool of moonlight, was a small dog.

'It's the one that got away this morning,' said Brian. 'That mongrel that got out of its cage.'

'Are you sure?' said Len nervously. There was something odd about the way the dog was looking at him. 'It's not a ghost, is it?'

'No, he's not a ghost,' said a voice.

Brian looked wildly round. 'Who's that?' he said. 'What d'you want?'

'I'll tell you what we want.' Rachel stepped into the

moonlight to stand beside Eric. 'We want to know enough about these dogs to return them to their owners. We want the collars and name tags you took from them, and we want to know exactly when and where you stole them.'

'Oh, that's all you want, is it?' Brian relaxed. The voice had startled him at first, but now he could see it was just coming from a girl. The two of them ought to be able to deal with a small dog and a girl. He gave a nod to Len and they both stepped forward.

They had barely started to move, however, when Len halted and gripped Brian's arm. From out of the shadows, on their right, stepped a large black Labrador. It gave a low, ominous growl and Brian froze. If the truth were known, he had always been a bit frightened of dogs, and there was something about this one that frightened him more than most. It was a solid, muscular-looking dog, but it was the way it stared at him with large, unblinking eyes, as if it knew exactly what it was doing, that really worried him.

'Is that your dog?' he asked Rachel, trying to keep the fear out of his voice. 'Because if it is, you'd better call him off before he gets hurt.'

'He's not my dog,' said Rachel calmly. 'Nor are any of the others.'

'Others?' Len glanced quickly around. From his left, an Alsatian had padded quietly into view. No, not one Alsatian, but two – and there was a St Bernard with them, and a beagle and a . . . Len stared around him in mounting panic. There were dogs everywhere. In a great semi-circle in front of them were dogs of every shape and size, who seemed to have appeared from nowhere out of the night.

The silence was the most frightening part of it for

the two men. Apart from that one growl from the Labrador, none of the dogs had made a sound. They just stood there in the moonlight, eyes staring, tongues hanging out, waiting.

It wasn't natural, Len thought to himself; ordinary dogs wouldn't behave like that. The wild thought flashed into his brain that he was in some sort of horror film and that these dogs had come for revenge for all the cruelties he had inflicted on their kind. Beside him, Len gave a little whimper of fear, and the two of them turned and fled.

If Len and Brian had stopped to think about it, they would have realized they had no chance of getting away. The dogs not only outnumbered them, they could see better in the dark, and they could run faster. But the men were too frightened to think at all, they just ran.

Len ran to the right. He was trying to get back into the house, but one of the Alsatians cut him off. He veered off to the side, trod on a rake he'd forgotten was there so that the handle came up and banged into his face, completely lost his sense of direction and ran straight into the side of the house before collapsing, quietly, into a flower-bed.

Brian ran to the left. On his way, he picked up a shovel and tried to swing it at the dogs following him, but a retriever grabbed it by the handle and tore it out of his hand. Wherever he ran, there seemed to be a dog waiting for him, trying to nip at his heels or running in front to cut him off. Panting heavily, he vaulted a wall in a desperate effort to get away, and landed in what had been, till very recently, a pig-pen. Covered in muck, he lifted himself up, to find a range of doggy faces looking at him from round the wall. In despair, he sat back down again in the ooze. He felt safer staying where he was.

'It's the oddest thing I've ever seen,' said the constable, when his sergeant arrived and asked what it was all about. 'We came out originally because there was a complaint about the noise – dogs barking in the middle of the night, you know – and we found all these stolen dogs.'

'How d'you know they've been stolen?' asked the sergeant.

'That's what's so odd,' said the constable, pointing to the dogs in the cages. 'They've all got labels on, saying when they were stolen, where from, what their names are . . .'

'Labels?' The sergeant sounded puzzled.

'That's right,' said the constable. 'And I think we've got the people who did the stealing.'

'You caught them?'

'Not exactly.' The constable grinned. 'They're locked up in the last dog cage. Not very keen on coming out, either. Say they feel safer in there.' He led the sergeant across the yard and pointed to two very bedraggled men in the end cage.

'My word,' said the sergeant, 'they look a bit of a mess. What happened?'

'They say it was dogs,' said the constable.

'Dogs?'

'That's right.' The constable frowned. 'They say a lot of dogs came out of the night, forced that one into the pig-pen, and then locked them both in here.' He paused. 'We found quite a few beer bottles in the house,' he added.

'We'd better get them back to the station,' said the

sergeant. He sniffed the air and pointed at Brian. 'I'm not having that one in my car.'

From their vantage point at the top of a nearby hill, Eric and Rachel watched it all. They had seen the flashing blue lights of the police cars as they arrived, they had heard the excited barking of the dogs as they were loaded into vans ready to be taken back to their owners and now, finally, they could see two tiny, bedraggled figures being led towards a police van. It was all very satisfactory.

If the police constable had been surprised by what he saw at the farm, he would have been even more surprised to see who was watching him from the top of the hill. Rachel and Eric-as-a-dog sat at the edge of a wood, and to either side of them were dogs. All of them were watching the events down in the valley with concentrated stares. Apart from an occasional twitchy nose or a quick scratch behind the ear, none of them moved. They just sat, and watched.

As the last police car drove away from the farm, there was a stirring among the dogs, a sense that their job was done, and that it was time to go home. Eric nudged Rachel's knee, and she stood up. Somebody ought to say something, she thought, and she had just realized that she was the only one with a voice.

'Look, I hope you don't mind,' she said, 'but could I just say something?'

Two dozen pairs of doggy eyes turned to stare at her.

'Woof,' said the beagle.

'It's just, well, I know Eric would like to say what I'm going to say, but he can't at the moment so I'd better say it for him.'

'Woof,' said Eric.

'We just want to say thank you,' said Rachel. 'I don't know who any of you are when you're not dogs, but I'm sure you're all very busy and we're very grateful for the way you came to help us. Particularly Mr Bentley, of course, who planned the whole thing and told us all what to do.' She glanced at the black Labrador, who was looking modestly down at his paws.

'I hope you can all get home all right. Does anyone need any help?' A chorus of soft 'Woof woofs,' went round the circle. 'No? Well, in that case, I think Eric and I had better be getting on. Thank you all again, and ... and I hope very much that we all meet again one day.'

The big St Bernard stepped out of the line and came over to Rachel. 'Woof,' he said, and held out a paw.

It wasn't a yes, Rachel realized, but a goodbye. She took the paw and shook it. 'Goodbye,' she said. 'Thank you again.'

The St Bernard turned to Eric. 'Woof!' he said, padded off into the woods and was gone.

Then all the other dogs came up, one at a time, to shake hands with Rachel, and to say goodbye to Eric (a lot of them did this by touching noses), before disappearing into the dark as mysteriously and as quietly as they had come.

The last of them was the black Labrador. 'Goodbye, Mr Bentley,' said Rachel, and she bent down and gave him a hug. 'We think you're wonderful.'

The Labrador gave Eric a wink, woofed softly, and was gone. Eric and Rachel watched him go. Even after the last rustle had died away and the night was filled only with silence, they sat there a little while longer, thinking.

Eventually, Rachel got up and the two of them walked back to where she had left her bicycle.

'You know, Eric?' she said, as she helped him up into the basket. 'You've got some brilliant friends.'

'Woof!' said Eric.

# WOOF!

## A TWIST IN THE TALE

by Andrew Norriss

# CONTENTS

Minding the Store                        249

Dad's Birthday                           262

School Trip                              274

The Haunting of Blocker      289

Mis-cast                               303

Badgers                               318

The Girl on the Horse        334

End of Term                           348

# MINDING THE STORE

Eric Banks was in the toy section on the third floor of the Co-op department store when he felt a tingling at the back of his neck. He knew at once what was going to happen.

He had come in to spend the last of his Christmas money and, after a lot of thought, had chosen an archery set. He had taken it over to the check-out, given it to the woman behind the desk, and was just reaching into his pocket for the money, when the itching feeling started on the back of his neck. It meant that some time in the next few seconds, he was going to turn into a dog again.

In case you've never heard of Eric Banks, or read any of the stories about him, I'd better explain that this had happened to him before – quite often. It had started when he was ten and, off and on, it had been taking place ever since.

If you're wondering why it happened and how, all I can tell you is that Eric had been wondering the same things. He had racked his brains over the last year and a half for an answer to both of those questions, but had never found one. All he knew was that it happened. It would begin with the tingling on the back of his neck and next thing there would be a pile of boy's clothes on the floor and a small, shaggy mongrel with large brown eyes and a short, wagging tail, sitting there. This might have looked for all the world like an ordinary dog, but it wasn't.

It was Eric.

Eric knew from experience that it was no good trying to stop the transformation once it had started. He had sometimes managed to turn into a dog when he particularly wanted to, but apart from that he had no control over it at all. It could happen at any time, anywhere and, once he'd changed, it might last for hours or just a few minutes. In the past year and a half, this habit had led to some very exciting adventures but it had also, as Eric would be quick to point out, put him in some highly embarrassing situations.

Like now.

The woman at the cash desk had taken the archery set, put it in a bag, rung up the price on the till and now held out her hand for the money. But the boy with the red hair and the freckles who had been there just a second before had disappeared. She looked right and left, but there was no sign of him. Then she looked over the top of the counter and gave a short scream.

'Everything all right, Miss Robinson?' Mr Norwood, the store manager, had heard her and was coming across.

'Yes, I think so,' said Miss Robinson, looking rather flustered. 'It's just that I was serving a boy, and I looked down and . . . and there was just this dog.'

'Dog?' said Nr Norwood, sharply. He didn't like dogs and he certainly didn't like them running around in his store. It wasn't allowed. 'What dog? Where?'

'Well, it . . .' Miss Robinson pointed to the floor in front of her desk, but Eric had sensed trouble and was already running off down one of the aisles. 'There he goes. Look! Over there!'

'All right, there's no need to shout,' said Mr Norwood. 'I'll deal with the dog.' He pointed to the pile of clothes Eric had left behind. 'Who do these belong to? And what are they doing scattered all over the floor?'

'I've no idea.' Miss Robinson was feeling worse all the time. 'They weren't there a moment ago, I'm sure.'

'Well, clear them away,' Mr Norwood told her angrily. 'Put them in the lost-property cupboard or something. I've warned you before about keeping the place tidy.' And he turned and walked off after Eric.

He didn't think it would take long to catch the dog. The aisle it had run into was a cul-de-sac, so all he had to do was follow the creature and grab it before it could escape. But to his astonishment, when he turned the corner, the aisle was empty. The shelves were lined with stuffed toys, boxes of games, dolls and even tricycles, but there was no sign of a dog.

There's something odd going on here, he thought as he walked away. Something very odd indeed.

Peering out from between a large teddy and a stuffed elephant, trying very hard to look like a stuffed dog himself, Eric sighed with relief when he saw Mr Norwood turn away. But he knew his troubles were not over yet. If only Rachel were still with him, he thought.

Rachel was the only other person who knew that

Eric sometimes turned into a dog. If she had been with him, she could have sorted things out, as she had done so often before. She would have gathered up his clothes, made some excuse to the store manager, got Eric outside and probably taken him back to her house where he'd be safe until he turned back into a boy.

But Rachel wasn't with him. She had got bored waiting for him to choose what he was going to buy and had gone off to look round the sports department. They had arranged to meet outside the main doors at a quarter past five.

The real problem, Eric thought, was his clothes. From his hiding place, he could see the store assistant gathering them up in a bag and then carrying them off to a storeroom at the far end of the toy department. He needed his clothes. Not while he was a dog, obviously, but when he turned back into a boy, he did not want to find that his clothes had been locked up for the night in a department store.

His first thought was to creep down to the main doors, find Rachel and ask her to come up and help. The snag was that, as a dog, he couldn't tell Rachel what he wanted her to do. They had a sort of code – one woof for yes, and two for no – but that wasn't much good for saying 'Please come up to the third floor and get my clothes out of the lost-property cupboard before the store closes.' Worse still, he could see from the clock on the wall that it was nearly half past five. Closing time was any minute now.

Eric made a quick decision. He would get the clothes himself. It shouldn't be too difficult, he thought, creeping cautiously out of his hiding place. The shop assistant had put them all in one bag and if he could pick it up in his teeth, he should be able to drag it off down the escalator without getting caught.

Cautiously, he followed Miss Robinson into the store-room. He was lucky. She didn't see or hear him and he was able to hide behind some boxes and watch where she put the bag.

Miss Robinson left the bag on a low shelf in the corner and went back out to the store. As soon as she had gone, Eric trotted over, pulled the bag off the shelf with his teeth and dragged it over to the door. That was when he realized it wasn't going to be as simple as he'd thought. The shop assistant had closed the door behind her and, even though he reached as high as he could with his paws, Eric found he just wasn't tall enough to turn the latch and open it.

He sat down. This problem was going to require some serious thinking.

Outside the main doors of the department store, Rachel was beginning to worry. It was gone half past five. The store was officially closed and there was still no sign of Eric.

When the lights in the store started going out and a man with a huge bunch of keys began locking and bolting the doors from the inside, she tapped urgently on the glass.

'Excuse me!' she shouted. 'You can't lock up yet.'

The man on the other side hesitated, then opened the door a fraction.

'What?' he asked.

'You can't lock up yet,' said Rachel. 'My friend is still inside.'

'There's no one left in here,' said the man. 'We check very carefully.'

'But he must be,' said Rachel. 'He said he'd meet me when he came out.'

The man shrugged. 'Perhaps he forgot.' And before Rachel could say anything else, he firmly closed the doors and bolted them.

Rachel knew Eric well enough to know he would not have forgotten when he said he would meet her. If he wasn't here, it was because something had happened to him, and she had a shrewd idea what it was. Eric must be stuck somewhere inside the department store as a dog, and it was up to her to help him.

But how? She was still trying to think of something when she heard two women, a little further along the pavement, admiring one of the window displays.

'Isn't he lovely?' one of the women was saying. 'Such a friendly looking dog. You'd almost think he was alive.'

The word 'dog' registered in Rachel's mind and, turning, she raced along to the window. Sure enough, sitting quietly amongst a display of fishing rods, raincoats and picnic hampers, was Eric.

She checked quickly that no one was watching before cupping her hands to the glass and calling, 'Eric! Eric, what happened?'

Eric looked gloomily up at her. How could he tell her about his clothes? Or about getting trapped in the store cupboard but eventually freeing himself by dragging a box over to the door so he could reach the handle and open it?

'They've just locked all the exits,' said Rachel. 'The staff are all going home – you're going to be stuck in there till tomorrow morning.' She looked at him anxiously. 'Will you be all right?

'Woof, woof,' said Eric.

Rachel thought quickly. If Eric didn't get home tonight – and she didn't see any way that he could – there was going to be trouble. Someone would ring the police. The police would want to know where he had last been seen and who with. They would come to Rachel and then . . . and then she had an idea.

'Hang on, Eric,' she shouted through the glass. 'Don't worry, I've got it. I'll go home, phone your mum and tell her you're staying with us tonight. You'll be able to get out in the morning and nobody'll know. Okay?'

'Woof, woof,' said Eric.

'It's the best we can do,' Rachel insisted. 'If you think of anything else, you can –' She stopped. A policeman was walking down the pavement towards her. 'I've got to run, Eric,' she hissed. 'See you tomorrow.'

Police Constable Briggs watched Rachel go and wondered what it was in the window that had attracted the young girl's attention. He stopped and looked. Maybe it was the dog; it certainly seemed remarkably life-like. In fact he could almost have sworn it blinked just then. But no . . . he must have imagined it.

At home that evening, Rachel waited till her mother was busy in the kitchen, cooking supper, before ringing Eric's parents.

'Hello, Mrs Banks, it's Rachel,' she said. 'I was wondering if it was all right for Eric to stay here tonight.'

To her relief, Mrs Banks said that would be fine. 'Would you like me to bring his pyjamas round?' she asked.

'No, no, it's all right,' said Rachel cheerfully. Eric's mother coming round was the last thing she wanted. 'Mum's got a spare pair we keep for visitors.'

'Well, thank your mother for me,' said Mrs Banks. 'Make sure Eric behaves himself and we'll see you tomorrow.' Then she rang off.

Rachel breathed a sigh of relief and went back into the kitchen. As she sat down to supper, she wondered how Eric was getting on in the department store.

As it happened, Eric got on just fine. At about seven o'clock that evening he changed back into a boy, and was able to ring Rachel on one of the phones in the electrical department on the second floor.

If you had to get locked inside a building, he told her, there were a lot worse places for it to happen than a large department store. If he wanted something to read, there were several thousand books in the book department. If he wanted music, there were whole shelves of cassettes that he could play on the stereo systems in the music department, and on the first floor, one huge counter had almost every computer game you'd ever heard of.

Eric began the evening, however, by getting himself some supper. Borrowing a basket from the gardening department, he carried it down to the food section on the ground floor and chose his supper from the shelves. He got a saucepan, frying pan, plate, knife and fork from China and Hardware, and then took the whole lot along to the kitchen department, where he set about frying his sausages on one of the cookers – a model used for demonstrations.

After supper, he carefully washed up all his pots and plates in the staff sink, left some money to pay for the food he'd taken, and then headed back upstairs to enjoy himself.

He started in the toy department, whizzing up and down the aisles in a battery-operated car that looked like a mini Rolls-Royce. Next, he tried out the fitness machine in the sports department and then, as a rest from that, settled down with an enormous pile of videos in front of a thirty-six-inch television screen.

With all this excitement, you'll understand why it was very late – well past midnight – when Eric finally decided it was time for bed. He picked up some pyjamas from Childrenswear, got himself a few books, a glass of milk and some biscuits and took the lift up to the top floor, where he settled down in a huge four-poster in the furniture department.

The result of being late to bed, though, was that Eric overslept the next morning. He had been sensible enough to borrow an alarm clock, but he must have been so deeply asleep that he didn't hear it go off. Instead, the first thing he heard was a man's voice shouting, 'Mr Norwood! You'd better come quickly!'

For a moment, Eric couldn't remember where he was. Then it all came back to him. He was in a department store, in borrowed pyjamas and big trouble. He tried to open his mouth to say, 'It's all right, I can explain everything,' but all that came out was 'Woof.'

'What is it?' Mr Norwood was walking over to see what the fuss was about.

'It's a dog,' said the man.

'A dog?' Mr Norwood quickened his pace. 'What's it doing?'

The sales assistant pointed to where Eric was sitting up in bed. 'It's wearing some of our pyjamas,' he said. 'I think it's been sleeping here.'

Mr Norwood looked at Eric. 'It's the same one as yesterday,' he muttered to himself. He looked at the empty glass of milk and the pile of comic annuals on the floor and added, 'There's something funny going on here.'

Eric looked at Mr Norwood and decided it was time to leave. Struggling free of the pyjamas, he jumped off the bed and headed for the stairs.

'Stop that dog!' shouted Mr Norwood. 'I want him caught. You hear me? I want that dog caught!'

At first, Eric was not particularly worried. As he raced off down the stairs, he consoled himself with the thought that he had been chased before and he knew that, as a dog, he was small, fast and very difficult to catch.

But Nr Norwood was no fool. The first thing he had done was order that all the outside doors be closed, so that Eric couldn't get out of the building. The people chasing him might not have been as fast as Eric, but there were a lot of them, and as time went on, Eric began to realize that he was going to get tired before they did.

He fought off the inevitable for a while by driving around in the car from the toy department, but when the battery gave out he had to abandon that. He tried hiding, but whenever he did, somebody always seemed to find him. Somehow, he had to escape. He had to get out of the building.

*

When Mr Banks pushed his way through the service doors of the Co-op that morning to deliver the post, he found the store in total uproar. Excited staff were running in all directions shouting things like, 'There he goes!' and, 'I'll stay here and block off the stairs.'

As he carried his two sacks of mail across the ground floor to the manager's office, Mr Banks wondered what could possibly be going on. He left the two sacks by the office door as usual, picked up the empty ones from yesterday and was about to leave when he saw a small dog racing down the aisles towards him. It skidded to a halt, darted behind a display of men's shirts and hid there, panting.

Mr Banks bent down in surprise. 'You're Rachel's dog, aren't you?' he asked.

'Woof,' said Eric, rather breathlessly.

'Are you what all this fuss is about?' asked Mr Banks.

'Woof,' said Eric.

Mr Banks put one of his empty sacks on the floor. 'Here,' he said. 'You'd better climb inside. I'll take you home.'

Gratefully, Eric crawled into the sack and Mr Banks swung him gently round on to his shoulder. He was just in time.

'Have you seen a dog?' Mr Norwood was leading a posse of staff along the aisle towards them.

'Dog?' asked Mr Banks.

'Scruffy, long hair, about this big.' Mr Norwood held out his hands. 'Possibly driving a car,' he added.

'Ah,' said Mr Banks.

'Never mind.' Mr Norwood was already moving on. 'Make sure the door's firmly closed when you leave, won't you?'

'I will,' said Mr Banks. 'I certainly will.'

Mr Banks stopped his post van outside Rachel's house on his way back to the sorting office. He let Eric out of the passenger seat and walked him up to the front door.

'I've brought your dog back,' he told Rachel. 'It is yours, isn't it?'

'Goodness!' Rachel tried not to look as astonished as she felt. 'Yes, it is. Thank you.'

'You'll never believe where I found him this time,' said Mr Banks. 'The Co-op department store. I think he must have been there all night. He gets into some scrapes, that dog, doesn't he?'

Rachel smiled weakly. 'Yes. He certainly does, doesn't he! Thank you for bringing him home.'

'No trouble.' Mr Banks turned to go. 'Eric all right, is he?'

For a moment Rachel didn't know what he meant.

'Our Eric,' said Mr Banks. 'He was staying here last night, wasn't he?'

'Oh, yes!' Rachel tried to look reassuring. 'Yes, he's fine.' She thought quickly. 'I would call him down, but he's not dressed yet.'

'That sounds like Eric.' Mr Banks grinned. 'Well, I'd better get back. Morning, Mrs Hobbs!'

Rachel's heart sank. Her mother had appeared behind her.

'Morning, Mr Banks,' she said. 'Got time for a coffee?'

But Mr Banks was already walking back to his van. 'Better not,' he called. 'Still on duty. Thanks for looking after Eric, though. I hope he behaved himself.'

Mrs Hobbs was rather puzzled. 'Looking after who?' she asked Rachel.

Rachel didn't hesitate. 'Looking after Eric.' She pointed down at the dog. 'I told him we'd look after Eric.'

'Oh, I see.' Mrs Hobbs waved cheerily at Mr Banks as he climbed into his van. 'He's no trouble at all,' she called. 'Always happy to have him.'

Rachel led Eric upstairs to her bedroom. She had a supply of Bonio dog biscuits there, and she thought he might need some breakfast while they worked out how to get his clothes back.

'You know, Eric,' she said, as she watched him scrunching crumbs all over the carpet, 'you lead a very complicated life.'

'Woof!' said Eric.

# DAD'S BIRTHDAY

It was Mr Banks's birthday soon and Eric had decided that this year he wanted to get him something really special. 'After all,' he told Rachel, 'if Dad hadn't rescued me from that department store, I would have been in real trouble. I want to say thank you.'

'You can't thank him,' said Rachel. 'He doesn't even know you were there. He thinks he rescued a dog.'

'But that's why I want to get him something special for his birthday,' Eric explained. 'Something he really wants.'

'Like what?' asked Rachel.

'That's the trouble.' Eric sighed. 'I don't know.'

His mother had suggested getting a pair of socks, but that didn't seem very exciting to Eric. He had spent days searching the shops before eventually buying one of those jokes that you clip behind your ears to make it look as if you've got a knife stuck through your head. It was a good present, Eric thought, but it still wasn't . . . well, special enough.

'You have to listen,' Rachel told him. 'My mum says if you want to know what someone wants for their birthday, you have to listen to them round the house.

Then, when you hear them say something like "I wish I had a decent book on train-spotting", that's what you get them.'

Eric listened. In the course of the next three days, he heard his dad say he wanted a bit of peace and quiet, to be sixteen again, and for someone to buy him a new car. None of which was very helpful.

But then on Tuesday, he struck gold. Mr Banks was sitting reading the paper over a cup of tea after his lunch when he said, 'I see Dave Barry's doing a gig at the Plaza again.'

'You ought to give him a call,' Mrs Banks told him cheerily. 'Ask if he needs you back in the band.'

Eric looked up. 'Dave Barry's band?' he said. 'Dave Barry the rock star?'

Mr Banks smiled.

'Your father was the one got him started,' said Mrs Banks. 'Helped him pay for his first guitar.'

Eric stared at the two of them, wondering if he was having his leg pulled.

'It was a long time ago,' said Mr Banks. 'And we wouldn't have been much of a band if the lead guitarist didn't have a guitar.'

Eric was more astonished than he could say. He looked at his father, with his elbows on the table, the sleeves of his postman's shirt rolled up and his quiet, friendly face. He didn't look as if he'd ever been in a rock band.

'You were in Dave Barry's rock band?' he asked again, just to make sure.

'No,' said Mr Banks. 'He was in mine. Charlie and the Barnstormers, we were. I've got a picture some-where, I'll show you.'

Unfortunately, he couldn't find it. He searched for over an hour before Mrs Banks pointed out that he was going to be late back for work, and he searched again that evening when he got home. But he still couldn't find it.

'It was probably thrown out years ago,' said Mrs Banks. 'It was only an old photo. I don't know why you're so bothered.'

But Mr Banks *was* bothered. 'It's not just the picture,' he said. 'Dave signed it for me especially.'

And that's what gave Eric the idea.

'If I go round to Dave Barry,' he told Rachel excitedly, 'and tell him what's happened, I can ask him to sign another picture for me, and then I'll give it to Dad.'

Rachel looked doubtful.

'I'll ask him to write, "Thank you, Charles Banks, I owe it all to you", or something like that,' Eric went on. 'I think he'd like it.'

'It's a nice idea,' said Rachel. 'I just don't think you'll get anywhere near Dave Barry.'

'Why not?' asked Eric. 'It says in the paper which hotel he's staying at.'

'Dave Barry's a rock star,' explained Rachel. 'You can't just walk up to him and start chatting. That's what everyone's trying to do. Pop stars hire men to keep people like you away. You'd never get near him.' She thought for a moment. 'I suppose if you wrote him a letter . . .'

'There's no time for that,' said Eric. 'It's Dad's birthday in four days.'

Rachel thought. 'I suppose it might be possible', she said eventually, 'to sort of . . . attract his attention.'

*

Dave Barry's room at the hotel was, as Rachel had predicted, guarded by a large man with a broken nose and muscles on his chest so big that his arms couldn't hang straight by his sides, but stuck out at a slight angle. His name was Lol, and in ten years nobody had ever got past him to see Dave Barry without his permission. Various fans had tried all sorts of tricks – dressing up as hotel staff or pretending to faint just outside the door – but Lol was not as stupid as he looked, and they were all quietly, but firmly, turned away.

Lol was sitting on a chair outside the hotel room when the patter of feet warned him that someone was coming down the corridor. He looked up, but relaxed when he saw it was only a dog. It was a small mongrel, with an oddly intelligent, purposeful air, but obviously nothing to worry about.

He was wondering, idly, why a dog should be wandering on its own in a hotel corridor, when it stopped in front of him and he saw it was carrying a note in its mouth.

Lol thought for a moment, then opened the door behind him and called, 'Message for you, Dave.'

Dave Barry appeared in the doorway, drying his hair with a towel. 'Who from?' he asked.

'I dunno,' said Lol. 'This dog brought it.'

'Dog?' Dave Barry looked at Eric and then at the message. 'What does it say?'

Lol took the note and read it aloud. 'Dear Mr Barry, I'm sorry to trouble you, but could you sign this photo for me. Thank you very much.'

'What photo?' asked Dave, but before Lol could reply, the dog at their feet had gone trotting off round the corner, reappearing almost immediately with a large brown envelope in its mouth. It dropped the envelope on the ground in front of them and sat down, waiting expectantly.

Lol opened the envelope and pulled out a photo of Dave Barry cut from a newspaper, with a second note attached to it by a paper clip.

'This is the photo,' he read. 'Please could you write "To Charles Banks, the man who helped me get it all started", and then sign it. Thank you very much.'

Dave Barry took the note. 'Charles Banks . . .' he murmured, thoughtfully.

'You want me to get rid of this dog?' asked Lol.

'No,' said David Barry. 'I want you to get me a pen.'

'Pen.' Lol patted his pockets hopefully. 'Right.'

He went into the hotel room, got a biro from one of the cases inside and came back out to the corridor, to find David Barry already at work scrawling something in a large bold script over the newspaper cutting.

'You're not quick enough, Lol,' he said cheerfully. 'The dog beat you to it.'

'The dog had a pen?' asked Lol. 'Where'd he get it from?'

'No idea,' said Dave. He finished writing, put the photo back in its envelope, bent down and gave it to the dog.

'There you are. All right now?'

'Woof,' said the dog. And taking the envelope carefully in its mouth, it carried it back down the corridor.

Round the corner, Rachel waited impatiently. 'Did he do it?' she asked as Eric appeared with the brown envelope in his mouth.

'Woof!' said Eric, dropping it into her lap.

'Brilliant, Eric. Just brilliant!' Rachel peered inside the envelope. 'What happened to the biro?'

Eric looked a bit sheepish.

'Don't tell me you left it behind.'

'Woof,' said Eric.

'That was a fourteen-colour biro!' Rachel looked down at him accusingly. 'Where am I going to get another –' She stopped. A hand was holding her fourteen-colour biro just in front of her. She looked up. It was Dave Barry.

'Is this your dog?' he asked.

'Sort of,' Rachel agreed.

'And you're the one wanted me to sign the photo?'

'Sort of,' said Rachel again.

'Perhaps you and I should have a little talk,' he said, and Rachel and Eric-the-dog followed him as he led the way back to his room.

Dave Barry's hotel room was large. It was several rooms really – a huge sitting room, two bedrooms, two bathrooms and a balcony looking out over the park.

'So,' said Dave Barry, 'you know Charlie Banks, do you?'

'Yes,' said Rachel. 'He's Eric's . . . he's my friend's father. You remember him, do you?'

'Remember Charlie Banks?' Dave smiled. 'I should say. He was the one got me started in all this.' He sat down opposite Rachel and Eric. 'So what's all this about?'

Rachel told him most of the story. How Mr Banks had been upset at losing the photograph and how Eric had wanted to get a replacement in time for his birthday.

'And you thought the dog might get past Lol here, is that it?' Dave asked.

'Yes. I hope you don't mind,' Rachel added.

'No.' Dave looked down at Eric. 'It's just I didn't know dogs were that clever.'

'Well, most of them aren't,' Rachel admitted. 'Eric is . . . exceptional.'

'I can see that.' Dave Barry was still looking at Eric.

'He's a great fan of yours, Mr Barry,' said Rachel. 'I'll show you.' She turned to Eric and pointed to a pile of compact discs on the floor over by the wall. 'Why don't you choose a record, Eric. Something Mr Barry might like to hear.'

Eric went over to the pile of discs, nosed around for a moment, and came back with one of them.

'He's chosen my new record!' said Dave Barry, in disbelief.

'Like I said,' Rachel smiled. 'You're one of his favourite singers.'

'I've never seen anything like it.' Dave Barry shook his head. 'Would it be all right if you asked him to do it again?'

'I think so,' said Rachel. 'You don't mind, do you, Eric?'

'Woof, woof,' said Eric.

'I tell you what,' said Rachel, picking up a pile of discs by different singers and spreading them out over the sofa so that Eric could read all the titles, 'we'll ask him to pick out the singer he thinks has the biggest talent, the best voice and the most charisma.'

Eric trotted over to the sofa, looked at all the covers for a moment, picked one up and brought it over to Dave.

'"Dave Barry's Golden Hits"!' A smile spread over the singer's face. 'I don't believe this dog!' He was grinning from ear to ear. 'I just don't *believe* this dog! Again. Ask him to do it again!'

'All right.' Rachel looked at her watch. 'Once more. But then we have to get home for lunch.'

An hour later, when Eric had demonstrated his ability to read cards, do mental arithmetic, tell the time and drink Coca-Cola from a can (not easy when you've got paws) – Dave Barry reluctantly allowed them to leave.

'What a dog,' he kept saying. 'What an amazing dog!'

At the door, he stopped. 'Look, I've got an idea,' he said. 'I don't want to interfere, but I've got hundreds of photos back at the office. Why don't I find one of Charlie and the Barnstormers, get it framed and bring it over to Eric's dad on his birthday?'

'That'd be wonderful,' Rachel smiled.

'Woof!' said Eric.

'When's his birthday?'

Rachel thought. 'I think it's Saturday, isn't it, Eric?'

'Woof,' said Eric.

'Right.' Dave showed them out to the corridor. 'See you on Saturday.'

As they walked back to the lift, they could still hear him talking to Lol. 'I love that dog. I just *love* that dog!'

Mr Banks had to go to work on his birthday, so he didn't get to open his presents until tea-time. He came in from his post round to find Mrs Banks had baked an enormous cake with thirty-seven candles, and while she went out to make the tea, he sat down and started opening his cards and parcels.

Eric gave him the joke knife-through-the-head and Mr Banks said it was just what he'd always wanted (and wore it for the rest of the day). Emily, Eric's sister, gave him an egg cosy she'd made that could keep four boiled eggs warm at the same time. Mrs Banks gave him six pairs of socks, but said she had another present that she'd give him upstairs later on. Then Rachel arrived with a book about Nottingham Forest football club which Mr Banks said he'd been trying to get for years.

Rachel quietly asked Eric if Dave Barry's present had arrived.

'Not yet,' Eric told her.

'He wouldn't have forgotten, would he?' she asked anxiously. 'I mean, he wouldn't say he'd do it and then forget, would he?'

'I don't think so.' Eric gave her a nudge and pointed to the window. 'Look!'

Rachel gasped. In the little street outside, an enormous Rolls-Royce had stopped outside the front gate. Lol, in a chauffeur's uniform, opened one of the back doors and Dave Barry, carrying at least half a dozen parcels and a huge bunch of flowers, got out and rang the door bell.

'Why do people always call in the middle of tea,' said Mrs Banks, laying out the cups. 'Whoever it is, Charles, tell them we're busy.'

Mr Banks went out to the hall and opened the door.

'Hi, Charlie.' Dave Barry handed over one of the parcels. 'Here. Happy birthday.'

Mr Banks's jaw moved up and down as if he was trying to say something but no sound came out.

'Who is it, Charles?' called Mrs Banks from the sitting room.

'It's . . . it's . . .' Mr Banks was still having trouble getting out the words.

'I think Dad would like to invite you in for a cup of tea, Mr Barry,' said Eric.

Dave Barry said that would be very kind, though he only had a few minutes to spare. So he came in for some cake and tea, and then he stayed a bit longer while Mr Banks opened his present. It was a picture of Charlie and the Barnstormers, beautifully framed, and in the corner it said, 'To my good friend Charlie, who helped me get it all started. Best wishes, Dave Barry.'

He stayed a bit longer after that, because he had presents for everyone else as well. The flowers were for Mrs Banks, and there were tapes for the children, and there was a bottle of champagne, which Mr Banks said they ought to drink right away, so Dave Barry stayed while they did that as well.

Then Eric asked him if he could remember any of the songs the Barnstormers had sung, so he and Mr Banks sang some of them, and then they had some sandwiches and sang a few more, and Dave Barry taught Eric and Rachel how to sing the 'doo wah, doo wahs' in the background.

In fact it was quite late when he finally left, and I don't think he'd have gone even then if Lol hadn't warned him he was going to be late for the concert he was giving that evening. So he said goodbye to everyone, made them all promise to come and see him in a month's time when he was playing at Leicester, told them it had been the nicest day he'd had for a long time, and then Rachel and Eric walked him back out to his car.

'Thanks again, Mr Barry,' said Eric. 'Thanks for everything.'

'Wasn't a bad afternoon, was it?' Dave grinned. 'Though I must admit I was hoping . . .' He hesitated.

'Yes?' said Rachel.

'Well, I was rather hoping to see that dog again.'

'I'm afraid he comes and goes,' said Eric.

'Yes.' Dave looked as if he was about to climb into the car, but then changed his mind. 'Look, you won't mind if I ask something, will you?'

'Anything, please,' said Eric.

'It's just . . . you don't have time for a family in my work. You're always travelling, moving around, never in the same place more than a few days. It's exciting and it makes a lot of money, but it'd be nice if there was someone to come back to and . . . well, I was wondering . . .'

It was Rachel who realized first what he was trying to say. 'You want to adopt the dog,' she said.

Dave Barry looked at her. 'Yes, I do.'

'I'm afraid he's not really mine,' Rachel explained. 'He's more Eric's, really.'

'Ah,' Dave turned to Eric. 'I'd look after him, you know. He'd have everything money could buy, I promise you.'

'It's very kind of you, Mr Barry,' said Eric. 'Very kind indeed, but I think this is sort of where Eric belongs.'

'Yes.' Dave Barry gave a sigh. 'I thought you'd say that. But you'll let me know if you change your mind?'

'We certainly will,' Eric promised.

Dave Barry climbed into the passenger seat of his car and looked back for a moment at Eric's house. It seemed very small and ordinary, with Mr and Mrs Banks standing in the doorway with Emily, trying to get her to wave goodbye.

'Belongs here, does he?' he said. 'Well, I think he's a very lucky dog.'

And he gave a nod to Lol, and they drove away.

# SCHOOL TRIP

Turning into a dog when you weren't expecting it could, as Eric had discovered, lead to difficult and embarrassing situations. But the worst time for it to happen, he decided, was while he was at school. It wasn't just the problem of finding somewhere to hide his clothes, or explaining where he'd been when he was late for a lesson – it was Mr Blocker.

Mr Blocker was the headmaster. He was not a bad man, but he did not like animals, he did not like dogs, and he particularly did not like the small scruffy mongrel which kept appearing in his school, causing nothing but trouble and chaos. Eric knew this and tried hard to keep out of the headmaster's way, but it wasn't always possible. Like the time he got caught in Mr Blocker's Scripture lesson.

It all started in the school library towards the end of break. One minute Eric was sitting there, quietly copying out some spellings, and the next he found himself on the floor, surrounded by his clothes and with a sharp pain in his head that turned out to be a pencil stuck up his nose. He shook out the pencil, dragged his clothes and shoes behind one of the book shelves and was on the way to find Rachel when he met Mr Blocker.

To be honest, Eric was rather unlucky. He saw Mr Blocker coming down the corridor and darted into a classroom to hide. Unfortunately, it turned out to be the very classroom the headmaster wanted to use. He came in and sat down at the desk with a book.

Eric couldn't escape, not without being seen anyway, so he decided, rather cleverly he thought, to hide himself under an upturned waste-paper bin and wait for Mr Blocker to go away. What Eric didn't know was that the headmaster had no intention of going anywhere; he was getting ready to take the Class Five Scripture lesson.

When Class Five started filing into the room and sitting down at their desks, Eric realized he was in a very tricky situation. If he came out of his hiding place, Mr Blocker would certainly see him; on the other hand, staying where he was could be even more dangerous. Supposing, some time in the next hour, he changed back into a boy? Suddenly appearing from under a waste-paper bin with no clothes on during the headmaster's Scripture lesson was not a situation in which Eric wanted to find himself.

He decided to make a run for it, or more precisely, a crawl. Peering out underneath the basket, he could just see Mr Blocker's feet, and whenever he noticed the headmaster was facing away from him, he edged himself slowly towards the door, like a snail carrying his shell, stopping whenever Mr Blocker turned round. It was a bit like a game of grandmother's footsteps and he nearly got away with it.

Mr Blocker was talking to the class about miracles when a boy called Simon Burgess put up his hand.

'Would a miracle still happen today, sir?' he asked. 'I mean, could it happen here, in this room?'

Mr Blocker said he thought God had better things to do than produce miracles for a class like Form Five.

'I only asked, sir,' Simon explained, 'because I thought that might be why the waste-paper bin was moving like that.' And he pointed at the bin, edging its way towards the door.

The headmaster stared at it. You have to realize that, to him, the upturned bin seemed to be moving entirely on its own; there was, after all, nobody else anywhere near it. The way it floated over the ground towards the door was rather sinister and frightening. The only explanations he could think of were that either the bin had been taken over by a ghost, or young Burgess was right and it was a miracle.

'Nobody move,' he said, trying to control the quaver in his voice. 'It could be dangerous.'

Keeping a safe distance, he followed the waste-paper bin out into the corridor, where he met Mrs Jessop, the games mistress and his deputy.

'It moves on its own,' he told her, pointing to the bin, and added in a low voice, 'You don't think it's a miracle, do you?'

'No,' said Mrs Jessop. 'I think it's a dog. You can just see its paws poking out under the bottom.' And she lifted up the bin to reveal Eric, blinking in the light, his tail wagging apologetically.

'It's that dog again!' Mr Blocker shouted. 'The one that caused all the trouble last term.'

He would have been angry enough just seeing Eric, but the added feeling that he had been made to look a fool in front of his class sent him into a fury. Snatching a hockey stick from Mrs Jessop's hand, he brought it cracking down on the floor where Eric had been sitting.

Eric, I'm happy to say, was already twenty yards down the corridor and running like the wind.

'Mrs Jessop told me she thought you should go into kennels for the next few weeks,' Rachel told Eric as they walked home after school that day. 'She thinks it's the only way you'll be safe from Mr Blocker.'

'She's probably right,' Eric sighed. 'But it's not that simple, is it?'

He was thinking particularly of what would happen that Friday. Avoiding Mr Blocker on an ordinary school day ought to be possible, as long as he was careful, but Friday was the school outing to the Nottingham Caves, and Mrs Jessop had already told them that Mr Blocker would be in charge.

'He'll be with us all day, Rachel,' Eric complained. 'If I turn into a dog then, I'm done for.'

Rachel thought. 'You'll have to get banned,' she said eventually. 'You'll have to get Blocker to tell you you can't come on the trip.'

'How do I do that?' asked Eric.

'It shouldn't be too difficult,' Rachel told him. 'Next time he shouts, "Who is responsible for this outrage?" you just put your hand up and say it was you.'

'Right,' said Eric. It would mean trouble, he knew, but it was better than being nearly killed by a hockey stick.

Next morning, when Mr Blocker demanded in assembly that the culprit who had wantonly mangled his bicycle the previous evening own up at once, Eric politely put up his hand and confessed. Mr Blocker was somewhat surprised, partly because people didn't usually own up when he asked them to, and partly because he didn't understand how Eric, who was not a large boy, could have bent a bicycle frame with his bare hands. Nevertheless, he gave Eric a stern lecture and told him that, amongst other punishments, he would not be allowed on a school outing for the next year.

He was even more surprised when Mrs Jessop told him later the same day in the staff room that the damage had really been caused by some council workmen felling a tree. They had rung up to say they were very sorry, a branch had accidentally fallen on the bicycle, and they would of course pay for the repairs.

Mr Blocker was puzzled. 'Why would Eric Banks own up to something he hadn't done?' he asked Mrs Jessop.

'Maybe he was worried about Friday,' said Mrs Jessop. 'Perhaps he thought you were going to cancel the school trip if nobody owned up – and he decided to sacrifice himself for the sake of the others.'

'Would a boy do that?' Mr Blocker sounded dubious.

'Eric might,' said Mrs Jessop.

So instead of getting banned, Eric got called to Mr Blocker's study, where Mr Blocker apologized for shouting at him.

'He gave me a toffee,' Eric told Rachel afterwards, 'told me I was the nicest boy he'd ever met, and hoped I'd have a good time at the caves tomorrow.'

'You'll have to try something else,' Rachel said. 'Do something *really* awful.'

Eric tried. His next plan was to write 'Blocker is a wally' in red paint on one of the corridor walls, at a time when the headmaster would catch him doing it.

Unfortunately, Mr Blocker was late. Eric wrote up the message as slowly as he could, but the headmaster still hadn't appeared before he'd finished. Since the whole point was to be caught actually writing it, Eric decided to wash it off and start again. It was while he was washing it off that Mr Blocker appeared.

'Good grief!' he said, gazing in horror at the wall. 'What exactly is going on here, Banks?'

'Ah,' said Eric. 'Well –'

'No, no,' said Mr Blocker. 'There's no need to explain. I can see perfectly well what has happened.'

'Oh, good,' said Eric.

'You came along,' boomed the headmaster, 'you saw someone had written something rude about me on the walls here and you nobly decided to wash it off before anyone got into trouble. Good lad.' He gave him a pat on the shoulder. 'Keep at it.' Then he gave Eric another toffee and marched off down the corridor towards his study.

'Never mind,' said Rachel, when he told her what had happened. 'Don't forget, you may not turn into a dog tomorrow at all.'

'I suppose not,' said Eric, but he was not convinced.

Eric has never really known when he'll turn into a dog, but he has noticed that two things make it more likely. One is getting over-excited about something, and the second is getting too hot. Rachel has always said he'll have real problems if they're right about the greenhouse effect.

It was very hot in the coach taking the school trip to Nottingham and Eric, who had taken the precaution of sitting by Rachel in a back seat, turned into a dog before they had even arrived. He tried to stay hidden under the seat while everyone else got off, but he had forgotten that Mr Blocker always checked the coach for litter after every journey. When he found Eric he went, quite literally, berserk. The veins in his neck bulged and throbbed, his face turned red and mottled, and his ears for some reason went white.

He lunged at Eric and very nearly caught him by the tail before he could scuttle off the coach. He chased him twice round the car park, trying to throw a jacket over him to trap him, and he chased him a full three-quarters of a mile down a path to the canal.

When he came to the water, Eric, desperate to escape, jumped on board a sight-seeing barge that was casting off. Mr Blocker was several seconds behind but, driven by a manic energy, leapt a gap of at least two metres to land in the bow of the barge.

'Right,' said Mr Blocker, looking round. 'Where is it?'

'Sit down in the front there!' called the man steering the barge from the stern.

'I am looking for a dog,' said Mr Blocker firmly. 'He jumped on to this boat and I'm not leaving till I find him.'

'For goodness sake, sit down!' shouted the bargee.

'I will not sit down!' Mr Blocker shouted back. 'I will not sit down until the dog on this boat has been handed over to me so that I –'

Mr Blocker never said what exactly he was going to do to the dog when he got it, because at that moment a low bridge hit him smartly on the back of the head and knocked him straight into the water.

*

While Mr Blocker was being hauled out of the canal, Eric was able to creep back and join Rachel. He knew he had no more than a temporary respite. Once Mr Blocker had been bandaged up and dried off, he would be back on the warpath, angrier and more dangerous than ever. The more Eric thought about it, the more convinced he became there was only one way to keep himself safe until he turned back into a boy, and that was to lose the headmaster in the caves.

In case you've never heard of them, the Nottingham Caves run for miles under almost the whole city. Dug out over the last few thousand years, they have been used as part of the castle defences, as storage space, and as air-raid shelters in the Second World War. The important thing from Eric's point of view, though, was that they were a maze in which it was very easy to lose all sense of direction.

Before she took the children down into the caves for a tour, Mrs Jessop gave them all a stern warning to stick to the main path and the signposts. 'If you start wandering round the other caves,' she warned, 'you could find yourself lost in no time, so be careful.'

That was what had given Eric his idea. If Mr Blocker could be lured off the main track into the uncharted section of the caves, Eric would be safe. Even a few hours would probably be enough. By then, hopefully, he would have turned back into a boy and there would be nothing to worry about.

Leading Mr Blocker into the caves, that was the answer!

When Mr Blocker emerged from the Red Cross station, his head swathed in bandages and his clothes still somewhat damp, his one aim, as Eric had suspected, was to settle accounts with 'that dog'. Maybe he should use some of the older children as a search party, he thought, as he walked through the caves' entrance to rejoin Mrs Jessop and the others. Maybe he should offer a reward. Ten pounds to the first person who brought him the dog, or part of the dog. Dead or alive . . .

He set off down the main tunnel. The guide at the entrance had told him that the school party was about half a mile ahead. He'd have to walk quickly to catch them up.

He stopped. Echoing round the damp walls came an unmistakable sound. It was a dog, howling. Mr Blocker knew at once who it was and, as if in confirmation, Eric-the-dog stepped out of the shadows into the centre of the path ahead of him and gave another eerie howl.

'You!' Mr Blocker gave a strangled cry. 'It's you!' And he ran towards him, hands outstretched. Eric darted down one of the tunnels to the left; the headmaster hesitated. He knew as well as anyone that if he chased the dog into any of the side caves he could become lost in no time. Unless . . .

From his pocket, Mr Blocker took a ball of string. He tied one end of it to a stone and started unravelling the other to leave a trail as he set off after Eric. 'Right,' he murmured to himself. 'Let's see if you can get away this time.'

Following Eric, he worked his way deeper and deeper into the caves. Always, just ahead of him, he would see the bobbing tail of the little dog. Or it might be to the right. Or the left. But however fast he ran, he could never get quite close enough to catch him. Finally his ball of string gave out and, panting and breathless, he knew it was time to admit defeat and turn back.

To his horror, he found that he couldn't. He followed his trail of string back a few yards to where the path divided, only to find the entire ball, still tied to its stone, in a rough jumble in the middle of the pathway. Someone must have got behind him to gather up the string trail. And Mr Blocker had a shrewd idea who it was.

'That dog . . .' he moaned, sliding wearily down the wall till he sat on the cave floor. He was tired, his clothes were damp and the caves felt chilly; he hadn't had any lunch and his head ached dreadfully under its bandage. Then, when he had decided there was nothing for it but to walk in what he hoped was the right direction, the battery on his torch gave out.

If you had been able to see Mr Blocker's face in the darkness, and if you hadn't known that he was a headmaster, you might have thought he was starting to cry.

Eric trotted back to the caves' entrance feeling distinctly relieved. As a dog, of course, he had no trouble finding his way round the caves. All he had to do was follow the scent on the ground and go back the way he had come. Safe in the knowledge that he could not be chased by Mr Blocker for several hours at least, he made his way back to the caves museum, where he had arranged to meet Rachel.

'Are you all right, Eric?' she asked him anxiously. 'Mr Blocker's not still chasing you, is he?'

'Woof woof,' barked Eric confidently.

Rachel was still rather nervous. 'Well, let's not hang around, just in case,' she said. 'Let's go and have lunch.'

'Woof,' said Eric, and they started walking out through the museum to the exit.

Before they had got there, however, Eric suddenly sat down in the middle of the floor and started scratching the back of his neck.

'Not here, Eric!' Rachel turned on him, appalled. 'You can't change here – there's people coming through!'

She looked wildly round for somewhere he could hide. 'There!' She pointed to a little side door that led back into the caves. The door itself had 'No Entry' written on it and was securely locked, but there was a gap between the bottom of the door and the floor that Eric might just squeeze through if he hurried.

Eric hurried, and Rachel watched in relief as his legs and tail disappeared under the door. She waited a few seconds before asking quietly, 'Eric? Are you all right?'

'Fine,' Eric's muffled voice came back from the other side. 'Just the one problem.'

Rachel looked down at the gap at the bottom of the door. It had been large enough for Eric to go under as a dog but, she suddenly realized, it was certainly not big enough for him to come back out as a boy.

'Eric!' Rachel felt a stab of guilt. It had, after all, been her idea to hide there. 'What're you going to do?'

'Well, I thought I'd get dressed for a start.' Eric was trying not to sound as worried as he felt. 'If you could just pass my clothes through. And a torch might be useful.'

Rachel took Eric's clothes out of her rucksack and pushed them, with her torch, under the door.

'Do you think you could find your way round to the main cave?' she asked. 'If you just started walking?'

Eric couldn't help remembering how easy it had been for Mr Blocker to become lost.

'I can try,' he said. 'But I think the best thing is to tell Mrs Jessop.'

'Tell her what?' asked Rachel.

'Tell her –' and Eric suddenly had a rather clever idea, 'tell her that Mr Blocker's got lost in the caves and that I went to look for him.'

'Brilliant,' said Rachel. 'Just brilliant!'

Mrs Jessop was back at the coach and just settling down to lunch with the other staff when Rachel brought her the news.

'Mr Blocker's got lost?' she asked. 'How do you know? Isn't he still being patched up?'

'No, miss. We saw him going off into a side tunnel, and that was ages ago,' said Rachel.

'I wonder why,' said Mrs Jessop. 'And why on earth would Eric go chasing after him?'

'I don't know, miss,' said Rachel. 'I suppose he was worried. He's very fond of the headmaster.'

'Is he?' muttered Mrs Jessop. 'I'm glad somebody is.'

They went to tell the manager of the caves museum, who seemed to take the news very calmly.

'There's always one in these school groups, isn't there?' he said, as he phoned for extra staff to organize a search party. 'Always some joker who thinks he's clever enough to go off the path without getting lost.' He pulled a large coil of rope over one shoulder. 'So, what does he look like?'

'Six foot tall, greying hair, and he's wearing a suit,' said Mrs Jessop. 'It's our headmaster,' she added apologetically.

The manager gave her an odd look. 'That's a new one,' he said, and put on a helmet with a light attached to the front. 'Right. Let's go.'

Meanwhile, Eric was still wandering in the caves. He had read once that you could solve any maze by always turning right whenever the path divided – and since the caves were in a sense a very large maze, that was what he had decided to do. (The book was quite right, by the way, but when the maze is spread out over several miles, solving it by this method can take a very long time.)

Eric, then, was not too worried. He had Rachel's torch, he knew that, if he didn't get out on his own, somebody would probably come and find him and, compared with the morning's excitement, strolling through caves on his own seemed quite peaceful.

Peaceful, that is, until he started hearing the noise. It was very faint at first, just a low moaning, like the wind sighing through one of the passages a long way away, but as he walked, it got louder and closer, until Eric was forced to admit to himself that it wasn't the wind. There was something in the passage ahead of him, and whatever it was sounded desperately unhappy.

It took all Eric's courage not to turn and run back

the way he had come. The noise was very close now, in fact it seemed to be just round the next corner . . . and then it stopped.

Eric stopped as well, his heart thudding in a silence that was eventually broken by a small querulous voice. 'Who's that? Is there anybody there?'

Eric gave a great sigh of relief. 'It's all right, Mr Blocker,' he said as he swung round the corner. 'It's only me.'

Poor Mr Blocker was in a dreadful state. His suit, which had already been soaked in the canal, was now streaked with mud and one of the pockets was badly torn. The bandage on his head had slipped down over one eye, and he was huddled in a corner of the cave looking frightened and miserable.

'Eric?' Mr Blocker blinked in the torchlight. 'Eric Banks? Is that you? Oh, how wonderful!' He clutched gratefully at Eric's hand. 'I got lost, you see. And then the torch gave out, so I've just been sitting here in the dark and . . .' He gave a little sob.

'It's all right,' Eric tried to reassure him. 'I think Rachel's gone for help. I'm sure they'll find us soon.'

Mr Blocker didn't seem to hear. 'It's not just the dark, you know.' His voice lowered to a whisper. '*He's* out there.'

'Who?' asked Eric.

'That dog,' said Mr Blocker. 'The one that got me in here. He's still out there, I just know it . . . padding silently through the caves, waiting his moment to strike.'

Eric reached into his pocket and took out some sweets. 'Have a wine gum, Mr Blocker,' he said.

\*

The rescue team found them at about three o'clock, and by quarter past they were back at the main entrance. In the end, they weren't even late back to school.

Eric had thought he might get into trouble for going into the caves on his own, but most people seemed to think that trying to rescue the headmaster had been a very brave thing to do. Mr Blocker himself said that he didn't know how he'd have managed if Eric hadn't turned up when he did, and that he was going to write a letter to his parents to say so.

'There you are, Eric,' said Rachel. 'It all ended happily and you needn't have worried about Mr Blocker at all. He thinks you're wonderful.'

Eric wasn't so sure. Mr Blocker might think he was wonderful as a boy, but as a dog, he knew he now had a dangerous enemy. He had overheard Mr Blocker telling Mrs Jessop what had happened, and he had finished by saying, with quiet determination, 'I'm going to find that dog, Victoria. I'm going to find that dog, and when I do . . .'

Eric had been watching the headmaster's face as he spoke, and there was something in his eyes as he said this that sent a shiver down Eric's spine.

'I shouldn't worry,' said Rachel. 'I mean, whatever he tries couldn't be worse than today, could it?'

But she was wrong. What Mr Blocker had planned was definitely worse. Much, much worse.

# THE HAUNTING OF BLOCKER

In the days that followed the school trip to the caves, Eric managed to ensure that Mr Blocker never even caught a glimpse of 'that dog', but it was clear that the headmaster had not forgotten him.

For a start, there were notices all over the school asking anyone who saw a dog on the premises to lock all doors and report the fact at once to the headmaster. Then there were the 'emergency' boxes that had been placed at regular intervals along the corridors. Mr Blocker wouldn't say what emergency they were meant to provide for but, when Rachel looked inside, she found each box contained a net and a baseball bat.

The headmaster had also taken up shooting. He had bought a shotgun and every day after school he could be seen practising out on the playing field, using balloons pegged into the ground as targets. Nobody could understand why he had suddenly become so keen on this particular sport, but Eric had a terrible suspicion. It wasn't, however, until he saw Mr Blocker in the Craft, Design and Technology workroom that he knew for certain.

It was a lunchtime. Most of the children were out of doors, in the playground or on the field, but Eric had been sent inside with a message for the staffroom. As he passed the CDT workroom, he saw the headmaster through a window in the door.

Mr Blocker had a packet of Bonios – the bone-shaped biscuits that people sometimes give to dogs as a treat – and he was taking them out of the packet, one at a time, and drilling a hole down the middle. It seemed an odd sort of thing to be doing, and Eric stayed to watch.

When he had drilled holes in about a dozen biscuits, the Headmaster reached for another box, marked 'Webster's Rat Poison', and carefully poured a little of the contents inside each biscuit.

At that point, Eric decided he had seen enough and slid quietly away.

'He's trying to murder you?' Rachel was understandably horrified. 'Are you sure?'

'It all fits.' Eric looked pale and shaken. 'All those notices, the shotgun, and now he's put those biscuits in little hiding places all round the school. He's trying to kill me.'

'Wow . . .' Rachel had always know that Mr Blocker felt strongly about Eric the dog, but had never realized the dislike ran as deep as this. 'It's just as well you saw him,' she said. 'At least you know now it's not going to work.'

'Not this time,' Eric agreed, 'but what about the next? Or the time after? You know what Blocker's like. He's not going to give up, is he?'

Rachel said nothing, but she knew Eric was right. Mr Blocker had a reputation for being determined and she had never seen him more determined than this.

'I'm dead,' said Eric hopelessly. 'If he doesn't get me this time he'll just keep on trying something different till he does.'

'Perhaps, in time, he'll calm down and forget all about it,' said Rachel. But she didn't believe that, even as she said it. Nor did Eric.

'I may as well die now and get it over with,' he muttered. 'Nothing else is going to stop him.'

There was something about those words that made Rachel pause. 'Maybe that's it,' she said, thoughtfully. 'Maybe that's the answer.'

'What is?' asked Eric.

'If you were dead —' A smile crept over Rachel's face as she spoke. 'If you were dead, Mr Blocker would stop trying to kill you, wouldn't he?'

Eric started saying he could see one drawback to this as a solution, but Rachel interrupted him.

'You wouldn't have to *be* dead,' she explained, 'as long as Mr Blocker *thought* you were dead.'

Eric looked at her. 'Go on,' he said, and listened carefully while Rachel outlined her plan.

By the time she had finished, Eric was smiling as well. 'Not bad, Rachel,' he conceded. 'Not bad at all.'

It was morning assembly two days later, and Mr Blocker had just started giving out the notices when the doors at the back of the hall burst open.

'He's dead!' Rachel's voice echoed through the building. Her face was streaked with tears and in her arms she carried the limp, lifeless body of a dog, loosely wrapped in a blanket. 'He's dead,' she repeated. 'Dead!'

'What is all this noise?' Mr Blocker put down the notices. 'Rachel Hobbs, is that you?'

'Somebody's killed him.' Rachel carried her burden down through the hall, past the shocked faces of the assembled school. She was getting into her stride now and rather enjoying herself. 'He's been poisoned!'

Eric, on the other hand, was distinctly uncomfortable. Part of the rug was tickling his nose and he was trying desperately not to sneeze and give the game away.

Rachel laid the little body on the stage at Mr Blocker's feet and the headmaster bent down to look at it. The dog's paws and face could just be seen at one end of the blanket and he recognized it at once.

'Who would want to kill a lovely, fluffy little dog like this?' Rachel demanded tearfully, sweeping the body back into her arms.

Mr Blocker stood up. 'Would you deal with this please, Mrs Jessop?' he said. Then, as Mrs Jessop led Rachel and her burden away, he turned back to the main assembly. 'All right, everyone, quieten down,' he called. 'It's only a dead dog. Nothing to get excited about.'

Later that morning, Mrs Jessop took the headmaster to one of the flowerbeds behind the science labs.

'I told Rachel she could bury him here,' she said, pointing to a mound of earth. 'She was very upset, and I thought it might help.'

Mr Blocker stared at the little grave. To do him justice, he had never really thought that the dog's death would make anyone unhappy. 'I don't see why she's upset,' he complained. 'It wasn't her dog, was it?

I mean, it wasn't anyone's dog. It just roamed around causing trouble.'

'The dog may not have belonged to Rachel, but she was very fond of it,' said Mrs Jessop. 'As were most of the children. That's why they brought flowers.'

Mr Blocker noticed for the first time that the ground was covered with little bunches of flowers. 'All this fuss over a scruffy little mongrel,' he muttered, but he was beginning to feel a little uncomfortable.

'The story is going round the school –' Mrs Jessop had turned and now looked the headmaster straight in the eye, 'that you killed the dog with rat poison.'

'Really?' said Mr Blocker. 'How extraordinary.'

Mrs Jessop was still looking at him. 'I have told the children that, although we all know you don't particularly like animals, you couldn't possibly have done anything like that.' She paused. 'You didn't, did you?'

'I can't understand it,' Mr Blocker blustered. 'That dog has caused nothing but trouble from the day it arrived here. All I did was . . .' His voice trailed off. There was something about the way Mrs Jessop was looking at him that made him feel like a very small first former instead of the headmaster.

'Look, I can explain –' he said.

'I'd rather you didn't,' said Mrs Jessop coldly, and she turned on her heel and left.

Mr Blocker glared angrily down at the little grave. 'I should have known you could still cause trouble, even from there,' he muttered, and stomped off back to the school.

From a distance, safely hidden by some trees, Eric and Rachel watched him go.

'I think stage one went rather well, Eric,' said Rachel. 'Now for stage two.'

'Woof,' said Eric.

At the end of the day, when everyone else had gone home, Mr Blocker sat in his study at the school, trying to work. It wasn't easy. His thoughts kept wandering back to the dog, and the way Mrs Jessop had looked at him when she realized what he had done.

The children were treating him differently as well. He knew he had never been the sort of teacher who got given little presents and cards, but today some of the smaller children had actually backed away from him in fear and the older ones had stared at him with undisguised hostility.

If only they knew, he thought, if only they knew what that dog had done to him. He remembered the time it had slipped a skateboard under his foot so that he fell in the pond, the time it had beaten him at chess, and the time . . . oh, the list was endless.

He had every right to get rid of the animal. It wasn't an ordinary dog. It didn't even have an owner you could complain to – and all animals should have an owner; it was the law, wasn't it?

But deep inside him, so deep that he was hardly aware of it himself, Mr Blocker was not convinced by his own arguments. He knew that what he had done was wrong, and the knowledge gnawed away at his insides.

With a start, he sat up in his chair. Was he imagining things, or could he hear something? There it was again! Someone was playing the piano in the hall. Mr Blocker stood up in annoyance. Nobody was supposed to be in the school at this time. Whoever it was, he would throw them out and give them a piece of his mind at the same time.

He strode down the corridor, swung open the door to the school hall – and the instant he did so, the music stopped. Mr Blocker stared through the dusk, but the place was empty. The piano stood up on the stage, but nobody was playing it. Someone had left a window open, though, and the huge curtains on either side of it billowed and swirled in the evening breeze.

Mr Blocker shivered. He must have imagined the whole thing, he thought. But even as he crossed the hall to close the window, the tune he had heard seemed to echo in his brain. It was like a voice, softly singing,

*'How much is that doggy in the window?*
*The one with the waggerly tail . . .'*

Mr Blocker shivered and decided it was time to go home.

The headmaster did not sleep well that night, and when he came into school next morning, his eyes were red and there was a dispirited droop to his shoulders.

Calling into the staffroom, he saw Mrs Jessop. 'Morning, Victoria,' he called, but he got no reply.

'Look, I've been thinking,' said Mr Blocker.

'Bully for you,' said Mrs Jessop.

'I've been thinking', Mr Blocker continued determinedly, 'that perhaps I was a little harsh on young Rachel. I know what it's like to lose a pet. I had a rabbit when I was little.'

'Did you poison that as well?' asked Mrs Jessop.

'Please, Victoria!' Mr Blocker was painfully wringing his hands. 'I'm trying to help. I was wondering if I could perhaps buy Rachel another little dog to replace the one she lost.'

Mrs Jessop picked up her briefcase and headed for the door. 'You'll have to sort that out with Rachel,' she said briskly. 'I have a class to teach.' And she was gone.

Mr Blocker asked Rachel to come and see him, and that breaktime she knocked at his study door.

'Ah, good,' said Mr Blocker, drawing her in. 'Splendid, yes, splendid. How are you feeling today?'

Rachel said nothing, but started crying quietly.

'Oh, come on!' Mr Blocker gave her a tissue from a box on his desk. 'It's not that bad. In fact that's why I asked to see you. I've got good news. I —'

He stopped and his jaw fell open. Behind Rachel, in the open doorway, sitting in full view, was . . . was the dog! It was impossible, quite impossible, but it was there!

'You said you had some good news, sir?' asked Rachel, blowing her nose.

'Look!' Mr Blocker could hardly speak. 'Look! Behind you!'

Rachel turned obediently and looked at the doorway. 'Look at what?' she asked.

'At the dog!' Mr Blocker pointed, squeaking with excitement. 'The dog, it's alive! It's right there!'

Rachel stared blankly in the direction Mr Blocker was pointing. 'Is this some sort of joke, sir?' she asked.

'Joke?' Mr Blocker looked at her in astonishment. 'But he's standing right in front of you! See? Now he's turning round and going back out . . . there!'

'Why must you torment me like this?' Rachel

sobbed. 'Haven't you done enough already?' And, grabbing another tissue, she turned and ran out into the corridor.

The headmaster slowly sat back in his chair. His face was drained of blood and his hands were shaking as he reached for his pipe. His worse nightmare had come true.

The dog had returned to haunt him.

Over the next three weeks, the children and staff of the school noticed a change in Mr Blocker. He didn't shout any more. He didn't bustle from classroom to classroom telling everyone to get on with their work, nor did he stride across the playground ordering people to 'stop doing that at once'.

In fact he hardly did anything. He spent most of the day shut up in his study, only coming out for meals that he would often forget to eat and speaking to hardly a soul.

He looked awful. His suit was wrinkled, as if he'd slept in it, his shirt needed washing, his shoes hadn't been polished and some days he even forgot to shave. If you'd seen him shuffling down the corridors, you'd have thought he was a tramp instead of the head-master, and you couldn't have helped noticing he had a hunted, haunted look, as if he were always frightened someone was following him.

Mr Blocker, in short, was not a happy man. Since that day when he had seen the little dog in the doorway of his study, he had known scarcely a moment's rest. He didn't just *look* haunted . . . he was.

The dog had appeared on a number of occasions. He had seen it sitting on the pavement ahead of him as he cycled home; he had seen it peering at him round the corner of a school corridor; once he had found it on his front lawn when he pulled back the curtains in the morning. He never knew when he might see it next, and the waiting and worrying were almost as bad for his nerves as when he actually saw it.

Mr Blocker tried to tell himself that, as a ghost, the dog couldn't actually do him any harm, but the way it sat and looked at him, the way its eyes followed his every move, had unnerved him completely.

Mrs Jessop got quite worried about him. Headmasters of busy junior schools are not supposed to spend most of each day shut up in their studies, with the curtains drawn, saying they don't want to see anybody. 'It can't go on like this,' she confided to Miss Staples in the staffroom one day. 'Something's going to crack.'

Eric and Rachel had come to the same conclusion. One more good haunting, they thought, and after that, if the headmaster ever saw Eric the dog around the school, he'd be too frightened to do anything.

I think what actually happened surprised even them.

Mr Blocker awoke with a start and sat up in bed. He'd been woken by a tapping sound and even before he looked at the window, he knew what it was.

His bedroom was up on the first floor, but staring at him through the glass, glowing in the moonlight, was the dog.

'Ooooh!' Mr Blocker moaned quietly and pulled the sheets up to his chin. 'Ooooooh!'

The dog was a ghastly luminous green and was swaying slightly from side to side. He was swaying, though Mr Blocker didn't know this, because he was trying to balance himself on a tray Rachel was holding above her head at the top of a ladder, but the effect was quite spooky.

The luminous paint had been Rachel's idea as well, and it was remarkably effective. Eric had been a little worried that when he changed back he would be a painted, luminous boy, but oddly enough that didn't happen. In the same way that Eric's clothes fell off him when he turned into a dog, the flakes of dried paint were to float to the ground when he turned back into a boy.

For Mr Blocker, however, there was only the terrifying sight of a ghostly dog, swaying in mid-air outside his bedroom window in the middle of the night.

'Why do you keep doing this to me?' pleaded Mr Blocker. 'What do you want?'

The dog just looked at him, saying nothing, and inside Mr Blocker, something cracked.

'All right!' he cried, almost shouting. 'I'm sorry, I'm sorry, I'm sorry. I shouldn't have done it, I was wrong. I admit it: I was wrong.'

Outside the window, the dog nodded its head.

'I promise I'll never do anything like it again.' Mr Blocker was kneeling up in bed, pleading. 'I'll change, I'll never hurt another animal in my life. I'll be kind to them, like I know I should have been. I'll do anything if you'll just please ... please ... go away and leave me alone.'

Slowly, the dog nodded again, and Mr Blocker closed his eyes in relief. When he opened them again, the dog had gone.

*

When Mr Blocker bustled into school the next morning, he looked quite different. Smartly dressed, clean-shaven, and with all his old energy, he arrived a little later than usual, carrying half a dozen cages.

In assembly, he told an astonished school that he was making a few changes. First, all the rules about no pets on school premises were abolished. In future, everyone was welcome – indeed, encouraged – to bring their animals in, so that pets could be looked after during the day. Second, he had decided there should be a gerbil in every classroom, for those who didn't have pets of their own – that was why he had the cages and he wanted someone from each form to come down to the pet shop with him that morning and choose them. Third, he announced he would be holding an animal surgery every Thursday morning. 'I may not be a qualified vet,' he told the children, 'but it's amazing how many problems can be solved by a talk and a little cuddle from someone who cares.' Then he announced the morning hymn, 'All things bright and beautiful'.

From that day on, Mr Blocker was a changed man. In some ways he was still the same – he could still be very fierce on occasion, but he was fierce in a different way. If he caught you running in the corridor or if you were a little late for his lesson, he might not say anything at all; but if he saw you trying to swat a spider, instead of picking it up gently and taking it outside, he would give you a long stern lecture on the importance of insects to the food chain.

The school became a different place as well. For a start, it was full of animals. Each classroom, as well as having a gerbil cage, slowly acquired vivariums for keeping stick insects and hatching caterpillars, glass tanks for frogspawn, and baskets and cushions in the corner for any visiting dogs and cats.

Mr Blocker even started talking of turning one section of the playing field into a farm and keeping sheep, goats and cows. You would hardly have known it was the same man.

Now, you're possibly wondering what was happening to Eric all this time. You'll have realized that Rachel's plan had been to convince the headmaster that, if he ever saw Eric-as-a-dog in school, he would only be seeing a ghost – but the situation had now changed. Mr Blocker had promised to be a different person as long as he never saw 'that dog' again – which meant that Eric was back with the problem he'd had at the start. How could he ensure that Mr Blocker never saw him as a dog?

The short answer was that he couldn't, but oddly enough it didn't matter. It happened like this.

Eric had changed into a dog just after a Domestic Science class (it was probably the heat of the cookers that had done it) and he and Rachel were eating a packed lunch, sitting on a little patch of grass behind the squash court. Normally nobody else went there, which was why they had chosen the spot, but today, with no warning at all, Mr Blocker suddenly appeared round the corner with Mrs Jessop.

When he saw Eric, Mr Blocker blanched. 'What . . . what's that dog doing?' he asked.

Rachel knew it was impossible to pretend that Eric was a ghost, especially when she was feeding him chunks of sausage roll. She opened her mouth to reply, but couldn't think of anything to say.

Then Mrs Jessop stepped forward. 'This must be your new dog, Rachel,' she said. 'He looks very like the old one, doesn't he, John?'

'I thought he was the old one,' said Mr Blocker.

'No, no,' said Mrs Jessop confidently. 'Look at his ears.'

Mr Blocker looked at Eric's ears.

'They're much longer,' said Mrs Jessop. 'And his tail's quite different, isn't it, Rachel?'

'Oh, yes, miss,' Rachel agreed. 'Yes, quite different.'

Mr Blocker was still studying Eric. 'Now you mention it,' he said thoughtfully, 'he's a darker colour, isn't he?'

'D'you know, I think you're right,' Mrs Jessop agreed. 'I hadn't noticed, but he is. Definitely darker.'

The colour had come back to Mr Blocker's cheeks and he was smiling as he knelt on the ground beside Eric. 'My name is Mr Blocker,' he said, holding out a hand. 'I'm the headmaster of this school, and I hope we're going to be friends.'

Eric held out a paw and Mr Blocker shook it gently.

'I want you to know', he went on, 'that you're welcome here at any time.' He stood up. 'Now, how about I take you along to my office and we find you some proper dog food?'

Eric the dog and Mr Blocker set off together, back towards the main building.

'You know,' said Mr Blocker, 'I think you and I are going to be good friends.'

'Woof,' said Eric.

# MIS-CAST

The phone rang in the hall, and Mrs Hobbs came out of the kitchen to answer it. 'Double six five four one,' she said briskly. 'Hello?'

'Woof! Woof, woof, woof!' said a voice on the other end of the line.

Mrs Hobbs put the receiver on the hall table. 'Rachel!' she called upstairs, 'it's for you,' and went back into the kitchen.

Rachel recognized Eric's barking at once. 'Is everything all right?' she asked.

'Woof, woof,' said Eric.

'Is there anything I can do? You want me to come round?'

'Woof,' said Eric, and something in his voice told Rachel that the quicker she got there the better.

'Don't worry.' She tried to sound calm and reassuring. 'I'll be right there.'

She put down the phone, reached for her coat and was just pulling open the front door when she remembered that she hadn't asked Eric where he was. Then she realized that even if she had asked him, he wouldn't have been able to tell her. One woof for yes and two for no is a very useful code, but it has its limitations.

She picked up the phone and dialled Eric's number. To her relief, he answered it almost at once.

'Woof,' he said.

'Sorry, Eric,' Rachel explained. 'I just wanted to check – you are at home, aren't you?'

'Woof,' said Eric.

'I'm on my way.' Rachel put the phone down. No doubt about it, there was something in his voice. It sounded serious.

Rachel had once been the National Juveniles Circuit Cycling Champion, and she covered the mile and a half to Eric's house in a little under four minutes. She left her bike in the garden, went straight round to the back and rang the bell. When there was no reply, she pushed open the door and went in.

'Eric?' she called. 'Eric? Where are you?'

'Woof!' said Eric, and Rachel found him in the hall. He was at the bottom of the stairs, the telephone beside him on the floor; when he tried to walk towards her, Rachel could see the problem at once. He was limping badly, hopping to keep his right back leg clear of the ground.

'What have you done, Eric?' Rachel knelt beside him.

Eric, of course, couldn't tell her, but as Rachel looked round, she began to guess what must have happened. There was a roller skate at the top of the stairs, another at the bottom, and Eric's clothes were scattered at intervals all the way down. It looked as if Eric had tripped on a skate at the top landing, and actually changed into a dog while he was falling down the stairs. Alone in the house, knowing he was hurt, he had telephoned the only person who might realize, just from his barking, that he needed help.

'How bad is it?' Rachel gently touched the injured leg with a finger and Eric gave a yelp of pain. She drew back. There was only one thing to do. Eric had to be taken to the vet.

She pushed him there in his sister's old pram, which Mrs Banks still kept in the cupboard under the stairs. Mr Drew, the vet, knew Eric and lifted him carefully on to the surgery table.

'So what's happened here?' he asked.

'I'm not sure,' Rachel told him, 'but I think his sister left her roller-skates at the top of the stairs, and Eric tripped up on them.'

'You've got a dog that roller-skates?' asked Mr Drew.

It was a moment before Rachel realized what he meant. When she had said 'Eric's sister', she had meant Emily, but Mr Drew had naturally thought she meant another dog.

'Oh . . . yes.' It seemed best to change the subject. 'His leg's not too bad, is it?'

The vet had to take an X-ray before he could answer that question properly.

'It could be worse,' he told her eventually. 'It's a fracture, fortunately not too severe, on the top half of the fibula.' He pointed to a faint line on the X-ray. 'Just there. You see it?'

'Woof,' said Eric.

'Will he need an operation?' asked Rachel.

'I don't think so,' said Mr Drew. 'If it happened to you or me, we'd have to have the leg put in plaster, but with dogs it's often best to let these things heal on their own. They can hop around on three legs, you see.' He was taking out a syringe as he spoke. 'I'll just give him his booster shot while he's here, if that's all right?'

'Woof, woof!' said Eric.

'He doesn't like injections,' Rachel tried to explain, but the vet only smiled.

'They don't really feel anything, you know,' he said reassuringly. 'Not like us.'

But Eric will tell you, from personal experience, that is not true.

The real trouble started when Eric changed back into a boy. As Rachel pointed out, the vet might not have had to do anything about his leg while he was a dog, but he had also said that a boy with the same injury would need to have it put in plaster. Eric thought they shouldn't do anything until his parents came back – they had gone to visit his gran – but Rachel argued that since they knew what *had* to be done, there was no point in waiting, and Eric eventually agreed.

As the hospital was only half a mile away, Rachel pushed him round there in the pram. She wheeled him into the Casualty department and straight up to the reception desk, where a nurse looked up from her notes. 'Can I help?' she asked.

'My friend's hurt his leg,' Rachel told her.

'It's a fractured fibula,' Eric explained. 'Fortunately not too severe, but it will need to be put in plaster.'

'Will it,' said the nurse. 'Well, I hope you won't mind if I get one of our doctors to give a second opinion?'

'Not at all,' said Eric. 'Good idea.'

Doctor Phelps took an X-ray, carefully examined Eric's leg and then delivered his verdict. 'It's a fractured fibula,' he said. 'Fortunately not too severe, but it'll need to be put in plaster.'

The nurse gave Eric an odd look, but didn't actually say anything.

'So what's the situation with your parents, young man?' the doctor asked. 'They know what's happened, do they?'

Eric explained that his parents had gone to visit his gran, and the doctor asked the nurse to ring and tell them what had happened. She came back a few minutes later.

'I've spoken to Eric's grandmother,' she said, 'and she told me she knows Mr and Mrs Banks told Eric that's where they'd be, but they're not there.'

'So where are they?' asked Doctor Phelps.

'Nobody knows.' The nurse shrugged. 'Apparently it's a secret.'

'A secret?' The doctor's brow furrowed. 'His parents aren't where they said they'd be, and where they are is a secret?' He turned to Eric. 'Isn't that rather odd?'

'I think so,' said Eric.

Rachel was allowed to wait in the day room while Eric was taken off to one of the children's wards to have his leg put in plaster, and while she sat there, she did some thinking. If Eric's accident had happened anywhere but at home, she would not have been able to help him. Even if he had been within reach of a telephone, Eric-as-a-dog would simply not have been able to tell her where he was. What they needed, it seemed to her, was a more advanced form of communication than one woof or two. But how could a dog say something as precise as where he was, when the only noise he could make was a bark?

Then, glancing round the toys that lined the shelves of the dayroom, she spotted a possible answer. On one box, she read, 'Electronics in action! Fifteen projects you can complete using this simple pre-wired circuit board' – and project number five was a Morse transmitter. It was perfect, Rachel thought. If they could just learn Morse, Eric would be able to press the key with his paw and say whatever he liked. She snatched up the box to take it in and show Eric.

The nurse told her they had finished Eric's plaster and that he was in the end bed with the curtains drawn. When Rachel got there, however, the bed was empty. Empty of Eric, that is, because the only thing lying on the coverlet, apart from a pair of pyjamas, was the plaster that had recently encased Eric's leg.

In an instant, Rachel realized what must have happened. Eric had turned back into a dog. Because his leg was a lot smaller as a dog than as a boy, the plaster had simply fallen off.

'Wow!' Rachel murmured to herself. 'How's he going to get it back on again?'

'Everything all right?' the nurse called from the other end of the ward.

'Fine,' said Rachel, 'just fine.' Poor Eric, she thought, this was going to take some explaining.

Eric the dog, meanwhile, had gone in search of something to eat. He hadn't had any lunch, and although a nurse had promised to bring him something, he doubted if she would give it to a dog, even one sitting up in bed wearing pyjamas. A hospital, how-

ever, is not an easy place for a dog to find food. In fact
Eric soon realized that dogs were not welcome in this
one at all. Everyone who saw him seemed determined
to chase him out of the building; the only person who
didn't seem worried by him was an old lady who gave
him a biscuit.

She was sitting up in bed, in a room on her own,
when Eric hopped up on to the chair beside her.

'Do you know what a whoopee cushion is?' she asked
him, putting down the letter she had been reading.
'My grandson wants one for his birthday, but I can't
get it if I don't know what it is, can I?'

'Woof, woof,' said Eric, and the old lady laughed.

'I know what you want,' she said, and gave him one
of her chocolate biscuits. She would probably have
given him another if a nurse hadn't come in just then
and chased Eric back out into the corridor. Running
on three legs, Eric decided the best thing was to try
and find Rachel, and he was just heading for the lift,
when he stopped dead in surprise.

Ahead of him in the corridor, getting a cup of coffee
from the vending machine, was his father.

Eric's first thought was that his father had come to
visit him, but then he realized that wasn't possible.
The nurse had told him only ten minutes before that
they were still trying to get hold of his parents, but
hadn't yet done so. If his father was in the hospital,
then it had to be the place his parents had gone to
when they had said they were visiting Gran ... But
why?

As Mr Banks set off down the corridor, Eric followed,
and when his father turned off through a doorway
marked 'Antenatal Clinic', Eric managed to sneak in

behind him without being seen. He found himself in a sort of waiting room, lined with rows of chairs, and he hid under one of them while he watched his father carry the cup of coffee over to where his mother was sitting.

The two of them were soon deep in conversation, and Eric was naturally very curious to know what they were saying. Crawling under the row of chairs that ran around the wall, he worked his way round the room until he was close enough to overhear the conversation.

'I was wondering', his mother was saying, 'if you'd mind if we didn't tell Eric and Emily yet.'

'We don't have to tell anyone,' said Mr Banks. 'Not for a while, anyway.'

'I'd like to keep it secret a bit longer,' said Mrs Banks. 'Just till we get used to the idea.'

'It'll certainly take some getting used to.' Mr Banks took a sip of the coffee. 'Who'd have thought it. Twins.'

Under the chair, Eric's chin sank to the ground and his paws covered his eyes. This whole day, he thought, was getting right out of control.

Eric eventually found Rachel in the children's dayroom. It felt good to see a friendly face, and felt even better ten minutes later when he turned back into a boy, and Rachel got him his pyjamas and dressing gown and then helped him hop back to his bed without being seen.

'You'll never guess who I saw downstairs,' he told her as she tucked the sheets in around him, but before he could say anything else, the nurse appeared.

'Doctor wants to see you, Eric,' she said as she pulled back the curtains round his bed.

'Doctor?' Eric sat up. 'Why? What's wrong?'

'Nothing's wrong,' the nurse assured him. 'He just wants to check the cast on your leg. Make sure it's comfortable, that sort of thing. All right?'

'Ah,' said Eric.

'It is comfortable, isn't it?' asked the nurse.

'I think so.' Eric wondered how to break the news. 'It's just . . . it's come off.'

'Come off?' The nurse pulled back the blankets and stared at Eric's leg and at the cast lying neatly beside it. 'It's come off!' she said. 'How?'

'It's a bit of a mystery, that,' said Eric. 'I just sort of . . . found it.'

'You must have been tossing and turning in your sleep,' Rachel chipped in helpfully. She turned to the nurse. 'He does a lot of that when he's asleep. Tossing and turning.'

The nurse said nothing. She picked up the cast and looked at it, and the more she looked the stranger it all became. It was definitely Eric's cast — she knew that because she had signed it herself — but how could it possibly have come off in one piece like that? It was impossible; there was simply no way that it could have happened — but it had.

'I'll go and get the doctor,' she said.

Rachel watched as the nurse carried Eric's plaster back down the ward. 'Close one, Eric,' she murmured. 'I thought you were going to be in trouble there.'

'I think I already am,' Eric replied, and he told her what he had heard in the antenatal clinic downstairs.

Rachel thought the idea of twins was very exciting. If anything, she was rather envious. 'What's the matter?' she asked. 'Don't you like babies?'

'I think babies are wonderful,' said Eric. 'But think about it, Rachel. I've already got one sister. I live in a three-bedroomed house. It'll mean sharing a bedroom, won't it.'

'Lots of people have to share bedrooms.' Rachel was about to add that some of them even enjoyed it, but she didn't. She had just realized why Eric was so worried.

If you are a boy who turns into a dog, it is not easy to keep the fact a secret; especially from your own family, and especially when you live in a small house. If Eric had to share his bedroom it would be virtually impossible. Rachel knew how important it was to Eric that he *did* keep it secret, and she could understand how he felt.

'Well, you seem to be causing us a lot of trouble, young man.' Doctor Phelps had appeared at Eric's bedside, holding the cast. 'Never mind,' he added, 'we're quite used to it. No need to look so glum.'

'He's not upset about the plaster,' said Rachel. 'He's just had some bad news.'

'My mother's having twins,' said Eric.

'It'll mean sharing his bedroom,' Rachel explained.

The doctor shook his head in sympathy. 'I know how you feel,' he said. 'I had to share with my brother when I was little. I've never forgotten. He trod on my Meccano set. Just came in one day and . . . trod on it.'

'We'll put a new plaster on Eric's leg, shall we, Doctor?' asked the nurse.

'Yes, yes. Quite right.' You could see the doctor's thoughts were still elsewhere. 'He always said it was an accident, but I know he was lying. It was quite deliberate. I'm sure of it.'

It's getting worse, thought Eric. It's just getting worse and worse.

Later that afternoon, Mr and Mrs Banks arrived. They called in at the office to ask how Eric was, and the staff nurse told them about the fractured fibula and assured them that he was doing well.

'We'll keep him in overnight,' she explained, 'just in case there's a possibility of concussion, but there's nothing to worry about, really.'

'Can we see him now?' asked Mrs Banks.

'Of course,' said the staff nurse and added, as she took them through to the ward, 'I gather congratulations are in order. About the twins.'

'You know about the twins?' asked Mr Banks.

'Eric told us,' said the nurse. 'Ah. Here we are.' She stopped at Eric's bed. 'Better not stay too long. We want him to rest.'

Mr and Mrs Banks sat down beside Eric, and the first thing they wanted to know was what exactly had happened. Eric told them how he'd fallen downstairs, how he'd phoned Rachel, and then how she had wheeled him up to the hospital in the pram.

Mr Banks said he thought they had both behaved very sensibly. Mrs Banks agreed, then added, 'I gather you've already heard our bit of news about the twins? Though I don't know who can have told you.'

'I think it was one of the nurses,' said Eric.

'She just said you told her,' said Mr Banks.

'It doesn't really matter who told him,' Mrs Banks interrupted. 'The point is, Eric, that it will probably mean a few changes for you.'

'What sort of changes?' asked Eric.

His father took a deep breath. 'Well, we weren't going to tell you just yet, but since you already know . . . it'll almost certainly mean moving house.'

'To somewhere bigger,' Mrs Banks explained. 'So the babies can have a room of their own.'

'You won't mind, will you?' asked Mr Banks anxiously.

'Mind?' said Eric, who felt as if a great weight had just been lifted from his soul. 'I think it's brilliant. Just brilliant.'

And he thought perhaps it wasn't going to be such a bad day after all.

Rachel came back that evening for a visit. 'I've been thinking', she said, munching her way through the grapes by Eric's bed, 'about what you can do in an emergency. About how you can let me know if you're in trouble.'

'If you mean the Morse buzzer,' said Eric, 'it was a good idea, but I don't think . . .'

'No, I know that wouldn't work,' Rachel interrupted him. 'I mean, you'd have to go round with all the electrics strapped to your paws and people would notice. No, I've got a new idea. Look at this.'

She pulled out a large map, pasted on to a board, and held it in front of Eric. 'I'm going to hang this up by the telephone at home,' Rachel told him, 'and if ever you're trapped anywhere as a dog, we can use this for you to tell me where you are. You see?'

Eric admitted that he didn't.

'Well, you phone me up, like you did today,' said Rachel, 'and I ask you questions. Like . . .' her finger pointed to the map, 'are you to the north of the A43?'

'Woof,' said Eric, helpfully pretending he was a dog.

'So I know you're in this area.' Rachel pointed again to the map. 'And then I ask, are you to the east of Penfield Ridge?'

'Woof, woof,' said Eric.

'Right.' Rachel studied the map again. 'I now know you're phoning from the middle of the reservoir, you're drowning, and I can come and rescue you.' She put down the map. 'What do you think?'

Eric thought. And the more he thought the more it seemed to him to be a very clever idea. It was simple, easy to remember and, as long as he could get to a phone, he couldn't see any reason why it shouldn't work.

It wasn't just a good idea, either. It occurred to Eric that Rachel had gone to a lot of trouble to think the whole thing out, to get a map and to stick it on the board, and he decided you could have a lot worse friends than Rachel Hobbs.

'It's a great idea, Rachel,' he said. 'I mean it. It's a really great idea.'

'Well, it's better than the Morse buzzer, I suppose,' Rachel agreed modestly. 'Which reminds me, I'd better take it back.' She reached for the 'Electronics in action' box on the bedside table.

'No, no.' Eric put out a hand to stop her. 'It's all right. I've got an idea, and I might need it.'

Late that night, all was quiet in the hospital, even in the children's ward. Staff Nurse was in her office, working on some papers while listening with one ear in case anyone should call, but the only sound was of gentle, peaceful breathing.

Her friend, Nurse Cox, knocked at the door. 'I don't want to disturb you if you're busy,' she said, 'but I wondered if you had an Eric Banks up here. Boy with a fractured fibula.'

'That's right,' said Staff. 'He's in the bed at the far end. Why?'

'It's an odd thing.' Nurse Cox came and sat down on the edge of the desk. 'I was in Casualty when he came in this morning and he seemed to know exactly what was wrong with him before the doctor had even seen him. He knew what was fractured and where – and what needed to be done about it.'

'If you think that's odd,' said Staff, 'take a look at this.' And she picked up Eric's cast and passed it across. 'He says it fell off in his sleep.'

Nurse Cox turned the cast over in her hands. There were no breaks in the plaster. 'But it couldn't have!' she said. 'It's impossible. Quite impossible.'

'I know.' The staff nurse shrugged. 'But you get a lot of funny things happening in the children's ward.'

'They happen everywhere in this hospital,' Nurse Cox sighed. 'Do you know Mrs Wilkins?'

'The old lady in the room on her own?'

'That's the one.' Nurse Cox lowered her voice. 'They found her this evening taking Morse messages from a dog. Seriously! One of the porters found her sitting up in bed wearing a set of headphones, while this little dog sat beside her pressing the buzzer on a Morse transmitter.'

'It was sending her a message?' asked Staff.

'Oh, yes.' Nurse Cox got up and walked back to the door. 'You won't believe it, but she says the dog was telling her what a whoopee cushion was, and where to buy one.'

When Nurse Cox had gone, the staff nurse tried settling back to her work, but she couldn't. She felt vaguely restless and decided to take another turn round the ward, just to check that all was well. It was very quiet, and all the children seemed to be sleeping peacefully. She stopped at the far end and looked down at Eric. He seemed a very ordinary boy, she thought. Rather a lot of freckles but otherwise nothing peculiar about him at all.

She was just turning to walk back to her office, when something caught her eye.

'He can't have,' she murmured to herself. 'I don't believe it.'

She pulled back the sheets, and there was Eric's new plaster cast lying empty in the bed beside him.

'He's done it again,' she muttered. 'He's done it again!'

# BADGERS

There were times when Eric wished that, if he did have to turn into a dog, it could be something bigger than a mongrel terrier. It wasn't that he wanted to be a Rottweiller or a St Bernard necessarily, just life would be simpler if he was . . . well, bigger.

If, for instance, he had turned into an Irish wolf-hound or a Dobermann, he would probably not have found himself, as he did this morning, being chased at top speed out of the park by a Great Dane. It was such an enormous dog, Eric thought, as he darted through the park gates and hurtled along the street. In terms of size, it was a bit like you or me being chased by an elephant. A very fit elephant that had recently been selected to run for its herd in the Olympics.

The one advantage Eric had in these circumstances, and they happened more often than you might think, was that he could usually think his way out of trouble. He knew where there were holes in fences that were too small for larger dogs to follow him through. He could sometimes dart into a building and close the door behind him. Or he could do what he did this time, and find somewhere to hide.

Running as fast as he could round the corner of Garston Avenue, he saw a woman standing on the pavement with a large canvas bag at her feet and, without a second's hesitation, he dived straight into it.

The Great Dane rounded the corner, raced off down the pavement, and had gone at least a hundred yards before its eyes and nose discovered that it had lost the trail. It looked round hopefully for a few minutes but could see no sign of Eric, and eventually shambled off down a side alley to find some other form of amusement.

Inside the bag, Eric waited until he was quite sure the Great Dane had really gone; but then, just as he was about to climb out, a man's voice above him said, 'Sorry to have kept you waiting, Miss Barrington. Is this your bag?' and he felt himself being picked up, swung through the air and then put down again. A door slammed shut and Eric realized he was in the back of a car, without the least idea where he was being driven or by whom.

It was a very large, expensive car, Eric discovered when he cautiously lifted his head and looked around. The bag he was in had been placed on the back seat, and the man who had put him there was now driving, with Miss Barrington beside him.

Eric wondered what he ought to do. The simplest thing would be to bark and hope they would stop and let him out of the car – but what if they didn't? What if they decided to take him to the police or the RSPCA? On the other hand, if he kept quiet and waited for a suitable chance to escape, he might have a very long walk home.

It wasn't an easy choice, but what eventually

made Eric decide to stay hidden was the telephone. The car had a phone – Eric could see it sitting in the gap between the two front seats – and a phone meant he might be able to ring Rachel for help. Quietly, he settled himself back down in the bag and waited.

Twenty minutes later, the car stopped on the edge of an enormous building site. By listening to the conversation from the front, Eric knew that this was how Mr Ashmore (that was the man's name) made his money. He built houses, hundreds of them, and Miss Barrington was his secretary.

Mr Ashmore got out, opened the door for Miss Barrington, and the two of them set off in the direction of his office, a large Portakabin that overlooked all the building work in the valley below. As the sound of their footsteps died away, Eric emerged from his hiding place, crawled on to the front seat and tapped in Rachel's number on the phone.

You may remember that when Eric fractured his leg and had to be taken to hospital, Rachel had worked out a system that would let him tell her where he was when he was in trouble as a dog. This was the first time since then that they had tried it, and to Eric's relief, it worked perfectly. Rachel answered the phone. When she realized it was Eric, she asked if he needed any help, and when he said 'Woof!', she pulled out a large map from behind the phone table.

Eric knew he was about five miles out of town, on the edge of Boyatt's Wood. He couldn't tell Rachel that directly, but when she asked, for instance, if he was to the north of Durnford, or to the east of the ring road, he could answer 'Woof' or 'Woof, woof', until Rachel finally worked out exactly where he was.

She studied the map carefully before deciding what to do next. 'I think the nearest I can get to you, Eric,' she said eventually, 'is a bus stop somewhere in Norland Lane. Can you make it there, do you think?'

'Woof,' said Eric.

'I should be with you in about an hour. Okay?'

Eric was about to woof that that was fine when he was interrupted.

'Goodness!' said Miss Barrington, who had come back to the car to get her bag. 'What are you doing?'

Eric didn't hesitate. He abandoned the phone, darted out of the open door and ran.

'Anything wrong?' Mr Ashmore called from his office.

'It was a dog,' Miss Barrington told him, somewhat dazed. 'Using your telephone.'

'Oh, yes?' Mr Ashmore obviously didn't believe her. 'And who was he calling?'

Miss Barrington listened for a moment to the phone Eric had abandoned. 'I don't know,' she said, sounding more puzzled than ever. 'But whoever it was just told me to get off the line so she could carry on talking to her dog.'

When Rachel got off the bus at Norland Lane there was no sign of Eric, and she was trying to think what might have happened to him when –

'Psst,' Eric said. 'Over here.'

Rachel looked round and saw Eric's face peering over the top of the hedge that ran along the roadside. 'Did you bring any clothes?' he asked.

Rachel grinned. 'I thought perhaps you hadn't been able to find the bus stop.' She unhooked a bag from her shoulder and slung it over the hedge. 'I should have known.'

'No trouble finding it, Rachel,' Eric assured her as he pulled on his shirt. 'It worked perfectly. And as a matter of fact, that's not all I found.'

'What d'you mean?' asked Rachel.

'There's a gate down there.' Eric pointed. 'Come and see for yourself.'

What Eric had found was a badger, a young one by the look of it, only a few weeks old.

'It was just lying on the verge,' he told Rachel. 'I reckon it got hit by a car,'

There was a bit of blood by its mouth and it lay on its side, still breathing, but making no attempt to get away when Rachel stroked it.

'What are we going to do?' she asked.

'We can't just leave it here,' said Eric. 'I think we should take it home. Then we can ask Mrs Jessop what's the best thing to do for it.'

So they laid the badger in the bag that had contained Eric's clothes and took it home with them on the bus.

Mrs Jessop carefully examined the badger and decided there was nothing seriously wrong. 'I think you just have to feed him up.' she said. 'Let him have a few days' rest to get strong again and if he's better by the weekend, I'll drive you back out to Boyatt's Wood and we'll set him free. Can you look after him till then?'

'No problem,' said Eric.

I don't know if you've ever had to look after a young badger for three days, but if you have, you'll know that it is not as easy as you might think. Its diet is not particularly complicated – mainly worms, snails and slugs, with some fruit and plenty of milk – but collecting it can be a messy business and feeding one in your bedroom can be even messier. Also, although badgers are very clean animals, they have what Mrs Jessop called a 'powerful scent' and what Mrs Banks referred to as 'that disgusting smell'.

Looking after the badger was an interesting experience, but Eric was not entirely sorry when Sunday came, and it was time to return him to the wild.

The one thing that bothered Mrs Jessop was where exactly they should leave him. 'The best thing would be to take him back to his sett,' she explained, 'but the trouble is, we don't know where it is.'

'I think we could find it,' Eric suggested. 'Well, I think Rachel's dog could.'

'Of course!' Mrs Jessop smiled agreement. 'A dog could track it by the scent.' She turned to Rachel. 'Do you think you could get him to do that?'

'I think so,' said Rachel. If the smell of badger in Eric's room was anything to go by, she thought, she could probably follow the scent herself. As a dog, Eric should have no problem.

'Right,' said Mrs Jessop. 'We take him home tomorrow.'

On Sunday evening, Mrs Jessop, Rachel, the badger (in a cardboard box) and Eric-as-a-dog set off in Mrs Jessop's car. They parked near the bus stop in Norland Lane where Eric had originally found the badger, and Eric-as-a-dog got out and started quartering the field. 'Quartering' means that he ran, not just anywhere over the grass, but in a sort of pattern that would give him the best possible chance of finding a scent if it was there.

It didn't take him long. He gave a brief 'Woof' to tell the others he was on the trail, then set off with his nose to the ground, in the direction of some trees on the far side of the field.

'He's heading for Boyatt's Wood,' said Mrs Jessop. 'Come on!' And gathering up the box containing the badger, she and Rachel set off in pursuit.

They caught up with Eric in a small clearing about half a mile into the wood. He was lying on his stomach, head on his paws, peering cautiously over the top of a slight rise in the ground. Rachel and Mrs Jessop crept quietly forward to join him.

Below them lay a deep hollow, about ten metres across. The grass covering it had been mostly worn away to bare earth, and scattered unevenly round its edge were the entrances to a series of burrows, a bit larger than rabbit holes. Some looked more used than others, but round all of them they could see the distinctive prints of badger tracks.

'Well done, Eric,' whispered Mrs Jessop, sidling up beside him. 'It's a sett, all right.' She turned to Rachel. 'Okay. You can let him go.'

It was a sight none of them will ever forget. Rachel lifted the badger out of his box and up to the lip of the hollow. He paused there for a moment, sniffing the air, before setting off down the slope in an unhurried fashion, straight over to one of the burrow entrances, which was directly under the roots of an enormous beech tree.

Another badger's face appeared in the entrance; it looked no bigger than the one Eric had found. The two of them touched noses, sniffed cautiously, and then suddenly fell on each other, biting each other's necks and rolling over and over down to the bottom of the hollow.

Mrs Jessop smiled. 'Just playing,' she whispered.

You may have seen pictures of badgers in books or on television, but Eric and Rachel will tell you there is nothing quite so magical as the real thing – watching animals as they go about their day-to-day lives in their natural homes.

Rachel, Mrs Jessop and Eric-as-a-dog watched in silence as the two badgers rolled around in the bottom of the hollow, to be joined, in the course of the next fifteen minutes, by a series of parents, uncles, aunts and cousins, all going about their ordinary tasks in the twilight – cleaning out their burrows, airing the bedding, gathering food – to the accompaniment of the most extraordinary gruntings and snufflings.

'Pity Eric Banks couldn't be here,' said Mrs Jessop quietly. 'I think he'd have enjoyed it.'

'Woof,' said Eric, and they turned to go home.

And that might have been the end of the story if, on their way back to the car, Eric hadn't gone scampering off to one side of the path, in the way that dogs always do, and discovered a freshly painted sign nailed to a tree.

'This wood has been acquired by Ashmore Homes Ltd,' it said, and went on to explain that Boyatt's Wood would shortly be replaced by fifteen luxury executive homes.

Eric was not able to tell Rachel what he had seen until the next day. As a dog, he couldn't say, 'Come and have a look at this, it's important,' though he tried his best to lead them into the wood so they could see the notice for themselves. But Mrs Jessop had insisted they go straight home. It was late and it was getting dark, she said, and whatever it was Eric had found would have to wait.

'But they can't destroy the wood!' Rachel protested when Eric told her next morning. 'Not with badgers in it. I thought they were protected. By law.'

Eric nodded. 'They are,' he said. He had done some reading on badgers and this was one of the things he had discovered. 'Except in special circumstances, you're not allowed to build where there's a sett. Even then they'll probably say you have to move the badgers to another site first.'

'Perhaps that's what they're planning to do,' said Rachel.

'Or maybe they don't know the badgers are there,' Eric suggested. 'I mean, I'm not sure we'd have found them yesterday if I hadn't been a dog. They're very well hidden.'

The more they talked about it, the surer they felt that the first thing to do was go back out to the wood. They should start by looking at the notice again and seeing exactly what it said; then, if they were still worried, they could go over to Mr Ashmore's office and explain the problem to somebody there.

They caught a bus out to Norland Lane and by lunchtime were back in Boyatt's Wood, staring at the notice nailed to the tree, advertising fifteen luxury executive homes.

'It doesn't say anything about badgers,' said Eric when he'd read through the whole sign carefully.

'No.' Rachel bit thoughtfully at her lower lip, 'And it says they'll be starting work here on the 26th. What is it today?'

Eric looked at his watch. 'It's the 26th,' he said, and as he spoke, a diesel engine started up somewhere on the other side of the trees.

'What's that?' asked Rachel, but there was no need for Eric to answer. They both already knew what it was.

The bulldozers were coming to Boyatt's Wood.

If they were going to do anything, Eric realized, it would have to be done quickly. There were only two of them, so it would be best if they split forces. Rachel should run to phone Mrs Jessop and tell her what was happening, while Eric himself would go to where the bulldozers had started work to see if he could do anything to stop them.

When he got to the edge of the wood, Eric found three bulldozers and two enormous diggers already flattening the undergrowth and tearing out trees. He was a sensible boy and he knew that his chances of stopping them were not good. Busy workmen with a living to earn are not inclined to down tools on the suggestion of a twelve-year-old boy.

But he felt he had to try. If he could just get one of them to listen to him, he thought, and if he could just persuade the man to come and look at the hollow containing the badgers' sett before it was crushed under the tracks of a bulldozer, he might have a chance.

And it's quite possible he was right. Unfortunately, he never got a chance to try. As he approached the first bulldozer, heart pounding and throat dry, Eric turned into a dog again. He thinks it may have been all the excitement and tension that made him change, but whatever the reason it couldn't have happened at a worse moment. It would have been difficult enough for Eric to stop the drivers as a boy. As a small mongrel dog, it was virtually impossible.

Even then, Eric didn't give up. If he couldn't explain the situation to the men in the bulldozers, he thought, maybe he could stop them just by getting in the way. If he stood in front of one of the machines and barked, they wouldn't actually run over him, would they? The driver would have to stop, get out of the cab and try to catch him. At least that might buy some time while Rachel tried to contact Mrs Jessop.

It was a very brave idea, though I don't think Eric had thought about quite how dangerous it was until he actually ran in front of the first bulldozer and sat down. The earth-moving machines that they use for clearing ground on building sites are very large, weigh several tons, and can run over dogs the size of Eric without even noticing the bump.

Eric barked to draw attention to himself – and whether the driver didn't hear him over the noise of the engine, or didn't see him, I don't know – but he certainly didn't stop. And at the last second, when the great metal blade was only a couple of feet away, Eric realized it was not going to work, and scampered sideways to safety.

His next idea was a rather better one. If he couldn't stop the destruction himself, Eric thought, maybe he could get someone else to give the order to make it stop. Abandoning the diggers, he raced up the track to the part of Mr Ashmore's housing estate that was already nearing completion.

Up there, he knew, he would find a Portakabin office and his one chance of saving the badgers.

Mr Ashmore's secretary, Miss Barrington, was making herself a cup of coffee when the door to her office was pushed open and a small mongrel dog came in, wiping its feet careful on the mat.

'I know you, don't I?' she said, bending down for a closer look. 'You're the dog that was using Mr Ashmore's car phone last week!'

'Woof,' said Eric.

'And what do you want today, I wonder?' She smiled at him. 'Type a letter? Sell you a house?'

Eric did not reply. Instead, he trotted straight over to Miss Barrington's desk, jumped into the empty seat, stood up on his hind legs and used his front paws to tap at the keys of the word processor.

The smile on Miss Barrington's face slipped away as she watched him. 'What are you doing?' she asked, walking back to her desk to stare in astonishment at the screen. It was quite impossible, she knew, but the dog had just typed a word. On the screen it said 'Badgers'.

'Badgers?' She looked at Eric. 'What about badgers?'

Eric tapped some more.

'In the wood,' Miss Barrington read from the screen. 'Badgers in the wood.' She blinked sharply a couple of times as Eric pressed the return key and went down to a new line. 'What sort of dog are you?' she asked him.

But Eric was still typing.

'Stop the diggers,' the screen now read.

'You want me to stop the diggers because there are badgers in the wood?' Miss Barrington asked faintly.

'Woof,' said Eric.

Miss Barrington took a deep breath. 'Okay,' she said, reaching for the telephone, 'I'll try. I'll try anything for a dog that uses capital letters and punctuation.'

And she started to dial.

From a hilltop overlooking Boyatt's Wood, Mr Ashmore and his site engineer watched with satisfied smiles as the bulldozers did their work. It was all going to plan. They should have the site clear by the end of the day and, if the weather held, they could start levelling the ground tomorrow and be digging foundations by the end of the week. It couldn't be better.

The cell phone in Mr Ashmore's pocket started ringing.

'What is it?' he asked briskly. There was a pause as he listened to the reply, and a frown spread across his face.

'Badgers?' he barked. 'Of course there aren't! I never heard anything so ridiculous. Who told you there were badgers?' His frown deepened. 'A dog? A dog came into the office and told you?' The frown had become a look of downright anger, and a red flush was spreading over his cheeks. 'Now you listen to me, Miss Barrington,' he snapped 'I have no intention of stopping expensive machinery just because my secretary thinks she can hear dogs talking to her.' And he switched off the phone and put it back in his pocket.

'I think you should take her advice,' said a voice

behind him. 'It could save you a lot of trouble in the long run.'

Mr Ashmore spun round. 'Who are you?' he asked.

Mrs Jessop told him who she was, and that what Miss Barrington had said about there being badgers in Boyatt's Wood was true.

'Why is everyone talking about badgers all of a sudden?' Mr Ashmore's face was getting redder all the time. 'Look, I promise you, we had a survey done. There aren't any badgers.'

'Yes, there are,' said Rachel, standing next to Mrs Jessop. 'We've seen their sett.'

Mr Ashmore looked at her suspiciously. 'Those are rabbit holes,' he said firmly.

'They're a bit big for that, I think,' murmured Mrs Jessop.

'They're big rabbits,' said Mr Ashmore. 'Look, have you any idea how much it would cost me to stop all this now? I could lose thousands. Thousands!'

'I know it will be expensive,' – Mrs Jessop sounded quite sympathetic – 'and I'm sorry about that, I really am. But if you don't stop the work, I shall be making a few calls to the press and the local television stations, and we both know that in the long run the publicity would cost you more money. Much more.'

Mr Ashmore stared at her, very hard, for several seconds. Then he reached into his pocket for the telephone.

'Arnie?' he said briefly. 'Stop the diggers.'

And that is the story of how Eric, Rachel and Mrs Jessop saved the badgers of Boyatt's Wood – though if you'd been watching the local news on television that evening, you'd have found that Mr Ashmore got most of the credit. Rachel and Eric watched it at Mrs Jessop's house. The cameras showed the badgers' sett, the silent bulldozers and then Mr Ashmore, talking to a reporter called Judy Parker.

'You see, Judy,' he was saying, 'my company has always been very concerned about the environment. As soon as my secretary told me about the badger sett, I immediately ordered all work to cease. I think it's very important we do all we can to preserve our rich country heritage. Never mind the cost.'

'He makes it sound as if he's the one who saved the badgers,' said Rachel indignantly.

Mrs Jessop shrugged. 'Well, I suppose he is, in a way,' she said. 'Don't forget, he stands to lose a lot of money by this. The cost of delay, the cost of not being able to use the land and build his houses. I think we can let him have his moment of glory.' She stood up. 'It's been a long day. I'll get some tea, shall I?'

On the television the reporter was still talking. 'I wonder if you'd care to comment, Mr Ashmore,' she was saying, 'on the story going round the site that the first warning about the badgers came from a dog.'

'You've been talking to my secretary, I think.' Mr Ashmore chuckled and gave the reporter a knowing wink.

'Not just your secretary,' the reporter said. 'We've been told that a little mongrel dog was seen leaping around in front of the bulldozers, trying to get them to stop. Then, when it discovered that didn't work, it went down to your office and typed in a warning on the word processor.'

Mr Ashmore laughed again. 'I don't know anything

about that, I'm afraid,' he said. 'But if the story's true, it must have been a very intelligent dog – and a very brave one.'

'That's the first thing he's said I agree with,' said Rachel, getting up to turn off the television set.

'Anyone hungry?' Mrs Jessop called from the kitchen.

'Woof,' said Eric. And they both went in for tea.

# THE GIRL ON THE HORSE

There was one occasion – and fortunately it was only the once – when turning into a dog nearly resulted in Eric getting drowned. It happened like this.

Mrs Jessop had taken the top two classes to the Water Sports Centre down on the river, and there they had been issued with lifejackets, helmets, paddles ... and canoes. It was wonderful fun, and in no time they were all out on the water practising rolls, turns and speed sprints, when Eric felt the familiar tingling at the back of his neck.

His first instinct was to head for cover, and he rapidly paddled his canoe out of sight round a bend in the river. He had to stop paddling when his hands turned into paws of course and then, as the current began to take him further downstream and he realized there was nothing he could do to slow down or stop, he began to wish he had stayed where someone could see him.

The current flowed faster and faster, rocking the canoe from side to side while Eric tried desperately to use his weight to keep it balanced. He was just wondering whether he should abandon ship, jump out and swim for the shore, when he found it was too late. A sign by the side of the river said 'DANGER – no swimming'. Two seconds later, he passed another sign which said 'DANGER – weir ahead' and two seconds after that, Eric and the canoe disappeared over a twenty-foot drop into a boiling mass of white water.

As a boy, Eric might have been strong enough to swim out of trouble, but as a little dog, the violent movements of the water were far too strong, and he was sucked irresistibly beneath the surface. In a moment, everything went black.

He recovered consciousness to find himself lying on the bank, while a girl looked down at him with an expression of deep concern. She was a very beautiful girl and for one moment Eric honestly thought he had died, gone to heaven, and met an angel. It was something to do with the way the sun shone just behind her head, making it look as if she had a halo. Then he became aware that he was still a dog, still on earth and still just about alive.

'Oh, thank goodness,' the girl said, as Eric opened his eyes. 'I thought you were dead. What on earth were you doing in a canoe?'

The voice was as beautiful as the face, Eric thought. Then he noticed her clothes were dripping with water and realized she must have rescued him. She must have seen him go over the weir and jumped in the river to save him. He felt a sudden rush of gratitude. What a brave thing to have done!

Eric struggled to his feet and shook the worst of the water out of his fur.

'I wish I could dry myself as easily as that,' said the girl, looking down at her clothes. 'Look at me. I'd better go back and get changed.

She turned and walked down the path to where a pony was tied loosely to a tree beside the river. Unhitching the reins, she swung herself up into the saddle. 'You look after yourself in future, all right?' she called back to Eric, as she turned the horse the way she wanted to go. 'No more canoe rides on your own, understand?'

'Woof, woof,' said Eric. And as he watched her ride off through the trees, he thought what a wonderful person she was. What a very wonderful person.

How Eric changed back into a boy, found his canoe, found his clothes and then got back to join the rest of the class without getting into trouble is a story in itself, but it's not this story. The fact is that he did, and that nobody ever found out what had happened to him except Rachel, to whom he told the whole story that evening.

'Sounds like a close shave, Eric,' she said sympathetically. 'Lucky that girl was there.'

Eric nodded. 'I was wondering', he said, 'if there wasn't something I should do for her in return. I mean, when someone saves your life like that, you ought . . . you ought to say thank you, at least.'

Rachel agreed, but pointed out that it wasn't easy to thank someone when you didn't know who they were or where they lived and when the only time you'd met them you'd been a dog.

Eric, however, was not to be put off. 'I'm going to find out who she is,' he said. 'Then I can write her a note or something. It's the least she deserves.'

And Rachel could see his point. If someone saves your life, a simple thank you is plain good manners, even from a dog.

Finding out who the girl was turned out to be a lot easier than either of them had imagined. The only thing they knew about her was what she looked like, and that she sometimes rode a grey horse along the path by the river. So they went down to the river and asked some of the people who worked or lived there if they knew anyone of that description – and it seemed almost everyone did.

Her name was Chloe Marshe. She was twelve years old, the daughter of Colonel and Mrs Marshe, and she lived in Woodfield. Eric and Rachel had no trouble finding Woodfield either. Everyone knew where it was, and when they saw it, they could see why.

It was a very large house. Standing on the road and looking through an enormous pair of wrought-iron gates up a gravel drive that wound through lawns and trees for at least half a mile, Eric and Rachel stared in awe at the house. It was a brick building the size of a county hospital.

'Wow!' said Rachel. 'You're going to go in there?'

'Yes,' said Eric determinedly. 'But not now. She rescued me as a dog, and I'm going to say thank you as a dog.'

'Yeah,' said Rachel. 'Well, good luck.'

Next Saturday morning, Eric-as-a-dog squeezed himself through the bars of the gates and set off up the drive. He was understandably nervous. If the house in front of him had looked big when he was a boy, it looked even bigger now that he was a little dog. Nevertheless, doggedly clutching a bunch of flowers in his teeth, he hopped up the steps to the front door and pushed the brass doorbell carefully with his paw.

The sound of the bell echoed inside the house. Eric was just wondering if he should press it again when he heard footsteps and the huge oak door swung open in front of him. A grey-haired woman looked out. Eric didn't know it, but this was Mrs Batcombe, the housekeeper.

'Is anybody there?' she called.

'Woof,' said Eric.

'Oooh!' Mrs Batcombe looked down at him in startled surprise.

'Who is it?' a voice called from inside the house.

'It's a dog, Mrs Marshe,' said the housekeeper.

'A dog?' A smartly dressed woman appeared in the doorway. 'Goodness! So it is.' She bent down for a closer look at Eric. 'He's carrying a bunch of flowers.'

Eric stepped forward and dropped them, politely, at her feet.

Mrs Marsh picked them up and then saw the note Eric had tied to them. 'They're for Chloe!' she said, when she read it. 'How extraordinary! A dog calling round with flowers for Chloe. What a shame she's not here.'

'I'll put them in water.' Mrs Batcombe took the flowers. 'She'll be back tomorrow, won't she?'

'Yes.' Mrs Marshe looked down at Eric again. 'What a pity we can't explain that to the dog. Such a clever little animal – she'll be sorry to have missed him.' She smiled at Eric. 'Thank you,' she said, and went inside and closed the door.

What Rachel couldn't understand was why Eric wanted to go back. 'You've already said thank you in the note,' she said. 'Why do you want to do it again?'

'It's not the same if I don't actually see her,' Eric insisted stubbornly. 'And anyway, I've decided flowers weren't enough of a present. Not for someone who's saved your life. I'm going to take her some chocolates as well.'

So next day, when Mrs Batcombe answered the door, she found Eric-as-a-dog sitting on the step with a box of chocolates in his mouth. 'Well, I'm blowed,' she said. 'You came back!' She pointed at the chocolates. 'Are these for Chloe?'

'Woof,' said Eric.

'You'd better come in and give them to her, then.' Mrs Batcombe held open the door and, as Eric padded in, called up the stairs, 'Chloe? Visitor for you!'

When Chloe arrived, she recognized Eric at once. 'It's the dog I pulled out of the river the other day,' she exclaimed.

'Well, it looks like he wants to show you he's grateful,' said Mrs Batcombe. 'He's the one turned up yesterday with flowers and today he's brought you some chocolates.'

Chloe bent down to take the chocolates and read the little note taped to the top of them. 'I just wanted to thank you again, Eric.' She looked up. 'That's you is it? Eric?'

'Woof,' said Eric.

'Well thank you,' she said, and gave him a little kiss on his nose.

'Why don't you take him in to meet your parents?' the housekeeper suggested. 'And I'll bring in the tea.'

Tea in the drawing room with Chloe and Colonel and Mrs Marshe was a great success. It's not every day that a dog comes to call, and when it turns out to be a dog that can ring the doorbell, wipe its feet on the mat, and bark to tell you how many sugars it wants in its tea, it's not surprising that he should attract a certain amount of attention.

They gave him some cake, and when Mrs Marshe said she was worried he might leave crumbs on the carpet, Eric got a newspaper and carefully spread it out on the floor. Colonel Marshe said 'that dog' seemed to have more intelligence than half the officers in his regiment.

After tea, Chloe devised all sorts of experiments to try and find out exactly how intelligent Eric was. She asked him to fetch things, find them, hide them or carry them to another room – and of course Eric did all those things with no trouble at all. Chloe thought he was wonderful. She had never seen a dog like it, she kept saying, and every time Eric counted the right number of coins in her father's hand or picked up the left-hand cushion from the window seat, just as her mother had asked, Chloe laughed aloud with delight.

And Eric enjoyed it as well. He liked being the centre of attention among these rich people with their enormous house and their beautiful daughter. Somehow it made him feel . . . well, special and important.

'They seemed to like me,' he told Rachel proudly the next day. 'They thought I was pretty clever.'

For some reason, Rachel was not impressed. 'Because you could count to five and pick up cushions?' she asked. 'Doesn't sound too impressive to me. Are you coming on Saturday?'

'Saturday?' said Eric.

'I'm racing at Hadley,' said Rachel. 'You said you wanted to come and watch.'

'Ah. I can't come on Saturday, I'm afraid,' Eric apologized. 'It's Chloe's birthday. She wants me to come up to Woodfield and meet all her friends.'

'Oh,' said Rachel.

'In fact,' Eric went on, 'that's really why I came round. I wondered if you'd help me choose a present.'

'You want to get her a birthday present?' said Rachel. 'Why?' She held up her hand before Eric could answer. 'Don't say it. I know. She saved your life.' And she went to get her coat.

Eric had decided to buy Chloe some perfume. He had never bought any before, which is why he had asked Rachel to help him, and the whole thing was not made any easier by the fact that he turned into a dog in the bus on the way into town.

She had done some embarrassing things in her time, Rachel thought, but standing at a perfume counter, asking for various perfumes for a dog to sniff at, had to be one of the worst. There was a whole crowd of people watching them by the end, and Eric simply wouldn't make up his mind.

'Look, Eric,' she hissed at him as he rejected yet another sample of perfume she had sprayed on her arm for him to consider, 'if you don't make up your mind in the next ten seconds, I am leaving, with or without any perfume. Understood?'

'Woof,' said Eric, and he paced up and down in front of the counter a couple more times before finally pointing with his paw at one of the bottles.

It was far too expensive, Rachel thought, but it was Eric's money and there was obviously no arguing with him in this mood. So she paid for it, took the box, and headed gratefully for the door.

'Well, now that's done,' she said, 'can we please go and get something to eat? I'm starving.'

'Woof,' said Eric.

Out on the pavement, Rachel was trying to decide where would be the best place to have lunch, when a voice behind her said, 'Excuse me.'

She looked round to see a girl of about her own age, with long blonde hair tied back in a ponytail.

'I don't mean to be rude,' the girl said, 'but your dog is . . . it's Eric, isn't it?' She bent down on one knee and gently scratched the top of Eric's head. 'Fancy seeing you here! How lovely!'

She stood up and held out a hand to Rachel. I'm Chloe Marshe,' she said. 'I'm the one who rescued your dog from the river. Did you buy those flowers and chocolates for me?'

'Well, it was Eric's idea,' said Rachel.

'Thank you very much,' said Chloe. She beamed down at Eric. 'So . . . he's your dog, is he?'

'Sort of,' said Rachel.

'Have you noticed', Chloe asked confidentially, 'how clever he is?'

'Not really.' Rachel shrugged. 'Falling in the river. Doesn't sound too bright to me.'

'Oh, we think he's super,' said Chloe. 'In fact, I wanted to ask if he'd like to come home with us now. I've got some cousins staying who'd really like to meet him.'

'I'm sure they would,' said Rachel, 'but –' She was about to say that she and Eric were just going to have lunch, when she changed her mind. 'You'll have to ask Eric,' she said instead. 'He'll have to decide. It's up to him.'

Chloe looked down at Eric. 'Would you like to come home with me for the afternoon?' she asked.

'Woof!' said Eric.

In the days that followed, Rachel saw very little of her friend Eric Banks, and nothing at all of Eric-as-a-dog. Whenever he changed, Eric went straight round to Woodfield, where Mrs Batcombe would let him in, lead him down to the kitchen to feed him if he was hungry, and then take him up to the drawing room to meet any visitors there might be in the house that day.

Woodfield was always full of visitors, a lot of them, Eric suddenly realized, the sort of people he'd seen on television or in the newspapers. Whoever they were, Chloe would proudly introduce them to Eric, then ask him to do one or two of his 'tricks'.

One of the most popular of these was to let the guest choose the name of a book in the library, and then ask Eric to go and get it. One visitor, a Member of Parliament in fact, spent an entire afternoon asking Eric to bring him books. He was convinced there was some trick to it, and was determined to find out what it was.

'Bring me *Treasure Island*,' he would say, and then watch intently as Eric looked along the shelves until he found the book, pulled it out with one paw, and carried it back in his teeth.

Chloe assured him that there wasn't any trick. 'It's just that Eric can read,' she explained, several times. But the Member of Parliament simply shook his head in disbelief, and asked Eric to go and get *David Copperfield* or *Puck of Pook's Hill*.

Rachel still saw Eric at school, but it wasn't the same. All he wanted to do, she thought gloomily, was tell her what had happened with Chloe last time he'd been up at Woodfield. It was as if the Eric who had been her friend for so long had been secretly replaced by someone she hardly knew. She had no idea why it had happened, and it left her feeling very unhappy.

About three weeks after the day Eric had been rescued from the river, Rachel answered the door to find him on the step.

'I've come to ask a favour, Rachel,' he told her. 'Can I come in?'

Rachel took him through to the kitchen.

'I've decided I want to meet her,' he explained. 'And I was wondering if you could introduce me.'

Rachel didn't need to ask who he was talking about, but she was puzzled as to why he wanted an introduction. 'What for?' she asked. 'I thought you saw her almost every day.'

'That's as a dog,' said Eric. 'What I want is to meet her as myself. As a boy. So we can really talk to each other.'

'I see,' said Rachel.

'She's going to be in the shopping centre on Saturday,' Eric went on. 'And you've already met her, so if we were both out there, you could sort of bump into her and introduce me.' He paused. 'Will you?'

Rachel hardly hesitated. 'Yes, of course,' she said.

They sat together on one of the benches in the shopping centre next Saturday morning, waiting. Eric was wearing a new T-shirt and had put gel in his hair. Rachel couldn't help noticing he seemed rather nervous.

'There she is.' She gave him a nudge and pointed at

Chloe, who had just walked in through the main doors.

'I think I've changed my mind,' Eric said. 'I mean, after all . . . I hardly know her.'

'You've sat on her lap and licked her face,' said Rachel. 'That's not bad for a start.'

'No, no, I mean it,' said Eric. 'I really have decided it's not a good idea. I think we should go home and –'

'Yoohoo! Chloe!' Rachel called, waving both arms to attract her attention. 'Over here!'

Chloe came over. 'Aren't you the girl who owns Eric?' she asked.

'That's right,' said Rachel. 'He's not with me today, but I want you to meet a friend of mine with the same name. Eric . . . this is Chloe.'

Chloe looked closely at Eric as they shook hands. 'I haven't met you before, have I?' she asked.

'I don't think so,' said Eric.

'It's just you look . . . familiar somehow.' Chloe shook her head. 'Well. Anyone fancy a coffee?'

'Goodness, is that the time?' Rachel looked at her watch. 'I'm afraid I have to go and buy some spot cream, but I'm sure Eric would like a coffee, wouldn't you, Eric?' She gave them both a dazzling smile, and was gone.

Mrs Jessop found Rachel sitting by herself on a wall outside the car park, and stopped to say hello.

'How's life?' she asked.

'Wonderful, miss,' said Rachel. 'So wonderful I think I'll have to rush out and jump off a cliff.'

'Ah.' Mrs Jessop put down her shopping and sat on the wall. 'You want to talk about it?'

'Not really, thanks, miss,' said Rachel.

Mrs Jessop said nothing.

'But what really gets me,' said Rachel, 'is when people are so stupid they can't see what's happening right under their noses.'

'Ah.' Mrs Jessop nodded sympathetically.

'I mean, you'd think a blind person would notice if they were just being treated as a lap-dog, wouldn't you? Anyone can see they're not real friends. They just *use* him.'

Mrs Jessop thought for a moment. 'Would you mind if we started this one from the beginning?' she said.

When Eric came back from town that day, it was to find Rachel waiting for him in the garden. 'I hope you don't mind,' she said. 'I just wanted to hear how it went.'

'How what went?' asked Eric.

'The meeting with Chloe.'

'Oh, that.' Eric sat on the grass beside her. 'It was fine. It went well.'

'So, what did you talk about?'

'Horses, mostly,' said Eric. 'She's very interested in horses.'

'I see,' said Rachel.

'Then we talked about show-jumping, grooming, pony clubs, saddlery, stabling . . . that sort of thing.'

'Sounds good,' said Rachel.

'Yes.' Eric picked thoughtfully at the grass.

Neither of them spoke for a moment, and then Rachel said, 'I met Mrs Jessop this morning. She's got a nephew from America staying, who's got one of those new stunt kites.'

'Really?' Eric's eyes lit up. 'Can we see it?'

Rachel nodded. 'She said any time. If we were interested.'

'What about now?' Eric looked at the breeze swaying the branches of the trees at the bottom of the garden. 'It's the perfect day for it.'

'Okay.' Rachel got up. 'I'd better ring Mum first, though. Tell her where I'm going.'

Eric whistled cheerily to himself as he waited in the garden for Rachel to phone her mother. The two of them had always enjoyed kite-flying – in fact, last holiday, they had built several of their own. He remembered one time he had tried to fly Rachel's box kite while he was a dog and a sharp gust of wind had swept him straight up into the air. Goodness knows what would have happened if Rachel hadn't grabbed hold of his back paw when she did and pulled him down to earth.

Rachel came back down the path into the garden. 'That's fine,' she said, 'but I have to be back by six for supper. She said you can come too, if you like.'

'Great!' said Eric. 'Good idea.' He followed her out to the road. 'You know, you look different today,' he added.

'Do I?'

Eric paused at the gate, trying to think what it was. 'Have you done something to your hair?'

'I don't think so,' said Rachel.

Suddenly Eric had it. 'You're wearing a dress,' he said.

'Am I?' Rachel looked down. 'So I am.'

And they set off down the pavement together.

# END OF TERM

On the first day of the new term, Eric told Rachel that he had decided to win a cup.

'Cup?' Rachel asked. 'What cup?'

In reply, Eric gestured round the school entrance lobby to the shelves of silver trophies in their polished glass case. 'I don't mind which cup,' he told her. 'As long as I win one of them.'

Rachel was puzzled. 'Why?' she asked. 'What for?'

Eric sighed. Winning a trophy might not seem important to Rachel – after all, she had won the National Juveniles Circuit Championship and had a photograph of herself in the British Cycling Federation's hall of fame – but Eric had never done anything like that. He had been at the same school since he was five and never won a single trophy. This was their last year before moving up to Senior school and he had decided that, before he left, he was going to win something.

'It's important to me, Rachel,' he told her firmly. 'I want my name up there. I want something that tells future generations "Eric Banks was here."'

Rachel looked at the trophies. Most of them were awarded for sport and the reason Eric had never won any of them was that he was not very good at games.

She didn't say this, though. Instead, she asked if he had any particular cup in mind.

'That one.' Eric pointed to a rather tarnished trophy on the top shelf. It was very large, with big silver handles, and at first Rachel couldn't remember what it was awarded for. She read the inscription.

'That's the rugby cup, Eric,' she said. 'It hasn't been awarded since 1955. Nobody plays rugby here any more.'

'Exactly!' Eric smiled triumphantly. 'That's what gives me a chance of winning it. All I have to do is get a team of eleven people —'

'Fifteen,' said Rachel.

'What?'

'You need fifteen for a rugby team,' she explained.

Eric's enthusiasm was not going to be dampened by mere detail. 'Right. I get fifteen people,' he went on, 'and I get to be captain, because it's my idea. We play a couple of games and that's it!'

Rachel had to admit it was rather clever. In all team trophies, the person who had captained the team had his or her name put on the cup. It didn't matter if you lost all the matches you played; if you were the captain, your name went on the cup. If that was all Eric wanted, the idea might work.

'You'll need a member of staff running it all,' she said, thoughtfully. 'And for a game like rugby, it'll have to be someone tough and aggressive . . .'

'I thought Mrs Jessop,' said Eric.

'Sounds perfect,' Rachel agreed.

Mrs Jessop was a little surprised when Eric told her that he and some of the other boys wanted to start a rugby team. However, she was always keen to encourage sport and suggested that all those interested should meet on the playing field at four o'clock the next Wednesday for a try-out.

Eric was looking forward to it. Getting enough people to join him wasn't easy, but he finally managed it, and at a quarter to four on Wednesday he was just heading for the changing rooms . . . when he turned into a dog.

There was nothing he could do about it, of course. Except find Rachel, who then had the job of explaining to Mrs Jessop that Eric wouldn't be at the practice.

'What do you mean, Eric won't be here?' Mrs Jessop was not amused. 'This whole thing was his idea!'

'I know,' said Rachel.

'And now he doesn't turn up himself – why not? Where is he?'

'His granny's ill,' said Rachel. 'He's very sorry, Mrs Jessop. He says he'll be here next time. Definitely.'

'Woof,' said Eric, sitting on the grass at Rachel's feet.

'Humph.' Mrs Jessop was not impressed. 'Will he really. Well, come on. Let's get on with it.'

The try-out session was not a great success. Eric's friends were keen enough but none of them had actually played rugby before, and few of them showed any instinct for the game. As Mrs Jessop was heard to mutter, the only talent they seemed to have was for dropping the ball whenever it came in their direction. At the end of an hour, Mrs Jessop sent them all back inside to get changed and Eric-as-a-dog, still sitting on the touchline, overheard her talking about it all to the headmaster.

'I'm afraid it's not on, John,' she said.

'Ah.' Mr Blocker absent-mindedly stroked a little hamster which had emerged from his top pocket. 'I thought they looked a bit shaky.'

'I don't mind them being hopeless.' Mrs Jessop pursed her lips. 'I mean, that's why we have practices. But the two things you need for a rugby team are weight and speed and we just don't have anyone big enough or fast enough.' She turned to walk back indoors. 'I'll have to tell Eric Banks when I see him to-morrow.'

Mr Blocker was about to follow when he saw Eric. 'Hello!' His face lit up in a smile, and he beamed down. 'Everything all right?'

'Woof, woof,' said Eric.

'Jolly good.' The headmaster bent down and scratched the top of Eric's head. 'And would my favourite dog like a biscuit?' he asked.

'Woof, woof,' said Eric.

'I thought so!' Mr Blocker reached into his pocket and produced one. 'Here you are.'

He gave Eric a cheery pat on the head and was gone.

Eric didn't give up. If Mrs Jessop said you couldn't have a team without weight and speed, then weight and speed were what he would find. There was one obvious candidate if you were looking for weight. Big Bernard wasn't just big, he was enormous. Still only a third-year, he towered above everyone else in his class, and was already bigger than the headmaster. On his own, he probably weighed more than the rest of Eric's rugby team put together.

There was a snag though. 'Big Bernard playing rugby?' Rachel looked at Eric in disbelief. 'He hasn't mastered tying his shoelaces yet.'

'Mrs Jessop didn't say anything about brains,' said Eric determinedly. 'She just said we needed someone big, and Bernard is . . . well, he's big.'

'You'll never get him to play.' Rachel was still not convinced. 'You know Bernard – anything faster than a quick walk down the corridor and he's demanding an oxygen tent.'

But Eric had thought of that as well.

One result of the headmaster being 'converted' to animals was that he insisted on vegetarian school dinners. Most of the children had got used to this very quickly, but not Bernard. Instead of steak-and-kidney pie, burgers and sausages, liver and rissoles, Bernard now had to eat salads, nut cutlets and pulses. For a boy his size, it was agony. Eric had actually seen him crying one lunchtime into a bowl of bean broth.

When Eric asked Bernard to join the rugby team, he took with him a pork pie, some chicken sandwiches, a couple of sausage rolls and a scotch egg (he had taken a levy on the packed lunches of everyone else in the team). He promised Bernard more of the same every day, as long as he turned out on Wednesday afternoons for rugby practice.

Bernard agreed without hesitation. In fact, he was so grateful for the food that he gave Eric a hug that lifted him several feet off the ground and bruised three of his ribs.

The next rugby practice was a considerable improvement on the first, and when Mrs Jessop tried Bernard in a scum, even she was impressed by the results. 'You know,' she told Rachel, 'If we can just teach him which direction to push in, we could be on to something here.'

She was even more impressed when David Gordon appeared and asked if he could join the team as well. David was the fastest runner in the school, a county athlete, and already captain of the football, hockey and tennis teams.

'I wonder how Eric persuaded him to join?' said Mrs Jessop, but Rachel decided not to tell her.

If Bernard's weak spot was food, Eric had discovered that David's was a girl called Lucy Finglis. David would do anything Lucy asked him to, and Lucy was a very good friend of Eric's.

'Where is Eric, by the way?' Mrs Jessop looked round the field. 'Not still getting changed, is he?'

Rachel, with a sinking heart, had just seen Eric-as-a-dog trotting over the grass towards them.

'Getting changed,' she murmured quietly. 'You could say that.'

'It's not good enough, Rachel.' Mrs Jessop sounded understandably impatient. 'He's team captain, after all. He's supposed to set an example and get here early. What's the excuse this time?'

Eric the dog had stopped at Rachel's feet. He was carrying a note in his mouth, and Rachel bent down to take it.

'He asked me to give you this,' she said, passing it to Mrs Jessop.

'Apparently his grandmother has taken a turn for the worse,' said Mrs Jessop when she had read it.

'I thought she might have,' said Rachel.

*

Eric's rugby team played their first match four weeks later, and Eric's greatest fear was that the same thing would happen to him again, and that he would turn into a dog before the match had even started.

To his great relief, however, he didn't. At two o'clock both teams came out on to the pitch, and by five past, to the delight of the crowd, Big Bernard had scored his first try. It began from a scrum, way down the field, and when the ball finally emerged, someone passed it to Bernard, who set off in the direction of his opponents' line with all the slow, unstoppable determination of a tide of volcanic lava.

His opponents tried to bring him down. They launched themselves determindedly at his legs and arms, which certainly slowed him up a bit, but they couldn't stop him. Like a bear surrounded by a cloud of wasps, Bernard doggedly made his way to the far end of the field, paused a moment to remember what he had to do next, and then touched the ball to the ground to score four points.

Great cheers went up from all the spectators, but by that time, Rachel was no longer watching. As the scrum had pushed forward, she had noticed that it left in its wake a trail of boots, clothes, and finally a small mongrel dog. While everyone else was watching Bernard, rumbling like a Chieftain tank towards his touchdown, Rachel dashed back to Eric, quietly gathered up his clothes, checked quickly that no one had trodden on his paws or anything, and then drew him off to the side of the pitch.

Mrs Jessop was cheering as enthusiastically as everyone else as Bernard went over the line.

'Not a bad start, eh?' she called cheerfully to Rachel.

'But I must get Eric to tell the others to spread out more. They're bunching up too much and –' She stopped, her eyes scanning the field for Eric. 'Where is he? I can't see him.'

'Eric's had to . . . I'm afraid he's had to leave, miss,' said Rachel.

'Leave?' Mrs Jessop stared at her. 'In the middle of a match?'

'It was an emergency.' Rachel tried to make Eric's departure sound reasonable.

'I don't care what it was.' Mrs Jessop obviously didn't think it was reasonable at all. 'This can't go on. It really can't.' She pointed down at Eric. 'Honestly, Rachel, that dog of yours is here more often than Eric. I shall have a talk with him. Tell him I want to see him in the morning.'

And she walked away.

When Eric went to see Mrs Jessop next morning, he knew what she was going to say and, however disappointed he was, he couldn't really blame her for saying it.

'I know how keen you were to get this thing started, Eric,' she told him, 'and I'm sorry. But there's no point having a captain who's never there for the practices, and who disappears after five minutes of the first match.'

'No, miss,' said Eric.

'You see,' – Mrs Jessop sounded more apologetic than angry – 'we actually won that game on Saturday – 33 points to 7. I think we could even have a chance in the Inter-Schools Tournament, but not with you on the team.'

'No, miss,' said Eric.

'I've decided that Bernard will be taking over as captain from tomorrow.'

'Bernard?' Eric could hardly believe his ears.

'Yes.' Mrs Jessop said nothing for a moment, tapping her pencil on the top of the desk, before going on, 'I'm going to tell you something, Eric – in confidence. Bernard's never been very successful at school. He's not very clever. People laugh at him for being so big. But for the first time in his life, thanks to you, he's found something he's good at.' She leant forward. 'You probably wouldn't know this, but there's a cup for rugby, and if Bernard got his name on it, it would mean a great deal to him. It would give him something to be proud of, something that told the world "Bernard was here." Do you know what I mean?'

'Yes, miss,' said Eric. 'I think I do.'

Eric tried not to let it show, but being told he was no longer captain was a bitter disappointment. Turning into a dog had got him into all sorts of trouble in the past, but I think that was the first time it had stopped him doing something he really wanted to do.

The worst part of it was that the rugby team, the team that had been his idea and his choosing, went from strength to strength. They certainly didn't win all their matches as easily as they had the first, but they won them. And their extraordinary success, as they clocked up one victory after another, was the talk of the school.

Bernard himself became something of a folk hero, and the effect it all had on him was extraordinary. It was the first time he had really succeeded at anything and, as Mrs Jessop had predicted, it gave him a belief in himself and a confidence that changed his character completely. When you saw him striding powerfully down the corridor, talking easily with some friends, it was as if he was a different person. Nobody laughed at Big Bernard these days. Even his school work had improved.

The fact that Mrs Jessop had been right didn't help Eric, however. Each Saturday he would watch the match from the sidelines and, while he cheered as loudly as anyone, his heart was not in it. Somewhere inside he could never forget that, if he hadn't been 'different', he would have been out there with them, leading them to victory as team captain.

The last match of the season was also the finals of the County Inter-Schools Tournament, and it was with a sense of irony that Eric found himself watching it, not as a boy, but as a dog.

'Eric not with you today?' Mrs Jessop asked Rachel as they stood together on the touchline.

'No, miss.' Rachel looked down at Eric-as-a-dog at her feet. 'He's . . . he's not quite himself today.'

'He's not still upset about being dropped from the team, is he?' Mrs Jessop asked.

'Woof,' said Eric.

'Well, a bit,' Rachel admitted. 'But I think he understands.'

Most of the school had turned out to watch, Eric noticed. They lined every side of the pitch in their hundreds, along with staff, relatives, neighbours and friends. Nobody wanted to miss this one.

It was a close-fought match. Other teams had learnt from experience that Bernard was the man they had to stop, and the days when he could simply bludgeon his way through any opposition had gone. For a match like this one, the home team needed skill and tactics as well as brute strength, but, over the weeks and with Mrs Jessop's training, that was exactly what they had acquired. At half-time they had a narrow lead of 13 to 12. Towards the end of the second half they had extended that to 25 to 17.

At that point, with only a few minutes left to play, Eric decided he couldn't watch any more. He turned, squeezing his way through the legs of the other spectators, and started walking back past the pavilion towards the school. He simply couldn't bear to watch his friends win. He was very glad they were going to, of course, but to see them do it without him was more than his heart could bear.

Nobody noticed him go, not even Rachel. They were all too busy shouting encouragement as the last minutes of the match ticked away. The sound of their cheering followed Eric as he padded slowly down the path that led to the main gates, and perhaps it was understandable that there was a distinct droop to his tail.

Suddenly he stopped. Lifting his nose, he sniffed the air. It was only a faint trace of that tell-tale scent in the breeze, but could he possibly be mistaken? He sniffed again. No, it was definitely there.

Eric turned back towards the school, and ran.

Mr Blocker was not watching the rugby match. He had been busy recently with several projects involving animals, and one in particular had taken a lot of his time and energy. For several weeks, he had been trying to breed hamsters.

Earlier in the term, it had come to the headmaster's notice that some of the children in his school didn't have pets because they couldn't afford them. This seemed very wrong to him, and he had decided to offer a free hamster to any child that wanted one. All he had to do first, he had told Mrs Jessop, was breed them in sufficiently large numbers to meet the expected demand.

It was a generous thought, but it had not been as easy as he had hoped. He had bought two hamsters, but for several disappointing weeks nothing had happened. Then, when he had discovered that both animals were female, one of them had died.

However, Mr Blocker had persisted, and today all his efforts had finally been rewarded. In a cage on his lap as he sat in his study, were seven tiny baby hamsters – each of them smaller than a 10p piece. The first brood had arrived, and Mr Blocker couldn't have been more delighted if he'd given birth to them himself.

He was very tired though. Not quite knowing when the babies might arrive, he had stayed up both of the previous nights to keep watch and hadn't slept for fifty-six hours. He gave a great yawn as he put the hamster cage gently on the floor beside him. He had locked the door to make sure he wasn't disturbed, and now he turned on the radio, took out his pipe and lit it. It had been a perfect day. Drawing gently on the smoke, he settled back in the armchair and closed his eyes.

A moment later, the pipe slipped from his fingers.

If he had been awake, Mr Blocker would have noticed that a little lump of burning tobacco had fallen into the waste-paper basket. But Mr Blocker was deeply asleep.

*

With a dog's sensitive nose, Eric could smell the smoke long before you or I would have done and, as he ran into the school building, he could even track down where it was coming from. He skidded to a halt outside the headmaster's study and saw the first tendrils of smoke creeping out from under the door. He jumped up at the handle to try and open it, and when that didn't work, started barking furiously to try and warn Mr Blocker inside. Unfortunately the noise from the radio drowned him out.

Eric turned and ran back along the corridor, through the changing rooms, and out on to the playing field. He needed to get help. Out on the field, the rugby match had just ended and everyone was busy cheering and clapping as Big Bernard stepped forward on behalf of his team to collect the Inter-Schools trophy and hold it triumphantly above his head.

Rachel heard Eric as he came running across the field, barking furiously. 'Hey, Eric!' she waved at him. 'We won!'

'Woof, woof, woof, woof, woof!' said Eric.

'What is it?' asked Rachel. 'Something wrong?'

'Woof,' said Eric.

Rachel had never seen him behave quite like this. 'Something serious?' she asked.

'Woof,' said Eric, and he started running back towards the school.

'Hang on,' said Rachel. 'I'll get Mrs Jessop.'

In the end, it was Mrs Jessop, Rachel and four of the rugby team who followed Eric back across the field to the school buildings. There aren't many teachers, Rachel thought as they ran, who will take you seriously when you tell them your dog says it's an emergency, but then Mrs Jessop had always been rather special.

Eric led them unerringly through the school corridors to the headmaster's study, where by now, the smoke was coming out from under the door in a continuous curl. Mrs Jessop didn't hesitate. She sent David to phone the fire brigade from the call box on the corner, told everyone else to stand well back, and tried to open the door. It was locked.

'John?' she banged on the wood. 'John, are you in there?'

'Woof,' said Eric.

'Eric says he is,' said Rachel.

Grim-faced, Mrs Jessop turned to Bernard. 'Over here, Bernard,' she called. 'I want you to break the door down.'

Bernard hesitated. 'That's the headmaster's door, miss. I don't think he'd like it if I —'

'Just do it, Bernard,' Mrs Jessop interrupted him sharply. 'Now!'

Bernard braced his feet against the floor and pushed with his shoulders and arms against the door, just as if he were in rugby scrum. At first nothing happened. Then the door creaked, groaned, and with a tearing, splintering sound, suddenly gave way and fell forward into the room.

Smoke billowed out of the open doorway as Mrs Jessop darted inside. 'John?' she called. 'John, where are you?'

Through the haze of smoke and flame, they could just see her desperately trying to lift Mr Blocker's body from the armchair in the middle of the room, but he was a large man and the weight was too much for her.

Fortunately, Bernard had followed her inside. He emerged a moment later with the headmaster, unconscious, under one arm and Mrs Jessop, coughing and spluttering, supported on the other.

'Are you all right, miss?' asked Rachel.

'Yes, I'll be fine,' said Mrs Jessop, when she had stopped coughing. 'Thank you, Bernard, I think you can put the headmaster down now.'

Bernard let go of Mr Blocker, who fell to the floor with a thunk. Mrs Jessop knelt beside him.

'How are you feeling, John?'

Mr Blocker slowly opened his eyes. 'What happened?'

'It's nothing to worry about,' Mrs Jessop told him soothingly.

'You just set the school on fire, sir,' said Rachel.

Mr Blocker sat up. 'The babies! Are they all right?'

It was a few moments before anyone realized what he was talking about.

'The hamsters! My little babies!' Mr Blocker was trying desperately to struggle to his feet. 'I can't leave them. They'll die. I have to get them, I have to –'

'No,' said Mrs Jessop firmly. 'Nobody's going back in there. It's too dangerous.'

But one person had already gone. Eric had decided, as soon as he realized what Mr Blocker was talking about, that he couldn't leave animals to die there in the heat and smoke. He knew, too, that he was the best person to rescue them. In a smoke-filled room, there is most air down at floor level and, as a dog, that was where Eric was anyway.

Before anyone could stop him, he had plunged into

the heat and haze of the burning study, found the hamster cage, and dragged it back out to safety with his teeth.

'My babies!' Mr Blocker cried out in relief when he saw him. 'You've saved my babies!'

The fireman arrived soon after that. Mr Blocker was taken to hospital, still determinedly clutching the hamster cage to his chest as they loaded him into the ambulance on a stretcher.

Apart from the headmaster's study, remarkably little damage had been done to the school.

'It was lucky you spotted the fire so quickly,' said the Chief Fire Officer. 'Before it had time to spread.'

'We have Eric to thank for that,' Mrs Jessop told him. 'He's the one who raised the alarm.'

The fireman looked down at the little dog. 'Did he now?'

'He rescued the headmaster's hamsters as well,' said Rachel.

'It was all very dramatic,' Mrs Jessop agreed. 'I think he deserves a medal.'

Rachel said she didn't realize they gave medals to dogs.

But they do.

If you walk into the entrance lobby of Oakwood Junior School you will see the trophy cupboard, full of silver cups and shields, standing on the wall to your right. On the opposite wall hangs a picture. It is a large portrait of a mongrel dog, and beneath it is a brass plate on which are written the words:

'This plaque is erected in gratitude to Eric, who

raised the alarm and saved the school from fire. V. XI MCMXCI.

As well as saving the life of the headmaster, J. Blocker, BA, Oxon., Eric dashed bravely through the flames at great personal risk to rescue seven hamsters. For this courageous action, he received from her Royal Highness the Duchess of Monmouth, the Pro Dog of the Year Gold Medal – the highest award for bravery given to dogs.'

Beneath that, in a little glass case, is the medal itself.

Rachel and Eric studied it in silence for a moment. 'I know it's not quite what you planned,' said Rachel, 'but you've certainly left something for people to remember you by.'

'Woof,' said Eric.

## YOUNG INDIANA JONES AND THE PRINCESS OF PERIL
by Les Martin

**Aboard the Paris–St Petersburg Express as it races through the night, Young Indiana Jones helps a boy to evade the secret police.**

So begins another adventure for Indy – but his new-found friend soon realizes the authorities are not so easily thrown off the track. Pre-Revolution Russia is a very dangerous place, especially for those who dare to speak out against the Czar . . .

When Indy steps in, the might of the Russian Empire is thrown against him, and even he begins to wonder if there is any way out of this one.


## YOUNG INDIANA JONES AND THE CRUSADER'S CROWN
by Les Martin

**On the trail of a medieval manuscript in the South of France, Young Indiana Jones finds himself drawn into the dangerous streets of the Marseille underworld.**

But Indy has somebody to 'help' him – his least favourite travelling companion in the entire world, Thornton N. Thornton. Together they unravel the mystery of the manuscript, to discover they are not the only people with an interest in its message.

They soon become involved in a sinister conspiracy that could lead to a new reign of terror throughout the whole of France . . .